RIVER
SING
ME
HOME

RIVER
SING
ME
HOME

ELEANOR SHEARER

BERKLEY
New York

BERKLEY

An imprint of Penguin Random House LLC

penguinrandomhouse.com

Copyright © 2023 by Eleanor Shearer

Library of Congress Cataloging-in-Publication Data

Names: Shearer, Eleanor, author.

Title: River sing me home / Eleanor Shearer.

Description: New York: Berkley, [2023]

Identifiers: LCCN 2022025625 (print) | LCCN 2022025626 (ebook) |
ISBN 9780593548042 (hardcover) | ISBN 9780593548059 (ebook)

Subjects: LCSH: Slaves—Emancipation—Caribbean Area—Fiction. |
Mother and child—Fiction. | Caribbean Area—History—19th century—Fiction. |
LCGFT: Historical fiction. | Novels.

Classification: LCC PR6119.H433 R58 2023 (print) |
LCC PR6119.H433 (ebook) | DDC 823/.92—dc23/eng/20220621

LC record available at https://lccn.loc.gov/2022025625

LC ebook record available at https://lccn.loc.gov/2022025626

Headline Review UK hardcover edition / January 2023

Berkley hardcover edition / January 2023

Printed in the United States of America

1 3 5 7 9 10 8 6 4 2

Map by Tim Peters

Book design by Katy Riegel

For Mum, Dad,
Cal and Jeanette

My aim in writing this novel was to bring to life a story about the Caribbean in the aftermath of slavery—a place and time that is not always well-known or well understood. Doing this history justice was incredibly important to me, especially given my family ties to the Caribbean. To make this story as accurate as possible, I have chosen to use some terms—such as "mulatto" and "Negro"—that are offensive to many people today, myself included. There are also characters who express deeply racist views, which were widespread at the time. I do not use these terms or write these characters to condone them, but I want readers to be clear-eyed about the extent of the brutality and oppression that enslaved people faced. As we excavate history through fiction, we can confront the injustices of our past as a way to shed light on our present and work toward a more equitable future.

Eleanor Shearer

A voice is heard in Ramah, mourning and great weeping, Rachel weeping for her children and refusing to be comforted, because they are no more.

JEREMIAH 31:15

Break a vase, and the love that reassembles the fragments is stronger than that love which took its symmetry for granted when it was whole.

DEREK WALCOTT,
"THE ANTILLES: FRAGMENTS OF EPIC MEMORY"

RACHEL'S JOURNEY, 1834–1835

ATLANTIC
OCEAN

LEEWARD ISLANDS

WINDWARD ISLANDS

CARIBBEAN
SEA

Guadeloupe

Dominica

Martinique

St. Lucia

Barbados

St. Vincent

Grenada

Tobago

Trinidad

VENEZUELA

Georgetown

BRITISH
GUIANA

N

W   E

S

0   100   200   300 miles

0   100   200   300   400 kilometers

RIVER
SING
ME
HOME

THE SOIL ON *the island was fertile, but everything laid down shal-low roots. When the hurricanes came, they ripped up even the stur-diest trees; and when the white men came, they tore children out of their mothers' arms. And so, we learned to live without hope. For us, loss was the only thing that was certain.*

Many of us had already lost one home. A home of deep roots and of ancestors delved down into history. Those roots did not save us. Those roots rotted in the hulls of the slave ships, in darkness and filth. We had little left to plant in the new world, and whatever we had was the white men's for the taking. So we tried to live only on the island's surface. We planted cane, but nothing of our own. Mothers turned their heads when a baby was born, refusing to meet its eyes.

We tried to glide through this half-life, this life without history or future, but our endless present had ways of stretching itself out, lying across time, until our lives had movement and color again. At night, we whispered stories to the children of old gods in our homelands, in a tongue the white men couldn't understand.

Still the hurricanes came. Still the children were taken away and sold across the sea. But they were sold with a little seed inside them that sang to them of another life.

Everything laid down shallow roots. But what couldn't go deep went wide, tapping the oceans, tunneling to the islands nearby, where others were also trying and failing to live without memory of yesterday or thought of tomorrow.

Without roots, things die. Many of us did die, at the hands of the white men or in the heat of the midday sun. The soil ran rich with our blood, and the roots fed on our bodies. It made the roots strong. Shallow, but strong.

There was hope for this new world, after all.

BARBADOS

AUGUST
1834

1

——

IT WAS THE blackest part of the night and Rachel was running. Branches tore at her skin. Birds, screeching, took flight at the pounding of her strides. The ground was muddy and uneven, slick with the residue of recent rains, and she slipped, falling hard against the rough bark of a palm tree. She slid down to the soil, to where ants marched and beetles scurried and unseen worms burrowed through the earth. With ragged breaths she gulped the heavy, humid air into her lungs. She could taste its dampness on her tongue, tinged with the acidic bite of her own fear.

What had she done?

She looked behind her. Looming in the darkness was the outline of the mill on Providence plantation, its arms splayed out like four sharp-edged daggers marking an angry cross into the sky. Terror clawed at her throat, as if the mill itself had eyes and could whisper to the overseer what it had seen.

It was not too late. She could still climb back over the wall and creep through the fields of half-planted cane, where gaping holes awaited young green stalks. She could return to her hut, one wooden square among many, and lie back on the sleeping mat that was worn thin from forty years of use. She could wait for dawn and another day of labor . . .

Scrambling to her feet, she kept running. Her legs plunged her deeper into the half-formed shadows of the forest.

Her chest ached. She wanted to collapse but could not; her body, unbidden, carried her farther and farther away from Providence. Every snap of a twig sounded like a gunshot; the murmuring of cane toads became the distant cries of searching men. She must keep running.

Alone, mud-streaked, with weariness sinking into her very bones, a question haunted her—

Was this freedom?

The empty forest. Her fleeing, sick with dread. Was this what they had hoped for, all along?

THE DAY BEFORE, all the slaves of Providence had gathered outside the great house. A stone-faced set of white people waited for them—the master, on horseback, flanked by the overseer, with the master's wife and three children standing on the steps of the house. The white people stared at the slaves. The slaves stared back.

They all knew what was coming. Some of the slaves even smiled. Rachel was among those who didn't. She was old enough to remember other times when there were whispers about the end of slavery. She would not believe it until she heard it for herself from the master's own mouth.

The master's balding forehead glistened with sweat in the heat. As he brought his horse forward, Rachel caught a glimpse of his wife's face, her lips pressed into a line of seething contempt. It was this sight, more than anything, that weakened Rachel's resolve. She dared to hope.

The master kept his remarks short. He told them that the king had decreed an end to slavery. As of the following day, the new Emancipation Act would come into effect.

They were free.

Some people cried. Others yelled and danced in delight. They were a mass of shouting, sweating bodies, a river bursting its banks. The master and the overseer barked useless orders, unable to be heard over the noise. Eventually, the master rode his horse through the crowd at a gallop, just to get them quiet again. Its hooves kicked one woman's head in, and she died instantly. But she died free.

There was more, the master said. They were no longer slaves, but they were instead his apprentices. By law, they would work for him for six years. They could not leave. When the sun rose, Rachel and all the rest would be going back out to finish the planting. They would tend to the cane until the next harvest, and the harvest after. Six years of cutting and planting and cutting again.

Freedom was just another name for the life they had always lived.

An ugly hiss went through the crowd. The overseer, gun slung over his shoulder, reached to bring it down. A hundred pairs of eyes watched the arc of his hand. The master's horse blew air through its nostrils, its reins pulled taut.

The hiss died, and the crowd was still.

Rachel heard the news of hollow freedom in silence. For years, she had lived in perpetual twilight. Those she loved were long gone. Her life had shrunk to the size of the plantation, the routine of endless toil and the long shadows of what had once been. So, there was sense to it. Freedom was an emptiness that could only be filled with sugarcane.

That night, everything was the same. The press of the ground on her back. The shape of her limbs, thin and knotted with sinew. The musty smell of her hut. Days of labor lay ahead, her life as neatly plowed as the furrows in the field.

In sleep, she dreamed of her mother. Or maybe it was the idea of a mother, an outline of warmth and kindness. She couldn't re-member her own mother.

The mother was there in front of her, but somehow Rachel knew that she was also not there. She was somewhere far across the sea. She was fragile, a wisp of smoke. She could not stay long.

The mother spoke a name, and Rachel knew that it was her name—the name she was meant to have before some white man called her Rachel. What the white man gave, he could always take away. But this other name—this was hers. Rachel repeated it. The syllables felt strange in her mouth, but as the thrum of speech vibrated through her, they gave her strength. She was able to stand without stooping. She could feel the pleasant weight of her body, solid and powerful.

The mother stepped back and began to dissolve, one drop at a time, soaking the earth underneath her. When she was gone, the soil glistened a deep, rich red.

Rachel had awoken in pitch darkness—wild, trembling and glistening with sweat—and her body could not be stilled. It moved without her asking it to; it moved on animal instinct alone, crawl-ing out of the hut, unfurling and flinging itself out of Providence and into the night.

In the forest, Rachel asked herself again: Was this freedom? A violent rupture, a body driven to flight, a mind paralyzed with hor-ror as it watched things unfold beyond its control?

The trees had no answer. Their leaves whispered in the wind, and Rachel imagined them taunting her—

What now?

Her body moved beyond the range of thought, with a desperate will of its own.

She kept running.

SHE HAD NO way to mark the passing of time on that moonless night, but by the burning in her legs Rachel knew she had traveled an hour or more when she heard it. So faint she thought she was imagining it at first. Singing.

She saw a speck of light, flickering between the tree trunks. She advanced slowly, her mind filled with thoughts of ghosts and nighttime spirits. But as the singing swelled, accompanied by drumming, filling the forest with sound, her fears receded. The noises were joyful and human and drew her in.

A clearing. A tight circle of bare earth in between the trees. At its center, dozens of people were dancing round a crackling fire, with still more lingering at the edge. As the dancers spun past, Rachel heard snatches of different words and melodies all blending into one. She heard some English, but also other languages, older languages that spoke not to her ears but to her bones.

Rachel stood in shadow, watching. She had been to dances before, as a younger woman, but not like this. Those dances had always been folded into plantation life. They took place in the slave quarters, or in the market square of a nearby town. At any time, a white passerby could appear, or the face of the master in a window of the great house, reminding all present that their joy was not boundless; it could not overflow the confines of slavery. The clearing sparkled with a different kind of magic. With no prying eyes to break the spell, the dancers moved with an unencumbered grace.

The insistent pull of the drums drew Rachel closer, closer, into the light. She found herself one body among many, swaying in time to the beat. She began to tap her foot and hum a song of her own.

A woman threw out her arm, her eyes wide and white, with glittering circles of firelight at the center. She seized Rachel by the wrist.

She sang the command, her voice low and sweet. "Dance!"

Rachel was swept into the throng. In an instant, she lost all sense of herself. She had no end and no beginning, no edges or limits at all. Her whole body dissolved into the rhythm. The dance rippled through the crowd as if through water, and Rachel gave herself up to the music.

Every ache in her body eased. She emptied her lungs of a song she had not even known was inside her. Someone was holding Rachel's hand; she reached out and grabbed another's hand, who grabbed another's hand. As the flames leaped into the sky, Rachel thought she could see the chain of hands climbing to the heavens, a line of people through time and space, united by a single drumbeat.

As THE LAST embers of the fire died, everyone stopped dancing. The dawn was beginning to break, gray light leaking through the trees, and the rising sun brought an end to whatever magic had bound them together. People began to leave, most of them tacking west, the sun on their backs, returning to their plantations. Hovering at the edge of the clearing, standing between two broad oaks, Rachel wondered momentarily if she should follow them. Her absence on Providence might not yet have been noticed. But she hesitated too long. Soon, everyone was gone and she was alone. She slipped eastward, back into the forest.

All of the running and the dancing weighed her down. She ached everywhere. It forced a slow pace. The terror of the first flight had faded to a kind of daze, and she stared up through the canopy at the sky. Somehow, the darkness had been easier—it had a kernel of mystery to it, a sense that the night held many possible worlds, their boundaries worn thin, so that anyone may pass between them. Sunlight was a reminder of the endless march of one day into the next, the unstoppable passage of time to which Rachel had been enslaved all her life.

Still the question plagued her—

What now?

It had a weary edge, a hopelessness. Her run from Providence had been pure survival. Now, she wandered aimlessly through the undergrowth; there was no path, and she stumbled over exposed roots. Her head throbbed with thirst and her limbs were heavy, but her body kept carrying her forward, away from Providence. Apart from the soft thud of her feet on the bare earth, the only sounds were the chattering grackles that flitted overhead.

She climbed the gentle slope of a hill. When she reached the top, suddenly there was the sea. The sight of it spread out below stopped Rachel in her tracks. She had reached the limits of the island.

The rising sun dipped its lower rays into the water on the horizon. Against the gray sky, the sea was a shocking shade of blue, dappled with white-gold sunlight. Its burst of color cut loose the fear that had wrapped itself around Rachel's throat the night before. As if she had plunged into the gently rolling waves, she felt at peace.

All her life, nothing had belonged to her, not even the children pushed out of her own body. With her world boxed in by Providence's walls, and its perimeter patrolled by the overseer's whip, it had seemed as if there was nothing the white men did not own. But now, here was the sea. Vast, defiant and unowned, for who, even white men, could claim it? However much they grasped at it, its waters would run through their fingers and plunge back into the depths.

At the plantation, Rachel had always been made to feel small. With the sea spread out in front of her, she felt small in a different way—not small in herself but a small part of everything that surrounded her. Immersed in the infinite sea. There was freedom in this new kind of smallness, an exhilarating sense that she was *in* the world, and not just passing through it at a white man's pace.

The question came to mind once again—

What now?

This time it had a new quality—it looked forward, outward, across the water. Not back over her shoulder to anyone who might be pursuing her.

Her lungs opened; she could breathe again. Her gaze wandered from the horizon down the hill. At first glance, the hillside was deserted. And yet . . .

She leaned forward a little, shielding her eyes against the sun. She thought she could see, nestled among the trees, about halfway down, the sloping roof of a hut.

Then rough hands seized her from behind, and her head was stuffed into a sack that smelled of smoke and damp earth.

2

———

THERE WAS A man on Providence who had tried to run. He was the only one Rachel had ever known who did. Of course, people talked about running—nighttime whispers, and quiet mutterings as they limped back from the fields—and there were always rumors of someone who knew someone on another plantation who had done it. But Barbados was small and densely settled. If you did run, where would you go that the dogs would not follow?

So, throughout her childhood, Rachel saw running as something beyond thought—an idea, too abstract to be made real. It seemed impossible until, suddenly, it wasn't. They woke up one morning, and he was gone. Rachel was ten years old.

Atlas was his name. He was a private man—quiet, ever since he lost his wife, who was sold away with his child inside her. Rachel had never heard him talk of running. He just slipped away.

For a whole day, the plantation felt different. The boundary walls looked weaker, and the cane no longer seemed to tower over their heads. Men and women stood up straighter. Something sparkled in their eyes. The overseer and the foremen saw it and they feared it, were even freer with the whip than usual. White and

Black alike felt like the world could change—until Atlas was dragged back at dusk, a seeping wound on his calf where a dog had seized him. The rupture in the expected order of things was only temporary; Rachel understood then that they could run but they couldn't hide. Their bodies would always return, dead or alive, to Providence.

Atlas had his nose sliced off as punishment. The wound had grown infected, and he died with foul pus oozing from the gaping holes in his face.

This memory—of Atlas, his flight, his capture and his agony—came to Rachel as she retched, the coarse cloth of the sack filling her nose and mouth. Calloused palms held her wrists tight—besides twisting her head and scrabbling against the earth with her aching feet, there was no way she could struggle. She had no sense of where these hands were pulling her—forward, backward or apart, ripping her in two. She tried to cry out, but she had no voice, and besides, who would hear? Who would come to her aid? Like Atlas, she had attempted the unthinkable, and the world must be put to rights.

She was no longer moving; the hands held her still. Rachel's breathing was ragged, catching on her fear. Something told her she had been brought inside—although she could not see the walls, she felt them pressing close.

There was silence. The grip on her was like iron. Fear kept her limbs twisting in vain—she could not free herself, however hard she tried.

Over the sound of her own heartbeat, Rachel heard soft footsteps.

A woman's voice—deep and close—said, "Well?"

A man's voice came from next to Rachel's ear.

"We find her near the forest."

"A runaway?" the woman asked.

The man gave no reply.

Rachel no longer struggled. She no longer even breathed. The course of her life was not in her hands. She waited.

The woman said, "Let me see her."

As quickly as it had descended, the sack was ripped away, and Rachel was left blinking, a shaft of harsh sunlight shining onto her face through an open doorway. They were in a hut, as small and anonymous as any in the slave village on Providence. But something was not right. The scent was not like Providence, where everything smelled of sweet cane and brutal despair. Fresh, salty air blew in from outside. And when Rachel craned her neck, she saw that the hands that held her were dark, like her own.

Before Rachel stood a tall woman, her hair shorn tight to her skull. Her skin was smooth, unlined and ageless, but something in her eyes betrayed that this woman had seen many years of life.

The woman looked at Rachel. Her gaze had a sharpness to it, something piercing. Rachel felt naked before it, whittled down to the barest elements of herself.

"You running?"

Rachel didn't dare speak.

The woman ran her eyes all over Rachel, taking in every part of her body. She nodded slowly. "Release her."

The hands did as bidden. Rachel tumbled forward, her knees sinking to the floor. She stared up at the tall woman, whose face was as impassive as if it was stone.

The woman took Rachel's chin in her hands. She had rough, worn palms, and her fingers were slightly cool against Rachel's skin.

"Me know why you here."

Rachel's voice was small, barely a whisper. "What you mean?"

"Me see it in your face. Your pickney. You want to find them."

THE HUT FILLED with ghosts. All of Rachel's lost children, crouching in the shadows. She did not have to turn her head to see them. She knew if she tried to look at them directly, they would disappear. They had been her companions, in the corners of her vision or on the cusp of sleep, for many years.

She counted them one by one. Eleven children in all.

Micah. Tall and strong. Taken from her before he'd even turned ten, because they knew he could pass as old enough for the first gang at the market.

Mary Grace. Never spoke again after the night the overseer ambushed her in the fields. Sold because they took her muteness as a sign she was damaged beyond repair. No good could come of a silent slave, who could not say *yes, massa, no, massa* and *right away, massa.*

Mercy. Almost as tall as Micah and also sold young—as soon as they saw a "breeding look" about her.

Samuel. Dead of a fever just after his second birthday.

Kitty. Dead at five of the same disease.

Cherry Jane. Taken up to work at the master's house on account of her honey-colored skin. Rachel saw her only in glimpses—riding in the cart with the other house slaves on the way to market, or tipping a pail of water out of the kitchen door. One day, even these occasional sightings ceased. Cherry Jane was gone.

Thomas Augustus. Small. Overlooked. He'd stayed with her longest of all, until he was fourteen, when they finally realized he was almost a man. They grumbled as they took him that he wouldn't fetch much of a price.

Then there were the unnamed ones. One born backward with the cord wrapped around its throat. Three that died inside her; blood-babies that ran out of her body into the ground.

Their round, watchful eyes prickled on Rachel's skin.

Is it true? she asked them. *That you are the reason I left?*

The instinct that had driven her from Providence was still coiled inside her like an animal. Rachel closed her eyes, tried to reach into herself, to understand. The sight of her children had not dulled this animal but roused it and caused its fur to stand on end. In her legs, worn down from running and dancing, she could feel the muscles tighten. The faces of the children who might yet live—Micah, Mary Grace, Mercy, Thomas Augustus and Cherry Jane—were etched behind her eyelids.

When Rachel opened her eyes, the ghosts were gone. The old woman was still standing in front of her. She nodded to the man behind Rachel.

"Me can take her from here, Gabriel."

Rachel turned, saw a stocky man bow his head.

The old woman held out a hand, with knuckles gnarled like tree roots.

"Come."

"Me name is Bathsheba, but they all call me Mama B."

Outside the hut, the older woman paused, allowing Rachel a moment to take in her surroundings. They were on the hillside, close to the sea. There were indeed dwellings here, as Rachel had glimpsed from the top. A large wooden house sat in the center of a circle of smaller huts, all supported by stilts on the sloping ground. Around them, the soil showed signs of cultivation, but not of the regimented, plantation kind. The furrows meandered, changing course to allow a few palm trees room to grow among the crops.

Rachel kept her arms folded tight across her chest. She felt Mama B watching her, waiting for her questions. A few men and women were at work weeding, moving between the huts, but there were no white people in sight.

"What is this place?"

"It was a tobacco plantation," said Mama B. "A small one. The massa get in some kind of trouble. He leave a few years ago, and we hear nothing since he gone."

Rachel watched a young boy, no more than ten or eleven, skip out of one of the huts, with the pang she often felt when she saw children of a certain age.

"This your family? Your pickney?"

"No. Me have no pickney."

"Then how come—" Rachel caught herself. There had been a sharp edge to Mama B's reply, and she didn't want to pry.

The older woman looked sideways at Rachel. "Then how come they call me Mama B?" Quite suddenly, she smiled, and deep lines formed across her face—the lines of someone who smiled often. "Me mother to no one, so me try to be mother to all. Me mother, Betsy, had twenty pickney. They call her Mama B before me, so in a way me inherit the title. Since the massa leave, me try and keep this place for them folks that have no place to go."

Mama B took Rachel into the main house. Rachel followed her slowly, carefully, ears still pricked for a sign that this was all a trick, that at any moment white men would come barreling out from the bushes with guns raised, ready to drag her back to Providence. Trust did not come easily to Rachel, but what choice did she have? There was nowhere left to run. The sea marked the outer boundary of Barbados—beyond it was nothing but deep water and sky.

The front door led to a large room, with a wooden table surrounded by chairs, stools and upturned barrels. A woman sat in one corner, pounding spices with a mortar and pestle. A few sleeping mats were pushed up against the walls, some empty and some still occupied. Two doors to the left and right signaled that the house had more rooms still, and through one door Rachel could hear the murmur of voices.

Mama B clapped her hands once. Activity in the room ceased, and heads were raised from the sleeping mats, eyes half-open. A man stepped through the door to the left, looking curious. Rachel, standing behind the older woman, felt hot under all these gazes. She stared down at her feet.

"This is Rachel," said Mama B. "She looking for her pickney, lost long ago."

From the way some of the faces in the room twitched, Rachel knew she was not the only one to have lost family, and perhaps not the only one to have tried to find someone again.

The woman in the corner had put down her pestle. She stood slowly—she was slight, young, and her hands were twisting together.

"Me think . . ."

Rachel's heart lurched.

"Yes." The woman came close, her eyes roving over Rachel's face. Her voice was light and gentle. "Me think . . . you have a daughter?"

Rachel nodded.

"Yes," the woman said again. "Me think me did see her. A few years ago, in Bridgetown. Your face have the same shape. Me remember because she don't speak."

Rachel did not move. She felt weak and light-headed. Her mouth was dry and her lip trembled. The image of Mary Grace flashed before her—a stronger, sharper picture than she had seen in years, more solid now that Rachel knew she existed in a particular place. Bridgetown. The other end of the island. In that moment, it felt an insurmountable distance away.

Mama B rested a hand on the small woman's shoulder. Then she turned to Rachel.

"Me planning to go down to Bridgetown. Me can take you. We can go tomorrow."

There was a hardness to the older woman's voice that quelled the protest rising in Rachel's throat. This was not an offer; it was a command. Rachel, her limbs slack with exhaustion, accepted it.

3

—

THE NEXT MORNING, the rain came. Rachel and Mama B had not yet reached the top of the hill when it began to fall, hard and angry, fat droplets boring holes into the ground. Soon, they were drenched, sinking step-by-step into the sodden earth, water clinging to them like a second skin. On the horizon, sea and sky bled together into the raging gray of an approaching storm.

"We must turn back," said Mama B.

Inside the house, the rooms were crowded but quiet. Rachel joined a group of women standing by a window, and stared out to sea. She took small comfort in imagining her daughter Mary Grace on the other side of Barbados, staring at the same forbidding mass of waves and hearing the same wind moaning as it ripped through the island.

By evening, the storm had blown itself out, but the rain lasted for three days. The thudding of water on wood began to make Rachel's head ache. To try to distract herself from the thwarted journey, she studied every inch of Mama B's house. There were three rooms in all—the main room with the broad table, and two side rooms, one filled with sleeping mats and the other serving as a food store. Rachel started in the corner of the store, and made her way around the house clockwise, tracing her hand over every crack and groove of the wall. She found the spots where water seeped in and dripped onto the floor. She found the places where the planks were uneven, or blackened with soot from candles. Next to the front door, she found a mark someone had carved into the wall—it looked like the beginning of a picture, curving gently back toward itself in a half-formed spiral, about the size of Rachel's palm. The line was deep and smooth, and it was the same dark color as the surrounding wood. A healed scar, not a fresh cut.

When the walls had no more secrets left to divulge, Rachel turned to the people. Many had unfinished carvings of their own that she glimpsed when they rolled over while sleeping, or turned to the window to watch the rain. Puckered skin patterned out the memory of whips, while the unmarked corners of backs and shoulders showed where freedom had cut short the process of searing slavery even deeper into their flesh.

Mama B was the center of the household. Everyone seemed to bring her their questions and their fears. Rachel often saw the older woman in hushed conversation with some frowning man or forlorn-looking child, someone who had braved the rain to come over from another hut and seek her counsel. These people always went away with their faces a little less downcast, thanks to whatever Mama B had said.

Mama B would nod to Rachel if their eyes met. One time, she came over and put a hand on Rachel's shoulder and asked if she was all right. Otherwise, Rachel spoke to no one. Being trapped inside made her uneasy—confinement felt similar enough to life on Providence that she reverted to her old self, withdrawn and quiet. For their part, the other occupants of the house paid her little attention. They seemed used to reticent strangers drifting in and out of the edges of their community. Rachel kept to the corners, out of their way, and waited for the rain to cease.

———

ON THE MORNING of the fourth day, Rachel woke to the sound of silence. The rain had finally passed.

Mama B was already up, sitting at the table, the hard obsidian profile of her face turned toward the sea. She did not seem to notice Rachel rise and take a seat beside her, waiting to hear if they might soon depart.

"One of the pickney sick," said Mama B, without turning to look at Rachel. The sentence rolled out of her mouth ready-formed. These words were not strangers to her. "A fever. It come in the night. We can't go to Bridgetown today."

Rachel nodded.

"Me must go into the forest." Mama B stood, taking a small sack from the table and tucking it into the waistband of her skirt. "There are some herbs that can help him. You can come with me if you like."

After days inside, Rachel was restless and eager for fresh air, but Mama B's mention of medicinal herbs made her pause. Rachel herself had never had that kind of knowledge, but on Providence there were a few who were rumored to be skilled with potions or spells. When she was a child, there was a man who everyone said was a witch in his homeland. He spoke very little English, and his unfamiliar words might have been attempts at conversation rather than curses, but people avoided him in fear. Rachel could still remember his eyes, the whites of them yellowing and bloodshot, with dark irises punched like holes in the center. Some of the other children said if you looked into them too long, you would drop dead. And Rachel had heard that once, when an overseer was galloping toward the man with the whip in his hand, the horse reared up and its rider was thrown backward, breaking his neck.

But Mama B's eyes did not look like they held the power of death, and through the window, the world looked inviting—pools of rainwater were scattered across the still-wet ground, glinting in the morning sunlight. This was enough to ease Rachel's childhood superstitions, and she followed Mama B out of the house.

THEY WALKED UP the hill and into the forest. The early-morning air was damp and humid, and everything smelled fresh. Under the canopy, the leaves dyed the sunlight a mottled green, and Rachel had to strain her eyes to avoid the roots that crisscrossed their path. Her head knocked against the low-hanging fruit of a calabash tree, and the fronds of ferns tickled her shins.

Mama B led the way by her hands, pulling herself from trunk to trunk. She was always touching something—bark, leaf, fruit, flower. At one with the forest. Rachel, who kept her own hands clasped behind her, watched the older woman at work. There was a language Mama B could speak that Rachel could not. Rachel was attuned to the rhythms of cane and the yams and cassava of the slave plots. Away from cultivation, the wild trees had shapes and secrets she did not know.

They came to a thick, knotted tree that had carved out a space for itself in the undergrowth; around it, nothing grew. Mama B patted it, as if in greeting, and turned to Rachel.

"Here." She held out the sack. "Take the bark."

Rachel stayed a few paces back. "You want me to do it?"

"Yes."

"But me don't know anything—about herbs, trees. How to heal."

Mama B laughed from the middle of her chest, and the sound vibrated through the earth around them. "You don't need to know all that. You can still help."

The warmth of Mama B's chuckle caught Rachel off guard, pierced her defenses. And why not? Where was the harm? Her long-held fear of obeah still cast a shadow, but Rachel shook it off and took the sack from Mama B.

Even under the shade of the canopy, the constellation of dew-drops on the tree's trunk shimmered. Resting a hand against it, Rachel could feel its age—hundreds of years of growth twisted into the rough wood, spiraling toward the sky. A sense of reverence overcame her at being in the presence of something so ancient. The tree preexisted even her distant ancestors, and would remain long after her own death. She found a chink and peeled loose a small strip of bark, dropping it into the sack. Then, almost without think-ing, she traced the naked patch of yellow-green trunk she had left behind. The wound was clean; no sap leaked from it. She exhaled, satisfied. The tree would be fine without what she had taken.

Mama B was smiling at her. "You see? You don't need to know. You feel it."

"What?"

"The connection between all things. That we can't just take; we must also give." Mama B, too, touched the place on the tree where the bark had been peeled away. "All healing start from there."

They continued to forage through the forest. Mama B was more forthcoming now, crouching down and pointing out to Rachel the tiny shoots poking out of the earth, or pulling down fruits and flowers and pressing them into Rachel's hands, telling her to notice their color, shape or size. They filled the sack with roots, petals and leaves until Mama B was satisfied.

"We must head back," she said. "The pickney may not have long."

INSIDE THE HOUSE, Rachel could smell the sickness in the pallid air. The child had been laid out on a mat in the corner, eyes closed and skin glistening with sweat. Rachel glanced at him, then looked away. He had the same feverish sheen of Samuel and Kitty as they slipped into death, the same shallow breaths. He reminded her of everything she had lost.

Mama B took the wooden mortar and pestle and sat at the table.

Beside her, Rachel emptied the sack of the things they had gathered in the forest. A knot of people drew close around them. Rachel picked out the child's mother by her tearstained face, and the sight made her breath catch in her throat. It was the small, fragile woman from before, the one who had seen in Rachel's face an echo of Mary Grace, and who now stood to lose a child of her own.

Mama B took a flower, bright red at its heart with petals that faded to soft pink around the edges. She began to grind it into the mortar. Its sweet fragrance soon cloyed into sickly fumes that stuck in the back of Rachel's throat. Mama B then added handfuls of the other herbs they had gathered, which tempered the scent of the flower with an earthier smell, like freshly cut wood. Finally, she added a handful of berries that burst under the pestle, their dark juice running like veins through the mixture.

Mama B leaned over the bowl. Her nostrils flared as she inhaled deeply, eyes closed. She murmured something under her breath in a language Rachel didn't understand, but the phrase had a warm familiarity like the face of an almost-forgotten friend.

Through the window, a fresh breeze pierced the stale air of sickness in the room. Mama B sat upright.

"It ready." She looked at Rachel. "Bring the bark."

Mama B knelt beside the child, whose eyes flew open as he sensed her approach. The little boy triggered a flood of memories that Rachel could no longer hold back. She saw Micah in the angle of his eyebrows, Mercy in the fingernails on his small hands, and Samuel in the way his ribs rose and fell. She saw them all. Time bent back on itself, and suddenly it didn't matter that the boy's eyes did not have the glassy, vacant look of the dying, or that his lips still sucked air greedily into his lungs. The cycle was doomed to repeat itself, over and over. Sickness and death. Tears pricked Rachel's eyes. Only loss was certain. Nothing would change.

A touch on her arm pitched Rachel out of her memories and back to Mama B's house. The child's mother was beside her, pressing the strip of bark into her hand. The viselike grip of past grief loosened its hold on Rachel, and the little boy no longer had the look of her own children. He was someone else's son, and his future had not been set.

Rachel took the bark, and gave the child's mother a small smile. The younger woman's lip was trembling, but her eyes shone with hope—hope that Mama B had the cure, but also hope that Rachel could help. Stirred by this trust, Rachel knelt beside Mama B.

"What can me do?"

Mama B instructed Rachel to lay the bark across the child's forehead. The older woman guided Rachel's finger into the herbal mixture, and then had her trace a line across his top lip and another down the middle of his chest. Finally, Mama B poured the remaining mixture into his mouth. The child gagged slightly at the taste but did not resist. Mama B rested a hand on his shoulder, her expression so tender and full of love that Rachel felt she had to look away—it was too private a moment to be shared.

"Sleep," Mama B whispered.

The child closed his eyes. The room stayed still as his ragged breathing slowed. Only when he had been asleep for some time did Mama B move. She touched Rachel first, a gesture of thanks, then stood and took the child's young mother into her arms. Those who had gathered to watch began to disperse, heading back out to work, or off into the other rooms. A few muttered prayers; one man crossed himself, his eyes cast toward the ceiling. Rachel also lifted her gaze and silently willed the child to live, though she had lost faith in praying years ago. Something about the moment, about the innocence of the child's face, rekindled a tiny spark of her faith.

For the rest of the day, everyone moved slowly and spoke in hushed tones. They waited. The child slept. Rachel took one of the blue-black berries Mama B had not mixed into the medicine, and rolled it between finger and thumb, careful not to let it burst.

4

——

THE CHILD LIVED. After a day of feverish sleep, he woke up with a smile that cracked the dried herbal mixture crusted on his lips. Everyone in the house allowed themselves a brief moment of celebration—the gripping of another's arm, or the raising of eyes skyward in thanks. The child's mother held him and wept softly into the dark curls on his head. Watching them, Rachel felt a weight being lifted. The wheel had broken. The endless tide of seasons spent planting and harvesting and planting once more—the cycle of harsh life and early death—these had lost their power. There was nothing inevitable in the child's survival, but there was nothing impossible in it, either. Things were not so set as they had once seemed.

RACHEL AND MAMA B set off for Bridgetown. Stepping outside the boundaries of the old tobacco plantation, Mama B's little sanctuary, Rachel felt uneasy. The road to Bridgetown would take her back toward Providence. Were they searching for her? Did they have dogs following her scent? But then the cool shadows of the forest swallowed her and she felt not safe, but hidden. Shielded from the exposing heat of the sun.

The forest path was close to the cliffs. Rachel could not see the sea, but she could hear it, breaking gently against the rocks below. Mama B led as they picked their way through the undergrowth. They said little to each other, but there was a comfortable ease between them. The child's sickness had brought them closer together. Rachel recognized in the older woman a boundless capacity for love that she had once felt herself, long ago. But Mama B also had a steel to her, a quiet strength that Rachel admired. She had the hardened edges of a survivor, but she had also helped others to survive. For Rachel, who had tried to teach herself to love less, help less, close herself off from others, this expansive survival offered hope. There was another way.

They turned inland and, still sheltered by the trees, headed for the hills. The path began to widen; branches had been hacked away to allow people to pass by easily, and on either side the trees grew into one another, interlacing to form a barrier against the road. As the forest shrank back, Rachel's fear grew. They walked now in a bright strip of sunlight, and Rachel kept seeing movement in between the trees, or hearing the sounds of leaves whispering. For a sickening moment she imagined her former master bursting from the shadows. She took short, shaky breaths, trying to calm herself, trying to rid herself of the feeling of being watched. The only eyes on them were the eyes of a solitary snail kite, nesting in the branches on the verge of the road, its head twisting to stare at them as they passed.

Rachel and Mama B reached the top of a hill, and quite suddenly all the trees fell away. Below them, sugarcane fields spread like a rash across the flat landscape. No inch of land had been spared—it had all been forced to submit and produce. The cane was the white masters' dominion over the island made manifest. The sight of the plantations made Rachel sick with fear.

"What if we seen?" she whispered.

"We might be," said Mama B. "But this the quickest way to Bridgetown. You want to get there, you gon' have to travel this road and take the risk."

As Rachel stared at the cane fields, imagining white men descending on horseback to drag her by a rope back to Providence, something else rose inside her. A kind of longing mixed in with her fear, tugging at her heart, pulling her back to her old plantation. Back to familiarity, and the soil that held the bodies of Samuel, Kitty and the stillborn child. There was certainty in their bones, unlike the vast unknown that lay ahead. A weary ache settled over her. She felt the old smallness again—a sense that she was nothing, had nothing, except the buried bodies of her dead children. Whatever else she had lost was lost forever.

Rachel turned her head. Mama B was looking at her, without impatience or expectation. There was no command anymore; Rachel knew that if she asked to turn back, they would. And yet something about Mama B's face, immovable as rock but carved with kindness, gave Rachel the strength she needed. She breathed in, feeling her chest expand. She took one step, then another, until they were walking again.

They went down the bald hillside and followed the road between the plantations. On either side, great houses squatted over the workers in the fields, watching. There was little shade, and the morning sun was burning fiercely. These were places made for surveillance, and Rachel felt observed. She kept her head down, her hands across her chest, keeping herself as small as she could.

No-longer-slaves tended the cane. Rachel watched a man walking with a bucket balanced on his head—he was close enough that the smell of fresh dung wafted onto the road, making her gag. She knew that smell. She knew how it felt to walk through the fields with excrement on her head.

Some of the workers glanced over as they passed, their eyes

glazed with exhaustion. Most never looked up. There were so many fields, and so many faces, that they all began to blur together. The lurch of terror each time Rachel saw someone look their way faded to a background hum of quiet dread. She almost felt resigned to her fate. If someone saw her who knew her—who shouted out what she was, a runaway—then so be it. She would be dead. Until then, all she could do was keep walking, staring numbly ahead at the road, letting the identical scenes pass through the corners of her vision.

Close to midday, with the heat from the sun unrelenting, Mama B slowed their pace. Rachel's mouth was dry, her head pounding. The island seemed vast—infinite rows of cane, and a wall of blue, cloudless sky.

"We must rest," said Mama B.

Rachel looked at the road ahead. It, too, was endless, squeezed between the fields and sky, narrowing into a single speck in the distance. "How long to Bridgetown?"

Mama B squinted into the distance. "Three hours or so. But we gon' go quicker if we get out the sun awhile."

Mama B walked off the side of the road, toward the nearest field. With a careless irreverence for the boundary of the plantation, she slipped under the thin fence. Rachel waited for the shout of a foreman or an overseer, but none came. The workers ignored Mama B, who continued around the edge of the field toward some stone buildings on the far side. It took the older woman turning and waving impatiently for Rachel to follow her.

When they reached the buildings, Mama B sat and motioned for Rachel to do the same. The sun was directly overhead, and they had to draw their legs into their chests to keep themselves in shade, but it was noticeably cooler, even with the stone radiating some of the day's absorbed heat into their backs.

Mama B shared out some provisions—mashed yams, salted fish,

plantain—and they ate in silence. Being back on a plantation, even one so far from Providence, left Rachel rigid with fear. Her shoulders, neck and jaw were clenched tight, and she kept glancing around for any sign of trouble. She noticed a man in the field stop working and lean against his plow, staring in their direction. Rachel dropped her gaze quickly, afraid to meet his eyes. When she dared to look up again, he was already halfway over to them.

He made his way slowly. By furtive glances, Rachel noticed that he limped. From far away, his height and breadth had led her to assume that he was young, but as he drew closer she realized she was mistaken. He was at least a decade older than her, if not more. His flesh had withered on his large frame, leaving behind sagging skin, but age made him even more imposing, as if strength had set straight into his bones and he had no more need of muscle. In spite of an ankle that was swollen, he looked powerful. A long scar ran down the left side of his face, cutting through an eye that was milky white. He stopped a few feet short of Rachel and Mama B, and his right eye regarded them shrewdly.

"Bathsheba."

Mama B looked up from her food. "Tamerlane."

The man's face split into a grin, his scar curling up toward his ear. Laughing, Mama B leaped up and they embraced.

"Rachel." Mama B released the man and turned to her. "This is Tamerlane. Me brother."

In spite of their skin—Mama B's smooth and Tamerlane's heavily lined—when they stood side by side, Rachel could see the resemblance between them.

"Hello, Rachel," said Tamerlane. "What bring you and me sister this way?"

Rachel forced herself to focus on his good eye, and not on the ruined left one twitching in its socket. "We going to Bridgetown."

In the pause that followed, Mama B did not supply any further detail, and Tamerlane did not pry. Rachel was glad. She sat with her knees guarding her chest. She bore no ill will to Tamerlane, but the thought of speaking her quest out loud, naming the true purpose of their journey, chilled her. She was afraid—of capture, of failure or even of judgment for not having been brave enough to attempt the search sooner.

Mama B brushed Tamerlane's arm tenderly. "Come. Sit."

He joined them in the thin strip of shadow. Mama B and Tamerlane sat with their bodies almost touching. In spite of the knot of anxiety still in her stomach, Rachel was entranced by their closeness. She let one of her legs stretch out, her ankle and shin slipping into the sunlight, though she kept the other against her like a shield.

"We grow up together," Mama B said. She spoke to Rachel, but also partly to the world. As if she had to speak to fix this truth in time, to defend it from some white man going back and stealing Tamerlane away from her. "On a plantation outside Bridgetown."

Tamerlane picked up the thread of her story and continued. "There were so many of us in the old days. The whole plantation talk of our mother's strength, giving the massa so many pickney to work in the fields."

Rachel said nothing, but she sat up slightly, straightening her back and leaning in. She was curious. She wanted to hear.

"We were happy as we can be," Mama B continued. "But one year, things get bad."

"Yes," said Tamerlane. "The massa in debt."

"He decide to sell two of our brothers."

Their sentences flowed into one another, matching in cadence and tone, as if coming from a single mouth.

"The loss of Ishmael and James kill our mother," Mama B continued. "We don' lose brothers and sisters to sickness before. But these were sons that live with her for twenty years—it was too much for her to bear."

"She pass away of grief. And there was worse to come."

"A few months later, the massa have our brother Samson drag out of his house and beaten. He say that Samson was plotting a rebellion to get revenge for our mother and brothers."

"They arrest Samson and execute him for his crimes."

The rhythm slowed to a funeral pace. Each syllable thudded like a drumbeat. They told the story with a practiced air—this was not the first time they had spoken of it. And yet Rachel could hear the roughness of their grief, which could not be smoothed away through retelling.

"After that, the massa vow to sell us all," said Mama B. "He don't want any more trouble from we."

"Me was brought straight here." Tamerlane gestured to the fields around them. "Me been here ever since."

"Me start out in Bridgetown," said Mama B. "When that massa die, me sold again to the north. Me lose hope that me gon' ever see me family again."

They lapsed into silence. Rachel, drawn in by their tale, could not bear the pause. "What then? How you find each other again?"

Brother and sister exchanged a smile.

"It was three or so years ago," said Tamerlane. "Me working in these fields and me see two people walking along the main road. The sun in me eyes, but me know it Bathsheba by the way she walk." He chuckled. "We sometimes call her 'mistress,' she walk so tall and proud. Me was ready to run to her, but with the overseer watching, me don't dare. She go past and she don't see me and me sure me never gon' see her again. Me don't know where she come from or where she going. Me think that one glance was all me get. One glance for all the years of praying."

"Tamerlane don' see me and the massa walking down to Bridgetown," said Mama B. "The massa had business in town. We due to stay a week, but the massa hear that his wife sick. He hire a horse, and tell me to walk back."

"This time, we lucky. When she pass, the overseer inside, and the nearest driver at the other end of the field. Me was still watching the road every day, though me try not to hope. When me see her, me run over, calling her name."

Tamerlane and Mama B closed their eyes, lost in the memory of their reunion. Written on their faces was the joy of the moment, mixed with the bittersweet taste of all the years they had lost.

"Since that day me come here when me can," said Mama B.

Tamerlane rested his hand on top of his sister's. Between them, stronger than the midday sun, burned the heat of a bond that no master could have broken.

Tamerlane got to his feet, supporting his weight on Mama B's shoulder to spare his bad ankle. "Me must work." He fixed his good eye on Rachel and nodded. "Take care, Rachel." Then, turning to his sister, "Me gon' look for you on the way back."

"Yes. Me gon' see you again." Mama B savored the certainty of her words.

As Tamerlane walked back into the fields, Mama B glanced at Rachel. From the glint in the older woman's eye, Rachel knew that the effect of the story had been intentional. The warmth that she felt, the sense that the impossible could become possible—that damage, once done, could be undone—all of this Mama B had planned. Rachel was thankful for it.

When the two women rose to continue their journey, Rachel kept her head down, and fear still quivered just below her skin. Still, they might be followed. Still, she might be found. And yet, her strides were a little longer. Barbados no longer seemed endless. With every step, Bridgetown seemed to be just beyond the horizon—and in it, Mary Grace.

5

———

THE ROAD SWELLED with people. Women carried baskets on their heads and hips, and men drove donkeys and pigs along with sticks. Horses trotted imperiously through the crowds, carrying soldiers in flaming-red coats. In the early-evening sun, everyone cast long shadows. The air thickened with the smell of sweat and manure, overlaid with the sweetness of ripe fruit. Buildings began to rise out of the ground. Small huts at first, no different than the ones on the plantations, but growing taller and grander as they walked.

"This is Bridgetown," said Mama B.

Rachel said nothing. She had always thought the plantation evidence of the white man's power over nature—his ability to enclose the land and force from the soil the things he desired. But Bridgetown was the real monument to the white man. Nothing grew here. Looking around, she saw only people, and the sprawling houses they had built.

The town was not designed with nowhere to hide, not like the plantations were. People dipped in and out of side streets and crouched in doorways. But Rachel could not shake the feeling of being watched. A white man on his horse fixed his eyes on her a moment too long, and she almost collapsed, dizzy with the thought that he knew she was out of place, knew she was a runaway, was about to leap off his horse and seize her by the wrists and drag her back the way they had come. But the man looked away, and they walked on.

"Me talk to Artemis before we leave," said Mama B. Artemis was the mother of the sick child, the one who had seen Mary Grace all those years ago. "She say she see your daughter at the market. Alone, but she dress smart. So most likely she a slave in a house somewhere."

Rachel could no longer see an image of her daughter. She no longer felt that Mary Grace was close. On all sides, there were streets filled with houses, any one of which could hold her daughter, and the scale of the task made Rachel feel light-headed.

Distracted, she almost walked straight into a cart that had stopped in front of them. Mama B put a hand on Rachel's back to guide her round it.

"Bridgetown not so big," said Mama B. "Don't worry. We gon' find her."

Mama B led them down a side street. It was quiet, and once out of the mass of crowds Rachel breathed a little easier. She tried to hold on to the way she had felt after seeing Mama B and Tamerlane together and hearing their story. By force of will, she stopped the last of her hope from ebbing away.

Mama B frowned at the front doors of the houses they passed. Eventually, one opened, and a woman walked out. Rachel couldn't help but stare. She had never seen a woman so dark dressed in such finery—a silk dress, pale blue, with a sash of red ribbon around the waist.

"Excuse me," Mama B said to the woman. "You know what place Hope live?"

The woman arranged her face into a haughty expression that

was undercut by the fact that she had to look upward at Mama B. "Who is asking?"

"Bathsheba. Me know Hope in the north."

The woman dropped her chin. "You are Mama B? Hope has mentioned you." She gestured to a house opposite. "She lives there."

The front door led them into a narrow hallway. A stout white woman leaning against a wooden desk straightened as they walked in. Rachel instinctively dropped her eyes, but Mama B stood tall.

"Can I help you?" The white woman had a nasal voice, and cold green eyes.

"We here to see Miss Hope," said Mama B.

"She's out."

"She back soon?"

"Maybe."

"Then we wait."

They stared at each other. After a while, the white woman shrugged and rested her chest back on top of the desk, opening a newspaper to signal that they deserved no more of her attention. Mama B leaned back against the shabby wallpaper, while Rachel hovered in the middle of the hallway.

They waited.

It wasn't long before the front door opened again. The woman on the threshold turned and waved to someone outside. Rachel saw the flash of brass buttons on a soldier's coat before the door closed.

The young woman sashayed down the hallway toward them. She was arrestingly beautiful. Her skin was the color of a pitch-black night—so dark it absorbed all the light around her, dulling everything she passed. Every single line of her body was soft, from the curve of each nostril to the gentle protrusion of her collarbone under a long, graceful neck. She wore a dress of dark emerald green, cut low across her shoulders.

Mama B stepped forward with a smile. "Hope," she said.

Hope gasped in recognition. The two women embraced. Hope

was a good deal shorter than Mama B, but somehow she was all
Rachel could see. Mama B was like the frame that Rachel's eyes
slid over in hungry search of the picture.

The woman behind the desk cleared her throat. Hope broke
away from Mama B and, reaching into the low neckline of her
dress, produced two silver coins, dropping them in the other woman's outstretched palm. Satisfied, the white woman returned to her
paper, and Hope turned back to Mama B.

"How delightful to see you!" Hope had grafted a lighter, more
refined accent onto her voice. The country tones were still there, but
the effect charmed more than it jarred. The different lilts blended
together in harmony. "And who is your friend?"

"This is Rachel," said Mama B. "She come with me from the
north."

"It is lovely to meet you, Rachel." Hope smiled at Rachel, and
the young woman's warmth was infectious. Rachel felt her own
shoulders relaxing.

"Come! You must be tired from your journey. Come up to my
room."

Upstairs, Hope's room was small and plainly furnished. A few
touches of luxury added a sense of character: a white lace bed-
spread, a patterned carpet on the floorboards and a red dress hanging across the front of a wardrobe. Hope grabbed two stools and set
them next to the bed, creating a tight, convivial circle for the three
of them.

"Come, sit down."

Hope positioned Mama B on the bed and took a stool for herself. Rachel sat on the other, so close to Hope that their legs brushed
against each other.

Mama B looked ready to speak, but Hope turned quickly.

"So, Rachel, did Mama B explain how we met?"

Rachel shook her head, and Hope leaned forward. Rachel mir-
rored the action, drawing their heads together.

"Two years ago, I ran away from my plantation. I headed north until I reached the sea. I had no food, no money, no plan—except a vague idea that I could drown myself!" Hope laughed and clasped her hands together, and Rachel found herself drawn into smiling before she could fully grasp the darkness of the younger woman's words. "Luckily, Mama B found me. She helped hide me until she could take me to Bridgetown herself." Hope cast her arms outward. "And now, here I am!"

Mama B looked at Hope with piercing eyes. "Me hear you in trouble."

Hope's face rushed through a few different expressions, too quick for Rachel to name them, before ordering itself into pleasant surprise. She laughed again. "Me? Trouble? Of course not!"

"Me hear you in jail."

Hope glanced one way, then the other, searching for an escape. She settled on a smile that was almost a grimace. "Oh, that old business. Well, I'm fine now."

"Hope."

Hope began to toy with the right sleeve of her dress, rubbing the fabric slowly between finger and thumb.

"It really was nothing." She looked away from both of them as she spoke. "I got into a fight. A man tried to hurt me, but I wouldn't let him." She looked back at Mama B. The soft contours of her body had hardened like granite. "He was white, so yes, I went to prison for a while."

The three women sat in silence. Hope kept her head held high.

"Well," said Mama B. "At least you all right. Me did worry."

Hope laughed and the hardness that had come over her vanished. "You don't have to worry about me, Mama. I can take care of myself. Oh, but, Rachel!" She turned on the stool, dexterously swapping one subject for another. "Why did you make the journey to Bridgetown?"

Even more than Hope's boundless energy, her sudden flash of

steel had worn down Rachel's defenses. Here was another woman navigating the world as best she could. Rachel felt that, young as she was, Hope would understand her quest.

"Me looking for me daughter."

"She is in Bridgetown? Would I know her?"

"She called Mary Grace." The words felt strange in Rachel's mouth. The idea of her daughter still felt like a dream, and something about Hope made it seem inappropriate to speak of dreams. She was too solid and too beautiful.

Hope frowned. "I don't know a Mary Grace."

"We gon' search for her," said Mama B. "Look around the market. Ask people. You think we can stay here while we look?"

"Of course! Anything I can do to help."

Rachel tried to protest but Hope and Mama B both shushed her. "It's the least I can do," Hope said.

Rachel cast her eyes downward. The sharing of her children, the precious memories she had, was still hard. But what she felt most of all was relief. Held between their three minds, Mary Grace felt closer. Mama B and Hope would help fill out the blurred edges until her daughter became real.

A voice from downstairs carried up through the cracks in the floorboards. "Hope!"

Hope sighed. "I have to go." She stood, smoothing out her skirt. "But please do make yourselves at home. I'll be back soon."

She walked over to the door and then paused, glancing back at Rachel. Hope's eyes held such intensity that Rachel felt heat rising in her cheeks. "Mary Grace," Hope said slowly. "I'll look out for her. Just in case." With Rachel's face committed to memory, Hope left.

Rachel went to the window. A white man in a dark suit was standing in the middle of the street. Rachel watched as Hope came out, kissed him on the cheek, and slipped her arm through his. Together, the two walked off down the road, and Rachel's eyes followed them until they were out of sight.

6

———

Rachel and Mama B slept on the floor with—at Hope's insistence—a dress for a pillow.

"Oh, that old thing!" she said. "I never wear it anymore anyway."

(Rachel thought she could see spots of blood around the collar, but it was hard to tell because the blue material was so dark.)

The next day, Mama B tried to teach Rachel how to navigate the bewildering web of streets. She pointed to the twin spires of St. Michael's and St. Mary's, jutting skyward, acting as a compass from any point in Bridgetown. Rachel tried her best to commit the town to memory, but she was as lost as she had been in the wild forest, painfully aware that she was in a totally unfamiliar place.

They went to a few of the grander houses on the west side of town, where they waited outside back entrances until the maids or manservants Mama B knew dashed out on an errand. Everyone was pleased to see Mama B, everyone looked on Rachel with sympathetic eyes, but no one had seen or heard of a woman called Mary Grace.

For the rest of the week, they split up so that they could cover more ground. At first, Rachel felt too shy to talk to anyone, but after a few fruitless days, her heart grew heavier with the fear that somehow they were mistaken and Mary Grace was not in Bridge-town, and she lost her shyness. She grabbed people by the arm in the street and asked, "You know me daughter? Mary Grace? She is mute," hoping that the desperation in her voice would encourage them to dig into their memories for an answer.

Her life began to take the shape of a waking dream. She felt as though the world wasn't solid—like Bridgetown kept shifting. Without Mama B, Rachel often got lost: a road she was counting on to take her back to Hope's house would turn out not to exist, or she would head in what she was certain was the direction of the pier, only to find herself on the opposite edge of the town. And the search had that dreamlike quality of sameness—like nothing she did could take her closer to her goal.

ONE DAY, RACHEL came home exhausted and found Hope alone in front of her dressing table, wearing a plain nightdress. For a moment, Hope looked drained, but when she smiled the warmth returned to her face.

"Any sign of her?" she asked.

Rachel shook her head.

"You'll find her soon." Hope spoke so earnestly that it was impossible not to believe her.

Rachel watched as Hope unscrewed the lid on a silver pot and spread a paste onto her hair, brushing it through slowly with a wide-toothed ivory comb. Rachel thought of Cherry Jane—as a child, the other women on Providence had admired her loose curls and declared that she had "good hair." Cherry Jane was beautiful, there was no doubt about it—but the idea that Hope's tight coils, which framed her face in a perfect oval, were somehow lesser was absurd.

Hope's eyes met Rachel's in the mirror. She laughed. "My hair is such a chore."

"It look beautiful."

"It's a pain! I've half a mind to chop it all off like yours." She turned and held out the comb. "Here. You can help me brush it if you like."

Rachel's hands still remembered the movement, though it had been years since she had pulled a comb through the hair of one of her children. Hope's thick strands rose and fell like waves, and Rachel's chest tightened. She forced herself to breathe through the pain, the echo of all the years of motherhood that had been taken from her. The paste from the jar smelled of roses.

Hope was watching Rachel in the mirror. For the first time, Rachel spotted little imperfections in Hope's ebony skin. A small scar nestled in her right eyebrow, and a thin line, the ghost of a frown, ran across her forehead.

"Can I ask you something?" Hope said. Her voice was subdued.

Rachel nodded.

"Do you think Mama B disapproves?"

"Of what?"

Hope gestured vaguely around the room. "Of this. Of me."

Without the peal of laughter in her voice, Hope was fragile. Young. Rachel wondered how old she really was—surely not much more than twenty.

"No," said Rachel firmly. And she meant it. Whenever they walked the streets together, Mama B often spoke about Hope. About how she had been when they met—a bundle of raw energy, hot-tempered, hurting. Mama B had known there was no taming her, but she had done her best to nudge that strong will toward life at a time when Hope wanted to destroy herself. Mama B spoke fondly to Rachel of how good it was to see Hope on her feet now. Of course, she still worried. But Hope seemed happier. If she was getting into fights, at least it was to defend herself. There was a time when she wouldn't have resisted an attacker. She would have joined him in bruising her and ruining her body.

Hope looked down at her lap. "I don't love what I do, you know," she said. "Some of the other girls do. They say it makes them feel powerful to be so desirable that someone would pay to have you." The corners of her mouth twitched into a wry smile. "The ones who say that are usually the ones who were born free." She glanced at Rachel again in the mirror. "We know that white men have paid to have so many of us. And to have all of us—everything we are and everything we do. I don't think the money says anything about desire. I don't mean to say that I hate what I do. But I certainly don't love it. I just do it. I'm good at it. I make money and that means I don't have to give myself up completely. Men can pay to own me for a while, but most of the day is mine." She turned and looked at Rachel directly. "Do you know what I mean?"

Rachel nodded. Some of the fire had returned to Hope's eyes, and Rachel knew that this fierce young woman was strong enough to carve out a space for herself in the world. She tried to imagine a man slipping inside Hope and managing to take something from her, but it was impossible.

Hope turned back to the mirror. Rachel looked at their reflections, side by side. Next to Hope's, her own face looked harsh and angular. Years of hard work and silent suffering showed in the lines on her skin. Hope was solid, her eyes shining; Rachel's reflection looked faint in comparison.

"You sure of yourself," said Rachel. "That's a good thing."

Hope laughed, and just like that her tiredness was gone. "Thank you! It took a long time, but I know my worth now—and I don't measure it by what men will pay for me."

Rachel went back to brushing. She watched her fingers slide easily into Hope's hair, as if the boundaries of her own body were permeable. Hope burned with the certainty of youth—of standing on the cusp of adulthood, clear about the path ahead, sure that the world would fall into place accordingly. Rachel had lived long enough to see certainty slip away. There were parts of her that were unfinished, like the half-remembered words of a prayer to the gods across the sea. There were parts of her that were dead and buried in the plantation life she had left behind. She was scattered, fragmented, torn.

But that was fine. She admired Hope's confidence, but it was in the same way as she admired the grand houses in the center of Bridgetown. Something impressive but alien, even a little frightening. Rachel did not mind that she lacked Hope's hard outlines and clear sense of self. That was how she had chosen to survive—by letting little pieces of herself fall away without resistance. She'd had to, or the grief would have killed her.

"I admire you, too, Rachel," Hope said. "Looking for your daughter. It's very brave." The light in her eyes flickered but did not fade. "I had a daughter once but she died. Not even a year old. Just before I ran away." She smiled, stretching her lips over the discomfort in her voice.

Rachel thought about what Mama B had told her—about the wild Hope, destined for death, trying to hurl herself into the waves. That was what grief did to hard edges that let nothing out and nothing in.

Rachel looked again at her reflection. Quiet, watchful eyes stared back. There was no fire in them, but they had their own kind of soft, pliable strength.

7

_____

THE SKY WAS slate gray and the air thick with humidity. The streets of Bridgetown were bustling, as usual, but they had a lifelessness to them. Rachel wandered listlessly, not quite lost, but without a clear sense of where she had come from and where she was going. From time to time, a face emerged from the crowd, unmistakably her daughter, but as Rachel rushed forward it melted into the face of a stranger.

She wandered west, along Constitution River and toward St. Michael's Cathedral. She stopped at a few shops along the way, describing her daughter but getting only blank stares. This was the town where people came to lose themselves—there was a reason why Mama B brought runaways here. It was easy to be anonymous. Mary Grace could be anywhere.

The crowd thinned in the narrow streets around the cathedral. Footsteps and voices echoed between the stone walls of the buildings crammed close together. Rachel moved slowly; it was late afternoon and she was worn out from a long day of searching. She let her gaze drift upward to the hazy clouds that hung low above the spire of St. Michael's, her mind empty of thoughts—hollow, like a coconut scooped of flesh.

Looking back along the road, she saw a man turn a corner ahead. Her eyes were drawn to the shock of his orange hair as it bobbed through a gaggle of women who were standing and gossiping together. He brushed two of the women roughly to one side, revealing to Rachel his sunburned face and heavyset brow. Recognition hit her, tearing her skin like the sharp edge of a whip.

One of the foremen of Providence. A white man from her old life.

He paused, took his time to look at the faces of the women he had barged past. He exchanged rough words with them—and though he was too far away for Rachel to hear, she knew with a fierce clarity that his quest was the cruel inverse of hers, its evil double, its cracked and distorted reflection in a ruined mirror.

He was looking for her.

Between two houses to her right was a tight alleyway, appearing to lead nowhere, piled with rotting timber and other detritus—things that people had forgotten. Rachel leaped sideways, squeezing herself in among these abandoned things and willing herself to disappear. She was able to wedge two planks of wood between her body and the street, but she still felt hopelessly exposed, as if the wood and all the walls around her were glass and she were trapped, in full view of the foreman, with nowhere left to run.

She pressed her eye to the gap in the wood, able to see only the barest sliver of the street.

She tried to mark time by counting her heartbeat, but it varied too raggedly for her to tell how long she stood there, watching.

Figures walked past. They appeared in Rachel's line of sight too briefly for her to process them—man, woman, old, young, Black and white all became only a flash of moving limbs. Her body stayed taut, ready to flee, though there was no way out but the way she had come.

No flash of red heralded the foreman passing by. Rachel strained her ears, but heard nothing of his bitter voice, which she had last heard spitting venom at a woman in the first gang on Providence who had fallen into a faint in the heat of the midday sun. Rachel tried to picture the street from which she had fled—were there other turnings he could have taken? Or was it possible he had already walked by and she had failed to notice?

Her jaw ached with the effort of clenching itself tight. She pulled her limbs close, making herself as small as she could.

She waited.

The memory of Atlas rose, unbidden—the man who had tried to run and paid for it with the disfigurement of his face, and with his life. She forced the memory back.

No.

The thought of her daughter, out there somewhere in Bridgetown's winding streets, strengthened her resolve. Her body began, slowly, to unwind.

The gray sky dimmed, little by little, as the afternoon ebbed away. A group of men came into view, and Rachel saw her chance for safety. She eased herself out of her hiding place and slipped, unnoticed, among them.

She kept her head bowed, matching their weary strides—she was just one of many, returning from a day's work. In their midst, she made her way to the end of the street. She risked a glance behind her. The road was empty. The foreman was nowhere to be seen.

On the corner, the group passed a man with one eye and one leg, sat in the dirt, his toothless mouth hanging slightly ajar, his palm outstretched and waiting for the kindness of strangers. Everyone hurried past him, their faces pulled taut with disgust—everyone except Rachel. In spite of the danger of being exposed, she hung back. She looked at the man and he looked back at her.

"A man pass this way?" she said. The first time it came out as more of a whisper—she had to repeat herself.

"What kind of man?" the beggar asked.

"Red hair."

The beggar exhaled. "Oh yes," he said. "He pass. Me hear him say something about some runaway."

Rachel could hardly breathe.

"He follow this runaway here?"

The beggar shrugged. "Don't seem that way. Reckon he know most of them end up here in the end."

He squinted at her, and Rachel was suddenly chilled by the thought that though this beggar might have skin the same shade as hers, that could all mean nothing in the face of some fat reward for her return. But then, the beggar man unwrapped the thin gray blanket from his shoulders and held it out to Rachel.

"Here," he said.

"What?"

"Take it."

Rachel shook her head—she couldn't. Not from someone who had so little. But he leaned forward to press it into her hands.

"Me think you gon' need it. Take it."

The sound of footsteps behind them sent Rachel's heart racing. She turned—but it was just some white woman hurrying home, who didn't give them a second glance. Rachel threw the blanket over her head, shielding herself as best she could. The beggar nodded to her. She nodded back. And she pressed onward.

IT BEGAN TO rain. All the streets had a damp sameness. Rachel's nerves were frayed from phantom glimpses of redheaded men at every turn; the blanket that she kept clutched around her head was sodden, and her clothes clung to her skin. For dryness and for peace of mind, she knew she had to take shelter.

She ducked into a shop, small but handsomely arranged. Flanking the door were two mannequins showing off dresses adorned with lace—not as ornate and ruffled as some of the dresses Rachel had seen around Bridgetown, but still beautiful in an understated way. Behind the shop counter, silks and cottons of all colors jostled for attention. A man was serving customers—a group of women, mostly Black or colored. He pulled out strips of fabric with a flourish, and Rachel caught some of his words as he held the material up to the light, painting a picture of the elegant gown it could become. He was dark-skinned but dressed like a white man, with the gold chain of a pocket watch glistening on his breast.

"May I help you?"

Rachel flinched. Distracted by the man at the counter, she had not noticed a woman standing behind one of the mannequins, copper-colored hands clasped in front of her and resting lightly on her skirt. Her expression was not unkind—she regarded Rachel with the polite disinterest of someone who spent many hours each day attending to strangers.

Embarrassed, Rachel averted her gaze. "Sorry, me—me come in because of the rain."

The woman smiled politely. "I don't blame you." She glanced behind Rachel, where the rain still fell like a heavy gray curtain, dulling the colors of the street outside. "I sent our servant girl out over an hour ago and she will be quite drenched when she returns."

The woman continued to stare thoughtfully out at the rain. She seemed in no hurry to leave Rachel and see to her other customers. In the end, Rachel felt she must speak—if only to acknowledge the woman's courteous attempt at conversation with someone who had clearly spent life in the fields and not dressed in silks.

"This your shop?"

"Yes." The woman turned her light brown eyes back to Rachel. "My husband you see over there. I sew all the dresses myself. It has been ten years since we opened, and we have done quite well. Many of Bridgetown's most fashionable mulatto women shop here, and even a few—" She interrupted herself, distracted by something over Rachel's shoulder. "Ah, here she is at last."

Rachel turned.

A young woman walked through the door clutching a shopping basket. Strands of dark, wet hair clung to her forehead. Her eyes slid from the seamstress to Rachel. A mouth, with lips thinning from lack of use, quivered in shock.

The shopping basket tumbled to the floor.

Rachel and Mary Grace bounded across the years that separated them. They embraced and Mary Grace felt like water, pouring into every crevice of Rachel, filling her, quenching her thirst. They knitted their limbs together and Mary Grace rested her wet face on Rachel's shoulder. Tears and raindrops ran down Rachel's skin. She held her daughter close. Her knees shook, but did not give way. She could feel Mary Grace breathing into her, slow and steady. There was no sound in the world but those breaths, and the beating of both of their hearts.

8

———

THE MAN BEHIND the counter was impassive as Rachel explained how far she had come to find Mary Grace. The shop was rather busy, he said in a level tone that suggested he was keen to get back to his customers. Perhaps Rachel could come back after closing time, and see her daughter then?

His wife was kinder. She introduced herself as Elvira Armstrong and her husband as Joseph. She said it was nice to meet Rachel, and she seemed to mean it. She also suggested that Rachel and her daughter could sit in her sewing room at the back of the shop so as to be out of everyone's way.

"You must have so much to catch up on," she said.

"Although Eliza doesn't speak," said her husband. "Perhaps you already know that."

Rachel looked from the man to her daughter. "Who?"

Mrs. Armstrong frowned. "Eliza. That's what we have always called her."

Mary Grace dropped her gaze to the floor. Rachel, reaching out, lifted her daughter's chin with her hand.

"Mary Grace," said Rachel, loud enough that a knot of customers by the front door turned and stared. "Her name is Mary Grace."

Mr. Armstrong's face betrayed no flicker of emotion, but his wife repeated the name with a smile, letting the rich syllables fill her mouth. Mary Grace's lip trembled, and tears threatened to spill once more from her eyes. Rachel wondered how many years it had been since her daughter had heard her own name.

Mrs. Armstrong's sewing room was small, lit by a single high window. It felt warm, lived-in, as if it was used to having bodies in it. Spread across a worktable was a length of lilac fabric, marked and pinned, a dress about to form.

Mary Grace was smiling, but her lips did not stretch very far. Her drooping shoulders made her look smaller than she was. Rachel noticed how age had changed her daughter. As a child, Mary Grace was thin, with jutting bones and awkwardly proportioned limbs. Now, the different parts of her flowed together more easily, and she carried more weight around her hips. The sight pleased Rachel but unnerved her, too. It was the body of a young woman, not of the child who had been taken from Providence, all those years ago. It was, made flesh, the years of Mary Grace's life that Rachel had missed.

Rachel waited. Part of her expected Mary Grace to speak. Surely, after everything, she would have something to say? But Mary Grace said nothing, and Rachel herself was lost for words. How could she begin to describe the scars on her heart that she once believed would never heal, and how the sight of Mary Grace, the smell of her, the feel of her skin, had made whole what was once broken beyond repair?

Eventually, taking Mary Grace's hands in her own, Rachel said, "Me find you." This was the only way she could think to express how she felt. The antithesis of loss; a joy and relief as deep as the pain of the initial separation. In the ringing silence after these words, Mary Grace's eyes filled once more with tears, and Rachel knew her daughter understood.

Mrs. Armstrong came into the sewing room first, followed by her husband. She was smiling.

"It must be such a pleasure to be reunited with your daughter," she said. "How long has it been?"

"Twelve years," Rachel murmured. She could feel every day of them.

"My goodness."

Mrs. Armstrong's face was mercurial—it jumped through warmth, curiosity and concern in an instant. Beside her, her husband's face hardly moved at all.

"What is your plan now?" said Mr. Armstrong.

Rachel had no answer. *Plan* implied a structured sequence of events, ordered by her own will. The search for her children was less a plan than a desire. Something insistent but unformed, vague in the details.

"Me don't know."

Mrs. Armstrong was looking at Rachel's hands, still holding Mary Grace's. "Will you stay in Bridgetown?"

In that moment, looking into Mary Grace's eyes, Rachel couldn't imagine being anywhere else.

"Yes."

"And do you have work?"

"No."

Something dark flitted across Mrs. Armstrong's face before she wrestled it under control—something like grief. "Would you like to work here?"

"Elvira." Mr. Armstrong touched his wife's wrist.

"Joseph, it makes sense." She shrugged off his arm. "We talked about having Eliza—" She broke off and glanced at Rachel. "We said that Mary Grace might assist me with my sewing. If she does, we would need someone else to run the errands."

Mr. Armstrong stayed quiet, though Rachel noticed the slight twitch of his eyebrows, forming a crease in his otherwise immobile forehead.

"So, it is settled," said Mrs. Armstrong. Her tone, and the way she clasped her hands together, suggested that she settled things often. "Rachel, you will come and work for us."

A plan. A future given to her, fully formed, with Mary Grace in it. What could she do but accept?

RACHEL AGREED THAT she would stay one more night with Hope, while Mrs. Armstrong made arrangements for her arrival at the house on Cheapside Street. After embracing her daughter one last time, holding her close to preserve the memory of her until morning, Rachel left.

The rain had broken, and the clouds had parted. The sun was setting, its rays brushing against the tops of the buildings crammed together along the streets. St. Mary's Church, silhouetted by the red sky, looked forbidding and beautiful in equal measure. Even at this time of evening, Bridgetown was bustling with workers and lovers and drunken brawlers. For the first time, Rachel did not mind the crowds or the smell of sweat. With the beggar's blanket still clutched to her head, she could move through the busy streets feeling less exposed, less vulnerable. She still kept an eye out for the foreman—she could not afford, even for one second, to forget that, at any point, the long reach of Providence could suck her back into the life she had once known. But in the soft light of evening, Rachel couldn't help feeling a little stirring of calm, an easing of the fear that had kept her in its grip all afternoon. How could the town that had given her Mary Grace betray her now? The evening shadows covered her, and the mass of bodies was her shield.

Rachel found Mama B alone in Hope's room. As soon as she saw Rachel's face, the older woman beamed. She stood and spread her arms wide.

"You find her."

At the sight of Mama B sharing in her joy, just as she had shared in the whole journey, Rachel was overwhelmed by how much the older woman had done. She thought of Hope, and she wondered how long it would have been before she herself, after running from Providence, had ended up at the sea, thinking of death. She would not have hurled herself violently into the water like Hope had planned to, but it would have enticed her nonetheless—she could have walked out and slipped quietly under the waves, and found a kind of freedom there. Instead, she had found Mama B, and Mama B had led her to Mary Grace.

Rachel tried to convey, by placing her hands on the older woman's shoulders, the strength of her gratitude. They stood this way in silence for some time, before Hope came back and greeted the news with gasps and laughter and tears, and the stillness of the moment Rachel and Mama B had shared was gone.

Mama B rose early to make her way back to the north. She and Hope said their goodbyes, but Rachel offered to walk with Mama B awhile. She lied and said they were heading in the same direction, though the Armstrongs' house was on the other side of town.

Rachel hoped to use their walk to express herself better than she had the night before. But when she began, "Mama B—" the older woman cut across her.

"It was no trouble."

Rachel felt she had no choice but to accept the lie.

When they reached the outskirts, Rachel could no longer pretend she was still going Mama B's way. The two women stopped and looked at each other.

"You know," the older woman said, "ever since me was a pickney, me have a gift. Me can read in a face the pain somebody feeling, but me see the hope in them, too. Me see the things they want the most. Even behind eyes that seem dead, all fill up with sadness, me always catch something burning in there. That's why me did see it in you. Your pickney."

Rachel nodded. "Thank you."

The words were small, hoarse, inadequate, but they were all Rachel had.

Mama B's face was as still and watchful as ever as she looked over Rachel.

"We all got our gifts—the things we see that others can't. All we can do is use them when the time come."

Mama B smiled, and it seemed to overflow her face, spilling out into the world. A woman who gave so much, and was prepared to keep on giving.

"Take care of yourself, Rachel."

"Goodbye, Mama B."

On Providence, every goodbye had felt like an almost-death—a passing out of each other's lives, likely forever. Even though Rachel had no idea if she would ever see Mama B again, this goodbye didn't feel as painful. The memory of Mama B would always be with her; not a ghost of a memory, but a living thing, like a branch grafted onto her that would keep growing after they parted.

As she watched Mama B walk away, Rachel heard an echo of the other woman's voice in her ear.

The connection between all things.

Rachel had been holding the beggar's gray blanket; while she walked with Mama B, she felt brave enough to leave her head uncovered. Now, she pulled it back around her—the streets were filling with people and there could be danger waiting for her around any corner. Moving carefully, trying her best to remain unobserved, Rachel began the walk to the Armstrongs' house, and to Mary Grace.

9

———

THE ARMSTRONGS LIVED in a simple house: wooden, single-storied, with a narrow hallway that ran like an artery through the middle. A small parlor, a dining room and a bedroom were the rooms where Elvira and Joseph spent most of their time. At the back of the house, Rachel and Mary Grace had the kitchen and a small second bedroom mostly to themselves—although Mrs. Armstrong was no stranger to a stove, and when the Armstrongs entertained she would often come back and supervise the cooking.

Mrs. Armstrong kept her house with the pride and attention to detail of someone who once had little to keep, and Mr. Armstrong leaned back in his armchair with the ease of someone who was born to expect a comfortable home and a wife to maintain its order. These were Rachel's first impressions of working for the Armstrongs, and over the following weeks she had them confirmed: Mr. Armstrong had been born free and Mrs. Armstrong had not.

At the shop, Mr. Armstrong had his study for doing accounts, which none of the women ever entered. Mrs. Armstrong had her sewing room. This was, of all the rooms that were now part of Rachel's new life, her favorite. If Rachel had no errands to run, Mrs.

Armstrong often encouraged her to sit on a little stool in the corner and see the dresses take form. Rachel loved to watch the tiny needle and thin thread pull the fabric together into a garment.

Rachel knew what it was to work hard, but hers had been the hard work of the endless cycle that sugarcane demanded: planting, tending, harvesting, crushing. There was skill in it, but it was the skill of forcing aching muscles to repeat a movement to the point of exhaustion. Mrs. Armstrong's sewing was a completely different kind of work. No dress was the same. Customers demanded embroidered details on the bodice, or a particular gathering of lace around the sleeve. There were whole hours where all that moved would be Mrs. Armstrong's nimble fingers as she created a dress just as the customer had imagined. This was the skill of executing minute, precise and constantly changing movements. It was hypnotic to watch.

Mrs. Armstrong talked intermittently while she worked, whenever the task at hand wasn't too absorbing. She explained to Mary Grace the different kinds of stitches, and how each fabric had its own quirks and obstinacies that required patience. Or, unprompted, she would tell Rachel about her past life. She would start with a particularly vivid memory—the smell of muslin or the sight of blood swelling out of a needle-pricked finger—and work her way outward. There were gaps, and the stories never flowed in sequence from one day to the next. But slowly, Rachel was able to assemble the pieces.

Elvira had been born on a plantation in the southwest of the island. Her mother was a slave, and her father was the master's youngest son. She had no memory of him, as he was sent away to England to be educated soon after she was born. Her mother she did remember. She was broad-shouldered, striking, and African-born, which even in those days was rare. The overseer treated her harshly, and the drivers taunted her weak grasp of English, but she commanded respect in the fields, working side by side with the strongest men in the first gang. Some of the other slaves believed that in her homeland she had been a queen. This was not true, but she did not care to correct them.

When Elvira was five, she was taken from her mother and given to one of the house slaves. It was common for fair-skinned children to be taken out of the fields; she was not the first of the master's sons' indiscretions, nor would she be the last.

She was given to a woman called Peggy, who came from a long line of house slaves. Peggy had recently lost a daughter to a fever, and perhaps the mistress felt that she would benefit from a replacement child. What, after all, was the difference between one young slave girl and another? If the plan had been for Peggy to adopt and nurture Elvira, it failed. She was not a cruel woman, but she was cold. The maternal part of her had died with the child, and at night she often slipped out of the house to meet with a field slave who knew how to keep a womb barren.

Once, when Peggy caught Elvira sneaking out to visit her mother, she slapped her.

"Your place is here now," Peggy said. "Inside. That dark-skinned savage gon' fill your head with trouble."

Until she was ten, Elvira worked with Peggy in the kitchen. She was in charge of cleaning and similar tasks that the rest of the house slaves considered to be beneath them. As she got older, she gained a reputation for having quick and steady hands, so when one of the other kitchen girls sliced off the tip of her finger, Elvira took over the job of chopping and peeling vegetables.

Her skill caught the attention of another house slave, Old Molly Rose, who had tended to the master's wife for as long as anyone could remember. Old Molly Rose was in charge of altering the mistress's dresses when money was too tight to ship the latest fashions from London, but her eyes were growing weak, and her withered fingers shook when they held the needle. She was looking for a new assistant. Peggy, uninterested to the last, had no problem letting Elvira leave the kitchen and take up a new post. From Old

Molly Rose, Elvira learned the art of sewing, and when Old Molly Rose died, she took on her duties as the seamstress of the house.

The old master passed away, and his eldest son inherited the plantation. Much to his mother's horror, he took a slave woman openly as his mistress. He began to place his own offspring in the positions of greatest authority in the house. One day, he summoned Elvira and a few of the other slaves. Waiting for him to speak, she realized she was surrounded by the sons and daughters of his brothers.

"You are all to be sold," he said curtly. "I cannot stand to have my brothers' bastards in my house."

And so it was. At seventeen, her life was uprooted. Though Elvira had no great love for the plantation, she cried as she left. The walk to Bridgetown was long and hot, and they were not allowed to stop for food or water.

It was as a slave in Bridgetown that Elvira met Joseph Armstrong. At the time, he worked as an assistant to a fabric merchant. Their early romance was not a subject Mrs. Armstrong regularly discussed. Whenever she drew close to it in one of her stories, her voice softened before trailing off, and she would lift her eyes from her work and gaze upward as if the memory of those days was etched into the ceiling. Some things, if shared, risked being diluted, and Rachel guessed that Mrs. Armstrong wanted to keep the experience of falling in love to herself.

Mr. Armstrong was a hard worker, and he had saved as much money as he could, ever since he was a young man. He had dreams of opening his own shop, one day. Instead, he took all his savings to Elvira's master and offered to purchase her freedom. Her master, after some haggling, accepted. She was free.

She and Mr. Armstrong married. He continued to work for the fabric merchant, and she earned what she could with her sewing. When they had saved anew, they purchased the shop, where they had worked ever since.

This was the story Rachel stitched together from the many afternoons spent in Mrs. Armstrong's sewing room. Rachel never knew why Mrs. Armstrong wanted to pour so much of her life into someone else. Perhaps she liked talking to Rachel because they shared a plantation past, which she and Mr. Armstrong did not. It meant that there were things she could leave unsaid—details that hung in the humid air of the sewing room.

"I remember my mother being beaten," she said once. "It's one of my earliest memories . . ." She fell silent.

Rachel's nostrils filled with the sickly smell of blood from an open wound. She nodded. She understood.

Mrs. Armstrong sighed, holding the dress she was sewing up to the light, the dressmaker's scissors poised in her right hand.

"You see, Mary Grace," she said, snipping the delicate fabric with care. "This way, the curved seam is quite flat. But you must mind not to cut the stitches themselves."

Those were the stories that Rachel suspected Mrs. Armstrong did not share with her husband. How could she? He would not be able to fill in the gaps. Fragments of her past would be lost forever. In Rachel, the memory was better preserved.

MARY GRACE HAD been in the Armstrongs' service for five years. Mrs. Armstrong—sensing Rachel's desire to know more about her daughter's life after Providence—tried her best to describe the white man from whom they had purchased Mary Grace. She even laid down her sewing, the better to recapture the memory, casting her eyes up to the ceiling.

"He lived in Bridgetown," she said. "I don't recall his name. He was rather"—Mrs. Armstrong glanced at Mary Grace, but quickly looked away—"forceful. About the sale, that is. He was in need of money to pay off some debts. Gambling, perhaps. Or drink. He seemed that way inclined."

Mary Grace kept her head bowed. Something like shame flickered across her face, as though to be owned by such a man was to be in some way defined by the measure of him—the act of being his property forcing her to carry his sins.

At night, in their little bedroom, Rachel and Mary Grace lay in silence. Rachel was still waiting for something—anything—that her daughter might want to say.

After a week of nights where nothing was spoken, Rachel tried a different approach. She began, falteringly, to tell Mary Grace about her own life. She told her about the sales of Mercy and Cherry Jane and Thomas Augustus. She told her about the grinding loneliness of the plantation when all her children were dead or gone. She spoke of the hollow promise of freedom on Emancipation Day, and of her sudden urge to flee. She described Mama B, and all the wisdom she possessed. She told her daughter of the days spent wandering Bridgetown and sleeping on Hope's floor.

Her story took three nights to finish.

On the fourth night, neither spoke.

On the fifth night, Rachel said, "If you got something to say, me will listen. You know that?"

Mary Grace did not reply.

Sighing, Rachel turned over onto her side. Her mind filled with memories of Mary Grace as a child with serious eyes and a bright smile, before speech was taken from her by the unspeakable cruelty of a man on a dark night. Rachel tried to recapture the sound of her daughter's voice. Slow, taking time over words, tending to drift upward at the end of each sentence as if everything was a question—not because Mary Grace was unsure of herself, but because she wanted everything she said to invite an answer. She wanted to keep others talking as long as she could.

Rachel remembered the night Micah was taken. The first loss of so many. There was an emptiness to her hut that night, though at that time it was still rammed with bodies, a gaping hole that sucked her into its nothingness and from which she feared she would never escape. Rachel had lain as still and silent as a corpse, with no tears left to shed, waiting for the release of sleep or death. It was Mary Grace who had been lying closest to her and who had known, even though her mother no longer wept, that the worst was not yet over. She had slipped her tiny hand into her mother's and kept it there as the night passed slowly, until dawn finally came and Rachel knew she must rise and live another day. That touch was what had kept Rachel anchored to this world. And that morning, when Mary Grace had whispered, "You gon' get through today, Mama," for once there was no question in her voice.

These were the memories that kept Rachel company in the Armstrongs' house as she waited for sleep, with a faint ache in the hollow of her chest, right in the pit of her collarbone.

RACHEL DREAMED OF Mary Grace. Her daughter was younger than she was now, but older than when she had been taken away. This was the Mary Grace of the lost years. Her head was bowed. Rags, torn and gray, were the only thing covering her body. A drop of blood tracked down her inner thigh.

Rachel stretched out her hand but it was no use. Her arms were not long enough. She could not reach.

Mary Grace raised her head. Lips, cracked and bleeding, spoke.

"Me have so much me want to forget."

RACHEL JOLTED AWAKE. Mary Grace's face was inches from hers, eyes open and brimming with the same pain as the dream-daughter's.

Rachel touched Mary Grace's cheek.

"Me understand," she whispered.

Some things were best left unsaid.

10

———

RACHEL KEPT THE thin blanket given to her by the beggar. Whenever she went out, she used it to cover her head. She shielded herself from the world as best she could. Every time she saw white skin, her hands would tremble. This was the real power of slavery, the long shadow it could cast after its formal end—that even with all this distance between her and Providence, Rachel still lived in fear.

Gradually, her other children began to creep back into her life. She was used to seeing them in the shadows, or standing around her as she slid between sleeping and waking. This was how they had appeared to her in Providence. Now, in Bridgetown, they were bolder. Behind a market stall piled high with dead, glassy-eyed chickens, she saw Cherry Jane, staring at her with a somber look on her face. Walking on a bridge over Constitution River, she saw Micah and Mercy holding hands as they stepped off the side and were swallowed up by the waters below.

And there were the nightmares. More feelings than visions—like the feeling of being eaten from the inside out, or of hands wrapping around her throat to choke back her screams. Guilt inched over her, day by day, starting deep in her gut and crawling through her veins. She was aware of what was still missing, the emptiness that Mary Grace alone could not fill. The question plagued her—

How could she find the others?

On Sundays, Mr. and Mrs. Armstrong went to church in the morning, and Mary Grace would go with them. Mr. Armstrong had always taken her, as a point of principle.

"The Lord knows neither slave nor free," he explained to Rachel.

Rachel chose not to mention that, as she was no longer a slave, the Lord could not judge her for being so. She politely declined the invitation to join them, telling Mr. Armstrong that she worshipped in her own way.

Instead, Rachel began to use her sliver of freedom on Sunday mornings to wander the streets. It was risky—perhaps even reckless—to leave the safety of the Armstrongs' home when she did not have to, but there was another force within her that was stronger than fear. The need to find her other children was growing ever more urgent. She courted capture for their sake. With the blanket to shield her, she went looking for them. Bridgetown still seemed so large, seemed to Rachel to contain almost everything, and yet it did not contain any trace of Micah, Mercy, Thomas Augustus or Cherry Jane.

Most Sundays, after hours of fruitless wandering, she would go to the harbor. The sea smelled stale, like fermented sweat, and its brine burned the insides of her nostrils on windy days. Rachel remembered Hope, back in the days when they were all together, saying that the harbor was one of her favorite places—and now she understood why. She was awed by it. The pier felt like the ending place of the island, the whole of Barbados sharpened to a single point spearing out to sea. It was a place of beginnings, too. Whatever came to the island came through the harbor. She liked the days when ships moored and disgorged hordes of grime-streaked men onto the shore, men who diffused and spread out into the labyrinthine alleyways around them. On those days, there seemed to be no limit to what Bridgetown could absorb.

What the ships gave they also took away. Some days, columns of people lined the harbor—mostly men, withered down to skin stretched over protruding bones, dressed in rags and with eyes sunk so deep in their skulls the sockets looked hollow. Rachel watched them shuffle slowly into the bellies of waiting ships. The first time she saw it, she thought for one wild moment that history had folded back on itself. Here were the slave survivors, the ones Caribbean life had spared, boarding the ships that would take them back to Africa. But, drawing close, she heard one man turn to another and mutter, "This ship for Jamaica?"

The other man shook his head. "Trinidad."

"Oh. Me thought this the Jamaica ship."

The other man shrugged. "Me hear they got work in Trinidad, too."

The first man sighed but stayed in line. So, no Africa for him— just another island and another life spent tilling someone else's land.

ONE MORNING, COMING back from the fabric merchant with ten yards of lace, Rachel saw Hope framed in the shop doorway, standing next to Mary Grace.

"Rachel!" Hope clapped her hands when she saw her. "This must be your daughter! She is beautiful."

Mary Grace wasn't beautiful—she was plain and her features were spread a little too wide across her face. But, as always, Hope's words rearranged the world, and for a moment Mary Grace was beautiful. Her eyes sparkled, reflecting the light of Hope's smile.

"These dresses are divine." Hope lifted the sleeve of a cream-colored gown hanging on one of the mannequins. "I cannot believe I've never been here before."

Mr. Armstrong came out from behind the counter. "Can I help

you?" he said smoothly. If he knew who Hope was—what she did—he didn't show it. Mr. Armstrong remained mostly a mystery to Rachel, but the philosophy by which he ran his shop had not escaped her notice. He took pride in his work but he was not proud. No one was beneath him. His customers ranged from the most elegant and aloof mulattoes to recently emancipated women who had saved for many months to buy a single dress. Every one he treated with equal respect.

"You must be Mr. Armstrong," Hope said, delighted. "My name is Hope. I am a friend of Rachel's, and as of today a loyal customer of yours."

The corner of Mr. Armstrong's mouth twitched upward, his only concession to Hope's charm.

"You are most kind." He ran a dispassionate eye over her. "Was there a particular dress you had in mind today? Or I can suggest something—we have just had some fabrics shipped from America."

As Mr. Armstrong led Hope to the back of the shop to show her, Rachel drew close to Mary Grace.

"So, you meet Hope."

. . .

"Yes, she is beautiful."

. . .

"There was a time she got pain, me think. But she happier now."

. . .

They often conversed this way, with Rachel leaving space for where Mary Grace's reply would be.

"You like her?"

Mary Grace nodded, with a shy smile.

They watched Hope gush over each of the fabrics Mr. Armstrong brought out from the back. She particularly liked a blue cotton printed with red cherries, but she also adored a cream silk detailed with small yellow flowers. Drawn by the peal of Hope's laughter as she and Mr. Armstrong discussed the relative merits of each, Mrs. Armstrong appeared from the sewing room.

"Hello," she said. "I thought I'd come and introduce myself."

"This is my wife," said Mr. Armstrong. "It will be through her great skill that your dress takes shape."

Hope sprang over to Mrs. Armstrong and took her outstretched hand. "A pleasure to meet you."

It was only next to Hope that Rachel realized quite how beautiful Mrs. Armstrong was. It was not like Hope's beauty—fierce, conspicuous. It didn't demand to be noticed. But somehow Rachel found her eyes drawn, again and again, away from Hope and toward the easy symmetry of Mrs. Armstrong's face, like slipping into a cool river in the heat of the midday sun.

At Mrs. Armstrong's gentle insistence, Hope ended up ordering a dress in each fabric at a very favorable price.

"You are too generous," Hope said.

"Not at all." Mrs. Armstrong smiled. "Just be sure to tell anyone who asks where you got the dresses. On you, I have no doubt they'll look their best."

RACHEL WAS PREPARING dinner that evening when Mr. Armstrong walked into the kitchen. She dropped her gaze to the stew she was stirring, to hide her surprise. She had never known him to venture to the back of the house, to the world of women and servants.

"Good evening, Rachel." He glanced languidly around the kitchen.

"Good evening, Mr. Armstrong."

"What are you cooking?"

"Beef stew, sir."

"Good."

He had a way of holding her at arm's length like this whenever they spoke. Even after a month, she barely knew him.

"Mary Grace is helping you tonight?"

"She off setting the table."

"I see. And are you settling in well?"

"Yes, thank you, sir."

"It must be nice to be with your daughter again."

Rachel turned the word *nice* over in her mind. Here was a man who knew dozens of words for what to Rachel looked like identical shades of blue—who could fashion out of his vocabulary elaborate gowns trimmed with lace, sporting a sash made from some daring color of contrasting ribbon—and he asked her if it was *nice*.

"Yes," she said finally. "It is."

He nodded.

She continued to stir the stew.

"And your friend," he said. "Miss Hope, who came by the shop today. How did you make her acquaintance?"

His tone was as bland as ever, but Rachel—staring into the stew—frowned slightly. As innocent a question as any of the others, but she noticed how it burrowed a little deeper. They were no longer dealing in the mundane details of the present, of her life and work in his household. Mr. Armstrong was trying to creep into her past.

"We meet in Bridgetown."

"I see." Whenever Rachel glanced up from the cooking, his eyes were there, unwavering. "And where did you meet?"

"In her house."

They stood in silence. Rachel kept stirring the stew.

Mr. Armstrong sighed, a tiny movement of breath through his nostrils. "Rachel. May I be direct?"

"Yes, sir."

"What your friend Hope does for a living is her business." He was treading delicately, she could tell. Every syllable was enunciated with a light precision. "I have customers of every kind. But my own home I wish to keep as respectable as possible. I was a little concerned that you had met Hope"—he cast around for the right word—"professionally."

Rachel leaned the ladle against the side of the pot and stood upright. She was a little taller than him. "Me was a field hand," she said, flattening all of her history into those two words. "That's all me ever was."

"I meant no offense," said Mr. Armstrong.

"Of course, sir."

She held his gaze for a few more seconds. His eyes, like hers, were dark brown, flecked with dashes of gold.

I know the smell of blood, she thought, forcing the words out through her eyes and into his. *I have seen skin stripped off flesh.*

So has your wife.

Men have been inside me just as they have been inside Hope, even though I'm the one who paid for it.

You are no better than any of us.

Letting the corners of her mouth curve upward into a smile, she went back to the stew. Mr. Armstrong lingered for a moment and then left the kitchen.

IN THE SEWING room, the next day, Mrs. Armstrong had seemingly exhausted her memories.

She said, "What about you, Rachel? What about your life before this?"

Rachel shifted on her stool, twisting her hands together in her lap. After all Mrs. Armstrong had shared, the sewing room had a kind of gentle magic; within its four walls, the women were caught in the threads of something much larger than themselves. They were weaving something precious out of memories. If there was ever a place in which Rachel could dare to reveal a part of herself, it was in this room—but she couldn't quite find the words. She said nothing.

Mrs. Armstrong kept her eyes on her work. Her next question was low, quiet and more searching—as if she wished to move softly around the edges of what Rachel might be ready to bare.

"You have other children?"

This cut to the heart of it. There was no time to trade stories of whippings, or to reminisce about nights spent in the stocks; Mrs. Armstrong wanted the most precious parts of Rachel's history.

Rachel looked down at the floor. Mrs. Armstrong held the hem she was stitching close to her face. She sewed in silence, waiting.

Eventually, Rachel spoke.

"Yes."

Still, Mrs. Armstrong waited. Rachel watched the needle pierce the fabric, counting the stitches—all the way up to ten. Then she found the courage to speak again.

"Micah is the eldest." His name caught in Rachel's throat. How long had it been since she had spoken it? She had whispered it in the dark to Mary Grace in those first few weeks together, but otherwise she had guarded it jealously inside her all these years. She hadn't even told Mama B the names of her other children.

"Micah," Mrs. Armstrong repeated.

Hearing his name in another's mouth didn't hurt like Rachel thought it would. Mrs. Armstrong spoke it quietly, like a blessing or a prayer.

"They take him young," Rachel continued. "But me can remember . . ." She faltered. "Me can remember his laugh. Just like a donkey." She was laughing herself now, with the echo of Micah in her ears. "When he laugh, everybody who hear laugh, too.

"And Mercy. She kind—so kind. One time, she find a baby bird that fall out its nest. She take care of that bird. Get up early in the morning to find worms to feed it. The bird die, and she cry when she bury it.

"Cherry Jane." The names flowed with ease now. It felt like a dam breaking as the past poured out of her. Rachel understood in that moment why Mrs. Armstrong had shared so much. There was a heady sense of release. "They take her to the great house young. But me remember how she did charm everyone she meet. All her brothers and sisters adore her. She can talk and smile just so, and make anyone love her.

"Thomas Augustus. He ask so many questions. He don't speak until he was three, then his first words, 'Where Mary Grace?' Then he keep asking. 'Where the sun go at night?' 'How come we cut the cane if it only gon' grow again?' He stay with me a little longer than the others. Me think . . ." She paused. "But they take him away, too.

"And there were others. Some that die. Some that never born."

Mrs. Armstrong nodded, her eyes still on her work. She understood.

Rachel exhaled. Micah, Mercy, Cherry Jane, Thomas Augustus—they were all living now in someone else. She no longer carried their weight alone.

"Mrs. Armstrong?" Rachel said slowly. "You ever . . . ?" Before she had finished, she saw a cloud pass over Mrs. Armstrong's face. She swallowed the unspoken words and waited.

Mrs. Armstrong tied off her thread and laid the dress down on her lap. "My husband and I have tried, but . . ." She turned her face upward, eyes closed, to where the light spilled into the workroom from a high window. "I don't think I can." Her skin gleamed, and it was hard to tell where the sunlight ended and she began. "On the plantation, one of the other women used to prepare herbs for those who . . ." She sighed. "They worked, but they've gone on working, all these years."

A hot, barren silence followed. It was broken by the sound of Mr. Armstrong's voice drifting in from the other room, describing how a simple stretch of cloth might be transformed into a pale pink dress trimmed with blond lace and red ribbon knots on each sleeve.

AT THE END of the day, with the light in the shop fading, they heard Mr. Armstrong retreat into his study with the day's accounts, the sign that the shop was closing. Mary Grace helped Mrs. Armstrong pack away her sewing things and fold up the half-finished dresses. Rachel still sat in the shadows, thinking of her children, and the children of Mrs. Armstrong who would never be—

The sound of footsteps and knuckles rapping on the counter. Mrs. Armstrong raised her head. Through the doorway, they could all see a figure stood in the shop, though with the sun setting behind, they could make out little more than a silhouette.

Mrs. Armstrong went through, leaving Rachel and Mary Grace to finish the tidying.

"Good evening, sir. I'm afraid we were just closing."

"I won't need long."

Rachel was rolling a long strip of lace. She did not freeze, but her hands came slowly to a stop. Dread came over her at a creeping pace.

That voice.

Could it be?

"What can I do for you?" said Mrs. Armstrong.

"I'm looking for someone."

Rachel shrank backward, into the shadows of the sewing room. She pressed herself against the back wall—as though with enough force she could simply melt through it and escape.

"An apprentice," the man in the shop continued. "A runaway."

"I see," said Mrs. Armstrong.

The voices seemed very far away. Almost all Rachel could hear was the sound of her own breathing—it seemed deafening. Surely he would hear? Surely he would know?

A touch on her arm. Rachel had forgotten Mary Grace was there. Her daughter was holding a pair of sewing scissors, with a half-pinned stretch of fabric folded over her arm. She looked at her mother. It was not a look of comfort, nor of hope. It was the look of someone who had endured much, and was resigned to enduring more in the future.

Rachel had to hold back her tears. She could not make a sound. Mother and daughter stood together at the back of the sewing room and they waited.

In the shop, the foreman of Providence was describing Rachel. Her age and build. The brand on her shoulder.

Mrs. Armstrong interrupted him. "And does she have a name?"

"Rachel."

A long silence. Rachel felt exposed, flayed of flesh, a wounded animal caught in a trap. She was sure that the man was looking through the doorway and right at her. That she could not hide. That she had only moments left with her daughter before his hands came reaching through the darkness and seized her. She held Mary Grace's arm and gripped it tight.

Then Mrs. Armstrong said, "I'm sorry. I can't help you." There was a cold edge to her voice.

Rachel heard the foreman grunt in annoyance.

"I'm heading back north," he said. "Needed for the harvest. But if you see anything—you just send word. MacLean. Providence plantation."

"Of course," said Mrs. Armstrong. "Good day, sir."

Footsteps again—the hard thud of his boots on the wooden floor. The shop door opened and closed. Then—silence. A stillness. Rachel felt herself sliding slowly to the ground as the muscles of her body gave out, one by one. She was shaking. Her breath came in short gasps.

Mrs. Armstrong appeared in the doorway. Shadows fell across her face; Rachel could not read the woman's expression. But there was something in the way she stood . . . Rachel found she was able to breathe again. So much had passed between these two women in the sewing room. So many secrets that its four walls would keep.

Mrs. Armstrong nodded once.

She understood.

A man's voice. "Ah, Rachel, there you are."

Rachel was on her feet in an instant. Mr. Armstrong was standing behind his wife.

"I was hoping you might be able to run to the tanner before he closes."

"Of course, sir."

Rachel was unable to keep the tremor out of her voice.

Mr. Armstrong's lips twisted upward into a smile. "Very good."

A pulse of fear ran through Rachel. Mrs. Armstrong had shown herself to be on Rachel's side. There were things they both knew that bound them together. But Mr. Armstrong?

When the foreman had come, had Mr. Armstrong been listening from his study? How much had he heard?

As ever, his face gave nothing away.

11

———

Weeks ago, in the early days with the Armstrongs, Rachel had been serving at dinner with a guest—a mulatto woman, a regular customer turned friend. The woman was dressed in such a way as to accentuate the lightness of her skin, to exaggerate the differences between herself and the others of her race who were in bondage.

As Rachel ladled soup into everyone's bowls, this woman had been talking about her planter friends in the south of the island, and the trouble they were having with their apprentices.

"Honestly, Joseph, the Negroes are deserting their duties at an alarming rate." The woman leaned forward, animated by her subject. "It can't go on like this."

Rachel's fingers trembled, and the ladle clinked often against the china, but no one paid her any mind.

"I hear that the governor will be introducing heavier penalties," the woman continued. "Punishments for these runaways. Fines for those who harbor them. Anything to make sure that the law is obeyed. Sugar has been, and always will be, the lifeblood of this island, and the interests of sugar must be defended before all else."

This memory visited Rachel often in the days after the foreman came to the shop, as she waited for the blow to fall—for the fragile life with her daughter to be shattered. In the true memory, Mr. Armstrong had not looked at Rachel at all, and she had slipped out of the dining room unnoticed to take refuge in the kitchen and slow her racing heartbeat. But the memory began to distort as it haunted her, until Mr. Armstrong's eyes were on her all the while, watching her every move, unblinking, the weight of his gaze unbearable and his mouth curving downward in displeasure.

ON SUNDAY, AS on every other Sunday, Rachel ended up at the pier. There were no ships that day, and Rachel perched on an upturned crate, staring out at the sea as it undulated like a living, breathing being—always moving, never still.

"Nice view, isn't it?"

Unnoticed, Mr. Armstrong had walked up beside her. Shielding his eyes against the sun, he was also watching the waves.

Rachel said nothing.

"You come here often?"

Rachel knew she couldn't duck a direct question, but she let the silence linger a little before answering. "Yes. On Sundays. Me like to watch the ships."

"Ah yes. There's always plenty to see at the pier."

Rachel kept her eyes directed out to sea, but the side of her face grew hot; she knew Mr. Armstrong had turned his gaze to her.

"I saw something interesting in the newspaper," he said, with his customary smoothness. "It was a few weeks ago now, but I still remember. They publish notices from the plantations sometimes— asking about runaways, people trying to escape the apprenticeships."

Cold dread washed over Rachel. Her body was taut, ready to run—to cast itself into the water, if need be. If that was the only place left she could go. But Rachel forced herself to be still. She imagined Mr. Armstrong's face as her own, completely unmoving, without even a quiver to give away what lay beneath.

"There was a notice about a woman from the north," Mr. Armstrong said. "No name given, but it listed her age as about forty. Tall, it said. And strong, too. A field hand."

Rachel could not look at him. She did not dare. The power he had over her in that moment was too great; like the sun, she feared that meeting the force of it directly would blind her. All she could do was watch the movement of the sea, as if in slow motion, waves gently cresting and falling.

She wanted to ask—

What do you want from me?

But it took all her energy to keep from sobbing or screaming or sprinting away. So she sat in silence.

When Mr. Armstrong spoke again, his voice had a different quality to it. Rougher. A hint of pain.

"You know, I remember when the slave ships would land here."

The surprise was enough to release Rachel from the bind of terror. She was finally able to look at him. He was staring at the pier, at the point where land met sea. The corners of his mouth twitched, twisting his features into expressions more intense than she had ever seen on his face before.

"I was still a young boy when they stopped the new ones coming in," he continued. The rhythm of his words, usually so flat and metronomic, began to rise and fall with the memory. "But I still remember. My father used to bring me down here from time to time, to watch them come in. I will never forget the sight of the slaves being taken from the ships. Some would try to run. I remember one man who leaped off the gangplank, taking with him every other slave he was shackled to. The white men tried to dredge them out of the harbor, but it was too late. Their irons dragged them down."

Rachel was following his gaze now. She saw, as he did, the wooden ships, rotting away from the inside after their long journey, unloading their cargo of ghosts onto the pier.

"If I tried to turn away from them, my father would say, 'You must look. These are your people. Those are the ships that brought your great-grandfather to this island, all those years ago. We may be free, but we will never forget where we came from.'"

Rachel nodded. She did not know his story like she knew Mrs. Armstrong's stories of beaten backs and herbs that could make a womb barren. But she understood.

"I know my wife appreciates your company, Rachel," Mr. Armstrong said. "It's good she has someone she can talk to . . ." He paused. "She has told me a little about your children. They are the reason you ran?"

Rachel had glimpsed the layer underneath his cool exterior, the raw memories he held inside him. What she had seen was enough to lower her defenses.

"Yes."

"And do you know anything about where they are?" he asked.

"No."

"Have you looked? Asked around?"

"Me ask. But nobody got the answer."

They fell silent again. Both kept their eyes on the sea. In the corners of Rachel's vision, Bridgetown life seemed to move slowly, at the crawling pace of a receding tide.

Finally, Mr. Armstrong spoke. "Has my wife told you about her mother?"

"A little."

"Did she tell you we went back for her?"

"No."

Mr. Armstrong sighed. "It was after we were married. We were saving everything we had to get enough for a shop. One day, she came to me and asked if I could bear to wait for the shop a little longer. She told me that she wanted to use our money to buy her mother's freedom, as I had bought hers. 'My mother was born free,' she said. 'I never really knew what that meant until I was free myself. I do not want her to die a slave.' So, we walked to Elvira's old plantation. But when we got there, we found that her mother had been dead many years."

Rachel could hear the echoes of his wife's pain as he spoke, and her heart broke for Mrs. Armstrong.

"I know, Rachel, that when Elvira thinks of you and your children, she remembers her mother. We were too late, but you don't have to be."

He looked at her—not through her, like he usually did, but truly seeing her.

"I want to help you."

Rachel was lost for words. She hugged her arms closer to her chest. She held his gaze, cautious, hardly daring to hope.

"What can you do?" she asked.

"Have you heard of the slave registers?"

Rachel shook her head.

"When the ships stopped coming from Africa, the government made everyone register their slaves. They wanted to stop the trade carrying on in secret. Every few years, you had to go and declare which slaves you had, and they'd check their names against the list of slaves you said you had before. If you had more or fewer than last time, they'd check that any changes had been legal."

Rachel tried to imagine such a thing. In her mind she pictured a huge book, as thick as it was wide. Each page was a little slice of the island's life; its people, frozen in stasis, pressed into a list of names scrawled onto the yellowing paper. To turn the pages of such a book would be to gaze down on Barbados from high above, like God, watching as people were shunted from plantation to plantation to grave. As if the only question that mattered was: Who owns you? She thought of her own name, written again and again in the same place under the same master. If she died tomorrow, was that what would be left of her? Just her name in this book the white men kept to remind them of what was theirs?

"You know when your children were sold?" Mr. Armstrong asked.

"Yes."

"You know your master's name?"

"Yes. Carrington."

"Good. Then I think we could consult the registers and find out where they were sold."

Rachel couldn't quite believe it. This loathsome register that, in her head, was heavier than anything she had ever carried in her life, that could crush her to nothing under the immense weight of its thousands of names on thousands of pages—this was what would take her to her children?

She looked at Mr. Armstrong. His face still moved too slowly for her liking. Could she trust him?

"You gon' look at this register?"

"I can't directly, but I know a man who has worked at the records office. He should be able to help."

"And you know," Rachel said slowly, "that me gon' want . . ."

Mr. Armstrong smiled. It was not his shop-smile—smooth lips stretched over even teeth. It was a smile from the heart.

"I know. You would want to leave. And you would take Mary Grace with you, I expect."

She nodded.

"I will not stop you," he said. "There are many people in this town in need of work. Elvira and I will manage."

He spoke, as he always did, with a tone of authority and confidence. He arranged her future like the verbal folds of a dress he would conjure for a customer. There were no holes, no uncertainties in the dresses he sold. Only beauty—something elegant, well-made and meant to last.

———

THAT AFTERNOON, RACHEL sat with Mrs. Armstrong in the sewing room.

"My mother . . ." Mrs. Armstrong began. But she got no further.

A long look passed between her and Rachel. No more was said. They both understood.

Mrs. Armstrong bound off her thread tightly, pulling hard so it would not fray, and then tucked the seam away behind the ornate lace trim so no one would see it.

12

A T THE SHOP, Mr. Armstrong called Rachel into his study. It was a room she had never entered in all her time working for him. It was smaller than the sewing room, and without a window; its disorder took her by surprise. She had always imagined that it would be a neat room, sparsely furnished and austere. Instead, she found papers piled in uneven stacks in every corner, and books spread open on the floor, their pages overlapping. A large desk and three chairs had been squeezed somehow into the chaos, leaving little space to move about.

Overall, it made her more disposed to like him. Ever since their conversation at the harbor, they spoke with something approaching familiarity in the house, but at the shop he was still distant. When at work, he was like an automaton, repeating with perfect consistency his polite service to each customer. Only when he was back home would he become human again, through a light touch of his wife's arm or a sigh of contentment as he sank into an armchair. Seeing this cluttered study, a little sliver of imperfection, allowed Rachel to bring together these two men—the salesman at work and the man he was at home.

"Sit, please." He smiled, the wrinkles around his eyes like little cracks in an otherwise smooth facade. "I have news."

Rachel had imagined this moment, over and over, since they had spoken at the harbor. She had tried to practice holding back tears of joy or of sorrow. But now there was no racing heartbeat. Her eyes were dry. Cool and clearheaded, Rachel listened.

"My friend has consulted the registers," he said. "He managed to find mention of all of your children. Micah and Thomas Augustus were sold overseas, to the colony of Demerara. Your daughter Mercy was in another plantation in Barbados for a time, before she, too, was sold to another colony—Trinidad."

Still, no tears came, but the names of these far-off colonies cut into Rachel like shards of glass. It was worse than she had feared. Barbados she could cover on foot in a matter of days. But Trinidad? Demerara? They might as well have been Africa or England. These were not places she could go.

"And Cherry Jane?"

Mr. Armstrong frowned. "Cherry Jane was initially sold to a man in Bridgetown. We traced her through the years, right up until 1829, but in the next register she disappears."

The air was still, disturbed only by Rachel's breathing.

"Dead?"

Mr. Armstrong shook his head. "She was not listed among the dead, nor among those sold or gifted to others. The man she belonged to is a white businessman of some renown—his name is Lancing. Were he not as prominent in Bridgetown, the discrepancy would have led to questions, but somehow he managed to get away with it. Her trail stops there. He may have sold her and failed to report it. Or, he may have freed her."

Rachel closed her eyes. She tried to picture her children—her sons in Demerara, Mercy in Trinidad, Cherry Jane in some unknown place—but it was impossible. She saw only formless shadows.

"I'm sorry," she heard Mr. Armstrong say. "I wish I could tell you more."

THEY HAD REACHED the limits of what the slave registers could tell them, but there were forms of knowledge not written in books.

That night, after hearing the Armstrongs retire to their room, Rachel crept out the front door. She had run an errand to the butcher's in the afternoon, and the man behind the counter had told her the way to Mr. Lancing's house. It was late enough that the streets were almost empty—though gaggles of men were visible in the windows of firelit taverns, and desperate souls huddled in the doorways of shops to sleep. In the moonlight, the town looked softer. The daytime sounds and smells of hard work faded; even the most dilapidated buildings had a subtle charm.

After all this time, Rachel still kept her head covered with the blanket the beggar man had given her. The foreman might well have gone back north, but Rachel was starting to realize that Bridgetown—that all of Barbados—might never be safe. That she would always be glancing over her shoulder, always jumping at shadows, always waking from nightmares of being dragged from her bed.

Whenever anyone rested their eyes on her for too long, she thought: *This is it. They know.*

The Lancing house was stone, gray and imposing. Its tall windows were all shuttered; on the second floor, chinks of light appeared through the cracks, but on the ground floor, everything was dark. An alleyway along the side of the house led to a servants' entrance. Rachel knocked once, with no answer. From within, she could hear the clatter of pots and pans. She knocked harder, a frantic note to the rhythm as she pounded on the wood.

The woman who finally opened the door had a gaunt, pinched face and lines around her downturned mouth. She looked Rachel up and down with unfriendly eyes.

From inside, another woman shouted, "Leah! Who that at the door?"

Leah sucked her teeth and shouted back over her shoulder, "Hush up and me can find out." She glared at Rachel. "What you want?"

Rachel kept her voice steady and respectful. "Me looking for someone who once work here. Cherry Jane."

Leah narrowed her eyes. "Why?"

"She me daughter."

Leah's frown deepened. "That can't be. You too dark."

"So you know her?"

"Maybe me did."

Not a single fissure appeared in the sour expression on Leah's face.

"Please. You know where she is?"

Tight-lipped, Leah gave no reply. She folded her hands over her chest with a note of finality. Behind her, the other woman called out again.

"These pans aren't gon' wash themselves."

Desperation rose within Rachel.

"You have pickney, Leah?"

Leah was not expecting this. The frown stayed on her face, but her arms dropped back to her sides.

"Yes. Me do."

"Still with you?"

"No. They gone."

"You miss them?"

Leah's mouth twisted in a violent, involuntary movement, before settling back into its downward curve. She did not reply.

Rachel tried one more time. "Please. Me just want to know what happen to me daughter."

There was a softening behind Leah's eyes. It flickered there, for an instant—but then her face hardened again.

"Me can't help you," she said, and she slammed the door in Rachel's face.

A PAINFUL MEMORY surfaced—the day Cherry Jane was taken up to the great house. It was a year after Micah had been sold away. Two of the house slaves came to Rachel's hut early in the morning, and Rachel knew as soon as she saw them why they were there.

Rachel thought she would fight them—that she would hold Cherry Jane close and tell them they could not take her daughter. But then these women's arms were on Cherry Jane, and Rachel was standing in the corner of the hut doing nothing. Saying nothing. She had thought of Micah, and the great emptiness her heart had become, and she had stood still and let them take her daughter. Cherry Jane had been so afraid, but in that moment, in the shadow of Micah's loss and in anticipation of all the losses yet to come, Rachel had become one of the mothers she never thought she would be—the ones who could not look their own children in the eye.

As Rachel moved slowly through the dark streets of Bridgetown, her throat tightened, remembering that day. Her whole body ached with regret. After Cherry Jane started work in the great house, Rachel rarely saw her—and then, only in flashes, from a distance, too far away for Cherry Jane to know her mother was looking. In fact, Rachel and her daughter locked eyes only once more before Cherry Jane was taken from Providence altogether, when Rachel had snuck to the side of the great house one day and peered through the kitchen window, hoping to catch a glimpse of the radiant, light-skinned child she had not fought to keep. Cherry Jane was inside, smiling as two of the kitchen girls fussed over her, and she turned her head to the window and met her mother's gaze. Three months later, Cherry Jane was gone.

Rachel walked to the harbor. She couldn't think of anywhere else to go. She sat and she allowed herself to mourn—Cherry Jane, lost, not once, not twice, but three times over.

Rachel watched the movement of the waves. Moonlight glinted off the water as off steel. The pier pointed out into the unknown, reminding her that out there, across the sea, were Micah, Thomas Augustus and Mercy. The path ahead forked—one side following the slave register to distant lands, the other creeping slowly, blindly, in search of the cold trail left by Cherry Jane.

Rachel weighed each choice in turn. Could she sail away? The island was her whole world; all of her life had been contained by its shores. It was a warm, humid night, but Rachel felt a chill of fear, and though the sea was calm, it looked forbidding. What mysteries lay beneath its silver surface?

She remembered Mr. Armstrong's story of watching the slave ships coming in. At night, the ghosts of the past seemed closer; the membrane between the worlds of the living and the dead wore thin. There were skeletons in the harbor, still wearing their chains. Rachel tried to imagine boarding a ship for Trinidad or Demerara, but she kept coming back to those old bones under the waves.

Rachel turned her face from the sea, back toward the shadow of Bridgetown. Cherry Jane might yet be somewhere in Barbados. So should she stay and find her first? Rachel turned the idea over in her mind—but she felt its false promise, the way it threatened to disintegrate like a wisp of smoke at her touch. Bridgetown was where the runaways came, to hide among the crowds. If Bridgetown itself was what Cherry Jane had sought to escape, where on the island would she have gone? All across Barbados, the plantations gave precious little shelter.

And then there was Providence. Rachel thought of the foreman. The endless hunt. Fear on the island; fear across the sea.

"Rachel?"

A voice sliced through her thoughts. She knew, right away, from the warmth that spread over her, that it was Hope.

"How funny to run into you!" Hope exclaimed as they embraced. "You know how I like it here."

"Yes," said Rachel. "Me like it, too."

They both looked out to sea. Rachel wondered if Hope was thinking of her old life—the urge to drown herself. It suddenly struck her as strange that this place would be so dear to Hope, but then Rachel knew some people preferred to keep painful memories close.

"But what are you doing out so late?"

"Me was just visiting someone."

"Well, I was on my way home. But I can sit with you awhile, if you like?"

Behind the smile that flashed a row of perfect teeth, there was a watchfulness to Hope's expression. Rachel accepted her offer of company, and the two of them sat cross-legged on the ground.

"How is Mary Grace?" Hope asked.

"She is well."

"It is so good that you found each other again."

"Yes."

The memory of the reunion flooded through Rachel. The relief. The filling of a hole in her heart, bringing color to the world again. But then that moment became bittersweet. An ocean lay in the way of her ever experiencing that feeling again.

"You have other children, Rachel?"

From the tone of Hope's voice, it was a question, but from the look she gave Rachel, it was not.

"Yes."

For once, Hope was still. No clapping hands, no cocked head, no laughter. Wind whispered over the waves. Around Hope's throat, the ruffles on her dress danced in the breeze. She dropped her gaze.

When Hope spoke, it was as if all the joy had been stripped back from her voice, leaving behind something rough, something animal. "If my daughter had lived, I would do whatever it took. I would find her."

There was so much about them that was different. If Hope was a whirlwind, Rachel was the calm after the storm. But Hope's words, and the way she spoke them, called to something deeper. Rachel had it in her, too.

She would go. Of course she would. Part of her had always known it, had always brought her back, again and again, to the harbor. Not an ending, but a beginning. Distance didn't matter. Nothing mattered. In her, as in Hope, was a hard, harsh, unforgiving will, bent but not broken by slavery. She would choose the unfamiliar fear, and she would put an ocean between herself and her old master on Providence plantation.

Hope smiled, and it was as if nothing had happened. All her softness and delight returned. She got to her feet.

"It's late. I must go." She took Rachel's hand. "I'm glad I saw you tonight." Her lingering touch said that they would not meet again. She knew Rachel could not stay.

"Take care, Hope."

Rachel watched Hope walk away. There was no chill in the harbor now. The dead, if they were still watching from the ocean's depths, did not frighten Rachel anymore. They had died because they dared to fight against the path that had been chosen for them, that led down the gangplank of a ship and away to a plantation. The thought thrilled Rachel. There were other paths. Things could change. The island that had bound her need not bind her forever.

DESPITE THE LATE hour, Mrs. Armstrong was waiting, framed in the narrow hallway in all her quiet beauty. She looked at Rachel. Rachel looked back, and saw that she knew.

"You will go?"

"Yes."

Mrs. Armstrong grabbed Rachel's shoulders, the grip of her fingers passing on her grief for her own mother, and her hope that Rachel might yet avoid this fate. "You must do what I could not." She dropped her hands, and smudged away the tears that were spilling onto her cheeks. "I will ask my husband about passage to Demerara or to Trinidad. We will find you the first ship out of here. And we will pay your fare."

Rachel opened her mouth to protest, but Mrs. Armstrong silenced her with a wave of her hand.

"I insist," she said. "*We* insist." Her eyes were gleaming, the lower lashes wet and clumped. Her voice shook. "I hope you find them, Rachel. I hope you find them all."

13

SOMETHING VISCERAL INSIDE her body rejected the ship. They boarded in Bridgetown in the early afternoon, and as soon as they left the dock, Rachel's legs gave way beneath her and she began to retch violently. Mary Grace and one of the crew helped carry her below deck, where she lay in darkness, shivering and feverish, the unsteady rocking of the boat sloshing the bile in her stomach. That night, she did not sleep, but open-eyed she dreamed a visionless dream of groaning despair and stinking death. The dark, putrid air in the hold of the ship pressed down on her throat like the limbs of a still-warm corpse.

After what felt like a lifetime lost in the thick, cloying blackness, she crawled above deck as the dawn broke. Her legs still useless, she managed to sit herself upright against the side of the ship. She closed her eyes and tried to block out everything but the familiar sound of the waves and the taste of salt on her tongue.

"First time at sea?"

Opening one eye a crack, she saw a man standing over her, with skin the same color as the damp wood of the planks along the deck. The outer corners of his eyes sloped gently downward toward the curve of his smile, leaving his expression somewhere between somber and kind.

Rachel nodded. She didn't dare open her mouth, for fear that her insides would come spewing out over this man's boots.

"It can be hard, the first time." He had a solemn voice, without the usual island lilt. His consonants were hard like a white man's.

He plunged one hand into the pocket of trousers that were torn and frayed around the ankles. "Here." He offered her a small piece of something gray and wrinkled. "Ginger. Chew on it to help the sickness."

Rachel opened her mouth just enough to slip the ginger in. It was old and tough, but as she chewed, it began to leak its juice, which she swallowed with some difficulty.

The man waited patiently as she continued to press her head to her knees. But soon, she felt something working outward from the pit of her stomach, radiating down her shaking legs. It felt at first like a tightening, a firming up of all her muscles—and then, suddenly, everything relaxed. Supple and calm, her body was able to absorb the movement of the boat without complaint.

The man's smile widened. "Feel better?"

Rachel nodded again, and even managed to croak, "Yes."

The man gestured to the spot of deck beside her with a large, calloused palm. "May I sit?"

"If you like."

He sat close enough for her to feel the heat from his body.

"So," he said. "Who are you?"

There was a depth to his eyes that was unlike anything she had ever seen. His pupils were caverns, rolled into twin black circles. She couldn't look directly into them too long without experiencing a sense of vertigo.

"Rachel," she said. "Me traveling with me daughter."

"Good to meet you, Rachel. My name is Nobody."

Rachel looked Nobody up and down. He was more solid than she would have expected from someone with such a name. His shirtsleeves were rolled up, and muscles wrapped their way down his forearms like vines.

"Perhaps you are wondering how I came by my unusual name?"

A little embarrassed, Rachel averted her gaze, but he did not seem displeased.

"Well, I will tell you. On my old master's plantation in Antigua, a woman was accused of witchcraft. They claimed she had been burying things in the corners of the field to cast a spell—the heart of a goat, the berries of a poisoned bush and the afterbirth of one of the slave women, still wet with blood. Rather than denying the accusation, she accepted it proudly. She told the master that she had cursed the land, and that nobody would be born on his plantation again.

"The master's wife was at that time with child. A week later, the baby was born too soon—misshapen and dead. For many years, the curse appeared true—the slave women were barren and the master's wife bore him two more dead children. But one day, I was born. And so my master told my mother to name me Nobody. For it was true that Nobody was born on his plantation."

He spoke with the easy rhythm of a frequent storyteller. His words rose and fell with the deck beneath them. All the while, he kept his deep, downturned eyes fixed on the sea.

"How come you traveling to Demerara?" Rachel asked.

"I am part of the crew. I have been at sea for many years."

Rachel tried to imagine such a life. She took a deep breath, letting the salty air fill her lungs. "Do you like it? Being at sea?"

"I owe my freedom to the sea," he said, after a pause. "So, I respect it for that. But it is not always an easy life."

"Your freedom?"

"Yes. When I was a child, barely ten years old, my mother told me, one night, that she had a plan, but I must do exactly as she said. She told me to lie on my mat and not to move a muscle. She went out in the cover of darkness to scoop up some waste from the latrine pit. She took a knife and cut herself on her thigh, and mixed the waste with blood and water. Then, the next morning, she poured the bloody mixture between my legs, and ran outside. I heard her crying, and eventually the overseer came. She told him that I was dying—that the curse had come to take me, after all.

"I heard the overseer come close to look at me. I kept my eyes shut and my breathing shallow. The hut stank, and he did not stay long. That night, my mother whispered to me: 'Run.'"

Nobody closed his eyes for a moment, overcome. Rachel could feel his body tense up next to her, the mere memory of the command enough to make him prepare for flight.

"And so I ran. I found a road, and followed it until I reached a town with more people than I had ever seen—that was St. John's. I spent three days roaming the streets, not daring to stay still. On the third night, a man stumbled out of a tavern and saw me crouching by the doorway. He told me I could get food and shelter if I came on his ship, sailing from Antigua to London, the next day. That was my first of many voyages, and now here I am. I have not set foot in Antigua since."

Nobody kept his face blank—aside from the brief flash of pain, he might have been telling a myth or a fable. But etched into his features was the ghost of a frightened ten-year-old boy. Rachel imagined the grief his mother must have felt, sending him off to freedom while knowing she would never see him again.

"London?" she said. "You been all the way over there?"

"I was not there for long. But I remember it was cold—so cold that it pulled the clouds down from the sky and they wrapped themselves around everything so that you couldn't see."

"What other places you been?"

"Mostly to Europe and around the Caribbean," he said. "Once

to Africa, to the port of Popo." He looked down at the weathered wood of the deck. "I was on a Spanish ship, taking slaves to Cuba."

His words sent a chill through Rachel, but she felt no anger toward him. The image she had conjured of a daring life at sea, exploring the corners of the world, vanished. In its place, she saw a young boy again, buffeted across oceans on journeys he could not control. Every freedom had its price.

"And what takes you to Demerara, Rachel?" Nobody asked.

Leaning back, Rachel's face caught the sun's rays as they began to unfurl, burning off the dawn mists that still lingered around the ship. Their warmth, and Nobody's story of being separated from his mother as a child, softened her. Although something still felt secret about her search, she decided to tell him.

"Me sons. They was sold there many years ago."

They were interrupted by a white boy, not much older than twelve, appearing from below deck. His thin face was streaked with grime and sweat.

"They need you below."

Nobody got to his feet. "Perhaps we will speak later," he said, as though this was something he would like but had no control over. Ultimately, they were all at the mercy of the sea.

ALTHOUGH HER SICKNESS had subsided, Rachel still found it hard to be below deck for too long. Ancestral pains, sedimented somewhere inside her, continued to twist her stomach in knots as soon as she lost sight of the sun, and the phantom smell of rotting flesh haunted her down there. She and Mary Grace spent as much time as they could out in the open. Rachel introduced her daughter to Nobody, the next time he appeared on deck. Mary Grace held his gaze, unafraid of losing herself in those deep, cavernous eyes.

They were being blessed with a good crossing, and it looked set to stay that way—or so Nobody told them. The prow of the ship cut through the water with barely a murmur. He told them of great storms he had sailed through, where rain gouged your skin and raging waves, taller than the ship, threatened with every crack against the deck to splinter the boat in two.

Whenever they saw him, he would tell them a different account of one of his many journeys. If another crew member came by and snapped at him to stop slacking, the tale would be short—the time he saw a whale leap out of the water only yards from the boat, or the time a gust of wind blew a man straight out of the rigging and onto the deck, the crack of his bones only just audible above the noise of the gale. When he was able to stay with them longer, he had enough time to tell them about being harassed by a pirate ship all the way along the coast of Cuba, or about the attempted mutiny he helped a captain suppress on a journey to Brazil. Mary Grace listened with rapt attention whenever he spoke, and he seemed to enjoy her audience. When Rachel saw the looks that passed between them, she felt a pang of maternal mourning for the child her daughter had been. But she was glad, too. In all their time in Bridgetown, Rachel had never seen her daughter listen without a lowered gaze, but now she kept her eyes fixed on Nobody. With him, Mary Grace's muteness no longer seemed like timidity; it seemed like wonder.

For three more days, they saw only sea and sky. Rachel liked to walk to the bow of the ship and see the ocean lapping against the horizon on all sides. In Barbados, she had never been more than a few hours away from seeing that the land did not last forever. But on the ship, it was easy to believe the water had no end. She wondered how anyone could last the long journeys from Africa or from Europe. She had only been sailing a few days, but already the idea of land—solid and firm underfoot—seemed a distant speck in her memory.

She asked Nobody what it was like to spend weeks surrounded by infinity in every direction—above, below and all around.

"A life at sea is not for everyone," he said. "It can make you feel very small. I have seen it drive people mad. Once, I saw a man jump overboard in despair, because he became convinced that the sea had swallowed up the whole world and everybody in it but us . . ."

He paused. The sun was low in the sky, almost brushing against the water's surface, and its dying light turned the waves into a shimmering, shifting mirror.

"I have always survived it," he said. "I do not mind feeling small. I do not need reminding that I am Nobody—as are we all."

ON THE FOURTH day, they sighted land. The coast of South America crept out of the waves and curled across the horizon. Rachel gripped Mary Grace's hand tightly when she saw it emerge. Immediately, she felt grounded, and it was easier to hold the images of Micah and Thomas Augustus in her mind than it had been when the only thing in sight was water.

They drew close enough to see the green outlines of trees along the shore. The boat turned eastward, and over the morning it skirted the coast. Nobody came and found them, and took them to the prow of the ship. He pointed into the distance.

"You see there? How the water has started to brown?"

Shielding her eyes, Rachel found she could indeed see a streak of muddy water cutting through the deep blue of the surrounding sea.

"That's how we know we're close," Nobody said. "That is the mouth of the Essequibo River. Not long now until Georgetown."

Over the next few hours, the coast began to fall away, forming the gaping mouth of the river. Little islands, like teeth, jutted out toward the sea. Rachel and Mary Grace stayed at the bow, transfixed, as the vastness of the estuary became clear.

"Enjoying the view?"

Nobody had returned. He stood beside Mary Grace, and Rachel noticed the back of his hand brush against her daughter's hip.

"Me never see a river so big," Rachel said. There was still no sight of the far bank on the horizon.

"The rivers of South America are quite a sight," said Nobody. "Farther along the coast, in Brazil, is the Amazon. They say it is one of the largest rivers in the world. Like a great wound in the shoreline." He smiled a little sadly. "Even more than all my time at sea, the sight of it humbled me. The life we make for ourselves on land is futile. In the end, the water will win."

Rachel stared in silence at the Essequibo. She, too, was humbled, but that feeling was not as dark as Nobody described. Where he saw the river as a wound, she imagined the land embracing it on each side as it ran deep into the country's interior. Where he saw water and earth locked in opposition, she noticed that things were not as simple as they appeared. The muddy, fresh water met the salt water of the sea, their colors blending and dissolving into each other at the river's mouth. The islands rising out of the depths were green and fertile, teeming with life. Coexistence was possible. No one had to lose for the water to win.

Nobody was called back to work, but he told them to keep an eye out for a second river—this would be the Demerara, on which Georgetown sat. Over the afternoon, the shadow of the ship's mast lengthened. To port, the shoreline reemerged as they put the Essequibo estuary behind them.

Eventually, Mary Grace saw something, and she pointed out into the distance. Squinting, Rachel could just make out the Demerara, disgorging a thick vein of brown water out to sea.

The ship turned, swinging its bow toward the shore. A few other curious passengers had wandered over to watch their final destination crawling toward them across the horizon, and one young woman caught Rachel's eye. This woman stood apart from the others on deck, self-consciously so, her eyes darting often to the people around her and adjusting her position if anyone came too close. She was strikingly beautiful—tall, slender, fair-skinned, with gentle curls that she wore loose around her shoulders. Rachel was reminded of Cherry Jane, though this woman did not really resemble her daughter—her nose was too narrow, her eyes too dark and her skin a shade too light. But there was something in the way she carried herself, upright and deliberately graceful, as if she knew she would draw attention and had to be ready at all times to be looked at and admired.

What held Rachel's gaze was not this woman's beauty, however, nor her echo of Cherry Jane. It was her dress. After months with Mrs. Armstrong, Rachel could recognize great artistry when she saw it, and the dress was a thing of beauty. It was lilac silk, ornamented with a pattern of roses around the base of the skirt. Short puffed sleeves were overlaid with a sheer oversleeve that glimmered in the sunshine, and the neckline was adorned with lace. This was a dress that reveled in its own expense, a dress designed with the goal of advertising its wearer as a woman of good taste and considerable means.

And yet . . . Rachel looked closer. She tried to see what Mrs. Armstrong would see. The patches around the bodice where the color had faded. The fact that the skirt had been re-hemmed, and unevenly at that. That the shape of the sleeves had not been in fashion for some years now. And that, around this woman's waist, the dress was not the fit you would expect if it had been tailored for her by an expert seamstress.

The young woman turned her head, and her eyes briefly met Rachel's, but she turned away again hurriedly, and Rachel could see that she was afraid because she knew—she saw in Rachel's face that her disguise was not enough, and that whatever life she had fled from, and whatever she was trying to pass herself off as now, some small part of her true self would always shine through.

Nobody appeared again at Mary Grace's shoulder, and Rachel tore her gaze away from the woman in the lilac dress.

"How long?" Rachel asked.

"About an hour," he replied.

Mary Grace looked at her mother. Over the last few days, Rachel had noticed how her daughter's shoulders had unclenched and her lips were always on the cusp of a smile—especially when Nobody was around. Rachel saw the hope that had been building in Mary Grace's eyes flickering, like a flame on the verge of being extinguished.

"How long you gon' stay in Demerara?" Rachel asked Nobody.

He shrugged. "I have a little money that could last me a month or two. Then I will find work on another ship."

"You been good company to us."

"Thank you."

The mouth of the Demerara inched closer. Mary Grace dropped her gaze to the deck. Her lips started to curve downward and her back began to stoop, and Rachel knew there was no time to be indirect.

"Maybe you can stay with us awhile. In Georgetown. We can all find a room together."

Nobody said nothing. He was staring out at the sea, the waves reflected in miniature in his pupils.

Rachel took his hand. He looked from the ocean to her and back again.

"Listen," she said. "Me understand how hard it is to leave behind what you know. But it is time." She squeezed his hand tighter, and he looked back to her. "You can stop running now."

The smooth skin on his face quivered, holding back the tears that, aged ten, he had never had the chance to shed. Rachel could see his mother in his eyes—a faint outline, a distant memory with her features blurred—and she knew that he could see a piece of his mother in her, too. Together, these echoes of his mother were enough. They released him from the decades-old command.

"All right," he said. His voice was thick with the ache of memory. But there was relief in it, too. "I will come with you."

Mary Grace's head was still bowed. Nobody, the pain of the past still showing in his eyes, looked at her, and his face grew still. The tears not yet spilled ebbed away. He allowed himself, just for an instant, to smile.

BRITISH GUIANA

JANUARY
1835

14

THERE WAS AN eerie orderliness to the streets of Georgetown. As they sailed down the estuary, the buildings lining the riverbank stood neatly to attention. The dock was on the downriver edge of the town, and beyond it were strips of plantations, running in straight lines away from the water's edge. After their days on the open sea, it was jarring to see a landscape so carefully planned and tidily arranged.

Nobody led them down the gangplank. A small gaggle of people stood to greet the arrivals—mostly Black, still as lean and angular as the people who had left Barbados, but with clothes that were newer, and without that sunken hopelessness in their eyes. Rachel noticed the beautiful young woman in the lilac dress edging her way around this crowd. The woman walked quickly toward the nearest side street, and disappeared into its shadows.

"I know a place," Nobody said. "A tavern with some rooms. Cheap but not too seedy. They might take us there."

As they walked away from the river, tall buildings with stone facades gave way to shabbier, squatter ones with windows un-paned and gaping into the dusk. The street they walked down was almost empty. They passed a white woman, leaning against her doorframe, chatting away to a man outside in a language Rachel didn't recognize. Harsh words, spilling over with consonants, were softened by occasional peals of laughter from the pair.

Rachel frowned. "Me thought Georgetown was English?" She would never be able to find her sons in a foreign language.

"It is," said Nobody. "But it was once Dutch. A few of them are still around."

Before too long, they reached the tavern, relieved to find it still open. About a hundred yards away, the arrow-straight road ran out abruptly, replaced by a flat, barren field.

"I wouldn't go down that way if I were you," Nobody said. "A burial ground. And the dead don't rest easy in it."

Inside, the tavern was poorly lit but clean. A few men sat drinking at the bar, and another group huddled around a corner table with playing cards in their hands. There were two soldiers at the table, one fair-skinned and one dark. Otherwise, the men looked to Rachel like sailors or roving laborers—they gave off a shifting, impermanent air, and their eyes didn't stay fixed in one place for long. She had noticed the same sort of energy in Nobody, ever since they had left the ship.

Nobody went over and spoke to the barman. After a brief exchange, he turned and beckoned Rachel and Mary Grace over.

"You see?" he said curtly to the barman. "Both good, respectable women."

The barman was short, heavyset and balding. He wheezed slightly every time he exhaled. He looked them up and down with dark, beady eyes pricked into a face the color of molasses.

"And how they gon' earn a living?" he said, the question directed at Nobody. "How me know them won't turn to that line of work, if they desperate enough? They wouldn't be the first."

Nobody went to speak, but Rachel cut across him.

"Me daughter can sew a little. Me was a servant back in Barbados, but me have also been a field slave. Me no stranger to hard work."

The barman continued to stare. Eventually, he said, "If it's hard work you want, you gon' find it here. We looking for someone to serve and move the barrels when they come in. You strong?"

"Yes, sir."

"Well, me can talk to the landlord tomorrow. And if he take you, he let you have the room instead of wages."

Rachel shrugged. It seemed a reasonable trade.

The barman jerked his head toward a door in the corner. "The room's through there, up the stairs." He turned to Nobody. "Me need your money for tonight. No free board until she work a day here to earn it."

Nobody reached for his knapsack, but Rachel moved more quickly. She counted out coins—left over from the money Mrs. Armstrong had pressed upon her—into the barman's hand. She took the key and led the way up the stairs.

The room was small, square and perfectly anonymous. Two beds flanked the window on each side, but otherwise it was empty. Nobody hovered on the other side of the door. He was good at controlling his expression, but Rachel could still sense something was wrong. She guessed he was bristling at the fact that she had taken work and had paid for their room. If his pride was wounded, it was to his credit that he did not show it, but it was no surprise. He was unused to relying on anyone but himself, Rachel thought. Since he was a child, all he had known was the friction of a life at sea, where salt water ate away at weakness. The only relationships he had known were either contractual—between captain and crew— or fleeting—between mariners who would sail together once and then go their separate ways.

Rachel was thinking of a way to say delicately that she and her daughter did not need his money or labor or protection, only his company, when Mary Grace brushed a hand against Nobody's wrist. A tiny movement, before she moved away to look out the window, but Nobody's hands, which had not been still since they left the ship, stopped clasping and twisting. He finally stepped through the door.

RACHEL SLEPT WELL that night, after so many evenings spent avoiding her bed below deck. Nobody had insisted on sleeping on the floor.

"I've slept in worse places," he said.

On the cusp of sleep, Rachel caught a glimpse of him gazing up at Mary Grace. Her daughter's eyes were closed, and the moonlight shot streaks of silver through her dark, close-cropped hair. Lying there, Mary Grace had a soft beauty, and Rachel could tell Nobody was entranced by it.

In the morning, Rachel rose early. Nobody was still sleeping, half-curled like a question mark on the floor. Mary Grace was awake, and watched Rachel tiptoe over to the window. Leaning out of it, Rachel could see the burial ground at the end of the street. She inhaled, letting Georgetown's humid air fill her nostrils. The smell reminded her of Bridgetown—cluttered and dusty—but there was an unfamiliar edge to it, harsh and acidic, that told her she was far from Barbados and everything she had known.

Mouthing to Mary Grace that she would be back soon, and taking care not to disturb Nobody, Rachel stepped out of the room. She passed through the empty tavern, a forest of upturned stools resting on the tables, and out onto the deserted street. She retraced their steps from the night before, along the road to the river, but as she walked she grew uneasy. She saw so many things she did not recognize that at times she feared she had taken a wrong turn, even though she kept walking straight. The strangeness of it all was a reminder that it would take time to know this place.

She passed a man wheeling a cart of fruit, and a woman, gaunt and haggard-looking with a baby swaddled on her back. Otherwise, she saw no one. The quietness unnerved her. When she reached the grander buildings near the dock, their windows were mostly still shuttered. Only one house had a ground-floor window uncovered, and inside Rachel glimpsed an old woman with a white bandanna spreading a spotless linen tablecloth over a breakfast table.

In the corners of her vision, she caught glimpses of her sons, her shadow-companions on the quiet street, though never at the same time. Even in her own imagination, it was beyond Rachel's power to bring these two boys together, for they did not know each other—at least, not yet. Thomas Augustus had been born after Micah had gone and knew his brother only by the stories Rachel told. As a young child, Thomas had loved these stories; Rachel suspected he did not quite understand, back then, that Micah was a real person. This mysterious older brother was more like something out of a folktale, just one of the many characters Rachel summoned to lull her youngest son to sleep each night. This was after Mary Grace was sold, but Rachel was sure Thomas thought his sister was only months away from returning. To be told that there was another child gone, too, and gone far longer—perhaps that was too much for Thomas to bear. It was easier to think that Micah was his mother's invention, and that Mary Grace would come back to them soon, because the alternative was the harsh truth that any of Rachel's children could be taken at any time, and there was nothing she could do about it.

But it wasn't long before Samuel and Kitty were dead and Mercy was gone, and Thomas—not even seven—understood how fragile their family really was, how easily broken. Soon, he stopped asking for stories of his older brother.

When she reached the dock, a cool breeze from the river helped dispel the ghostly quality of the morning. A few men milled around near the water's edge. There were no ships yet, but they looked as though they were waiting for something. Two of them were standing closer together than the rest, with their backs to the sea, their heads bowed in conversation. They looked like father and son. The younger man had a round, innocent face. There were echoes of that face in his father's, but it was as if age had sanded down its soft edges until his jaw jutted prominently outward, and deep indents were hollowed into his temples.

Figuring she had to start her search somewhere, Rachel walked right up to them. The old man broke off and looked at her suspiciously.

"Yes?" he said.

"Sorry. Me looking for me sons."

"Well, we not your sons." The old man had a quiet, gravelly voice.

"You might have seen them—heard of them?"

The younger man answered. There was a hint of pity in his eyes. "We not been here long. What they called?"

"Micah and Thomas Augustus. One tall, the other short."

The younger man shook his head. "Sorry. We don't know anyone of those names."

It was as she expected, but a small sigh still escaped her lips.

"How long you been looking?" the young man asked. His father, still sour-faced, turned toward the sea.

"Many years they gone," Rachel replied. "But me only get to Demerara yesterday."

"Well, me sorry we can't help." He glanced at the sea. "We looking for someone, too."

"Not looking," said his father sharply. "Waiting."

The young man closed his eyes for a moment, a pained expression flashing across his face. Rachel tried to guess his age. Probably around the same as Thomas Augustus, wherever he was now.

"Who you waiting for?" she asked.

"Me mother," said the young man. "We come from St. Lucia

about a year ago, because we hear they pay a little more here. Me mother say she gon' join us when she can." He gave Rachel a sad smile.

"Her ship come in today?" Rachel asked.

The old man said, "Yes," as the young man said, "We don't know."

The young man cast his eyes downward, embarrassed. "We hope she gon' come today," he said. "We always come in the mornings and wait, just in case."

Rachel took a step toward the old man. He must have felt her closeness, because he turned to stare at her.

"Well, me hope today is the day," she said to him gently. "Me hope the next ship that come in is hers."

But deep in his eyes she could see that same void that had filled the eyes of her dying children, Kitty and Samuel. The same awful emptiness written on the face of the stillborn baby as it left her body. It broke her heart to see it—the pain she felt for him in that moment, and for his son, was so acute that it almost bent her double. Underneath it all, the old man had no hope left. His heart had died because he believed his wife had died, all those hundreds of miles away from him and his son.

The old man said nothing.

The young man said, "Sorry," again. And then, as Rachel was walking away, he called after her. "Me hope you find your sons!"

Rachel felt her heart throbbing at his words, forcing out a pulsing beat to keep alive her belief that her unfound children were living. She hurried back down the road to the tavern.

15

ON THE WAY back, there were a few more open shutters and smoking chimneys—the town was starting to creak to life. The streets were no longer deserted; Rachel passed a group of silent, stony-faced men with spades, and a young boy on crutches with a left foot that twisted awkwardly out of his ankle, toes splayed in all directions.

Back at the tavern, the barman from the previous night had returned, wheezing louder than before as he went around setting the stools on the floor. He glanced up when Rachel came in.

"This the one," he said, looking toward the corner. Turning, Rachel saw a white man sitting at one of the tables with an account book open in front of him. The nib of his pen hovered above the page as he peered at her over the tops of his glasses.

"Come closer," he said. "Let me get a proper look at you."

He wasn't at all like she had expected the landlord of a tavern would be. He had a long nose that pointed downward at the tip, inviting attention to a mouth that was so thin it was almost lipless. His face was framed by limp, graying sideburns. He looked prim and fastidious—Rachel tried to imagine him sitting down for a drink with any of the men she had seen in the tavern the previous evening, and found she could not.

She stood in front of him as he swept his eyes up and down her body, hands clasped tightly behind her back to keep them still.

"So," he said, finally. "You want a job?"

"Yes, sir." She avoided his eyes. It was always a split-second decision, whether to look at white people directly or not. Some of them got intensely irritated if she did; others found it the height of insubordination if she did not. This man struck her as the type who would want her to keep her gaze deferentially lowered.

"And you were a slave, I hear?"

"Yes, sir. A field hand in Barbados. Then a servant in Bridgetown."

"Good." He rested his pen back in an inkpot, freeing up his hands to gesticulate firmly. "I have always made a point of hiring ex-slaves here. Some said I was quite mad—that they would make bad, insolent and rebellious workers. But I found the opposite, as long as one isn't afraid to demonstrate a commitment to discipline and order." He bared his teeth in a grimly satisfied smile. "Once they've seen you're willing to have them arrested if they step out of line, they tend to be most obedient. No one knows the value of freedom more than an ex-slave."

Rachel realized after a pause that he was expecting some reply. "Yes, sir."

"Well, then. You can work here a week, and we will see how you do. Albert can supervise you." He nodded over toward the barman, who had finished setting down the stools and was now rubbing the bar with a damp cloth.

"Thank you, sir." Rachel hesitated. "And . . . the room?"

The landlord waved a hand dismissively. His veins were visible through the translucent skin on his wrists. "Yes, yes, Albert mentioned that. You may have the room in lieu of wages, as long as your companions behave themselves."

Rachel bowed her head even lower. "Thank you, sir."

The landlord picked up his pen again. Albert, treading heavily, came out from behind the bar and shoved the cloth into her hand. "Keep wiping everything down," he said.

Rachel did as she was told. As she made her way around the room, cleaning the tables, the landlord paid her no further attention—not even when, after she stumbled over a crack in the flagstone floor, her hip collided noisily with one of the stools. From time to time, she glanced over at his pinched face, frowning down at his figures, and could not help thinking of Mr. and Mrs. Armstrong. Their kindness was thrown into sharp relief by this mean-spirited white man. But the flash of their memory was brief, and quickly set to one side. This landlord was not the first unpleasant employer she had known, and she was not so naive as to think he would be the last.

After cleaning, she helped Albert lug fresh barrels of ale up from the cellar. When he suddenly slackened his grip, shunting the brunt of the barrel's weight into her arms, Rachel knew he was testing her. The first time he tried it, at the bottom of the cellar steps, she was unprepared and almost tumbled backward. But she held her footing and, afterward, kept herself braced against the barrel, jaw clenched, back straining and bent legs rooted into the floor. By the time they brought up the fourth and final barrel, which Rachel had all but carried herself, sweat was dripping down her forehead and stinging the corners of her eyes. As they lowered it, she looked Albert directly in the eye and kept staring, forcing all traces of effort from her face, until the barrel had reached the ground.

About midmorning, Nobody appeared from upstairs. Nodding to Albert and to the landlord—who shot him a brief look of disdain before returning to his books—he perched on a stool while Rachel wiped the sticky traces of last night's ale out of the tankards.

"Mary Grace is just changing," he said. "She will be down soon."

Rachel smiled to herself as she turned to place a tankard back on the shelf.

"You two been talking?" she asked.

Nobody shrugged. "Not really. It doesn't seem fair, somehow, for me to always talk and her to always listen. So this morning we sat in silence for a while." He looked down at his hands as he spoke. "It was nice."

With a soft thud, the landlord closed his book and began to buff his glasses on the sleeve of his shirt, his eyes on Nobody as he did so.

"This is one of your companions, I presume?" he said. "Albert mentioned you had brought a man and a woman with you."

"Yes, sir. Me son and me daughter." The lie slipped out easily, bonding the three of them more tightly together. Just in case.

"I see. He has work?"

"I am a seaman by trade," Nobody answered. He kept his voice small, steady, unthreatening. He also knew how to appease a white man. "The wages from my last voyage will go a little way, then I may seek work in town."

The landlord nodded. "And the daughter? What will she do?"

"She can sew, sir," said Rachel.

The landlord put his glasses back on his nose. Through them, his green eyes were bulbously enlarged.

"I shall consult with my wife," he said. "God knows, the tailors and seamstresses in this town charge a fortune, so it may be she has some acquaintances with clothes that need mending or retrimming for the new season."

Rachel was momentarily stunned by this offer of genuine assistance. But then he said, "Idle hands only turn to trouble, after all," and she accepted there was a less charitable reading of his words. In his eyes, the Negro was a brute kept in check only by the wiles of white men like himself, who found ways to control them. She thanked him anyway, and continued cleaning the glasses as vigorously as she could, in case he decided to watch her.

———

THE LANDLORD'S NAME, Rachel learned from Albert, was Mr. Tobias Beaumont. Mr. Beaumont never asked for her name, and Albert told her not to expect him to.

"It was many years me work here before he ask me," he said.

After Rachel had carried most of the weight of the barrels up and down the stairs for a few days, Albert began to warm to her in his way. He was a man of few words—he would often ask her a question, or otherwise make a remark of some kind, only to fall silent after her reply. He would then pick up the same theme later in the day or the following morning. They could stretch a whole conversation out for almost a week in this manner.

Whenever Rachel told Albert about herself, she interwove truth with fiction. This was partly out of caution but also, sometimes, just for the sheer thrill of it. She was now an ocean away from her old life, and anyone who knew her. The freedom to reinvent herself, even if in the most inconsequential ways, gave her a rush that felt like being untethered, floating a few inches above the ground. She told Albert that her old master's name was Williams rather than Carrington. She said that, other than Mary Grace and Nobody, she had no other children. One night, when the last patrons had finally stumbled out onto the street and it was just the two of them stacking stools onto tables, she said in a whisper that Mary Grace and Nobody's father had been killed in a fire on their old plantation, and her voice choked with imagined grief.

Despite the lie, Rachel had not forgotten her other children. But Mr. Beaumont was a waspish and unpleasant master—hard to please and quick to cast a critical eye over anything that crossed his path. He left Rachel no room for error, so once again, her life was forced to conform to the exacting demands of another master. Though she was far away from Providence, and cleaning tankards and tables bore no resemblance to cutting sugarcane, she felt a creeping sense of familiarity. Work had a numbing effect; giving herself in service to Mr. Beaumont dulled the exhilarating urgency she had felt when she first stepped on the boat and sailed away from Barbados. Fear, too, dulled the desperate edge to her quest—fear of the unknown and of the vast, foreign land in which she found herself. It was easy to let weeks slip by, with avoiding Mr. Beaumont's displeasure as her only task.

When Rachel did manage to snatch an hour away from the tavern, she would wander the streets. She stopped passersby and described her sons—or, rather, described them as they might be, trying to imagine how the years had changed them. But, like the long hours of labor, the searching felt more and more like an empty repetition, devoid of any real meaning. She inhabited her body only as a tool, and not as an end in itself.

ONE DAY, AN early-morning walk took her right to the edge of town, to where houses gave way to plantations. It was a chilling sight. The mills, the boiling-houses, the rows of cane—all reminded her of Barbados. Suddenly, the distance between the two colonies did not seem so great. Suddenly, it did not seem so unlikely that her past could follow her here. Everywhere, the long shadow of slavery was the same.

In spite of the humid, sticky morning air, Rachel shivered.

But she had not walked all this way for nothing. She shielded her eyes against the sun; in the distance, she thought she could see workers tending the cane. Stepping off the road, she crossed into the plantation. She looked around carefully—but no sign of an overseer. She made her way across the fields.

It was the smell of it that unsettled her the most: the sweetness of the juice that leaked from fresh-cut stalks, and the manure that caked the earth. She closed her eyes, just for a moment, dizzy with the sensation that she was still on Providence, hundreds of miles away, and all that had come before—perhaps even emancipation itself—was simply an illusion. Maybe she was still there, without her children, and maybe she was still a slave.

She opened her eyes to dispel the thought, and there was a white man standing in front of her. Loud, red-faced.

"You," he said.

Rachel took a step back. The man had a gun.

"Who are you?" He spewed flecks of spit as he spoke. "What are you doing here?"

Rachel opened her mouth, as if to speak, before cold certainty descended on her. An angry white man with a gun could not be reasoned with.

She must run.

She turned, almost tripping over her own feet, and scrambled away. Behind her, she heard the man roaring.

"Trespasser! Thief! Stop!"

Every word urged her forward, bile surging up her throat, her hands scrabbling to part the cane, to make a path back to the road.

A gunshot.

How long until Rachel realized she did not bleed? She was so certain of death that her vision went black. Her knees gave way. She crawled on her hands and knees.

But then . . .

Tumbling out of the cane and into the road. Slowly, sight returned. Daring to glance back, she saw the white man in the distance, his gun pointing to the sky. A warning shot—but a reminder. For if he had shot to kill, who would punish him? What did her life matter here?

She had been careless—too careless. It was not a mistake she could afford to make again.

She got to her feet. The sun was now over the horizon, the morning light harsh and bright. Work would be starting back at the tavern soon. She began the walk back toward Georgetown, her hands still trembling.

MR. BEAUMONT WAS already waiting, swinging a pocket watch between thumb and long, thin forefinger.

"You're late," he said.

Rachel bowed her head. "Sorry, sir."

"I do not pay you to be *late*."

He was not paying her at all, except in the use of a room to sleep in, but Rachel kept her mouth shut and her head bowed. She heard the sound of Mr. Beaumont's footsteps on the flagstones as he marched toward her.

"Look at me when I'm talking to you."

He jabbed a finger under her chin, forcing her head upward, and then withdrew his hand sharply, as if touching her repulsed him. Rachel, shaken, stared up at him in stunned silence. Everything was out of joint. Her ability to read the face of a white man, honed over years of enslavement, had failed her. Instinct had told her to look down, but now Mr. Beaumont had commanded her otherwise.

"Where have you been?" he pressed. "Have you been out all night?"

"No, sir. Me—me just go for a walk."

"Well, if I catch you out walking again . . ." His lip curled as he trailed off, as though he found everything about this encounter distasteful. He wielded his power bluntly—nothing about his tone made the threat less clear—but he seemed to take no pleasure in it.

Rachel was lost for words. The plantation, the gunshot—now this. She felt as if she had stepped from solid ground into deep water. She was sinking into fear—the old fear, the Barbados fear. In Mr. Beaumont's sneer she saw the foreman from Providence.

"I know what you are, you know," Mr. Beaumont said in a low

voice. He was still standing close to her, their faces only inches apart. His pale, watery eyes were filled with malice. "I know what you've done."

Rachel said nothing. Still sinking, sinking—until there would be no light, no hope left.

"Where was it you came from?"

Rachel opened her mouth, but was too slow to answer.

"I said—where?"

"Barbados, sir."

He nodded slowly. "You think I don't know people in Barbados? You think I couldn't write to them if I wanted to? Have them send me the runaway notices? You think I couldn't collect your reward?"

All Rachel could do was stare mutely back at him. But of course, she had known. Of course, she had always known she would not be safe. How could she have forgotten it?

There was a long silence. Then Mr. Beaumont stepped back and pocketed his watch, as if to say that the matter was closed.

"Sorry, sir," Rachel said, her voice cracking. "Me not gon' do it again."

After that, she did not dare go out searching for her children.

THEY HAD BEEN in Georgetown a few weeks when Mary Grace came and sat at the bar. It was the middle of the morning, and Rachel was cleaning the tankards just as she had done in the middle of every morning since they arrived in Demerara.

Mary Grace gave her a long look.

Lowering the tankard in her hand, Rachel sighed. "Me know," she said.

Mary Grace raised an eyebrow. In the time they had been in Georgetown, her face had grown more expressive. Underused muscles twitched beneath her skin, stretching her mouth into wider smiles than Rachel had ever seen before, so wide they made the features spread across her face seem in perfect proportion. Back in Bridgetown, Mary Grace had been able to make herself understood, but it was always through her eyes—two eloquent orbs set in the middle of an otherwise passive face. Now, her feelings spilled out of her eyes and spread around the rest of her body—she even moved her hands more, to touch Rachel's arm in the middle of a conversation, or to point out the window at a beautiful sunset. Rachel credited Nobody for the change. Her daughter suddenly had to marshal more expressions as she plumbed new depths of emotion in her heart.

"Me do what me can," Rachel said. "But me can't—me don't know where they—"

Mary Grace reached out and brushed the tips of her fingers against Rachel's wrist. The feeling of her daughter's skin on her own sent a jolt through Rachel, flooding her empty body with warmth. Hands that had been reaching for another tankard without the need of thought to guide them, so familiar had the work become, stilled themselves. Rachel was aware of the way she was standing, shoulders hunched over to make herself smaller than she was. She let herself stand upright. This small act of unbending herself was not enough to undo the weeks in Georgetown, and years in Barbados, spent being subdued by labor. But it injected her with fresh hope. She felt the ache that usually only came at night, and she welcomed it. Her body was trembling, and she claimed her ownership of it. Her hands, arms, legs, took new shape, as instruments of her own will.

Before Rachel could reply to her daughter, Albert came trudging up from the cellar. Never wanting to be caught in a moment of inactivity, Rachel set to work again. She could feel her daughter's eyes on her as she stared intently at the damp cloth, smearing away the sticky residue clinging to the sides of the tankard. She tried to convey, with her still-straight back, that she understood what her daughter had tried to tell her, and was grateful for it.

After a while, Rachel heard Mary Grace push herself up off her stool and go back upstairs. She was left alone to finish her morning's work.

16

———

QUIET TONIGHT," SAID Albert.

It was dark outside, approaching midnight. An old white man with three fingers missing on his left hand was curled around a tankard in one corner. In another two younger men sat in morose silence, speaking only when it was time to order another drink. Otherwise, the tavern was empty.

Rachel and Albert stood for a moment, staring at the unoccupied tables. Then Albert said, "You go. Me can manage tonight."

Rachel searched his face for any sign that this was some kind of test—that if she said yes, Mr. Beaumont would emerge from upstairs and say that he always knew she was lazy. But Albert, leaning against the edge of the bar with a dishcloth dangling from the crook of his arm, looked as if he bore her no ill will.

"You sure?"

"Yes. You can cover for me next time."

Rachel glanced over to the stairs leading up to her room, but found herself walking out from behind the bar toward the exit.

"You going out?" Albert asked. She didn't turn, but could hear the frown in his voice.

"Me gon' be back soon."

It had been a long time since she had dared to walk the streets. The night air cut through her lungs as she made her way down the road. Her mind was curiously empty—clean, unsullied by any thought further ahead than placing one foot in front of the other. She sensed the vague outline of an intention to walk to the dock, but no sooner had it begun to crystallize than she turned left, off the road that she knew would lead to the river, and down a narrow side street. A thin sliver of moonlight fell between the buildings on each side, like a glowing thread pulling her down an unknown path. She felt a mass of contradictions—pure will, unbridled spontaneity, brimming with possibilities, but at the same time unformed, purposeless, with a life that was outside her control.

The street intersected with another, almost as narrow, so that the thread of moonlight split into three. Pausing, Rachel looked left and then right. One way, she knew, must lead to the river—that road was empty. The other would lead back toward the burial ground. Down that path, standing just outside the strip of silver light, was a crouching shadow.

She knew immediately that it was a child. She stared at the shadow, and though she could not see the child's eyes, she felt them staring at her.

The shadow-child began to run. It moved awkwardly, lurching slightly from one side of the street to the other, the moonlight slicing a line down its back. And Rachel was running, too, her body carrying her forward, as it had done out of Providence, frightening her with its speed. The pounding sound of their feet echoed off the walls of the surrounding buildings. Arms pumping, chest heaving, she strained to keep up.

She could not let the child get away. Not again.

Rachel tried to work out which of her children she was pursuing in this dreamlike chase. The shadow-child was small and slender— could it be Thomas Augustus? Or maybe Cherry Jane, for they had been almost as tall as each other.

They were running out of road. Ahead lay the burial ground. Exposed to the full illumination of the moon above, it had been turned a washed-out, sickly gray. They were close enough that Rachel could see the grass rippling as a gust of wind shivered through it.

Panic bubbled up from the pit of her stomach—a thick, glutinous panic that gummed her throat shut in terror. She knew that she must not let the child get to the burial ground. She could not let the dead take what was hers.

Adrenaline spread through her body, bursting through her boundaries. Uncontained, she moved along the street as sheer force, streaking toward the child, closing the gap between them.

"No!"

She heard herself cry out, and felt herself grab the child by the arm. Her fingers closed around something solid and firm—she was no longer unrestrained energy, and the child was no longer a wisp of shadow, but stood, full-blooded, panting, at the precipice of the burial ground. The child twisted in her grip.

"Let go of me!"

A boy's voice, the accent unfamiliar. Rachel drew back her hand as if scalded. It was not Cherry Jane, or Thomas Augustus, or any of the phantom children who so often haunted her. This child was not hers at all.

"Sorry," she said, stepping back.

The child drew himself inward, coiled like a spring on the point of release, but he did not run.

"You chased me."

The boy's face was framed by dark, straight hair that had been unevenly hacked away near the base of his neck. He was not white or Black but something else entirely—skin the color of a mulatto, streaked with grime, with a narrow nose and wild eyes, too big for his emaciated face.

"Me sorry," she said again, keeping her voice low and gentle, like he was a startled animal. "Me did think you were . . ."

She trailed off. The boy said nothing.

"What you doing out so late?" she asked. He looked to be only eleven or twelve.

Still, he said nothing. Despite his strangeness, accentuated by the shadows that fell across his face, Rachel felt a stab of pity. She could see a little of her children in him, after all.

"You have anywhere to stay tonight?"

Slowly, the boy shook his head.

"You have anything to eat?"

He shook his head again.

Rachel held out her hand. "Come."

The child did not move.

"Me not gon' hurt you," she said. "But me can get you some food, and someplace warm to sleep."

The child simply stared at her hand. Rachel waited, holding herself as still as she could. Beyond the road, in the burial ground, she could sense the shifting presence of the dead. She no longer feared them—they would not take the child—but their whispers made her uneasy. The living should not outstay their welcome, so close to this place of ghosts.

Still, the child showed no sign of wanting her help. Meeting his wild eyes, Rachel decided on a different approach. She began to walk slowly back the way they had come.

"Well," she called over her shoulder, without looking back. "You can come if you want to."

The night was silent enough that, straining her ears, she could hear the soft pad of feet behind her.

Inside the tavern, the two younger men had gone. The old man was slumped against the wall, with his eyes closed and his mouth open, and his tankard of ale, half-drunk, perched precariously on his lap. Albert nodded to her as she came in, but his face hardened when he looked behind her.

Rachel spoke quickly. "It's all right. Me bring him here."

Albert drew himself up taller and pursed his lips, the better to glare down at the boy.

"We got food?" Rachel asked.

Besides ale, the tavern had only meager offerings at the best of times. Mr. Beaumont said that he could only tolerate so many sins under one roof, and he was not in the business of facilitating gluttony. Stale bread, slices of beef so thin that light could pass through them without trouble and watery soups with a shimmering film on their surface were usually all any patron could hope for.

"He got money?" Albert shot back.

"Me gon' pay for him."

With a wheeze of displeasure, Albert pulled out a misshapen loaf from under the bar. It made an audible crunch when he thrust it onto the counter.

Rachel took the bread and sat at one of the unoccupied tables. The boy was still hovering near the door, his arms drawn tightly across his chest. In the candlelight, she could see all the bones of his face under his rust-colored skin.

She slid the bread across from her, so that it rested in front of an empty stool. "Sit," she said. "Please."

Slowly, the boy made his way over. He moved stiffly, emphasizing the sharp angles of his limbs, and with a slight limp in one leg. He perched on the stool, perfectly still, before falling upon the bread and beginning to rip it apart. Rachel watched him as he devoured it.

"What's your name?" she asked.

The boy kept his eyes on the bread, chewing manically, and did not reply.

"Me name is Rachel," she said gently. "Me come from an island, many miles away, called Barbados."

The boy's eyes darted up from the bread and then back down.

"You also far from home?"

The boy was nearing the end of the bread. Slowing down, he considered the final chunk in his hand. "Yes."

"What place you from?"

He began to tear tiny pieces off the last bit of bread, savoring every bite. Between mouthfuls, he said, "A village up the river. But many people got sick and died. My mother died. It was hard. My father brought me here. We would work, any work we could find . . ." He paused, chewing on another morsel of bread. "But my father died. There is no work for a child. No money for our room. So I stay on the street."

He spoke in a quiet, monotone voice—it sounded like the prayers Rachel had sometimes heard the Armstrongs murmur late at night before bed. She longed to reach out and brush a lock of his hair away from his forehead, but she forced herself to keep her hands resting on top of the table.

"Me sorry to hear it," she said.

She watched him eat the final piece of bread, and then fold his arms back across his chest. He looked across the table at her with his dark, serious eyes, and she shifted a little under the full force of his gaze.

"Who are your people?" she asked. "Up the river. You have other family—brothers, sisters? You can go back."

The boy shook his head. "No other family. Everyone left. Some came north, like us, looking for white man work. Some went looking for better places, farther upriver, in the forests. My people are Akawaio—Indian. This was our land first."

Rachel nodded. She had heard stories in Barbados about the ones who were there before, though there were none left on that island. On Providence, there had been one man convinced that there was a patch of forest in the northern hills where some of these people who predated the white men were still living. He believed that if you ran you could reach them, and live in safety in the last little strip of the land that was still free. He died, not from running—he never did try—but a quiet death from overwork and slow starvation, the sort of death that struck often on the plantations. The feverish dream of freedom among the last survivors of the Carib Indians could not sustain him.

Rachel glanced over her shoulder. Albert held her gaze long enough to make sure she knew he had been staring at them, and then looked away and busied himself with putting the lid back on a barrel of ale.

"You can stay here tonight," she said to the boy. "With us. If you want."

The boy drew his arms in a little closer. His eyes flicked over to the door. The tension came back over him, as if he was about to flee. But he nodded.

Rachel led him upstairs. She knew Albert's disapproving eyes would be following them out of the room, but she ignored him. In her mind, she was already testing out what she could say tomorrow, to try to persuade him that the boy should stay longer.

At the top of the stairs, the boy suddenly stopped. "You want to help," he said. "Why?" His tone was perfectly flat, without any trace of suspicion. If he had been betrayed before by the false kindness of strangers, he did not show it.

Rachel thought of Mama B, all those hundreds of miles away. "Because someone help me when me need it. And you should not take help if you not gon' give it when the time comes."

She held open the door to the room. The boy seemed satisfied, and he slipped inside.

Mary Grace was already asleep, with her back to the room and her face close to the wall. Nobody was lying on the floor, but he pushed himself up as they came in. He looked from Rachel to the boy. Rachel waited for his questions, but none came. Nobody nodded at the boy, and then stretched himself back out on the floor with his eyes closed. Somehow, one lost child had recognized another through all the years that separated them.

Rachel pointed to the bed that was usually hers, but the boy shook his head firmly and pointed to the floor at the foot of it. She tried to pile her blankets into a sleeping mat, but he tossed them back to her. He lifted his chin, and in spite of his small, fragile size, she knew he would not do things her way. She watched as he curled himself up on the bare wood, before lying down herself.

Waiting for sleep, Rachel listened to the overlapping rhythms of their breathing, like the changing tides of four different oceans. She heard the boy's breath—sharp and shallow—even out until it was as gentle and slow as a lullaby.

At the very beginnings of a dream, with the solidity of the room around her just starting to shift, there was a whisper.

"Nuno. My name is Nuno."

In the morning, when they all woke up, the boy was gone.

WHEN ALBERT ARRIVED, he gave her an accusatory look but said nothing. They went through the morning routine in silence. After they had set down the last barrel behind the bar, Rachel said, "Albert, me did not tell you true. Me have more pickney—two sons and two daughters. Me think me sons are in Demerara. That's why we come here, to find them."

Albert gazed out the open doorway onto the dusty street outside. He had a faraway look in his eye that told Rachel he understood. She wondered who he had lost, or who he still hoped to search for, but she was sure he would never tell her.

After a long pause he said, "Me hope you find them."

For the rest of the day, they settled back into their old routine, letting pieces of fractured conversations ebb and flow over many hours.

17

RACHEL FOUND MR. Beaumont's presence in the tavern incongruous at the best of times, but never more so than on the infrequent occasions he was there in the evenings, when it was busy. He would stand at the end of the bar, stiff and upright, and if any man came stumbling over to order a drink he would direct them distastefully to either Rachel or Albert. As the night deepened and the patrons grew louder and more raucous, his nostrils would flare and he would glance frequently up to the ceiling as if appealing to God for the strength to tolerate the noisy, dark, stuffy room. The busier it was (and therefore the more money he was making), the more put out he would seem.

Rachel tried to glean from Albert why a man so ill at ease in a tavern had ended up running one—a mystery compounded by the fact that Mr. Beaumont was white and seemed well-to-do, but his patrons were mostly Blacks, mulattoes and the odd unsavory white man. She first asked early on, when Albert did not quite trust her—not meeting her eye, he had said gruffly that he supposed the money was good, and left it at that. But a few weeks later, unprompted, he had leaned close to her and said quietly that Mr. Beaumont used to own a shop on the other side of town, but that there had been a rumor he was not white.

Over the next few days, the full story came out in snippets from Albert. Mr. Beaumont's great-great-grandfather had been Black—or so a man who happened to run a rival business had said. Mr. Beaumont had wanted to go to court and prove his innocence, but the damage had already been done. People began to whisper. Wasn't there something of the Negro about his shifty eyes? Wasn't his head a little too narrow, hiding a smaller-than-average brain inside? Mr. Beaumont had moved across town, purchasing the tavern from the previous mulatto owner—Albert's former master. Mr. Beaumont was a shrewd businessman, and made a tidy profit on the place, but he knew that it would be impossible to significantly raise the class of patrons he served. White society in Georgetown had a long memory, and even the whisper of a fraction of Blackness was enough to taint Mr. Beaumont for life.

It was on one of the evenings when Mr. Beaumont was standing at the end of the bar, looking displeased, that Nobody came in with a white man. They sat close together in a corner, deep in conversation. The white man had a long, scraggly beard that was just turning to gray. It quivered when he laughed—a loud bark of a laugh that drew the attention of the other men packed on the tables nearby. At one point, Rachel saw Nobody point toward her, and the white man stared at her with a furrowed brow before shaking his head.

Rachel wanted to get closer to them to overhear what they were saying, but with Mr. Beaumont behind the bar she was too busy trying to look hardworking, and she didn't dare seem distracted, even for an instant. The men nursed their ales slowly, but eventually, craning her neck, Rachel could see that their tankards were empty. She slipped out from behind the bar and went to collect them. As she drew close, she heard the white man's gravelly voice.

". . . sure it will come to me in a moment. Let me see. You know, I can picture the exact snooty expression on his face, right down to the little hairs coming out of his nostrils, but what was his damned name?"

"Rachel." Nobody touched her on the arm. "This is Captain Grafton. We sailed together, a few years ago."

"Ha!" The captain barked a laugh again, dusting Rachel's hand with a fleck of spit as she reached out to take his empty tankard. "Sailed together? To put it mildly." He looked at her, his eyes a sludge-colored mix of brown and green. "This boy saved my life."

"The mutiny," Nobody said. "I told you about it before. That was Captain Grafton's ship."

The captain bared his teeth and grinned in Nobody's direction. "And to think," he said, "before that journey, I always said that nobody mutinied on my ships. Turns out Nobody was the only one who didn't bloody well mutiny!" He slapped the table to drive home the force of his pun.

Rachel glanced behind her. The tavern was crowded, and there were other, noisier patrons who had attracted Mr. Beaumont's disapproving gaze. She could linger a little longer.

"Captain Grafton has sailed often to Georgetown," Nobody said, leaning toward her. "And he has come a few times from Barbados. Including once in 1817."

A tremor spread through Rachel's body, as easily as if Nobody had spoken her son's name. In her mind, the year and the name were one—Micah.

"Nobody says you're looking for a son, came to Demerara around that time?" If Captain Grafton felt any awkwardness, to be confronted with a mother whose son he was complicit in tearing away and casting across the sea, he didn't show it. His muddy-eyed stare was unblinking. "Can't say I remember anyone of your resemblance. Don't usually pay much attention to the cargo, unless there's trouble. But I do know we sold almost every slave on that ship to this one man—uppity sort of fellow, flashy with how he bought them all. He wanted the whole town to know he could afford it—you know the type."

In Rachel's hands, the tankards finally stopped clinking together. She was no longer shaking. The same sense of cool clarity that had come over her in Mr. Armstrong's study descended. She grew still.

"You remember the name of this man?" Her voice rang in her own ears, like the voice of a stranger. She felt as if she was somewhere across the room, watching herself watching Captain Grafton, as she waited for his reply.

The captain frowned, carving deep creases into his wide forehead. "I've been trying. I can picture the fellow, but the name . . ." He lapsed into silence.

Glancing behind her again, Rachel saw that Mr. Beaumont's eyes were trained firmly on the three of them. She snapped back into herself; her calm demeanor evaporated, and she was trembling once again. Mr. Beaumont's lip curled in venomous displeasure, but Rachel dared to turn away from him. This was too important.

Captain Grafton was twisting a strand of his beard between finger and thumb. Suddenly, his fist came down on the wood of the table.

"Braithwaite! That was the name."

Rachel inhaled. She could not look either Captain Grafton or Nobody in the eye; she turned to go, keeping her head down. Slightly stooped, avoiding Mr. Beaumont's gaze, she slipped back behind the bar, and was immediately accosted by a man who complained that the bread he had been served was so stale he had chipped a tooth on it. By the time she had successfully placated him, when she looked back at their table, Nobody and Captain Grafton had gone.

———

WHEN RACHEL CAME upstairs that night, she found Nobody and Mary Grace still awake. They sat on the bed, cross-legged, with their knees touching. It was not the first time she had seen them like this, gazing into each other's eyes, but usually she only got a fleeting glimpse before Nobody would jump guiltily to his feet or hastily snatch away a hand that had been resting on Mary Grace's cheek. This time, he did not move.

"I was just telling Mary Grace the news."

Mary Grace beamed at her mother, and Rachel couldn't help but see the echo of Micah in her daughter's face. It was not the first time she had seen a shadow of her son that evening—ever since she had heard the name *Braithwaite*, he had appeared even in the faces of strangers. He seemed closer than ever.

Rachel sat at the edge of the bed, close to the place where Nobody's and Mary Grace's bodies met. "How you—? Where was—?" All her questions for Nobody threatened to tumble out at once, but she managed to settle on one. "You already know? About the captain?"

"I knew he had done the journey between Barbados and British Guiana before. But there were others—a few different men I knew or had heard of—who also might have made the journey in that year. I've been asking around, investigating."

His eyes were shining with all the youthful energy of a child. She saw, in that moment, how much that little lie had meant all those weeks ago, when she had told Mr. Beaumont that he was her son. Leaning toward him, she patted his thigh, trying to convey the maternal warmth she felt toward him, to breathe life into the lie and bring it closer to truth. He was most welcome in her family.

"We should find out where this man Braithwaite has his plantation," Nobody continued.

"Me already speak to Albert. He hear of the name Braithwaite—his plantation, Bellevue, is about seven miles from Georgetown."

"Then we should go there. Tomorrow." The next day was a Sunday.

Rachel looked from Nobody to Mary Grace, their faces eager and full of hope. Mary Grace had not seen her brother since he was taken, when she was only eight years old. Nobody did not know Micah, but Rachel saw how he loved her daughter, and that love was ready to spread to anyone Mary Grace loved, in turn. They were restless, ready for the journey, ready to find what had brought them to Georgetown in the first place.

And yet, if Rachel tried to picture it—Micah appearing over the horizon, bent over, toiling in the fields, then raising his head, seeing her, running—it was no use. All she could see was herself and her son. The joy would be shared in time, but the moment when he reentered her life—somehow, she knew that was something for the two of them alone.

In her vision, Micah wrapped his arms around her, and at his imagined touch the memory of his birth burst forth. Every detail was still fresh. The way Great Polly, who usually acted as a midwife for the slave women, had looked at Rachel one afternoon and seemed to sense it. "It will be soon," Great Polly said, and she slept with Rachel in her hut that night, so as to be ready.

But when the labor pangs came, jolting her awake, Rachel was seized with a sense of terror that expunged any reason from her mind. She stumbled out into the night, gulping its cool air into her lungs. Little more than a child herself, she crawled into the rustling cane and lay there as the pain washed over her in escalating waves. She inhabited her body as a stranger. Even while pregnant, as her belly swelled and she felt the flutter of the child kicking inside her, she had started to feel helpless, out of control. But at the labor's crescendo, she felt truly possessed. Iron hands gripped her abdomen, forcing out the child, and there was nothing she could do to stop it.

Finally, he came. Wet, hair slicked to his skin, surprisingly solid as she scooped him out of the soil. Trembling, she watched as he took a breath and then began to cry. She held him as though he might break—he was still attached to her by the cord, and a futile wish entered her mind that they could stay that way forever.

Great Polly had appeared, breathing heavily. Rachel thought that the old woman might scold her, but she just took the child in her wrinkled hands, inspected him closely, and then handed him back with an approving nod.

"Strong lungs," was all she had said. She helped Rachel bind off the cord—for they could not stay fused forever, however much Rachel had wanted it.

Looking back, Rachel could hardly believe the risk she had taken, to spurn Great Polly's midwifing wisdom and have a child all alone in the middle of a field. When Mary Grace was born, Great Polly had helped to turn her while she was not yet out, saving her from being born feetfirst. Rachel had no doubt that if she had fled Great Polly a second time, Mary Grace would not have survived. And yet, she did not regret it, even for a second. To be the first hands that held Micah, to sit in the cane field and imagine they were the only two living things in the world—that would never leave her.

The memory settled it. He was her firstborn. The moment he was taken was the first time her heart shattered. Rachel was now so far away from that young girl who had given birth to Micah, but she felt the same wish for it to be her and her son, and no one else.

"Me think me must go alone," she said.

Mary Grace lowered her gaze. Nobody looked ready to speak, but seemed to think better of it. The force of the memory was still strong in Rachel, and she was sure the others could sense it. It was beyond reason, that all-consuming will of a mother to be with her child. Rachel had crossed an ocean for it.

"Me grateful for what you do," she said, smiling at Nobody. "And me sure we all gon' be together in time. But me must go first. Just me."

Her eldest son, the longest gone. She would go to him, she would find him, and they would be whole again, as if the cord had never been cut.

18

RACHEL ROSE BEFORE the sun and made her way east toward Bellevue plantation. The road from Georgetown was set back from the coast, shielding it from the empty wilderness that was the sea. Like everything in Demerara, it was straight and orderly, and Rachel found herself yearning to leave it and take her chances hacking through the rough, uncultivated land closer to the cliffs. But she persevered, knowing that the neater path would be the quicker one.

It was early, but there was already a steady stream of people heading in the opposite direction as Rachel, carrying their wares to Georgetown for the Sunday market. They came spilling out of the strips of plantations that sprouted off the side of the road—some talking, some laughing, some tight-lipped and limping. Rachel kept her eyes out for Micah, or even for Thomas Augustus—her heart would leap whenever she saw a man of a certain age in the distance, only to return to its habitual steady rhythm once he came close and she realized it was another stranger.

The edge of the sun began to crown over the horizon, silhouetting the figures coming toward her. Most of the travelers paid her no attention, too absorbed in their own conversations or too focused on keeping baskets balanced on their heads, but a few did stare at her as she passed. One man, hobbling along with the help of a wooden cane, called out, "The market that way!" but she just smiled and kept walking. As the morning drew on, the road grew ever more crowded, and was not wide enough for everyone. People began to walk on its grassy edges, or through the fields alongside it. And the coast began to curve toward the road, close enough that Rachel could hear and smell the sea.

She guessed by the sun that she had walked about an hour, so she began to ask the people she passed whether she was close to Bellevue.

"Oh yes," said a woman whose daughter hid from Rachel behind her mother's skirt. "Not far now. You will know it by the coffee that grow right by the road—the other fields are just cane."

Rachel walked onward. The morning sun's heat had begun to seep into the ground, making the dusty earth of the road feel warm underfoot. Sweat beaded on her skin as, impatient, she refused to slow her pace. The road grew quieter—by now, the market in Georgetown would be in full swing, so it was only the stragglers who were still out walking.

The reunion with Mary Grace kept playing, over and over, in Rachel's mind. The way it had felt when her daughter's skin had pressed against her own again, after all those years—that feeling was still with her, as if the embrace had never ceased. It was as though her body was rehearsing, readying itself to see Micah. Little by little, the notes of caution she had been repeating to herself— that Captain Grafton did not know Micah, could not know for sure where he had gone, and that Micah could have been sold again to another plantation or another colony—were drowned out by the warmth that spread over her. Although she was hot and thirsty, and her eyes ached from the glare of the sun as it climbed high in the sky, she pressed on even faster than before, hungry for the euphoric touch of reunion.

She kept her eyes on the plantations, but saw nothing except cane. Just as she started to wonder if she could have missed Bellevue, she heard a cheerful whistle from the distance. A young man strolled onto the road from the farthest plantation she could see, ambling at a pace that suggested he was in no great hurry. He had shed his shirt, which he was carrying under one arm, and the sunlight rippled off the skin of his torso.

"Morning," he said, when she was close enough to see the outlines of his ribs and the mottled scar of a brand on his shoulder.

"Good morning," she replied. "Me looking for Bellevue plantation?"

"Me just come from Bellevue, back there." He gestured back up the road, before looking closely at Rachel. "Me don't know you—you gon' visit someone?"

"Me son—Micah."

The man's demeanor changed. It was subtle—he kept a smile frozen on his face—but Rachel noticed. He pulled away from her ever so slightly, and he hugged his unworn shirt across his chest like a shield.

"You know him?" Rachel asked.

"Me . . ." Rachel could see dozens of tiny muscles working in the man's face. He swallowed. "Me do, ma'am," he said. Then, quickly, "Me must go." He started to walk away, his pace more hurried than before, but something stopped him in his tracks after a few yards. Turning, he said, "Ask for Orion. He can tell you about your son."

A LITTLE PATH snaked down the side of Bellevue plantation, past the coffee and the cotton and on to the cane. A patchwork place— Rachel imagined the slaves who must have been punished for fumbling over the unfamiliar plants after months spent tending to a different crop.

She walked a little slower beside the deserted fields. Part of it was caution—she still remembered the gunshot, remembered that she could not afford to let her guard down. But also, she wanted to draw out the ambiguity, the time when she could still believe that Micah would be waiting for her somewhere in this long belt of land. She knew that he had probably been sold—somewhere far away, judging by the look on the face of the man she had met on the road. But there was enough uncertainty that she didn't have to accept Micah's likely fate, not just yet.

The soil under her feet became stony and hard. Wedged in between row upon row of crops, there was a strip of land that was harsher and less forgiving. Rachel could see that the slaves had once kept their gardens here, eking what they could out of the cracked and dusty earth. Some of the plots had been abandoned, but a few still had green shoots springing out of them, against the odds. A woman was uprooting yams near the path, and Rachel stopped to ask if she knew of this Orion.

"He just over there, tending to his patch," the woman replied. She pointed across the field, where a man was standing with his back to them, leaning against a spade.

Rachel picked her way over to him, taking care not to step on anything growing, knowing the work that must have been done to coax life from that soil.

"Orion?"

The man turned. He was about her age, maybe a little older, with cracked and weather-beaten skin that suggested a lifetime of hard work. His head was framed by a halo of dark hair that he had let grow longer than most men who worked in the fields. His eyes, of a brown so dark that it blended into his pupils at the edges, scanned her face, waiting for recognition but finding none.

"Who want to know?"

She took a deep breath. "Me name is Rachel. Me travel here from Barbados. Me looking for me son, Micah."

As soon as she spoke her son's name, Rachel saw pure, abject

grief seeping into every pore of Orion's face. The lines on his forehead deepened as his eyes screwed shut to hold back tears. His
mouth trembled. His hands tightened their grip around his spade
until his knuckles looked ready to split his skin.

That was when Rachel knew. She knew that Micah was not just
somewhere else.

He was nowhere.

He was gone.

She felt the ghost of the cord that Great Polly had helped her
cut—the connection that had never quite left her, after all these
years—evaporate, sending a shaft of sharp steel up between her
legs until it cleaved her heart in two.

Orion could see that she knew. His spade fell to the ground and
they embraced—Rachel clung to him tightly, trying to absorb what
little was left of her son from the man who had known him all the
years she could not. Their tears salted the ground beneath their
feet. For a long time, Orion's arms were the only things that contained Rachel. Without them, she would have dissolved into the
thick fog of sorrow that filled her mouth and nostrils, ready to
drown her. But as her body threatened to disintegrate, she could
still feel its resilience. The thudding of her heart. Not shattered, not
split—still whole, and still beating.

She reassembled herself from the heart outward. She thought of
Samuel. She thought of Kitty. She thought of the unnamed children. She was no stranger to death.

And then Mary Grace—her daughter's face flashed vividly in
front of her, with eyes that glowed with soft but powerful love.

Finally, she thought of herself, and she was able to stand, supporting her own weight, no longer reliant on Orion's arms. She
gave herself permission to live, as she had given herself permission
to live before. There was a kernel of something indestructible inside
her, that neither slavery nor grief could shatter.

Rachel was a survivor. And she would survive.

———

As they broke apart, Orion dabbed at the corners of his eyes. "Me sorry," he murmured. "Me sorry." The pain in his face had receded, lingering only in the deep corners of his mouth. "Even after all this time, it hurt. He was like a son to me."

Rachel had exhausted all her tears. Her body felt whole again, but hard, like a shell, with a cold emptiness inside.

"When he die?" she asked. All that was left of her son were the memories, of which she had so few. She wanted—needed—to collect the remaining pieces, right up until his death. She had to know.

"It was twelve years ago," Orion replied. His skin was wet, glistening with a mixture of Rachel's tears and his own. "The uprising."

Rachel nodded slowly. She remembered news of the disturbance in Demerara, whispered fearfully between the white people when they didn't realize a slave was in earshot. The wounds of their own uprising were still fresh in Barbados then, on both sides. Just saying the name "Bussa" could get you a day in the stocks, as if the masters believed the slaves had the power to resurrect his bones from Bayley's plantation. The Barbados rebellion had claimed many lives, and some of the slaves on Providence took grim pleasure in hearing that the Demerara rising had met the same fate. Now, knowing that Micah had been among the dead, Rachel's grief thickened at the memory of them shaking their heads with a world-weary expression, condemning the foolhardy rebels who were no match for the white man's militia.

Orion was watching her closely. "There is a fallen tree just at the edge of this field," he said. "We use it like a bench. You can sit with me—if you like."

They walked over the uneven ground in silence. The tree of which Orion had spoken lay on its side, its roots naked and withered by their exposure to the air. The mottled bark of its trunk had been worn smooth in the places where people had sat over the years, resting from hard work on their meager plots of land.

"Me still can't believe you here." Orion released a long, slow breath, letting it whistle between his teeth. "He always talk about you. How one day, when we free, he gon' go back for you."

Rachel tried to keep her head high, and quickly brushed away the tears welling in her eyes. She was determined not to break down again, no matter the details of her son's life that confronted her. There was a time to grieve and a time to listen. She had grieved—briefly and acutely—and now she would listen.

"Tell me everything," she said. "Me want to know."

And so Orion told her Micah's story.

19

MICAH CRY THE first night he come to Bellevue. And not the silent tears we all cry to ourselves now and then—these were loud sobs that echo through the whole village. He was in the hut next to mine, and me wait for someone to shut him up. But the sobs keep going on and on, until me get up and go over there meself. He was curl up in a little ball, hugging his knees into his chest. Me stand over him and say that he can't let anyone see him cry like that, especially not the white man. He can't let them know they won.

"He stop crying. Me turn away to go back and sleep, but something stop me. Me think it was the way he was still curl up—he look even more sad when he quiet than when he cry. Me kneel beside him and me ask his name and he whisper it to me. Me ask if he was far from home. He say he was. Me ask him where he from, and bit by bit he tell me everything he remember about his home, right down to the ditch at the bottom of the plantation that the pickney splash about in when it fill up with rainwater. Eventually, he talk himself to sleep.

"On the next day, he come out in the fields with the rest of us. In the daylight, it wasn't his height that struck me first—though, by God, he was tall, even then. It was his face. He was so young. Me know none of the white men see it—not when they take him from Barbados, not when they sell him in Georgetown. They see only strong limbs and black skin. But me see it in the softness of his eyes. His mouth not yet get twist up with bitterness. There was innocence in that face.

"It was the time of year that we harvest the cotton. Me stand near him in the field and see his hands trembling as he work. Me ask him if he ever pick cotton before. He say no. Me ask if he ever work in the first gang before, he say no. He was a pickney, that much me could see. He had no place being in the first gang, no matter how tall was he.

"Now, back then, me already know a thing or two about love and loss. Me don' marry a girl at nineteen, and a year later she gone, sold away to the other end of the land. Every Sunday for a month me try and walk to her. If me walk, day and night, me can only get halfway to her and back again in time for work on Monday morning. It hurt, me tell you true. After that, me don't want to love because me don't want to lose again.

"It don't happen all at once. On that first day me don't look at Micah and know right away that he gon' help me love again. But me did feel something. Me want to stand close to him. Me shield him from the drivers, so they can't see how slow he work. Me give him some of the cotton me pick, just enough that he not gon' be punish for slacking. And at the end of the day, me sit down and me eat with him. Me try to use his name often—yes, Micah, no, Micah, that's how things are round here, Micah—so that he can feel a bit more at home.

"It come on slow. There was long days in the fields, and long walks to market on a Sunday. He take a plot next to mine and me show him how to make things grow. And always, me was looking into his eyes. Me realize that everything me do was to try to keep the softness in those eyes. Me want to protect him the best me can.

"The years pass. He lose his innocence, but his eyes shine as bright as ever. He talk to me about the future—me wasn't used to that. Me have no future until Micah draw me into his. When we free, he say. When we free, we gon' go and find me family. We gon' go and find your wife. We gon' have our own land. We gon' have pickney, and our pickney have them own pickney, and none of us gon' work in the fields again.

"He make me say me wife's name. Me not say it since me lose her. Susannah. It was our evening ritual, when we make our way back from the fields. We whisper the names of the ones we love like the words of a song. That was the taste of freedom to us, those names on our lips.

"And as he get older, Micah like to meet people. He like to talk to them and hear what they dream. There was even some nights he sneak out without a pass to visit friends in other places. You gon' find there's many folks round here with a kind word to say about Micah. He was a part of so many lives.

"It was three years or so since he come when he start going to the chapel at a plantation a few miles from here. He was there most Sundays. He wasn't so sure about this white man God, he say, but the chapel was a social place. Folks come from all over to that chapel, and Micah like to meet them. Me did go with him a few times. Me remember, once, the preacher man say that there was a man, very long ago, who don' part the sea so that slaves can walk through it. Micah turn to me and he tell me that even the white man's God know what we know. That one day we gon' walk through the sea to freedom.

"Soon, Micah have the shape of a man—tall and strong. But he was still so young. Six years, me don' watch him grow, afraid that the whip gon' drain the life from him. It did not happen. Nothing dim that fire in his eyes.

"He come back from chapel, one day, and rush to find me. There was talk, he say, that we gon' be free. England decree it. He pace in the hut as he tell me, already thinking of the next ship to Barbados, but me was not so sure. This wasn't the first time me don' hear such talk. Me old enough to remember when they stop the ships coming from Africa. Back then, folks say this was only the beginning. Africa was the root and we was the branch. Cut us off and we die. They say slavery not gon' last. But then it did last. Me try to tell Micah that me have doubts, but he don't want to hear it. This wasn't just a rumor. The free men in the chapel don' hear it from the free men in Georgetown. The women with foremen and overseers and managers and even massas for lovers don' hear it, too. Everybody hear it. The white men in England want us free.

"The weeks pass. Freedom never come. Micah come back from chapel and this time he look angry. He say that while England want to end slavery, the planters in Demerara want to keep it. Now, Micah was not a fool, you understand. He always thought we gon' be free, but he did not believe that the white men just gon' lay down the whips one day. But me think he believe that it was not up to them. The white men own us, but they not free, either, because of England. We know England was where the power lie. We know they don' stop the slave ships when the Demerara men want to keep them coming. And so when Micah hear that England want to free us, he was sure it gon' be so. What he realize, over the weeks, was that maybe it was not up to England after all. Maybe the white men in Demerara have more power than we think. Maybe they don't want to give up.

"Soon after that, Micah come to me hut in the middle of the night. We sit in the dark and he whisper that there is a plan. He hear it from one of the men at the chapel. Romeo, me think was his name. This Romeo, he don' notice Micah. It was hard not to notice him, when he stand inches taller than any other man for miles around, but Romeo also notice how Micah sing the hymns in such a way, the force he put into certain words, that led this Romeo to believe that Micah want to be free.

"Micah explain that the massas don't want to give us our freedom, so we gon' have to take it instead. The plan was to all lay down our tools together and refuse to work until we free. Me was not sure at first. But Micah say that it not gon' end like the other rebellions. We have England on our side—for back then, all of us still think that England really did want us free. And we not gon' fight. We just gon' stop work. The plantations, they can't run without us. That was our power.

"Me agree to help Micah spread the word. We was cautious, and we speak only to those on our plantation that we trust. But they speak to the folks they trust, who speak to the folks they trust, and so on. Soon, everybody know. Everybody was ready.

"A few days after Micah first tell me about the plan, we went to a secret meeting. We slip out of the plantation at night and walk to a place beyond the road, in the wild land on the coast. Men and women come from many plantations. Seeing so many others, the plan finally feel real to me. All those years Micah talk of when we free, me never quite believe it gon' be so, but then me dare to hope that slavery gon' end.

"We wait for someone to speak. Finally, Romeo step forward. He run through the plan as me don' hear it from Micah—the strike and how it gon' lead to freedom. Most folks seem to agree but then others begin to speak. There was an old man with a leg that look like it break once and never heal right. Me don't remember his name, but me do remember people listen to him. He say that we think too small. There are more of us than of them, he say. Many more. If we try, we can take the land. Look at Haiti, he say. We all shiver when we hear that name.

"But the white men have weapons, another man say. There is more of us, but a single bullet from a white man's gun can pass through the flesh of ten men. He claim he don' see it with his own eyes.

"Everybody start talking at once. So many questions. How many white men, how many guns? There gon' be enough of us? How many

of us can they kill? Then Micah speak. There are the runaways, he
say. The men and women in the bush. Could be hundreds of them,
could be thousands. And them might have guns.

"Several folks try to shout him down. The bush Negroes are a
myth, they say. Runaways either caught or they die. But the old man
with the crooked leg say that Micah was right. Men and women do
live deep in the forests, he say. He know a man who run away, only
to come back many years later for his wife. No one see him that
second time except me, the old man say, slipping away with his wife
on a night with no moon. But he was proof. There are folks that live
free, beyond the plantations. If we call to them, they gon' come.

"After the old man say that, it was clear that folks was coming
round to this idea. The plan begin to change. Rather than stopping
work in the morning, we gon' gather the night before. We gon' am-
bush the massas while they sleep. We gon' seize them weapons and
we gon' be ready to fight. Meanwhile, two men, both free men, agree
that they gon' go into the bush and bring back an army of runaways.

"You must understand, the goal was not to kill. Romeo insist on
that point. He was clear that the point of the plan was the same—
to win our rightful freedom. Anything we do that England not
gon' like, such as murdering the massas in them beds, gon' threaten
that. It was just that, rather than refusing to work, we want to make
them scared. Make them see that they have no choice.

"Me can still remember the night before the rising. Me have
dreams of white men bursting into the hut and dragging me away
because they hear about the plan. So when me see a shadow creeping through the hut, me was scared. It was not until it curl up next
to me that me realize it was Micah.

"We lie close. By then, it was six years me know him, and me
love him like a son. As he lie there, me want to hold him, but we
don' never touch like that before, so me did not. Me gon' always
wish me did embrace him then—that me did hold him while me
still can.

"Micah ask what me gon' do in a few weeks, when we gon' be free. Me say me gon' go and see Susannah. Me ask him, expecting he gon' say something about family, too. But he say he don't know. That's the beauty of freedom, he say. You never know what gon' happen next.

"The next night, it all go as planned. It start a few plantations over and spread with the sound of shouts and gunfire. There are no words that can describe the sound of a battle cry carrying in the wind. The scream of freedom. Me tremble even now when me think of it.

"We march on the great house, almost two hundred of us. Some don' bring tools and sticks that they hold like swords, but most of us have nothing. We raise our fists in the air, and all the fists make a forest. Me can only imagine what it look like from inside the house. The white folks had them faces press to the window, pale as ghosts.

"Me don' never been in the massa's house. Most of us never see how he live, all the things he own. We run round and try to grab whatever we can find—candlesticks, kitchen knives, pokers. Me was in the dining room, and me can almost see me reflection in the table, that's how much it shine. Me hear a scuffle and a gunshot in the other room. Me run in just in time to see Micah leap on the man with the gun—it was one of the massa's sons. One of our women lie on the floor clutching her arm, but she was not hurt bad. Me reckon the white man's hands trembling too much to aim. All them worst fears was realized.

"We round up the rest of the house and bring them outside. There was still a few people was cautious—they say to be careful, not to hurt them, and so on. But me did feel something seep into the crowd. Something old, something dark. It was like those myths me mother don' tell me when me was a pickney, where day become night and night become day. Gods come down to earth as men, and men rule as gods, and chaos come over everything. The world was upside down.

"Someone grab the massa. Me can remember his wife was crying. We drag the massa to the stocks, lock him in. Behind him, me
see that someone don' start a fire in one of the fields. The cane was
burning.

"The crowd was silent. We just stand and watch the smoke bil-
lowing over the massa as he hang in the stocks.

"The rest of the night pass in a blur. The question that hang over
everything was—what now? The thrill of the first strike fade away
and we get left with some scared white folk, a few guns, and a dying fire in the cane fields. When the dawn break, a few of us gather
outside the big house to talk things through—those of us that don'
know about the plan earlier than the rest. Me guess you can say we
was the leaders.

"A man called Azor spoke first. He was a driver—Micah don't
want to tell him about the rising at first. Anyone who don' hold the
whip gon' be against us, he say. But me know Azor a long time. Me
don' see the overseer rape Azor's wife and then free her and carry
her off when she pregnant with his pickney. Azor never complain
and he always work hard, but a deep hatred lodge inside him after
that. Me know he gon' be with us.

"Azor say we must go to the other plantations and see if they
overthrow the massas same as we. And did the runaways come
from the forest? We need to know how big the rising—how far the
fire spread. Micah speak next. He agree with Azor, and offer to go
himself and see how the night don' turn out. He say that the rest of
us must share out the weapons and guard the white folks. We must
wait, he say. Wait for the governor to give in and accept that we
free. Or—he don't say, but we all think it—wait for the militia to
come and hope that our guns gon' be enough.

"The next few days feel like an in-between time. We do everything that Micah and Azor say. We take the massa out the stocks
and put all the white folks in one of the huts. Some of us take it in
turns to guard them. Micah return after a day with news of the

other plantations. For as far as he walk, the slaves don' rise. In some place, like us, they capture the massas and some weapons, too. But in other place the massas don' barricade themselves in the house with the guns, and the slaves was armed with nothing but sticks. Micah don't get all the way to Georgetown, so he can't say for sure how far the rebellion spread. And he say there was no sign of the runaway army.

"We take it as good news that we not alone—that for a few miles around, the rest of the world the same as us. But we know that this not finish. If this was a revolution, the wheel still turn—we all feel it. So, we wait.

"We hear them before we see them. It was night—quiet and still. Then, the sound of gunfire carry along the coast. We gather outside the village and the hut where the massa was. Who we hear shooting? The bush Negroes? The militia? That night even the wildest ideas seem true. One woman say that the white man don' raise an army of demons to kill us all.

"Then a boy come running from the west. He can't have been much older than thirteen. Me remember that he look scared, and he was clutching a gun to his chest. He tell us the gunfire was the militia. He come from Bachelor's Adventure, about a mile away, to warn us. The soldiers already don' pass through the first few plantations on the way from Georgetown, and everybody give up without a fight. But the men and women of Bachelor's Adventure was in no mood to surrender. They was gathering whoever was left, the boy say. Come, stand with us. Fight. The runaways did not come, but there was still more of us than of them. We still gon' win.

"Me remember how hollow that word sound when the boy say it—*win*. Before then, me can see how winning gon' look. An English ship coming to order the governor to free us. Or the bush Negroes charging out the forest with guns and spears, killing all the whites. But one by one, these futures gone, and what we got left

is marching against the militia. At best, we gon' kill them before
they kill all of us. What then?

"At the same time, me know we have no choice. How can we go
back when we don' glimpse the world as it might be—massas in the
stocks and cane fields burning? Even if that world now beyond our
grasp, we all know we gon' die for it if we must. Me look across at
Micah and me see he feel the same. The softness don' burn out of
his eyes. Now those eyes like coal—dark and hard.

"We walk the mile to Bachelor's Adventure. The road fill with
slaves. There must have been two thousand at least. An army. We
don't have many weapons, and we ache from years of work. Many
stoop or limp or got limbs missing. But we was an army just the
same.

"The sound of gunfire draw closer. We stand in the road, packed
shoulder to shoulder. Micah get called to the front because he have
a gun. Me only have an iron poker, so me stay farther back. We all
quiet because fear was the best weapon we have. We know the militia don' march from plantation to plantation and see groups of
fifty or a hundred slaves. They gon' expect more of the same. While
the horizon still cover us, we want them to believe it would be so.
When they see us, in the thousands, we want them to be afraid.

"Me was squashed in the middle of the crowd and me can barely
see the road ahead, but me can hear and me can feel. Me feel it when
the folks at the front see the militia. Everyone hold them breath. Me
hear the stamp of boots and then silence. Me push on the shoulders
of the man in front, and me can just about see the red coats of the
soldiers. They huddle together a few hundred yards away from us.
Me can't see the faces, but me do believe them was afraid.

"Me don't know how long we stand like that. It feel like hours.
Me can't hear them, but the soldiers seem to be talking about what
to do. We all stay silent. Me remember it feel as if me whole life get
roll up into a single moment. Every time me close me eyes, me can

see Susannah. Me can see blood on the backs of friends me don' see get the whip. Me can see sugarcane and smell coffee growing. And yet, some of the memories was strange. All the bodies press close around me. Sometimes, me think me can hear the voice of a child that me don't recognize, or see the smile on the face of a mother me don't know. Such was the power of the crowd. We don' share our memories.

"At the very moment that it become too much to bear—the silence and the memories—a voice ring out. Someone near the front. A man's voice, and it sound young. Me don't think it was Micah, but me can never be sure. The voice say SHOOT THEM—and like that, the gunfire start.

"When a crowd move, it's like water. You get swept along, but you also the one who push ahead and carry others with you as you go. We charge at the enemy, screaming with one voice. For a few seconds, with the bullets roaring in me ears, me feel it again. That deep, honest belief that we gon' be free. It pass through me right down to me bones.

"Then the pressure break. Bodies pull apart. Some fall on the ground, clutching limbs that get explode open by bullets. Others scatter. Folks was running for the fields, running for the sea, running back down the road. Me was running, too. Me feel like an animal. Me get ashamed to remember it now, how me did climb over the bodies, not caring if they die, only that me can live.

"When me can't run no farther, me collapse on the side of the road. Me realize that the gunfire stop. All me can hear was a woman weeping across the road and the faint cries of the dying, back the way me did come. Me don't know how long me sit there. Me remember how me feel nothing—no memories of the past and no hope for freedom. Me feel empty.

"Then me hear someone calling. Me look up and see Micah limping toward me, the rising sun behind him. Me can see where he get graze by a bullet on his leg, but the wound was not bad—already the blood around it begin to dry.

"We stand facing each other. It don't feel right to embrace. But, with a nod, we show that we glad we both make it out alive. Me ask him if he know how many die. He shrug. A hundred. Maybe more, he say. We begin to walk back to our plantation. At one point, me remember we pass some parakeets that was singing. The morning was beautiful, but everything seem dull. Me feel flat. Tired.

"When we reach the plantation, we go back to our huts and sleep. After a few hours, we wake up—and me and Micah walk around to get a sense of what happen the night before and what gon' happen now, on this new day. Not everyone don' go with us to Bachelor's Adventure, and some get anxious for news. A few folks ask whether we come back with them husband or son or brother. We can only shake our heads.

"In all the excitement of the night before, the massa and his family don' escape from the hut and flee back to the great house. Sometimes we see a face appear in a window and stare. But we pay them no mind. It no longer feel like the world get turn on its head, with Blacks on top and whites below. It feel, somehow, like white folks don't exist. Like the world is just us. It don't feel like we won, but it don't quite feel like we lost, either. It was like after a hurricane, when you first step outside and see all the things it wreck.

"Me can remember the last time me speak to Micah. Me gon' remember it until the day me die. We sit and watch the sun rise the second day after the battle. We close enough to smell the cane from the field that burn, what seem like a lifetime ago. Already when me look at the burned cane, me know me gon' clear it. All the futures we dream of during the uprising was gone, and only one path left. Back to the fields we gon' go.

"Me ask Micah if he think it all over. He say he don't know. Me ask Micah if he regret anything. He say no. But then he sigh, the

sort of sigh that had no business coming out of the mouth of somebody his age. He was only sixteen. Me did think it gon' be different, he say. Me know, me reply. Me did think it, too. And that was
it. The last words we speak to each other. We sit in silence as the
sun climb higher and higher in the sky.

"It was afternoon when the soldiers come. We don't know they
arrive, but we hear something up near the road—folks shouting, a
pickney crying. We run over and find most of the plantation rushing up to the edge of the fields. Azor, someone shout. They get
Azor. We push to the front and we see the militia, and two soldiers
holding Azor by his arms. People around us was screaming, plead-
ing, but one of the soldiers lift his gun to the sky and fire it. We all
go quiet. The soldier step forward—me think he was the captain.
He have a soft voice, but it carry over the crowd as he read a list of
charges. He accuse Azor of being a leader of the rebellion and of
plotting to murder all of the whites in the colony.

"We say nothing as the captain speak. We know how this go.
We don' see overseers and massas make accusations and drag off
slaves to throw them in jail. The wheel come full circle and bring us
back to a familiar world. What can we say that can save him? We
all stand, waiting for them to take him away.

"The captain pause when he finish the list. Then he say that
Azor is guilty. And he tell his soldiers to kill him.

"It was like time get stuck. Me can remember things moved
slow, so that me see the way Azor's eyes widen, and the way he
fight against the men that hold him. Then, as if bursting free of
whatever hold it back, time leap forward. Blood shoot in the air as
a bullet rip through Azor's neck. A woman jump forward, screaming, but get kick back by a soldier's boot. The captain turn and
point straight to me.

"The two soldiers who hold Azor let his body fall to the ground
and rush forward, but it was not me they seize. They grab Micah.

They drag him in front of the captain. They stand him next to Azor. The captain open his mouth to speak.

"A voice inside me say: This real? This happening? Before me can answer, the captain already start to repeat, word for word, the charges he don' lay against Azor. Micah stand still as the captain speak. He keep blinking. He look down at his arms and see the soldiers' hands around them. Then he look to me.

"Finally, me can move and me can speak. Me run forward, only to get struck down with the butt of a rifle. On the ground, me try to crawl toward him as the soldiers kick me back, over and over. Me plead for them to let him live. Me tell them it's all wrong, that me is the one they want, that me is the one they must kill. Me is the guilty one, not him. He just a pickney, me say. Just a pickney. That was the only time the captain look at me, when me say that. He pause and look from me to Micah, and his eyes say that this *thing* is not a pickney, it is a killer.

"All the while, Micah silent. He still stare at me. The captain come to the end of the list of charges, and he say that Micah was guilty. He turn away from him, and tell them . . . tell them . . .

"Me did beg them, Rachel. You must understand. Me try to have them take me instead of him. But me fail. They—"

(Orion's tears were flowing again like rivulets. They fell down familiar paths, threatening to erode gullies in his cheeks, for he had wept these same tears before, and would weep them again and again until the end of his life.)

"—they shoot him right in front of me.

"He was just a pickney.

"Me sorry."

20

ORION INSISTED ON walking Rachel back to Georgetown. He seemed unnerved that she had listened to his story without emotion, without so much as a flicker of pain crossing her face. He had quickly wiped away his own tears, as if ashamed to show his grief any more outwardly than she did.

For Rachel, the story had sounded alien, like it was the story of a complete stranger. Or perhaps, as the name "Micah" cut through to her heart every time, it felt like a folktale or a myth featuring a god or creature she knew in a story that she did not. It was in this numb, detached way that she took in the details of her son's life and death, feeling ever more cold and distant as Orion recounted her son's final moments.

Sometimes, on Providence, Rachel had imagined what it would be like to live differently, feel differently. To not always be small and quiet. Usually, it was brought on by a dream. This could take any shape whatsoever but would always end with her crying. The sort of tears that choked all the breath out of her, that bent her double and contorted her face and forced out a scream from the hollow part of her chest that seemed like it would never end. She would always wake up feeling disorientated by the sudden change, from a body overtaken by sobbing to one that was lying, silent and still, on a sleeping mat. It was in those moments, letting the echo of the dream linger, that she would imagine that she really might let it all go one day. That she might surrender her body and let emotion rend her in two.

In parts of Orion's story, she remembered those dreams. The echo of them was with her still, a slight constricting of her throat, a throbbing behind her eyes. These echoes were the closest thing she felt to mourning as he spoke.

On the road back to Georgetown, Rachel lifted her face to the sky, willing the heat of the midmorning sun to seep under her skin. She could feel Orion's eyes on her, still waiting for any sign of anguish.

"Your wife," she said to him, breaking the silence. "What happen to her?"

The emotional toll of recounting Micah's story was still written on Orion's face, but he managed a small smile. "She live with me now. We both work on Bellevue. When me hear we gon' be free, me go to the massa and ask if me can go and find her. He don't want me to go at first, but me say that me can bring her back with me, and he want the extra hands for work. Me do it for"—his voice wavered, but he swallowed and continued—"for Micah. Because he was right. After he die, me stop believing, but then it happen— we free."

Rachel did not smile, still could not express any emotion in her face, but she was happy for him.

They walked onward, treading in reverse the path of the militia, twelve years later, their feet falling into the ghostly imprints of the soldiers' footprints. Then Orion said, "What happen to the others?"

"The others?"

"Your pickney. Mercy, Mary Grace, Cherry Jane." He seemed to say the names without thinking, his voice soft and lilting as his tongue rolled over their syllables. He caught himself. "Sorry. It's just me can still remember them after all these years, we did talk of them so much."

Rachel looked down at the cracked earth of the road. "Mary Grace with me now," she said. "The others me still try to find."

Orion surprised her by taking her hand gently in his. "Micah know it," he said. "Micah know that one day you gon' all be together."

Rachel opened her mouth to tell him they could not all be together because Micah was dead, but she closed it again. He was looking at her so earnestly that she felt compelled to say, "Me hope so." And she repeated the names, his little prayer. "Mercy, Mary Grace, Cherry Jane, Thomas Augustus."

Orion stared at her. His tired eyes, still bloodshot from crying, widened. "You say Thomas Augustus?"

The dark cloud of grief reassembled itself, and for one moment Rachel was convinced that Orion would tell her that he had also seen Thomas Augustus killed, many years ago. But there was none of the pain in Orion's expression that she had seen when she first mentioned Micah, so, breathing deeply, she forced the grief to dispel.

"Yes. Him born just after Micah was taken, so Micah don't know him. But he come to Demerara, too, in the end."

Orion was blinking slowly. "Thomas Augustus your son?"

Still, Rachel searched for any sign that he had more bad news— another death story for another son. But he looked, if anything, excited.

"It can't be . . ." he muttered, more to himself than to her. "But then . . ." Noticing Rachel's growing distress, he snapped his attention back to her. "There was a Thomas Augustus at Felicity, a plantation just to the east of Bellevue. Me don't know when he come, and me never meet him. But he well known around here."

"What happen to him?" Rachel pressed. "He still there?"

Orion shook his head. "He run away. That's why we all know him. Not many folks that manage it, not anymore. After the rising, we give up our faith in the bush Negroes. Thomas Augustus's massa search and search for him, and talk to slaves from every plantation along the coast, but he was never found."

Rachel's heart was pounding once again. It was not death. Or, at least, not certain death. A lost son was better than a slain one.

Orion looked agitated, shifted from foot to foot. "Me wish me can tell you more," he said. Having delivered news of the death of one son, he clearly wanted to give her more than the hint of the survival of another to make up for it. "But that's all me know."

They resumed their journey back to Georgetown in silence. Orion kept glancing over toward the sea, where the smudge of silty brown water from the Demerara River was just visible, snaking its way down the coast.

"The river," he said, under his breath.

Rachel said nothing, but gave him a curious look.

"Me was just thinking—how he get away? The land route is just plantations, and no one say they see him. There's the canal but it only go so far inland. Me think if he went up the river—but maybe the current too strong?" Orion lapsed into silence again. Then, slowly, "Although. There was once a man me meet at the market. One of the Indians, them folks that was here for thousands of years before the white men come. Me can remember . . ." He screwed up his eyes with the effort of recollection. "Yes, me can remember we did speak about the river. Me tell him about me wife. As well as the distance, it was crossing the river that stop me being able to get to her all those years. Me don' try to walk south up the river once, for many miles, thinking perhaps me can find its source, or a narrow point where me can wade across. When me tell the native man this story, he laugh and say the Demerara go farther than me can ever walk." Orion sped up as the memory came flooding back to him. "Yes. And he say his people don' paddle it in canoes, up and down, me sure of it. If you walk far enough, it must be that the current is no match for a paddle."

Orion looked at Rachel decisively. "The river," he repeated. "If Thomas Augustus escape, he don' escape upriver."

Perhaps it was the grief, still casting a long shadow over her judgment. Perhaps it was the heat or her aching legs—she had already walked many miles today. Perhaps it was the hunger and thirst settling in the pit of her stomach or the ache in her head. She knew that all she had was the conjecture of an almost-stranger, many years after her son had disappeared. And yet, she would go. Her mind was made up, and she felt the decision settle deep inside her, tightening her jaw and clenching her fists. She would go up the river and she would find her son.

RACHEL AND ORION said a muted farewell on the outskirts of Georgetown. Rachel wanted to thank him for looking after Micah for all those years, and for keeping her son's memory alive, but she couldn't quite manage it. She thanked him for walking her back to the town and hoped, somehow, that he would feel the deeper gratitude without her needing to say it. Orion, too, looked like there was more that he wished to tell her than just the words "good luck." He kept his lips parted after the last word, and Rachel hovered by him just in case. But, eventually, he closed his mouth, nodded to her, and turned to start the long walk back to Bellevue.

Watching him walk away, Rachel was seized violently by the thought that this was one of the last people to see her son alive, that as he left he took all the memories that Rachel would never have of Micah, the young, hopeful man. But the cry of "Wait!" died in her throat and, shuddering, she closed her eyes and let the wave of pain pass through her. What good would it do if she sat down again with Orion and made him relive every moment of Micah's life? Pressing him to recall every smile, every sigh, every word Micah had spoken? Memories cannot raise the dead. Orion had given her enough to know the man Micah became after he left her, and that was all that mattered. She must let Orion, and the shadow of Micah that lived on inside his head, have peace.

When she got to the tavern, Nobody and Mary Grace were waiting for her outside. She didn't know how long they had been standing there in the heat—perhaps since she had left—but as soon as she saw them as two tiny figures in the distance, her knees almost buckled.

Rachel's whole world had been so profoundly shaken when she learned that Micah was dead, it was like her life was split into *before* and *after*. The knowledge was so cruel, so wounding, that she had not really thought that she would have to tell anyone else. In those moments when Orion had held her, weeping, in Bellevue, she had felt like the last person in the world to know.

But it was not so. Nobody and Mary Grace did not know, and she would have to tell them. Nobody, who believed he had earned his place in their family by helping her find Micah. And her daughter Mary Grace. Barely two years Micah's junior. Who had wept every night for a week when he was taken, losing her appetite, growing thin and withdrawn. Rachel's heart threatened to wrench itself apart all over again as she walked slowly toward those waiting figures. She ached to protect them both from the grief she felt.

There must have been something in the way she moved—head down, dragging her feet in the dust of the road. Mary Grace stepped forward as she approached, her brow furrowed and her lips parted, her question unasked but clear.

"Did you find him?" Nobody, less able to read the movements of Rachel's body, looked from her to Mary Grace for answers.

Rachel said nothing. Stopping in her tracks, a few paces away from them, she could not bear to say the words. Her face began to crumple.

"He was not there?" Nobody's voice grew increasingly anxious, perhaps afraid that the information he had hunted out for her had proved worthless.

Still Rachel said nothing. She was looking at Mary Grace, seeing the tiny, quivering movement of her daughter's mouth. Mary Grace took in her mother's face, her gaze boring under Rachel's skin to seek out the raw lacerations of grief underneath. It took a few moments, but then Mary Grace understood. Her face, mirroring her mother's, contorted wildly. She sank to her knees, and began to sob—loud, croaking sounds, almost animal, completely devoid of any of the shape of human speech. It was as if her mouth had forgotten how to form words after so many years of silence, and could now only make this howl of pain. Rachel, silent, closed her eyes so she could imagine that her daughter's violent, embodied anguish was her own. For ever since the hollow, empty, hard feeling had descended, she had almost longed for her fierce weeping into Orion's chest, when she had felt as though she might shatter from the weight of Micah's death. She had no more tears left to shed, so she let herself feel her chest vibrate and her throat constrict as though she, and not Mary Grace, was able to cry.

THAT NIGHT, RACHEL prepared herself to see Micah in her dreams, but he never came. After a dreamless sleep, she woke in the early hours of the morning, to see only the shadows of Mercy, Cherry Jane and Thomas Augustus standing by her, while Nobody and Mary Grace lay next to each other, sharing the bed for the first time.

For Micah to have left even her unconscious—that was too much. Finally, tears flowed again. She sat there in the dark, stifling her sobs to avoid waking the others, while her still-lost, maybe-dead children looked on gravely.

21

I T WAS NOT until the next morning that Rachel told Nobody and Mary Grace about Thomas Augustus. Hoping that they would not notice her red-rimmed eyes and her throat hoarse from muffled crying, she told them everything that Orion had told her.

"We must look for him," said Rachel, exchanging a glance with Mary Grace. She knew her daughter agreed.

Nobody stood.

"It won't be easy," he said, but it was not a warning. He savored the words. He began to pace the short length of their room, turning every few steps. In his eyes was an expression Rachel recognized—it appeared whenever he told them his wildest stories of the dangers he had faced at sea. His body radiated a fierce energy that the four walls could barely contain.

Rachel rose, too, as if ready to leave, that instant. Nobody, sensing her desperate impatience, softened. The fire went out of his eyes.

"This will all take time," he said. "We must prepare carefully. Fear never stopped men sailing even the roughest seas, but every ship charts its course ahead of time, and every crew member knows the role he must play to avoid disaster."

After the deadening effects of dull routine in the tavern, the sense of urgency overpowered Rachel, coursing through her veins, quickening her breath. Her grief was kept at bay only by the thought that Thomas Augustus might be found, and soon. But Nobody was right. She sat again on the bed, and accepted Mary Grace's hand on her shoulder. They needed to prepare.

"We would need provisions," Nobody continued. "Weeks' worth of them. And a canoe." He paused, drumming his fingers against the palm of one hand, thinking. "Going up the river would put us in wild, unfamiliar country. This land is not like Barbados, or some other island where white people have tamed every inch. And there may be Indians still living deep in the forests, who might not look kindly on our intrusion."

At the mention of Indians, Rachel's mind went to the young boy. Nuno.

"What if someone help us?" she asked. "The boy who sleep here a few nights ago? He tell me his people from upriver."

Nobody nodded. "It wouldn't hurt to have someone who knew the way."

Rachel's heartbeat began to slow. The urge to find her son was still strong, but more immediate thoughts were able to channel her restlessness—food, a canoe and the boy. All this they must arrange. Then they would go upriver.

OVER THE NEXT week, life continued as it had been before. Albert, sensing that something was wrong but lacking the social dexterity to probe into what that might be, was even more taciturn than usual, and they mostly worked in silence. Rachel went through all the same motions of cleaning the tavern, serving patrons, avoiding the beady eye of Mr. Beaumont. The routine did little to calm her impatience, and much to inflame her fears. In her darkest moments, after long days on her feet, Rachel lost all but a sliver of hope that Thomas Augustus could have survived as a runaway among the mythical bush Negroes.

But even in these moments, Rachel fought hard to keep that sliver of hope alive. She would not let herself succumb entirely to an empty life. Outside of her work, a plan and a future began to take shape. Between the three of them, Nobody, Mary Grace and Rachel began to stock up on food—meats coated in a thick layer of salt to keep them from spoiling; grains and hard, dry beans; anything that could last the unknown length of their prospective journey. Nobody began to make inquiries among all the carpenters he could find, haggling to get the best price for a small boat that could carry them upriver. And Rachel, whenever she could snatch a moment away from work and all of this planning, looked for Nuno.

She was now known by some about Georgetown. People at the market or in shops, or waiting by the dock for the chance of work on a ship, would greet her warmly and ask how things were with old Mr. Beaumont. These were the people she started with, asking them if they had seen a little native boy, gangly limbed with tangled hair and wide, dark eyes. Every time, they shook their heads in surprise, but promised to keep watch for such a boy.

Over the course of a few weeks, a food supply was amassed, a canoe secured and everything carefully prepared for their departure. Nobody had even managed to pry from the network of naval men in Georgetown a rough description of the Demerara River. One or two of the mariners claimed that they had once sailed with a man who had sailed with a captain who had gone up the river almost fifty years ago, searching for a city made of gold. In those days, most men thought they might find the fabled city on the Essequibo, for the other river was larger and seemed a more fitting site for such a place. But this captain, determined to prove them wrong, had taken a small band of men to explore the Demerara right up to its source. He had not found the city of gold, but he had come back with tales of a winding river, fed by hundreds of tributaries, fiercely defended by native tribes and even by crocodiles as long and thick as the boat they had paddled in. The stories made Rachel shiver, mostly with fear. But there was another feeling, rusty and underused after years of a small and regimented life—a longing for adventure.

When Rachel was young, before she had children, she used to love to hear the older women telling stories. Myths, folktales, often a heady mix of African names and biblical themes, or vice versa. With a sense of wonder, she had imagined herself as the daring protagonist of her own myth, her own life. This wonder had faded with age, and she had thought it extinguished until now. Was Rachel afraid to paddle the length of an unknown river and face its monsters and its terrors? Yes. But below the fear was a thrill at the thought of plunging into the wilderness.

In all the time they were preparing, Rachel had only one dream of Micah, a quick flash of an image before she jolted awake and he was gone. She saw her son, grown, his face set with determination, waving a musket at the head of a Black army.

Maybe they could make their own stories, after all.

IT WAS JUST as Nobody and Rachel were getting most restless to depart that a slender figure appeared in the doorway of the tavern. It was morning, and Rachel was still wiping down tables, not noticing the figure at first.

"People say you look for me."

Turning, she saw Nuno. He still had that same wary, tightly wound quality. Even though he was upright, he held himself like he was crouching and ready to flee at any moment.

"You look well," said Rachel, after a pause. It was true—he was not as stick thin as before, though his face was blackened with what looked like soot, and his hair was still tangled.

Nuno shrugged. "I find some work. A blacksmith. I pump the bellows. Hard, hot work, but I can get food now. And sometimes I sleep in the smithy."

They stared at each other, neither sure how to proceed.

"People say you look for me," Nuno repeated.

"Me gon' go to find me son," Rachel said. "Me was thinking you might come."

Nothing about Nuno's demeanor changed to indicate an answer one way or another.

"Why?"

"We gon' go upriver. Me son, he run away. We think he living in the forest somewhere."

Nuno nodded slowly. "My village was not so far along the river. But we know stories of what is farther. When people were sick and many died, some said we should go up the river. Find more of our people. My mother, she believed, she wanted to go. But my father, after she died, he did not believe. There is nowhere left for us that the white man will not take, he said. So we came downriver."

"You believe it?" Rachel asked. "About the folks in the forest?"

Nuno's dark eyes, which had been darting around the room, rested for a moment on her face. "I believe some places left are safe. Our own. They will not last forever, but they are there."

Rachel was overcome with maternal instinct in the face of this child without a home. "Come with us," she said. "Please. We can search together. For me son and your people."

Nuno cocked his head, considering her request.

She added, "We need your help. To show us where we can paddle the river—if you know the place?"

Nuno flashed a smile, white teeth glinting in his soot-covered face. For an instant, he reflected back to her the same wild excitement, tinged with foreboding, that she felt at the prospect of their journey.

"I know it," he said. "So yes. I will come."

———

RACHEL SENT NUNO upstairs to fetch Mary Grace and Nobody. Their things were all but packed—they had been ready to leave for many days—and now that Nuno was with them, there was not a moment to lose. The sooner they set off, the more likely it would be that they could reach the shade of the forest before the worst of the midday sun.

Rachel's cloth lay abandoned on one of the tables; she had set it down with a satisfying air of finality. She would not miss this place, and she would not miss cleaning it. She allowed her mind to lose itself in the vision of Thomas Augustus, out there in the forest, living free. She was not blind to the scale of the journey ahead, but she clung to the feeling that her youngest son might be found, and that he might be happy. She had to keep her thoughts on this determined path, or they risked wandering back to slave armies, executions and burning cane fields. She did not have the strength to think of that—not yet.

Rachel's back was to the front door as she waited for the others to descend, so she did not know until he spoke that Mr. Beaumont had come into the tavern.

"Is it really the case that you have exhausted all possible tasks for today, or do you merely believe that it is your job to stand around doing nothing?"

Rachel scrambled instinctively for the cloth, ready to stammer a response—but then caught herself and made herself be still.

"Well?" he prompted.

Rachel met his accusing gaze.

"We leaving," she said. Through sheer force of will, she kept her voice from shaking.

"Excuse me?"

"All of us. We leaving Georgetown. Today."

Mr. Beaumont had been caught off guard; he visibly struggled to make sense of what Rachel had said. She had always known him to be sensitive to slights from those he considered beneath him, so keen was he to distance himself from the race of which he was rumored to be a part, but with his eyes threatening to bulge out of his skull, his face tipped over from its habitual displeasure to something darker—now, he was truly enraged.

"The *audacity*," he spat. "The idea that you can just waltz away like this, after everything I've done—after all the sloppy work I've tolerated from you." With every word, he worked himself up into more of a frenzy. He was inching closer to Rachel, propelled forward by the strength of his anger.

Rachel stepped back, but it was not long before she was pinned against the bar, with nowhere left to go.

Mr. Beaumont jabbed a finger at her. "I won't allow it," he said. "You must stay."

For years, bitter experience had taught Rachel to fear the rage of men like Mr. Beaumont. They had the power to hurt her. Despite his fastidiousness, Rachel did not doubt, in that moment, as she watched a vein throbbing in his temple, that Mr. Beaumont would beat her. That he would fabricate some charge out of spite and have the Georgetown police arrest her and throw her in jail. That he would send word to Barbados and seek out her old master. There were no limits to his malice—and yet, though her heart was racing, Rachel stood tall. Her hands gripped the bar behind her, and she refused to blink.

"No," she said.

Whatever Mr. Beaumont had been expecting, this was clearly not it. They were so close they were almost touching—Mr. Beaumont was breathing hard, and Rachel barely breathing at all. His mouth hung open, but no sound came out. In the corners of Rachel's vision, the tavern grew warped and distorted, as though from some great rupture in the natural order. Rachel felt dizzy, but did not faint, able to keep her head held high. Everything about the weeks of working for Mr. Beaumont—the dull, numbing tedium of work that made her feel, once again, like she was good for nothing except serving another—sloughed off like an old skin, and she saw it clearly now.

She was not his slave.

"We leaving," Rachel repeated, her voice quiet but firm. "You can't stop us."

"Rachel?"

The others had appeared from upstairs. Nobody was at the front, looking from Rachel to Mr. Beaumont.

"Is there a problem?"

Rachel looked back to Mr. Beaumont, who was still flushed pink and seemingly lost for words.

"No," she said. She beckoned to the others. "Come."

She edged herself out from where Mr. Beaumont had pinned her to the bar, and led the way out onto the road. She walked steadily, and did not look back—but once they were several paces from the tavern, she bent over and retched onto the ground, as all the terror she had kept at bay came crashing over her, and it was all she could do to stay standing.

22

THE FOUR OF them put the neat streets of Georgetown behind them as they followed the public road alongside the Demerara. To their right, they could glimpse the brown churn of the river through the trees that lined its bank. To their left, flat plantation land extended out to the horizon—tall, imperious fields of cane, ordered and standing to attention like a green battalion. Dotted in the distance, boiling-houses belched columns of smoke into the morning sky.

Nuno and Nobody led the way, each holding one end of the canoe. Nuno had turned his nose up at it, telling them that he could have made a better one, but insisted on carrying it nonetheless. Rachel offered, every ten minutes or so, to take his place, concerned by the way the tendons strained along his thin arms under the weight of the canoe, but he had not yet given up. He seemed to have taken to Nobody much more quickly than he had taken to Rachel, especially once Nobody started to entertain them all with more stories of his fantastical voyages, as they walked along.

Rachel and Mary Grace followed behind them, listening with a smile as Nobody described a storm in which lightning cracked the mast of a ship clean in two. Nuno, awed, kept up a steady stream of questions at appropriate moments—"And then what?" "So the doctor cut it off?" "But how did you have enough food?" and so on. After a while, Rachel began to lose sense of their words and just listened to the lulling rhythm of their back-and-forth, Nuno's voice high and rapid, Nobody's deep and changeable, his speed ebbing and flowing with the path of his stories.

Rachel already felt weary, though they had not walked far. The sliver of hope for Thomas Augustus sustained her, but she was still carrying grief, like a dull ache in her bones. And not just for Micah, but for all the losses in her life—children, friends, lovers. She kept thinking of Samuel and Kitty, trying to reach back in time to see if the grief she felt now was stronger than the grief she had felt then, and if so, what that revealed about the amount of love she had parceled up for each of her children over the years. She thought of the unnamed children, the ones she had never got to love. The grief for them was different—more like a shadow than a sharp knife twisting in her guts. Was it fair that because they never drew breath, or never took form, their passing hurt less?

Rachel felt Mary Grace's hand brush against her own. Not for the first time since Rachel had returned from Bellevue, her daughter was watching her with serious eyes.

There was something about the way the morning sunlight lit her daughter's face that made Rachel still her racing thoughts and pull them back from the losses of the past. Here, in front of her, was her daughter. Beautiful, in her own way—a little plain at first glance, but with kindness softening her features into something that held a person's gaze, and persuaded it to reappraise what it had first seen.

The dark cloud of memory parted, but in its place came a tinge of remorse for the lost years and all that might have been. She thought of Micah, trying to seize freedom by his own hand. He had dared where she had not. Maybe she should have tried harder and sooner to look for her children. All those years, Mary Grace had been in Barbados. Not even a day's walk away from her.

But with the heat of the sun growing fiercer, and a long journey ahead, Rachel knew there was no time to dwell on such things. Shaking her head to dispel the tears and the regrets, she smiled at her daughter.

"Me wish me did find you sooner," she said. "Me hope you know that."

Mary Grace nodded. It was hardly enough, but Rachel had no more words to capture the confusing swirl of feelings. For now, this was all she could say.

They walked on. In time, the noise of the plantations—the rustle of cane; the slicing of scythes through the air; the groans, sighs and songs of workers—receded. The land grew wilder. Slowly at first, with the trees on the riverbank a little thicker, and the chatter of swifts and plovers and parakeets a little louder overhead. Then, all at once, the final plantation fell away, and suddenly they were walking through land that was British in name only. In place of cane were trees whose felling white men had not yet ordered, with thick, twisted trunks that split into a hundred branches. Grass, untamed and unkempt, overwhelmed the public road, narrowing it to a path beaten through the undergrowth.

Their pace slowed. Rachel and Mary Grace took over from Nobody and Nuno carrying the canoe. Nobody brought out a knife from his knapsack and went ahead to cut back branches where they grew too thick to allow the boat to pass. Nuno walked close to Rachel at the back of the canoe, his head turning this way and that as he gazed at all the trees and bushes and vines that surrounded them.

"My mother knew all the trees," he said. "But I don't remember."

Rachel, thinking of Mama B, replied, "Me wish that me know them, too."

They lapsed back into silence. They still didn't quite know how to be around each other. They were too wary, too hesitant. Here was a motherless child, and though Rachel was not a childless mother, there were plenty of holes in her heart where children had been. And yet they could not be like mother and son to each other—what they had lost was too precious, too raw. And so they kept each other at arm's length, out of respect for the dead. Eventually, Nuno drifted back toward Nobody, to ask him more questions about his life at sea, and Rachel was able, from afar, to feel a sense of maternal warmth toward them both.

Back where there had been plantations, the public road had run straight, ignoring the curves of the Demerara, as if being next to the river was an afterthought and the road must chart its own course. Now, the path hugged the river closely, following its every turn. They were no longer in a land where men made any pretensions to have dominion. They let the river guide them.

It was late afternoon when Nuno pointed ahead of them and said, "Look!"

Rachel could see nothing until they were in it—a clearing. The sudden absence of trees felt different than before, when they had walked past the plantations. The clearing was man-made, that much was true, but respectfully so. Where the plantations spanned acres and acres, this clearing was no bigger and no smaller than it needed to be. It had been carved lovingly out of the forest so that people and nature might exist side by side, in peace.

"The village was here," said Nuno. "They must be all gone now. Some dead, maybe some upriver."

He kept any trace of emotion out of his voice, but Rachel could see in the way he drew his arms across his chest the ache of rootlessness that was so familiar to her.

Mary Grace shifted the weight of the canoe into one hand, and placed the other gently on Nuno's shoulder. Too absorbed in the ghosts of the past, he flinched at her touch, but then slowly, as she circled her thumb on his skin, he unclenched his body.

"Should we rest here for the night?" Nobody asked.

Nuno nodded. "We can paddle the river soon, I think. A little farther. Better to go in the morning."

Nobody built a fire while Rachel and Mary Grace doled out their provisions. Nuno, darting around the edges of the clearing, gathered an abundance of fresh fruit from the trees to sweeten their meal. They sat and ate in silence, the exhaustion from the day suddenly settling deep into their bones. By the time the food was done, the sun had set and the forest around them hummed with the sound of crickets. Mary Grace leaned against Nobody, her eyes drooping. Rachel began to rub her aching feet, humming to herself as she did so. Nuno, hugging his knees into his chest, stared out toward the river, the water's edge just about visible in the circle of light cast by the fire.

"How about a story before we sleep?" Nobody said. "Though I imagine you are all tired of mine. Rachel? You must have plenty of stories."

At that, Mary Grace opened her eyes again. Rachel could see, by the flickering firelight, what she wanted.

"Me do have a story," Rachel said. "Not a happy one. Me want to tell you about Micah. Everything me know."

She started at the beginning, with the little boy who laughed like a braying donkey. Those were her own words, and they hurt. There were times when she faltered, but she made herself continue. When she spoke of the day she came home from the fields to find the other children from the third gang at her door, their little faces grave, waiting to tell her that Micah was gone, there were tears in her eyes. But as she began to retell Orion's tale of Micah's life and death in Demerara, it was easier. The pain faded. The words were not her own, not really. She was merely a vessel for Orion's memories, as he had been a vessel for Micah's. And now, Nuno and Nobody and Mary Grace would carry them, too. This was the only way that, in death, Micah could still grow.

By the end of the story, the fire had dimmed and Rachel could barely see the others. She saw the silhouette of Nobody raise his hands to dab at his eyes, and she heard Mary Grace release a long, shaking breath.

No one spoke—what else could they say? They sat with their own thoughts, each of them shaping their own vision of Micah in their minds. Then, by the time the fire had died and the only light came from the moon overhead, they all curled up on the ground and slept.

IT WAS STILL dark when Rachel woke. She lay on her back for a while, transfixed by the stars scattered through the sky. Then, sitting up, she saw the river, its surface dappled with pale moonlight. The movement of the water was still visible, though the current was not as fierce as it was closer to the coast. The river proceeded at a gentle meander here. Getting up quietly so as not to disturb the others, Rachel made her way toward the water and sat close to it, breathing in its damp, silty smell. On the other side, the bank was a steep, muddy cliff, as though the river had carved itself deep into the land over the years, but in front of Rachel the ground sloped gently downward, ending in a stony beach. As she stretched out her legs, Rachel's heels just kissed the water's edge, and she let the river lap away the final aches from the previous day's walk.

She felt rather than heard someone coming up behind her. Nobody sat beside her, just visible in the moonlight. He, too, put his feet in the water, and for a long time they sat in silence, watching the ripples on the surface.

Rachel was thinking about family. She was thinking about the river, flowing from source to sea. She was thinking about the arrow of her own life, flying through time on a course that had always seemed set. A course that ripped mothers and children apart—that brought only despair and the gradual decay of a body worked to death. Now, the current of her life had shifted. Or, rather, it had split. Since hearing of Micah's death, she no longer trusted that things would flow toward happiness and healing. But nor was it inevitable that children once lost were lost forever.

In the corners of her vision, Rachel could see Nobody's profile. Not for the first time, she wondered what secrets were held in his face—what echoes of his ancestors did she witness in it?

"You ever think about it?" Rachel asked him. "Going back to Antigua. To find your mother."

Nobody took a while to answer. "No," he said finally. "When I was young, I was too scared of being caught if I went back. After emancipation, I did think . . . but no." He sighed. "She's dead. I just know it somehow. I felt it, when it happened. I was in America, between voyages. It was winter, bitterly cold. I was staying in a run-down guesthouse a little way out of town. On that day, I woke up earlier than usual, before the light. I felt uneasy. So even though it was dark and cold enough to freeze a man's fingers off, I decided to go out and walk for a bit to calm my mind. I had only walked for a minute or so when I knew. It hit me with such a force that I sank to my knees. I've heard others talk about these moments in life, when the truth just comes to them. Many talk of visions, but it wasn't like that for me. I saw nothing except the darkened street ahead of me, but the truth just dropped itself into my mind—my mother was dead." His voice thickened on these last few words. He paused, drew breath and continued. "So, no, after that I never thought about going back. I could feel there would be no one there if I did."

Rachel closed her eyes. "Me don't think me did know. With Micah. Me did not feel it."

She opened them again, looked at him. "Me don't know what that mean." Gazing into the river, she managed to dislodge a memory, long since buried and still blurred. "Me mother . . . me was sold as a baby, so me never know her. But me think me feel it when she die, just like you say."

Rachel fell silent, and they both sat turning over these old memories in their minds, each reliving their own flash of certainty and grief. Leaning her head back, Rachel looked up at the sky, as stars formed and re-formed into the lines and corners of strange shapes before her eyes. How could it be, she wondered, that she could have felt the death of a mother but not a son?

Other memories began to reappear. Great Polly, who had helped cut Micah's cord on the night of his birth, had two daughters on Providence—Hannah and Queen Ann. Rachel had not seen it with her own eyes, for Hannah had been at work in the boiling-house and Queen Ann was in the second gang, with Rachel working in the first. But she had heard the stories of the day Great Polly died, of how both women, miles apart, suddenly straightened with tears in their eyes and whispered, "She gone."

And then there was Samuel. Taken to the putrid, festering sick house with his fever. He lay next to Old Joe, the toothless father of another slave called George. They both died in the same night, but Rachel had slept soundly, while George was jolted from sleep by a voice in his head that compelled him to go to the sick house. He was the one who found the bodies, and the one who broke the news to Rachel.

So there was something about the passing of a parent. A cosmic weight that shifted onto the generation below. A child could leave the world without a whisper, but a parent's death made itself known.

By rights it should have been the other way around, Rachel thought. Because losing a parent was natural, expected. And although on the plantations, where everyone was half-starved and sickness ran rife, losing a child was almost as common as losing a parent, it still felt wrong, like a tear in the expected tapestry of a life. Shouldn't that disruption tug harder than the inevitability of a mother's or father's death?

Perhaps, she thought, it was a kind of mercy. Your body letting you hold on to the lie that a child was still living until the last possible second. The body was a rhythmical thing, keeping time by the day's hunger and thirst, going to bed tired and waking up with the sun. It was attuned to the expected. But there were kinds of pain that it could not stand to look at head-on, not if it didn't have to. Rachel thought of those hours she had slept while George went to the sick house. She thought of all the years she had lived before Orion broke the news to her of Micah's death. Not knowing had given her peace. It was the peace that she had clung to on Providence, that kept her frozen to the plantation. She would rather not know, she had told herself. She would rather imagine her children living than know them to be dead.

But from where Rachel sat now, on the riverbank, it didn't look so much like peace. Though the wound from Micah's death was raw and painful, what had come before was more like sedation—like the thick, heavy fog of a dreamless sleep. Yes, the knowing hurt her—aching pain, searing pain, creeping pain: she felt them all. But if she could go back and erase the memory, erase Orion's story, and live her whole life in darkness, she would not.

Nobody broke the long silence. "It will be good to get on the river," he said, turning Rachel's thoughts from death to the day ahead of them. "Quicker than on foot."

Even in the dark, Rachel could make out the glint in his eye. "You miss it?" she asked. "Being on the water?"

Nobody, catching her hidden meaning, glanced back at Mary Grace, still sleeping. "Sometimes."

"What you know is wandering." Rachel, too, looked over at her daughter. "But she really care for you." She paused, forming her next words carefully. "Me just don't want her to wake up one day and find you don' run back to sea. Me don' know wandering men before, and me don' know them leave."

For a moment, Rachel thought of . . . but she quickly let the memory go, back to the dark place it lived and was rarely disturbed. No. That was long ago. No use dwelling on it.

A slow grin was spreading across Nobody's face.

Rachel frowned. "What?"

"It's just that here we are walking through miles of forest, after you sailed all the way from Barbados to Georgetown. And next, if I'm not mistaken, we'll be off to Trinidad." He laughed. "If anyone is wandering here, Rachel, it's you."

Rachel couldn't help but join him in laughing. "Me guess you right."

From the edge of the Demerara River, under the stars and with the cool water flowing over her feet, her old life did indeed seem far away.

23

As soon as they took to the water, Rachel felt as though they had ceded control of their journey. She had felt the stirrings of this when they left Georgetown and the plantations—that sense that the trees, river, bushes, birds, insects and even the sky were somehow reclaiming their power. But once they pushed their canoe away from the bank and began to drift back the way they had come, Rachel knew they were at nature's mercy. Yes, Rachel and Nobody quickly picked up their paddles to get the boat moving against the current, so they were not totally helpless. But with every stroke, as Rachel felt the pull of the water's resistance, she was reminded of the river's quiet strength. The smallness of their boat, and the emptiness of the river ahead of and behind them, made the man-made structures of Georgetown seem farther away than ever.

At first, it scared her. She was acutely aware of the few inches of wood separating her from the river, mud brown and of uncertain depth, and kept imagining that the water would suddenly surge over the sides of their boat. But in time, fear was replaced by acceptance, even peace. She realized that the river was neither malign nor benign—it simply existed, and there was nothing they could do to alter its course or stem its flow.

For the first few miles, the tug of the current was still noticeable, slowing them down even when they hugged the riverbank, paddles occasionally scraping along the bottom in the shallows. Nobody and Rachel, soon exhausted, let Mary Grace and Nuno have their turn at moving the boat upstream. However, by the time Rachel took over from Mary Grace again, paddling was a little easier. If some tree or bird on the riverbank caught their attention, they could even rest for a moment and let the boat drift without the river towing it backward right away.

It was in the middle of their second day on the river when Nuno, who was sitting at the front of the boat, suddenly snatched his paddle out of the water and waved at Rachel to do the same. He pointed a few feet away from them.

"There."

Rachel, Nobody and Mary Grace strained their eyes, seeing nothing but water.

"What?" Rachel asked, matching his hushed tone. But then she saw it—what looked like the tip of a drifting log opened a single, yellowing eye, with a black gash of a pupil in its center.

All the occupants of the boat were still.

"Crocodile?" Nobody whispered. The river had started to pull them gently backward, and the creature kept pace beside them, its long tail flicking languidly from side to side.

"We call them caimans," said Nuno.

"We safe?" Rachel asked. She could not tear her eyes away from it. Here it was, the embodiment of her sense that they were in wild and unfamiliar territory, the river's command over them made manifest in the creature's scaly flesh.

"We must stay quiet," Nuno said. "No splashes."

Rachel could feel every tiny movement of the boat as it bobbed along the water, one side and then the other dipping perilously close to the surface.

Over long seconds, the crocodile moved toward them—slowly and without any sign of exertion. It seemed as if the current brought it alongside the boat by chance. Only the unblinking stare of its eye, which never left Rachel's face, showed that it approached at its own will. Up close, Rachel could see every crevice of its mottled brown skin.

Rachel had glimpsed death before, but only in flashes. The overseer as he raised the whip in fury, before he decided these blows would be to punish, not to kill. A fellow slave as he set upon the man who had slept with his wife, before he was dragged away by the crowd of onlookers. Death, when it appeared in the eyes of a man, had seized her in its grip, hands closing around her throat, before evaporating into thin air. She had felt like she was seeing death where it had no place to be, as men descended into pure rage. Like an animal, she would have said of their anger at the time. But now, seeing the caiman's gaze fixed on her, she knew how wrong she had been. An angry man, hell-bent on killing, was not like an animal at all. The caiman's gaze was lazy, curious, and yet still filled with death.

There was no bolt of terror—fear came over her as a slow creeping sensation. Her breathing slowed as her heartbeat quickened. Every muscle was locked tight, holding her body still, and all around her the river was vibrant and heightened. The animal in her knew that it must strain its every sense to hear, to see, to smell. To survive.

A swirling burst of water. The caiman surged forward. Nuno screamed. The boat, knocked sideways, threatened to tip. They clung to each other, scrabbling to stay above the surface, and Rachel felt with the icy clarity of abject terror that she would die. Her body was ready to burst open with the certainty of it, her vision darkened at the corners, and all she could see was the caiman's jaws spread wide, sharp teeth seeking flesh, and the wet, pulsing pink of the tongue inside . . .

But the boat did not tip. Death did not come for them. The caiman was lunging for the bank, where a squat, four-legged animal, somewhere between pig and donkey, had bent to drink. The caiman seized its squealing prey and dragged it down into the river. Both creatures thrashed together as the water turned red—bile rose in Rachel's throat at the sight of it—until, suddenly, all was still except for the blood rippling across the surface. With a twitch of its tail, the caiman began to move downstream, clutching the dead animal in its jaws.

They all watched the caiman until it was out of sight. Nuno was gripping Rachel so tightly that his fingernails bit into her skin, but she felt nothing—she only realized once he let go and she saw the small red drops beading on her arm.

Rachel and Nuno began to paddle again, gently at first to avoid creating too much of a disturbance in the water, then faster, with a desperate edge, glancing often over their shoulders. Only after the river had long since curved away from the caiman did Rachel feel her jaw unclench and her shoulders loosen, and she could breathe easily again.

After Rachel and Nuno handed their paddles to Nobody and Mary Grace, sometime later, they sat together in the middle of the boat. Rachel noticed the way Nuno's head drooped and his hands twisted together in his lap.

"You all right?"

He looked up at her, head slightly cocked, his dark eyes boring into her. After a few moments of calculation, he said, "Yes." Then his mouth twitched slightly, its corners shooting downward before he managed to bring his face back to neutrality. "The caiman scared me, that's all."

Rachel put a hand on his shoulder, moving slowly as she so often did around him. He watched her closely, but accepted her comforting touch without a fuss.

"I saw one before," he said, his voice wavering. "They didn't come to our village much. The current is too strong." Then, leaning slightly toward her, he spoke in a voice low enough that the others would not hear. "I didn't want to say. I didn't want to scare everyone. My father, the others in the village who spent time on the river, they always said if you keep quiet and you respect the caiman, he won't hurt you, and I always believed them, but . . ." He closed his eyes, swallowed hard. "The one that came to the village. There was a baby crawling down by the riverbank. The caiman leaped out of the water and grabbed the baby. I was the only one that saw it happen."

Rachel's hand tightened around Nuno's shoulder before she could stop it, but he didn't shake off her grip. After a few moments, his eyes flew open and he shook his head, as if to banish the memory.

"So I know. Sometimes the caiman will hurt you."

He angled his body away from her to end their conversation, and stared out at the passing trees on the riverbank. Rachel, crossing her arms over her chest, felt a chill of terror, not as strong as it had been when she had stared into the caiman's yellow eyes, but enough to make her shiver.

That night, they dragged the canoe out of the water and set up camp under the fronds of a palm tree. Rachel dreamed, again and again, of a small child being seized from her arms—sometimes by the grasping hands of white men, other times by the jaws of a caiman, its teeth glittering in the moonlight. As the child was dragged away, it looked back at her with Micah's eyes, and Rachel knew that there was nothing she could do to save him.

Just as she had begun to adjust to this rhythm, of cradling the child, watching it be taken, then finding herself cradling it once more, the child looked up from inside the caiman's mouth and she saw it was Thomas Augustus. She stumbled forward—*no, not this one, you cannot take this one.* Then, she was awake, drenched in sweat, and the stars overhead had been blotted out by swirling clouds so that all she could see was darkness.

THE RIVER SLOWED, no longer recognizable as the churning es- tuary belching silt out to sea. Rachel had not forgotten their en- counter with the caiman, but as they set out on the morning of their third day on the water, she felt at peace.

She thought back to what Nobody had told them in George- town, the story of the men who had come upriver to find the city of gold. In this story, passed from sailor to sailor, the men were in- trepid explorers, alone in the wilderness, fending off animals and savages alike. Even Nobody, in his retelling, had succumbed to that sense of wonder. Here were brave men, his burning eyes said as he spoke. Men who had dared to venture into the dark heart of British Guiana with nothing but their paddles and their wits.

Rachel wondered whether these men had really felt as solitary as the story suggested. She didn't feel alone at all, though they had not seen another person since the last plantation outside George- town. The world around them was full of life. Even before they had seen the caiman, she had known it. She had heard the birds, and seen the insects that hovered over the surface of the water. After the caiman, she saw even more evidence of life—her eyes were drawn to the river itself, and she began to see that it was teeming with fish. Some were small and quick, and as they darted toward the surface, sunlight would glint off their silver scales before they dived back into the depths. Others were larger and stayed deeper in the river, visible only as dark shadows in the brown water.

All these, and more, Rachel saw as she became more attuned to the river, and she did not feel alone. It was humbling, this much was true. It reminded her that they were far from any human settlement, and it almost felt like a foreign land, though they were still in territory claimed by the British as their own. But to feel alone, as those men had done? To discount all the other life around her, to discount even the gently flowing water and the fertile earth itself as companions in her journey? That struck her as the height of arrogance.

The encounter with the caiman had shaken them, but it was hard not to find a little joy in it all—this magical, strange river world. The sound of the water as it lapped against the sides of their boat, and the calls of birds that flew low and skimmed the surface— it began to sound to Rachel almost like a song. She could not help but hum along with the river as they paddled, joining in with nature's melody as they plunged ever deeper into the forest.

THE FEELING CREPT over Rachel slowly—they were being watched, and not just by animal eyes. The gazes of creatures in the trees or along the shore slid quickly over them. This was a different sensation. The sensation of a focused, unwavering stare, prickling her skin.

Rachel was next to Nobody at the front of the canoe, and she felt him stiffen, too. The sound of a twig snapping, close, on the near bank—both turned their heads. Nobody stopped paddling, held his oar still. Rachel could see the rhythm of his breath as his shoulders rose and fell. But now, they could hear only the normal sounds of the forest.

Maybe nothing?

Then, a whistling sound. Rachel started backward. Nobody cried out, clutching at his arm, almost pitching sideways and into the water.

Buried in his skin—an arrow, still quivering.

Rachel whipped around, a scream catching in her throat, but all she could see were shadows.

Another sickening whistle. This arrow landed short, slicing into the water.

Nobody, blood seeping from where the arrow had hit, was trying to paddle with only one arm, saying "Go, go!"

But then the canoe lurched as Nuno leaped to his feet. He shouted something in a language Rachel didn't understand, but got the sense of all the same.

Stop!

A ringing silence after his shout. Then a rustling of leaves. On the bank, a man emerged from the tree line, narrow shouldered and lean, a bow and arrow still raised and pointing at them.

Nuno spread his arms, and said something in a low voice—something Rachel imagined was, *Do not fear, we are friends.*

Behind the man, half-hidden in the trees, Rachel could see the shape of a woman, almost as tall and with a baby balanced on her hip.

Nuno repeated his reassuring words. Slowly, the man lowered his bow.

The man called out a question. *Who are you?* Nuno answered briefly, pointing to Rachel, then Mary Grace, then Nobody, in turn. Finally, with his hand on his chest, he spoke a little longer. Rachel could hear in the strange language the outlines of his story. The village. The sickness. The death. The journey to Georgetown. More death.

The man said nothing. Nuno dropped back down into the boat and picked up his paddle.

"Come on," he said. "Let's go over to them."

As they neared the opposite bank, Nuno hopped out, the water reaching almost to his knees, and waded close to the river's edge. Rachel saw the man realize how young Nuno was. He asked a question, which she imagined was, *How old are you?*

Nuno answered, and the man shook his head in sadness. He asked another question, and Nuno, glancing at Rachel, pointed downriver, then upriver as he replied. Rachel knew that he must be telling them about their journey—where they came from, and who they were seeking.

When the man spoke next, Rachel's heart soared. She could hear the meaning in his voice—*I know the place you speak of.*

"He know where the runaways are?" she asked Nuno.

Nuno nodded. Then he continued in his native language. He and the man exchanged what sounded like directions.

Nuno turned back to Rachel. "We are close," he said. "Half a day more to paddle. We will see two streams meet the river, one on each side. We follow the one to the west. By nightfall, we come to their village."

Rachel exhaled. She nodded to the man. "Thank you." He bowed his head in return, to signal that he understood.

Nuno and the man spoke a little while longer. Rachel could hear weariness in the man's voice. The woman behind him had stepped forward into the light, and Rachel could see how thin and haggard they both were. The baby on the woman's hip was awake but made no sound, its sunken eyes staring out at the river.

Eventually, Nuno and the man exchanged what sounded like parting words. The woman with the baby said nothing, but she raised her hand and touched the man's arm. Then, reaching into her skirt, she pulled out a strip of cloth and held it out to Nuno, who took it and brought it back to the boat.

"For you," he said to Nobody. "Pull out the arrow. Then wrap the wound with this."

Nobody winced as he drew the arrow out, his hands slick with blood, but once the bandage was on, his breathing grew less ragged. Whatever balm was on the cloth worked its medicine. He turned toward the bank and managed a smile.

"Thank you."

Mary Grace took his paddle, and she and Nuno moved the boat off again upriver.

"They are living the life my mother wanted," Nuno said. "The inland life, far from the white man. But he says it is hard. Many of my people come from the coast, and sometimes they bring the white man's sickness with them. He says there were many of them in his village once, but now it is just him, his wife and the child.

They hear that the white man comes closer each day. People say they see boats on the river—not so far up as here, but in time they will come. He and his family will journey farther into the forest, because he fears this home will not last."

Rachel turned back to get a final glimpse of the man and his family, her heart aching for all they had already lost. Before the river curved and the family was lost from view, Rachel managed to catch the eye of the woman on the bank. She shifted the baby slightly on her hip and she held Rachel's gaze. Between them passed an understanding. They knew what it was to search for something—to be exhausted, bent double by the weight of loss, but somehow still crawling on their knees, hands outstretched, fumbling in the dark to find the pieces of whatever had been shattered.

A family.

A home.

Just as the woman disappeared behind the trees, Rachel saw a smile flicker across her face, and felt the warmth of the silent words— *go well*. The family slipped out of sight, and Rachel turned back to face the river ahead of them.

24

THEY CAME TO the two streams, just as the Indian man had described. The one that snaked westward was too narrow for the canoe, so they had to carry the boat alongside it. After all the hours spent on the river, the soil felt strange under Rachel's feet, solid and unyielding. The tree canopy soon swallowed up the sky, forming a thick, green ceiling over their heads as they walked. The stream cut a path through the trees, but barely—in many places the water was parted by tiny islets out of which ferns and bushes sprouted.

They became aware of nightfall slowly: the rich green hues of the leaf-filtered sunlight darkened and the songs of daytime birds gave way to the low calls of nocturnal ones. They kept as close to the stream as they could, traveling by sound more than sight, following the trickle of water over stone. Nobody and Rachel each carried an end of the canoe. Mary Grace kept one hand on the back of her mother's skirt, as Nuno kept a hand on Mary Grace's, in turn. In this way, as an unbroken chain, they moved slowly through the forest.

At every snap of a twig or rustle of leaves in the darkness Rachel felt a prickle of fear. It was as though she had been swallowed up into the belly of the forest, and her mind raced through all the dangers that might be lying just out of sight. She couldn't shake the image of the caiman from her mind. At times, she thought she saw its eyes, luminous and golden, before—blinking hard—she realized there was nothing there.

Nobody came to a stop. "Maybe we should rest here." He kept his voice hushed, but it still cut through the forest gloom. "We won't find them without daylight."

Rachel opened her mouth to reply, but before she could speak, a deep voice said, "Tell me who you are."

The canoe wobbled as Nobody almost dropped the end he was carrying. Rachel felt Mary Grace's fingernails in her upper leg as her daughter gripped her skirt even tighter. But somehow, of all the forest sounds, this one did not frighten Rachel. She replied with her voice unwavering, "Me name is Rachel. This me daughter, Mary Grace. This Nobody. We used to be slaves. And this Nuno, an Indian pickney. All his people gone."

Beside her, what she had thought was the outline of a tree shifted, and she realized that its branches were outstretched arms, ending in the curve of a blade.

"We hear of the end of slavery," said the man in the shadows. "We have no more runaways since. How come you here?"

"Me looking for me son. Thomas Augustus."

The man lowered his weapon. "Thomas Augustus say he born in Barbados."

"Me come a long way to find him."

The man came so close that she could feel his breath on her cheek. He moved slowly around her, taking in what he could in the dark.

"You have his nose," he said finally. "And his courage—he was not afraid, either, when me come up on him like this, all those years ago." Rachel saw his teeth flash in a smile. "Me name is Quamina. Me glad you come."

Quamina signaled that they should follow. Leaving the stream behind, they took a narrow path through the trees, and soon found themselves on the edge of a clearing. The silhouettes of tents and huts were just about visible by the light of the stars peppering the open sky.

"We safe," Quamina called out as they approached. "They are friends."

At his words, the clearing filled with people, stepping out of the blackest shadows or slipping through darkened doorways. They pressed together and pulled one another close, so it was hard to tell exactly how many there were. Fifteen? Maybe twenty?

"Thomas Augustus," said Quamina. "Where Thomas be?"

"Here."

One of the shadows separated itself from the crowd. Even in darkness and after almost four years, Rachel knew him instantly.

She breathed his name. "Thomas." The last one gone, the pain still fresh. Only twice when the white men took her children did she let them see her cry. Every loss had tears, but only twice did she fail to hold them back until she was alone. Once when Micah was taken, because she knew he would just be the start, and once when Thomas Augustus was taken, because she had no one left to lose. When he was marched off the plantation, it felt like the end, a final emptying out of her life.

But here he was. A new beginning.

"Thomas," she said again. "It's me." She spread her arms wide to welcome him back to her.

With a sob of recognition, he collapsed against her. She held up his weight as their bodies fused back together. It was as if he had never left her embrace.

The crowd closed around them, and Rachel could feel the hands of family, friends and strangers alike as everyone shared in the joy of their reunion. As her son's breath warmed her neck, his head fitting perfectly into the crook of her shoulder, the moment felt intensely intimate. It was the healing of something broken that she had buried so deep inside her that no one had ever seen it. And yet it felt right that they were surrounded by people, exposing private pain and joy, loss and restoration, to whoever wished to see it. For all the forest runaways, the fracturing of families was as familiar as toil in the cotton and cane fields or in the kitchens of the great plantation houses. But from time to time, the runaways got to see a family mend. It was rare, but it did happen. A woman limping out of the trees, drawing a gasp of recognition from her husband. Or a man returning to their village, scarred and bleeding, carrying on his back a child, much grown but still his.

Rachel had not been there to witness these moments as the runaways had, but she felt them in the elation of their touch, as she hoped they, in turn, could feel every memory she had of the child she had known—the child she could now know once more. Trembling, Rachel felt the threads of her life and her son's, finally able to intertwine. Their story was their own, and there was none like it, before or since. But she also felt the thousands of other threads, the collective weaving together of all lives. The beauty was that they would not be the first mother and son to find each other again, nor, hopefully, would they be the last.

RACHEL WAS EXHAUSTED. She could feel every step and paddle-stroke of the journey—but she knew that it was not yet time to rest. Quamina led the building of a fire to better cast light on the new arrivals. Once it was lit, Rachel was moved to tears again, able to see every inch of her son's face and mark how time had changed it. Mary Grace, sold away when Thomas Augustus was only a few years old, embraced her baby brother who had become a man, and he could finally put a face to the sister he knew only as a name and a warm presence in his earliest memories. Rachel introduced Nobody, who had turned away to dab at the tears in his eyes when he hoped no one was watching, and Thomas Augustus greeted him like an old friend.

Rachel beckoned forward Nuno, who was lingering in the shadows beyond the fire's light. She saw his hesitation, the way his eyes flickered from face to face. She realized, with a pang of guilt, that while she had found what she was looking for, he had not. The people here were mainly runaway slaves—this was not the sanctuary for his people that he had hoped. Life here would not replace life in the village he had lost.

Quamina, standing beside Rachel, bent down to bring his head level with Nuno's. "Welcome."

Nuno, saying nothing, pressed his lips into a thin line.

A woman slid out of the crowd behind Quamina. As soon as Nuno saw her, the tension in his body that kept some part of him ready for flight at any moment began to abate. Finally, all of his limbs unwound.

"This me wife," Quamina said to Nuno. "Her name is Tituba."

Tituba smiled. Firelight danced off each strand of her dark hair, pulled into a thick waist-length braid. She spoke to Nuno in the same gentle language of the man they had met on the riverbank. When he heard his mother tongue coming out of her mouth, Nuno's lip began to quiver.

Tituba held her arms out to him, and spoke again. Her soothing words transcended language, and Rachel understood her perfectly. *You are safe now.* In a few bounds, Nuno came to her, and let her hold him as he cried.

Tituba looked to Rachel over Nuno's head. "What is his name?" she whispered in English.

"Nuno."

"Nuno," she repeated. Then she switched back into their shared language to comfort him in a low voice, one hand smoothing down the tangled hair at the top of his head.

Once Nuno had emptied himself of tears, and Thomas Augustus, Rachel and Mary Grace had hugged and laughed and wept and held hands to their hearts' content, they settled with the runaways around the fire.

"Tell us your story," said Quamina. "How you get here?"

Rachel went first. She let it all pour out of her. It was easier, now. It had grown easier each time she retold it, re-stitching the pieces of her life together, first for Mama B, then for Mary Grace and the Armstrongs, then for Nobody and for Nuno, and now for the runaways. When she got to the part about Micah, Thomas Augustus seized her arm, his face twisting in anguish.

"Me did not know," he whispered. "Me was so close to his plantation, but me never know it."

After Rachel had told all there was to tell, she turned to Nobody. He picked up the story where she had left it and brought it back to the ship on which they had met. From there, he spoke of his life at sea, touching on some of his greatest adventures, stories now familiar to Rachel but that continued to thrill her even the second or third time she heard them. The crowd around the fire was enthralled, wide eyes reflecting the flames back to him as he described storms and shipwrecks and mutinies and battles with pirates. Finally, hesitantly, he told the story of the plantation. He kept the brushstrokes broad at first—just describing his birth, how he came by his name, and alluding to the fact that he had left the plantation as a child. Then, after Mary Grace placed a hand on his arm, he retraced his steps to fill in the gaps. Eyes wet with tears, he spoke of his mother and the manner of his escape.

A long silence lingered after he finished. Rachel could tell from the faces of the runaways that each one was reliving with Nobody the moment he had fled the plantation, colored with their own memories of leaving behind their former lives. And however empty their lives in bondage had felt, Rachel knew that everyone in that clearing would have someone—a mother, a brother, a wife, a friend—that they missed. The taste of freedom was bittersweet.

Finally, Rachel looked to Nuno. He was sat between her and Tituba, leaning back on his hands, his legs stretched out toward the fire.

"You gon' tell them?" Rachel asked.

He glanced up at Tituba, who smiled in encouragement. A few murmurs went around the circle—"We want hear your story, child," "Tell us if you ready," and so on.

Nuno sat forward. At first, after a deep breath, he said no more than Rachel already knew.

"I lived in a village with my parents. My mother died. My father took us to Georgetown, the white man's town by the sea. Then he died. Rachel found me and she helped me. I came with her up the river. Now I am here."

He sat back again. No one spoke. No one even moved, except for Tituba, who nodded ever so slightly to him. Expectant quiet settled over them all like the warmth from the fire. They waited.

Nuno looked down at his mud-streaked knees.

"I had a sister," he said. "She died, too. A caiman, it took her from the riverbank when she was very young. After, my mother was not the same. The sickness took her, but it was not really her anymore. Something died long before."

He stared across the fire at Rachel. In the pit of his eyes, she saw deep despair. Behind the flat voice and the cautious, guarded look on his face, there was pain—too much pain for his small body to contain. Rachel's lips had parted as he named the baby killed by the caiman as his sister, and the expression was now frozen in place. How else could she order her features to convey to him the strength of her wish—to reach back and rearrange time so that he would never know such suffering? He held her gaze a long time; she hoped that somehow he understood.

Nuno continued the story in this fashion—long pauses broken by little details of his life. Occasionally, he would turn to Tituba, supply her with a word in his native tongue, and she would tell him the English one. He spoke in detail of his mother's death. He spoke of the gathering of the surviving villagers, and of the argument that ran deep into the night over whether to head north toward the plantations or south into the forest. Of how his father's own brother had begged them to come south, but his father, hollowed out by grief and fearful of the river after what the caiman had done to his daughter, refused. He spoke of Georgetown, of the abuse and the stares, and the ache of a hard day's labor on the docks or on a nearby plantation. Of his father's slow slide into drinking, until a bar fight over a spilled pint of ale finally killed him.

When Nuno was finished, not a single eye around the fire was dry. Pain, loss, dislocation, a search for home—each one of them knew these, too, in their own way. They sat with the grief of it, but with the wonder, too—that somehow, all had survived.

Quamina began to sing. His voice was rich, deep, and he poured forth a haunting melody. The words were achingly familiar to Rachel, though she could not understand them, and did not recognize the song. This was a deeper kind of memory, held in body as much as in mind, an ancestral memory that time and distance could not erase, though white masters all over the New World had tried. Rachel felt the music vibrating in her throat, the words tripping off her tongue. Quamina smiled as her voice joined his. Soon, they were all singing.

As they sang, Rachel felt it. The tugging of the soil, rooting her down, calling her home. The forest clearing had a certain anonymity to it—there might be thousands of clearings just like it, scattered through thousands of miles of forest. No roads led to it. It was not marked on any map. No one had tried to name it like a plantation, with some grandiose title like "Endeavor" or "God's Grace." And yet, Rachel felt its power. She felt what had drawn the runaways to it, over decades. They had built a home in this nameless, nowhere place. The clearing was no one's, and yet it was theirs. And now it was offering itself to Rachel, in turn. Anyone lost or adrift was welcome to anchor themselves there.

Rachel took Thomas Augustus's hand. The other she rested on Mary Grace's thigh. She closed her eyes, and let the thought overcome her.

After all these years, a home?

25

THE NEXT MORNING, Thomas took his mother down to the river. They followed a track so narrow that to call it a path would have been generous. By day, Rachel could see what she had missed the previous night—the dozens of similar tracks that ran like capillaries through the undergrowth of the forest. The runaways had cut away no more than they needed to navigate through the trees, and also, Rachel suspected, had refrained from leaving any obvious roads back to the village, lest white men came looking for them.

Thomas led the way, and Rachel marveled at his ability to spot a tree with yellow flowers, or a branch that twisted just so, and alter their course accordingly. He moved with practiced ease; Rachel was reminded of Mama B, in the northern forest in Barbados, what seemed like a lifetime ago. Thomas Augustus and the other runaways were truly living by Mama B's philosophy: *the connection between all things.*

The river took Rachel by surprise. She was trying to build up a mental picture of where they were in the forest, feeling like she just about had a sense of their direction of travel and how much ground they had covered, when it suddenly appeared, long before she expected it would.

"Oh," she said, thinking of the hours they had spent the previous evening following the stream.

"Yes," Thomas said, pulling fishing tackle out of a pouch slung around his waist. "Much quicker, if you know the way."

They sat side by side. On the opposite bank, the trees dipped as if in prayer, offering their lowest branches to the glinting surface of the river. Rachel took a deep breath, inhaling the fresh scent of the water and the sweetness of nearby fruit trees. She watched the meandering current and the iridescent dragonflies that danced on the river's surface.

Thomas let his line drift out to the middle of the river, and they waited.

"Sometimes, we come down here with spears and catch the fish that way," he said. "But it's nice to do things the slow way. It give you time to think."

There was a long pause. As she had done with Mary Grace, all those months ago in Bridgetown, Rachel waited for Thomas to fill the silence. Like Mary Grace before him, he did not.

Eventually, Rachel spoke. "Last night, you hear me story. But me don't hear yours."

"Me don't have much of a story," Thomas replied, his eyes following the path of a green-winged bird that swooped low to drink from the river. "No great battles like Micah. No adventures at sea like your friend Nobody."

"Even still, me want to hear it—"

They were interrupted by the fishing line, which jerked in Thomas's hand. Jumping to his feet, he reeled it in and pulled out of the water a struggling fish, its silver scales scattering sunlight as it twisted about the hook. Thomas brought it to the ground, and after a quick blow to its head, it lay still. Thick blood pooled in its gills, staining the soil black. He cast out a fresh line.

"Well, if you must know," he said, "from Providence, they take me to Bridgetown. Then a white man bring me to a boardinghouse. He make me wash and give me clean things to wear. He tell me that we gon' go on a ship, and that me must keep me head down and me mouth shut. If anyone ask, me must say that me was his house slave. We sail to Georgetown, and from there, me come to Felicity. Me was not strong enough for the first gang, so me work in the boiling-house. One day, a man's arm get mash up in the rollers. Me cut him free with an ax, so the rest of his body don't follow. Me was thinking about running away for a while, but that was when me decide—after me hack off that man's arm."

He fell silent, as if that was the end of it.

"How you escape?" Rachel prompted.

Thomas shrugged. "Me just walk out one night. Me get lucky that the white men all sleeping, drunk after some big dinner they have. Me go to Georgetown, think about staying there, or getting passage on a ship, but me decide to go along the river into the forest. Me walk for many days with no rest. Me was getting ready to give up and die when me see a village across the river. An Indian man paddle over to me in a canoe and me get in. He take me to his hut, give me food and let me rest for the night. The next morning, he take me back across the river, and tell me to walk until me reach the stream. And so me walk, me find the runaways, and now me here."

They sat in silence again. Thomas told his story like it was one he had heard third- or fourth-hand, giving her only the bare bones and none of the flesh or the heart. His tone was flat, with none of the rises and falls of a practiced storyteller like Nobody. Thomas was more like Nuno—the words did not come easily. There was much he did not want to share. Rachel felt a pang of nostalgia for the chattering little boy with so many questions; he had become the man who now sat beside her, his face impassive, giving nothing away.

"You gon' find there's two type of folk in the village," Thomas said. "Some love the past. It's all they have left. They want to tell it and retell it. They want to pass it on, to keep it alive. Some do not. For us, what counts is that we escape." He interlaced the fingers of his free hand with Rachel's. The other held the line that was still slack and floating on the surface of the river. "We here now. That is what matter."

He spoke with a finality that, like his furrowed brow and hard jaw, belied his age. There was a weariness in him that Rachel had not expected. He had escaped, and yet he had the heavy voice of a man who had spent forty years or more in bondage. Something about the process of snatching his freedom had bruised him. Aged him.

Rachel looked down to where their hands touched.

"You ever think about us?" she asked. "Me. The others. You wonder what place we were?"

"You, me did think of," Thomas said softly. "Me never think of finding you, but your memory was always there."

Then he sighed. He was not yet twenty, but it was the sigh of an old man. Or was it? Rachel studied his face. She had heard the sighs and groans of many old men. She had heard the sighs of the dying. Thomas's face affected age but it did not embody it—there was something missing. So, no, not the sigh of an old man, but rather the sigh her son must have believed an old man would make.

"The others, Micah and Mary Grace and the rest?" he continued. "Me . . . On the plantation, me was so alone. Me lose hope. The work and the loneliness almost kill me. So me lose hope for them, too. Me figure they must be dead." He blinked a few times. He seemed to have surprised himself. "Me never tell anyone that before. Me don't even know it until now. But that's how me did feel. That they dead—or the plantation break them, so they may as well be dead."

A chill passed over Rachel. She let her hand slide limply out of his, but he didn't seem to notice.

"With you, it was different," he continued. "Me don' see how you survive. But with the others—me did not see how they gon' make it."

Rachel wrapped her arms around her chest. The weight of Thomas's words was pressing on her heart and lungs, but he seemed the same as ever, staring out at the river. Did he feel nothing? Did proclaiming the deaths of his siblings not move him in any way?

"Mary Grace," she said.

"What you mean?"

"She survive."

Thomas frowned slightly. "She did." But then, as if the puzzle was solved, "But she was in Bridgetown."

"That make it easier—?"

They were again interrupted by the line going taut, and Thomas pulling another fish out of the water. He laid it on the ground, but hesitated for a moment, watching it writhe and twist. Then, as before, he brought his fist down and ended its thrashing.

"It was different if we leave Barbados," he continued. "Me think that somewhere inside we all have the memory of when they take us from Africa. Getting taken again . . . it's too much. So, yes, Mary Grace survive. And me survive it, too. But the others?" He was still staring at the dead fish, its mouth agape and its cold, black eyes shimmering in the sunlight. "Me don't know."

Rachel said nothing. She could feel that there was nothing to say. Thomas no longer had questions; he had become a man with only one answer, and with lines gathering prematurely across his forehead.

She turned her eyes to the river. She noticed that, if she let the corners of her vision blur, she could imagine that it was the water that was fixed, and that she was the one drifting slowly toward the sea.

"This is why me don't like to do it," Thomas said in a low voice. "Think about the past. The memories too painful. The hope hurt.

All me want to do is live the life in front of me, because it's a miracle me make it here."

He waited for Rachel to say something. The exhaustion in all her muscles, which had abated after her long sleep, was starting to return.

Hope hurts. Her son had managed to express the truth that had governed her old life. The mantra that she had abandoned as soon as she slipped out of Providence to start her journey. She had survived for so long by suppressing hope, but when she left, she dared to believe her children might still be found.

Hope, rekindled, had propelled Rachel south to Mary Grace, and it had taken her across the sea to find her sons. Hope had brought her to Thomas. But the sad memories came to drown out the happy ones. Was it hope that had killed Micah? Hope led you to dream things that could not be, like freedom wrestled from the white man's unwilling hands, or a family reunited.

Rachel thought of Mercy and Cherry Jane, but the image of them was faint. Like the river, she lost sight of who was moving—her or them. Would hope be enough to get her to them? Or would hope have already destroyed them, as Thomas had foretold, before she arrived?

What brought Rachel back from the brink of her grief for Micah, and the pain of her still-lost daughters, was the sound of the forest. Behind them, in the trees, a bird started to sing. It was a light, chirping call that left no lasting imprint on Rachel's heart. Whenever it paused, she almost forgot how it sounded until it started up again. There was also the sound of the water as it lapped against each bank. There was the hum of flies and other winged insects. Gentle, cleansing sounds that led her away from introspection and pain. In them was the echo of Thomas's plea—forget the past, and live the life in front of you.

Since she had left the plantation, Rachel had felt, more than ever, that she was made of memories. They were the currency that she traded with the people she encountered on her journey—with Mama B, with the Armstrongs, with Quamina and the runaways. They sustained her. They were the essence of her quest to move backward in time, to recapture what had been lost, to make whole what had been smashed.

But where, in all of these memories, was she?

What life did she have in front of her? How did it differ from the life that lay behind?

Her mind supplied no answers. It only directed her ears to the sounds of the forest, and her eyes to the ever-flowing current of the river.

26

RACHEL LEARNED, DAY by day, how to live in the runaway
village. They were not quite closed off to the outside world—
they traded regularly with nearby tribes, who in turn traded with
other tribes, who in turn traded with some of the white men who
lived on the borderlands of civilized British Guiana. Sometimes,
Rachel saw little signs of this porosity—such as a beefsteak sizzling
in a cast-iron cooking pot over the fire—and was reminded that,
even here, white people could not be forgotten. But at night, when
the villagers gathered around a fire, it was easy to feel that beyond
the clearing there was nothing but trees. This sense of isolation
bred a close familiarity between the runaways, who accepted Nuno,
Rachel, Nobody and Mary Grace as their own, without question.

The new arrivals slept at first in a tent left vacant, and they were
comfortable enough, but Thomas Augustus suggested that they
start work on a hut. Nobody agreed to help, and the two of them
spent their days chopping wood in contented silence. Rachel
watched them sometimes and noticed how easily they worked with
each other. For all that Nobody loved to tell tales of his seafaring

days, she realized, he and Thomas were not so different. Living the life in front of them, having made their escape from the past.

Mary Grace's skill with a needle meant that she became a kind of village seamstress. Her main task was to patch over holes in the villagers' worn-out clothes, but when a roll of dyed fabric made its way into a bundle of goods bought from a nearby tribe, she cut it up into ribbons and offered to liven up trousers and skirts by sewing bright bands around their edges. That evening, Quamina brought a small drum from his hut and played while people danced, spinning so fast that they turned to dark blurs with strips of blue around their ankles.

Rachel did not have any particular responsibility in village life, but she did not mind. After the monotony of field work and domestic work and her time at Mr. Beaumont's tavern, Rachel enjoyed the fact that she could take on different tasks each day. Sometimes, she joined Nobody and Thomas, sawing and hammering as the hut took shape around them. Other times, she went fishing, or foraging, often with Tituba and some of the other women. She even went once with Quamina on a journey farther upriver, carrying some bottles of rum that they were able to exchange for fresh axes for Nobody and Thomas.

Nuno, meanwhile, mostly stayed close to Tituba, or to Kamu, the one other native man in the village. The boy seemed happy, and everyone in the village enjoyed having him around. He loved to ask questions, and he loved to listen to stories, be they mythical tales of gods and monsters or accounts of a person's escape from their old plantation.

There were no other children in the village. There were husbands and wives among the villagers, and even a father with his grown-up son, but it was as though there was a generation missing. Rachel didn't like to ask why, but she did wonder. She remembered how Nuno had said he thought the safe places, away from the white men, would not last forever. Perhaps the runaways felt they were living on borrowed time.

Below the tranquility of forest life, Rachel realized, the village felt like an ending place. The runaways had limped, staggered and crawled their way to it, and when they reached it, they could finally exhale. But the work of letting go, of starting afresh, could take a lifetime. And so, there were no green shoots in the village. No trees had been cleared to plant crops—even cultivation would have seemed too much like daring the fragile freedom, finally won, to shatter before their eyes.

A RECURRING DREAM: she was walking through the ruins of the forest after a great fire, seeing only charred and blackened stumps with burned-out branches jutting toward the sky.

Micah was with her. It was the first time she had seen him in a dream since Georgetown, and on the first night he was there her heart soared. But the joy was short-lived; the expression on his face was sad as he took in what was left of the trees. They walked. Always, at the first step, he was a young boy, no older than when he had been taken from her. She watched him grow the farther they went, past the age when he died, until he was almost as old as she was now. The only thing that did not change was the expression on his face—the lines deepened on his forehead, at the corners of his mouth and eyes, as he looked around, trying to puzzle out the destruction.

Finally, he would speak.

"This not how me did imagine it."

"Imagine what?" Rachel would ask.

But she would always wake before she heard the answer.

QUAMINA SAID, "ME notice how the song on the first night move you. You are Akan?"

"No," said Rachel, "me born in Barbados."

"Your mother was Akan? Your father?"

"Me never know them."

Quamina gazed intently at her. "You may not know, but you remember. Me see it in you." For a moment, the warm, wise smile slipped from his face. "Me was young when me come. But keep those memories in me head. Every night, before me sleep, me think of home. Family. Me whisper some words in Akan so that nothing fade." He smiled again. "Me can teach you about it. If you like?"

And so, most evenings, he would seek Rachel out and sit with her, telling her folktales and teaching her a few words of his language. At first, she wondered if time spent with someone who, unlike Thomas, reveled in revisiting the past would give her a different perspective, acting as a counterweight to the growing sense that forgetting about Trinidad and her maybe-living, maybe-dead daughters would be as easy as falling asleep. However, as Quamina talked, Rachel saw that he, as much as Thomas, led her to the same conclusion. If the village was an ending place, a place of rest, he was just as much at home in it as the others. It was just that, for him, the ending could be found at the beginning, by tracing time back to those first ten years before he was shackled and stuffed into the belly of a ship bound for the New World.

In exchange for his details about life in Africa, Rachel started to tell Quamina about Mercy and Cherry Jane. Not as they could be, somewhere in another part of the Caribbean, but as they once were. Their childhoods. She told him about the two girls wandering hand in hand through the slave plots, scouring the earth for wildflowers. Whenever they found some, Mercy would plait them into her sister's hair with a steady hand, and Cherry Jane's young face would shine with delight, more radiant than ever beneath her crown of petals: white, red, purple and blue. And Rachel told Quamina about the night—after Cherry Jane was taken to work in the great house—that she woke just in time to see Mercy creeping out of the hut. Rachel had rushed after her daughter, ready to drag her back inside; it wasn't safe for young girls to wander the plantation so late. But Mercy had held out a small bunch of flowers.

"Me pick these today," her daughter said in a small voice. "Me gon' leave them outside the great house, so Cherry Jane can have them."

Rachel, grateful that the darkness hid her tears, had walked with her daughter to lay the flowers by the kitchen door—though she never knew if Cherry Jane found them.

Telling Quamina these stories soothed the part of Rachel that was still restless, still eager for the search. And as weeks turned to months, she began to wonder if this could be enough, these evening journeys into history.

The ache in her chest, the one that had driven her out of the plantation so many months ago, never really left her. It was an ache she knew Quamina felt, too. She heard it in the wavering of his voice when he sang. But in their evenings together, Rachel realized they could dwell in the ache, live in the old wound, count their scars. The ache would never fade, but they could make their peace with it.

One evening, Rachel asked Quamina, "You ever think about going back?"

"Me think about it. But me ever gon' try it? No."

"How come?"

Quamina sighed. "Because when me think of home, me think of a place that no longer exist. Me think of me family, who most likely dead or gone. They must don' kill and make slaves of me people after me go. Me father say that ours was fertile land. The soil sustain us for thousands of years. But soil cannot protect you when the slave raiders come."

They were sat by the ashes of the fire, watching whispers of smoke float from a few still-glowing embers.

"Me don't want to see it," Quamina continued. "What become of it all. Maybe me too much of a coward. Me just sit here telling stories. The fear that nothing is left—that's why me know me never gon' go back. This me home now."

Rachel was tired. So tired. She moved slowly when foraging or walking down to the river. Her feet still throbbed for every mile she had traveled. Every night, as she lay down to sleep, the noises of the forest enveloped her, whispering,

Rest.

THE HUT, WHEN finished, was neither grand nor ornate. Inside, it was divided into two rooms, one for Rachel and one for Nobody and Mary Grace; Nuno decided he would rather stay in the tent instead.

Rachel ran her hands over the inner walls. Nobody and Thomas were not expert craftsmen, but despite the occasional uneven plank, the whole hut had a humble, functional beauty. It was not pretending to be anything more or less than it was.

Standing in her own room, she watched through the doorway as Nobody and Mary Grace laid out their sleeping mats side by side. Nobody was humming, and Mary Grace took great care in making sure the mats were straight, and that the wooden chair Thomas had made as a gift for them was in the corner where it looked best. It was the first time, Rachel realized, that any of them had lived in a place that was truly their own.

That afternoon, the rain came, but the new hut kept them dry. The smell of damp wood, the sound of raindrops on the roof and the feel of the cool air through the window—all of these brought a sense of calm to Rachel. She sat with Nobody and Mary Grace, eating a hot bowl of fish stew, and she felt safe.

After they had eaten, as night drew in, Nobody braved the rain to go and check on Nuno in the tent. When it was just the two of them, Rachel whispered to Mary Grace, "Are you happy?"

Rachel had noticed the changes that had come over her daughter. The way Mary Grace, beloved by Nobody and beloved by the village, opened up like blossom on a fruit tree. All the pieces of herself that she had made small unfolded as petals—still delicate, but bright enough that they brought a smile to the face of anyone who saw her. She had begun to laugh more often, and not the shy, muffled laugh she used to have but a sound that burst forth from deep in her belly, echoing around the forest. When she laughed, the village laughed with her.

Now, in the hut, Mary Grace's expression gave nothing away. If she was happy, sad, grieving or joyful, she did not show it. She kept her gaze fixed on the wooden bowl still in her hands.

Rachel leaned closer to her daughter. "You think we can stay here?"

Before Mary Grace could give any hint of an answer, Nobody came back into the hut, wiping the rain from his forehead. As Mary Grace glanced at him, Rachel saw something flash in her daughter's eyes. Love. The green shoots of a new life.

Hope.

Nobody touched the back of Mary Grace's neck, a small, tender brush of his fingers against her skin. Mary Grace closed her eyes, just for a moment, and her face was tranquil and still.

There was nothing that predestined the runaway village to be a place of endings, Rachel thought. Maybe she, with the bulk of her life behind her, could only see things drawing to a close, but it did not have to be this way. Not for her daughter. Mary Grace deserved hope. She deserved new beginnings.

Around them, the walls of the hut were solid. Under their feet, after all this time of running, the soil of the forest could keep them steady.

27

THE RAINY SEASON passed, and the villagers gave thanks that the storms had been gentle. Quamina told Rachel stories of the year when great winds had ripped huts and tents from the ground, and forced them to build everything anew. Nature could have a dark, indiscriminate power, he said, but this year they had been spared.

One morning, a week after the last rains had cleared, Rachel came out of her hut and saw Tituba sitting close by, showing Nuno how to whittle a shaft for an arrow. Tituba caught sight of Rachel and waved her over.

"I am going to the river this morning," she said. "Come with me? I always go after the last rains, to bathe when the water is cool."

Rachel had only ever used the stream to wash herself or her clothes, as it was so much closer to the village. The thought of being able to submerge herself in water was tempting. "Yes," she said. "That sound nice."

She and Tituba took the shortcut to the river, through the dense forest. Rachel almost knew the way now—trees that had once seemed interchangeable to her were now as different as human faces, and she could tell by the crooked growth of their trunks or the pattern of moss around their bases whether she was on the right path.

When they came to the river, Tituba untied her belt and slipped off the plain tunic she always wore. She waded into the water up to her thighs, and then turned to wait for Rachel with a smile.

"The water is perfect," she said. "As it always is."

Stripping off her own clothes, Rachel followed Tituba, enjoying the feeling of lightness rising up her legs. They went in up to their waists and then stood for a while, letting the water wash them clean.

Tituba put her head back and let herself float in the water, eyes closed. Rachel couldn't help but look between their bodies, noting the ways they were different and the ways they were the same. The obvious difference was in color, one bronze and the other closer to the dark brown of coffee beans or rain-soaked wood. Rachel also saw more softness in Tituba, in the curve of her shoulders and in the breasts that crested just above the surface of the river. Rachel's own body had been hardened and sharpened by field labor—muscles and sinews were visible through her skin, and her own chest was almost flat.

As Rachel's eyes moved downward, she saw something that surprised her. The lower part of Tituba's stomach was just visible before her hips and legs dipped down under the water. What appeared at first glance to be the effect of sunlight on the rippling surface of the river were in fact pale stripes of skin, running from Tituba's navel down toward her thighs. Rachel had these marks, too, a faded memory of when her belly had swelled in pregnancy.

In all the months she had now lived in the village, Rachel had learned little about Tituba. She had certainly learned *from* her; they often went foraging together, and Tituba would point out all the best fruits to pick and roots to dig. But, unlike her husband, Tituba showed no desire to share any details about her past. Now, looking at the marks on Tituba's stomach, Rachel almost felt embarrassed, as if Tituba's body had whispered a secret that Tituba herself would want to keep.

Afraid she might stumble on more secrets if she kept looking, Rachel followed Tituba's example and lay back in the water. The current was slow enough that, except for an occasional kick with her legs or push with her arms, she could lie still. Her ears were under the water's surface, blocking out all sound. She felt small, cut off from everything but herself, and at the same time completely infinite. Above her, the sky seemed endless.

She felt rather than heard Tituba speak, a distorted sound vibrating through the water. She got back to her feet. "Sorry, what you say?"

Tituba was also standing. Water from the ends of her hair ran down her chest, along the stripes on her stomach and down into the river.

"I said you are not happy here."

Rachel dropped her gaze, watching the water moving around her body.

Tituba continued. "It seems like there is something on your mind."

Rachel managed to look up and meet Tituba's eyes. She was afraid that admitting her unease was an insult, after all the runaways had done. But standing before Tituba, she felt stripped to a more revealing nakedness than merely being without clothes. She could not lie.

"You make me welcome," she said. "But . . . me can't settle. Something don't feel right. Me don't know why."

Tituba's eyes were piercing but held a warmth that was not unkind. They seemed to be liquid; her gaze pored over Rachel, assessing her.

"Many of us found it hard, at first. It takes time."

Rachel couldn't help glancing again at the stretch marks along Tituba's hips. She wondered what had brought Tituba to the village, but then felt ashamed for wondering, as if even the imagined question was an intrusion into the other woman's life.

They stood in silence for a while, letting the water lap against their skin. From opposite sides of the bank, two birds were chattering to each other, a bright back-and-forth that grew ever more urgent and excited, until the two songs became a single, continuous harmony. Tituba took one hand and moved it gently through the water—not enough to make a wave, but enough that the surface of the water twisted around her wrist.

"For those who were slaves, I think it is hardest of all," Tituba said. "There are things I can understand. The loss of family. The loss of a home. But loss of freedom, I have never known. It leaves scars."

Tituba was watching her hand in the water. Rachel watched it, too: the slow, deliberate movements, the care she took not to disturb the surface too violently.

"I have seen people struggle to live after they escaped," Tituba continued. "Freedom was what they wanted for so long. Freedom means stepping over the plantation boundary. But what then? It can be hard to live after freedom." She looked up, and Rachel felt the shock of her dark, probing eyes once again. "I think we have all known that gap between what is real and what we imagined, don't you?"

"Yes."

If Tituba had hoped for, or wanted, Rachel to say more, she didn't show it. She lay back again, and her long, black hair fanned out behind her. She closed her eyes, humming the first few notes of a song. The birds were still calling to each other, and Tituba's music layered itself underneath them. Everything about her—her body in the river, her hum that mingled with the birdsong—blended so easily into the forest. She looked at peace.

Rachel, too, floated again, letting herself be weightless once more. The unbroken blue of the sky overhead had a simple beauty to it. Empty without seeming hollow. With the water in her ears, Rachel could hear her own heartbeat.

She wondered if Tituba was right. Perhaps she, like so many others, was struggling with the gap between freedom as she had imagined it and freedom as it was. The question that had dogged her every so often, ever since the first morning after emancipation, resurfaced—

What now?

She had asked herself this, over and over. Was she afraid of the answer?

This. Only this.

But in the thick quiet of the underwater currents, something else whispered to her. The runaway village was not the world. There were other ways to be free. There were the apprenticeships—freedom in name only, still forced by law to work for a white master. There was a life at sea. There was even death—Rachel had known many who chose this as a kind of freedom.

The cool water against her skin brought clarity. Not the burst of light she had been seeking, but clarity of a softer kind. She knew now. Her question did not have a single answer. It had many.

A small wave told Rachel that Tituba was standing, and Rachel stood with her. Tituba's eyes once again ran over Rachel's face and body, searching. Rachel resisted the urge to fold her arms across her chest, and instead accepted the gaze. She almost welcomed the other woman's appraisal.

Tell me what you see.

Show me to myself.

"How long has it been since you learned that Micah was dead?"

Of course. It seemed like the most obvious thing for Tituba to ask, the most obvious thing for her to see. The pain was still written everywhere on Rachel's skin.

"Four months now."

Tituba nodded. "All grief has power, but the grief a mother feels for a child is the strongest of all."

Rachel was no longer afraid to look at the marks on Tituba's skin, the ghosts of past children. Tituba noticed her looking, and something passed between them, under the water, through the wells of pain in Tituba's eyes, before her face reassembled itself into a calm, almost regal expression. Tituba said nothing, but there was no need.

Rachel understood.

THAT NIGHT, THE same dream. The burned trees. Micah by her side.

He said, "This not how me did imagine it."

"Imagine what?"

This time, he answered. "Freedom."

Rachel looked at the dead forest around them. "No. This not how me did imagine it, either."

28

WHEN RACHEL TOLD Nobody and Mary Grace what she had decided, what had finally been revealed to her as she floated on the surface of the river, they were not surprised. They had all known what was coming. Nobody and Mary Grace must have sensed the shift in Rachel, and she in turn knew they would be with her. They were ready to leave.

But first, Nobody said, there was just one more thing he and Mary Grace wanted to do. The forest seemed the right place. Would Rachel allow it?

Her heart overflowed with joy; for once, all traces of pain and loss were cast out.

"Yes," she said.

Of course they had her blessing.

THE WEDDING WAS just before sunset. The trees cast long shadows like stripes across the clearing, and as Mary Grace walked from the hut to where Nobody stood, she moved through dark, then light, then dark, then light.

She wore a dress that Rachel had not seen before, unmistakably made by Mrs. Armstrong. Mary Grace was a good seamstress now, but Elvira's delicate hand, the artistry in every stitch, was hard to match. It was light blue, simple, unadorned with lace or ribbon. Mary Grace must have brought it with her from Bridgetown, wrapped up in her other clothes, untouched through all the months in Georgetown and in the village. Rachel imagined her daughter unfurling the dress in secret, holding it up to her body and then stashing it quickly away—no, not yet. Too beautiful, too sophisticated, too elegant, her daughter would have thought. She could not possibly wear it. Until now.

The villagers ringed the center of the clearing, dressed in their finest clothes. To the unfamiliar eye, they may not have looked so different than on any other day, but Rachel noticed the blue ribbons on their skirts and trouser legs, which Mary Grace had sewn for them, as well as flowers tucked behind their ears and braided into their hair.

Mary Grace stepped into their circle, where Nobody was waiting. Tears were falling freely down his face, their tracks blending into the corners of his smile. Mary Grace slipped her hand into his. He kissed the top of her head. All around, birds and crickets sang their blessings, and the sky, streaked with pink and orange clouds, was the perfect backdrop for the young couple's love.

Thomas Augustus led the ceremony. He had overheard Rachel telling Nobody about the church back in Bridgetown, wondering whether Mary Grace might want the wedding to honor this God that she and the Armstrongs had worshipped each Sunday.

"Me can lead it if she want," Thomas had said. "Me know a bit of the Bible. Me did go to chapel on the plantation." And Rachel had realized with great sadness that there was so much of her son that she did not know.

Thomas beamed at his sister and the man who was to be her husband. "Me don't know much," he said, "but me know that God love us. And we must take His love and use it to love one another."

Mary Grace pressed herself close to Nobody. Their bodies seemed to melt together until it was not possible to tell where her skin ended and his began.

Thomas continued, "Love is the heart of everything. God create us to love, and He send His son to us so that we can love one another better."

Mary Grace lifted her eyes to the sky, perhaps to where she felt her God would be. Rachel did the same, even though she did not believe in a sky-god. She felt that if any god or gods existed, they would be diffused throughout everything and everyone on earth, neither benevolent nor malign, but simply existing, drawing everything together, living and dead. But the sky was beautiful that evening, and for a moment the whole village cast their gaze to the heavens and let the last of the sunlight bathe them in God's love.

"Mary Grace," said Thomas, bringing them all back to earth. "Me sister. You love this man beside you?"

Mary Grace nodded.

"And, Nobody. You like a brother to me. You love this woman here?"

"Yes." Nobody's voice rang out, clear and unwavering, carrying over the animal sounds of twilight.

"Then you may be husband and wife, with God's blessing, and the blessing of us all."

They kissed to the sound of cheers and laughter—a brief flaring of human noise before everyone fell silent again and ceded the twilight air to the flap of bird wings, the rustle of leaves and the whine of mosquitoes. Quamina had offered to sing once the marriage ceremony had been performed, but as he came forward, Tituba caught his arm.

"Let me," she said.

Her voice was quieter than Quamina's, but no less arresting. Her song and her words were completely strange to Rachel—they had none of the ancestral familiarity of the Akan ones Quamina had sung—but the beauty was in the strangeness. Understanding nothing, Rachel could make her own meaning. She could let the music carry her up, away from buried bones and ancient memories. Each note burst open with possibility. There was no predetermined path. Quamina's songs always felt like the passing down of knowledge, feeling, pain and joy, from one generation to the next, to keep certain memories alive. Rachel received these gifts from the past gladly. But now she experienced the thrill of a music that ruptured, that took her out of herself rather than further in. As Tituba sang, Rachel felt the world open up to her in all its wonders. For the first time in months—years—her heart was light.

Mary Grace and Nobody danced. They swayed slowly, wrapped in each other. As Tituba finished her song, Kamu, the other Indian man, went into his hut and brought out a drum. He replaced the steady melody with a fast drumbeat that soon had the whole village jumping, twisting, clapping and laughing. Here was a language they all spoke, that needed no words. Mary Grace, spinning out of Nobody's arms into the center of the crowd, spoke loudest of all, letting her body say what her mouth could not. Rachel caught her daughter's eye, and there passed between them the recognition that they had just one more night. One more night in this dreamlike place, this deep forest, where the stars were brighter and the air sweeter and the flowers and fruit on the trees more vibrant than anywhere else on earth.

It's not forever, Mary Grace said with her circling hips. *Nothing is.* She lifted her hands to the sky, exalting the drumbeat and her God. With this movement, she said, *Tomorrow, we will go onward and onward and onward—until there is nowhere left to go. Of course I will come with you. How could I not?*

Night fell, and they were still dancing by moonlight. Rachel found Thomas on the edge of the crowd, his feet striking a complex rhythm in the soil. She tapped his shoulder, pointed to her own hut.

"Come inside? We can talk."

Thomas followed her in, wiping the sweat from his brow. His whole body glowed with the energy and heat of the evening's festivities. He looked happy. At ease with himself.

There was so much she wanted to say to him, but she forced herself to start at the end.

"Me must go," she said. "Soon. Tomorrow."

The smile vanished from his face. "Go? Where?"

"Trinidad."

He raised a hand to his hair, rubbed his head, somewhere between disbelief and distress.

"You can come," Rachel said. But she already knew the answer.

"No. This me home. It can be yours, too."

"You know it can't, Thomas."

It hurt. Rachel had swung from one extreme to another—an easy reunion with Mary Grace followed by the absolute rupture of Micah's death. This was all shades of gray. Her son lived and she loved him. But she could not stay, and he would not go.

"Me don't understand."

Rachel saw youth return to Thomas's face, usually old beyond his years. Stubbornness set his jaw, and he threw his arms wide, casting around for an answer that Rachel had lived long enough to know did not exist.

"Me must finish it," she said. "As soon as me leave the plantation, there was no other way. Me must find the others."

He was wounded; anger burst out of him. "Why can't you see that there's no hope? You not gon' find them. The white man gon' capture you and force you to work. You gon' be back where you start, working the cane 'til you die. But you can stay here. You can be free."

Rachel let him rage, though her eyes stung with tears. She had known from their first conversation, fishing on the riverbank, that a rigidity had developed within him, a desire to see and live life in only one way. He wanted her to stay because he could not fathom how she would want to go. Loving and leaving—they could not go together in his eyes. For him, what he had left behind in his old life had ceased to exist.

"Me don't see things that way," she said softly. "Freedom mean something different to me. The search, that is the freedom."

No recognition flickered in his eyes, but she knew she had to keep trying.

"The not knowing is what hurt me. That's what slavery take from me—me did not know. Me did not know where me pickney was. And if me stay here, me can never know. That is not freedom. Not to me."

Thomas said nothing. Rachel could see the stubbornness and anger slipping away from his face. He still looked young, but small now. Uncertain. Just like the boy he had once been. There were questions in his eyes.

"Knowing can hurt," Rachel said. "When me know that Micah . . ." She took a breath, steadied herself. "But me glad me know the man Micah was. Me rather know than avoid the pain."

Thomas looked at the floor. "Me can't lose you again," he said. "You, Mary Grace. Last time, it almost kill me."

Rachel took him into her arms. It was a spontaneous movement, but she had reached the limit of what she could say with words alone. He let her hold him close to her chest. She could feel his heartbeat and the raggedness of his breath. Gradually, she felt his body soften.

"Me love you," she whispered into the close-cropped curls on his head. "It's not that me want to leave. It's that me can't stay."

Thomas said nothing. Rachel pulled back from him enough that she could look into his eyes.

"You won't lose us," she said. "We don' make fresh memories here—better ones than from the plantation days. You gon' remember how we sit and talk by the river. You gon' remember Mary

Grace on her wedding day. You gon' remember laughing and smiling. And you gon' know that we are free."

They broke apart. Thomas no longer looked angry or hurt or
stubborn, too old or too young. He simply looked like himself.

"So, tomorrow?" he asked.

"Yes."

He nodded. He seemed like he had nothing more to say.

They walked back outside, Rachel leading and Thomas following. The night air, already close and humid, was filled with the
smell of sweat. Quamina had taken over on the drums, and Kamu,
Tituba and Nuno were all in the center of the dancing. They were
each performing steps that were different but that somehow echoed
one another. Rachel was reminded of when a stone dropped into
water and the ripples fanned outward, their bands distorting but
never quite escaping the original shape of the splash that created
them. With the moon casting soft light onto their gleaming skin
and the swing of Tituba's long plaits, the scene was so beautiful
that Rachel stopped to take it in.

"Me glad you come here."

Thomas had to lean in close to make himself heard over the beat
of the drums.

"Me glad, too," said Rachel.

"Me never hope . . . me did not imagine it. You, here. It seem
impossible. So . . . me glad."

Of all the words he had spoken to her since their first reunion,
this speech—quiet, fragmented, his voice cracking a little at the
end—moved her the most. Sometimes, it was impossible to see a
shadow before it was lifted, and Rachel finally realized that she had
been afraid. She had been afraid that coming here had made no
difference. This green world, cut off from everything, where life
was so strange—where people came to escape but ended up, in
some way, trapped in themselves. It took such wild courage to reach
the runaway village, Rachel knew, and yet people arrived already

diminished. They had won freedom, but at a price. Slavery had sapped their will to imagine any future other than this one—a life on the edge, on the run, that felt fleeting even long after the villagers had settled in one place.

When Rachel had imagined telling Thomas she was leaving, she had expected his hurt, his anger. But the fear that had gnawed away at her, without her even really knowing it, was that these feelings would fade in him once she was gone. She would go back to being almost nothing—a part of the past he took such pains not to revisit.

That fear held no power anymore. She had been wrong. She would not fade for him. She saw it in his eyes.

"Me gon' always remember this," Thomas said. He looked from her to the dancers. Tituba, Kamu and Nuno were now teaching Mary Grace and Nobody their steps, blending the movements from the different tribes into a single expression of everything in the world. Happiness, sadness, history, hope—they were all there in this dance, performed in the middle of this mongrel village of lost souls who had found one another.

"Yes," said Rachel. "Me gon' remember it, too."

Mary Grace saw them standing there and pushed her way toward them. She paused, taking a moment to read their faces. When she understood everything that had passed between them, she grabbed them by the wrists and pulled them into the crowd. The drum pulsed through Rachel like a heartbeat, and bodies pressed against her—Mary Grace, Thomas, Tituba, Nobody. She did not know the steps, but it didn't matter—no one did. In combining the dances, they had created something new, something that would never be seen again. Muscles that Rachel hadn't used in years—in her inner thighs, along the sides of her rib cage, between her shoulder blades—shook off their stiffness and allowed her to move in ways she had never moved before.

Tomorrow, she would be gone. She would leave the forest and return to the world of roads and plantations and towns where falling-down huts huddled in the shadows of grand houses and stern church spires. But she would never forget the village where she had laughed, cried, grieved, loved and seen her son and daughter grow. Not the quick growth of young children, who seem a little taller every day and whose life is sprinkled with "firsts"—first steps, first words, first day working in the cane fields. Thomas Augustus and Mary Grace were not much changed. When the stream of childhood widened out to a river, the flow of adult life cut deep into the soil. The course of such rivers was not easily altered, but the smallest nudge, one way or another, could lead the river to turn in surprising ways.

To see in Thomas that little glimmer of understanding—to see him consider ways of seeing the world that were not his own—in one sense made leaving harder. If he had resisted Rachel's attempt to account for her actions, she could have imagined him ten, twenty, forty years hence. Always taking his life one day at a time, undisturbed by thoughts of what lay behind or what might lie ahead. It stung a little, to lose that certainty. She had seen in him, that night, the possibility of change. What would he do with his life now? How far from its former destination would his river turn?

In the years ahead, if she thought of him, she would not have the comfort of knowing exactly where he was and how he was living. But nothing was ever fixed. She knew that, and now he knew that, too. As their paths diverged, she could not say where either of them were headed. She was simply glad for the time that they had walked together, side by side. In some small way, he would be with her, and she with him, always.

29

THE JOURNEY BACK to Georgetown was quick. The Demerara carried the canoe along with its current, requiring only gentle paddling on their part, and what had taken five days on their way into the forest took only two on their way toward the sea.

The boat was lighter now, too, which helped its speed. They had left Nuno behind in the village, as he had no desire to come back downriver to all the sites where he had suffered. On the morning they left, with the villagers assembled to say their goodbyes, Rachel found herself leaving Nuno until the end—save for Thomas Augustus, he was the last person she embraced. With her hands on his shoulders, she took a moment to appreciate how a few months in the village had changed him. His arms were still lean but no longer skeletal—good food and plenty of hours spent carrying baskets of foraged fruits, and chipping away at branches to make ax handles and arrow shafts, had helped put some flesh on his bones.

He held her gaze, and accepted her touch without tensing or recoiling, hinting at by far the biggest change within him. He had settled into himself, no longer a wild, lost little boy ready to fight or flee at a moment's notice, though his eyes showed that there was still a little of the old wariness left inside him. The forest had not smoothed all his jagged edges—nor would it, Rachel expected. He had known so much loss while still so young, and some of those wounds would never heal. But being loved and accepted by Tituba, Kamu and the rest of the village had done him good.

"Take care," Rachel said. Even after all these months, she never quite knew the right words to say to him. There was an undercurrent of cautiousness to all their conversations—not quite as acute as the first time their paths had crossed, but enough to make her wonder if he grasped her full meaning. They looked at each other like wounded animals of different species, recognizing what they had in common—the search for home after a family has been scattered—but not quite able to make themselves understood across all that separated them.

"Good luck," Nuno said, with a small nod of his head.

Nothing more passed between them, and the pang that Rachel felt was soon overshadowed by the need to say goodbye to her son for the last time. But there were moments on the river when she thought about Nuno and realized how much she would miss his sharp eyes and his quiet will for survival. Almost as much as her own son, she wished him well.

AFTER MONTHS IN the forest, being back in Georgetown was an assault on the senses. Rachel had forgotten how noisy it all was— carts clattering over cobbles, people leaning out of windows to strike up a conversation with someone on the street and the shouts of those drunk, brawling or calling out after a thief. Gone were the subtle smells of earth, wild fruits and fresh water. Instead, her nostrils filled with the stench of people, hundreds of them, unwashed and forced close together.

In spite of the noise and the smell, Rachel was glad to be back. Not to be back in Georgetown exactly—she had no particular attachment to it, and would not miss it once she was gone—but to be back among people and all the imperfections of a man-made world. It invigorated her, made her mind and her purpose sharp and clear. Her time in the forest had felt like floating, caught in the gaps between life's moments rather than inhabiting them in all their richness. The runaway village looked inward, and many of its villagers looked inward, too—seeing only their own pasts and their own futures. The messy, brash, stinking state of Georgetown pulled Rachel out of herself and back into the world again.

As soon as they arrived, Nobody headed for the docks, and managed to find work on the first ship leaving Georgetown bound for Trinidad. As a parting gift, Quamina had pressed on them some Indian-made cloths, and hawking these as well as the canoe raised a small amount of money, enough for Mary Grace's passage. Rachel, like Nobody, would have to work to be allowed on board.

The boat was taking livestock to Trinidad. Goats, pigs, chickens and cattle were rammed into the hold, which stank of their feces even before the ship left the pier. Rachel's job was to look after the animals. The captain, his skin beaten almost to the color and consistency of leather after years of salt and sun, eyed her sharply. In a crossing of two days, he would allow her two breaks of a few hours to rest, he said. Otherwise, she would have to be below deck at all times, keeping watch.

"And don't even think about napping," he said. "Last time, the boy I had down there fell asleep and one of the cows got loose. Trampled most of the chickens to death."

When Rachel descended into the bowels of the ship, the thought of waking up to the dying screams of chickens and the smell of their blood thickening the already foul air was enough to keep her alert.

Despite regular doses of ginger, the tight knot of nausea in Rachel's stomach never quite abated. The animals didn't help—it was not just their smell, but their fear. They snorted and jostled one another, and in the darkness she could see the whites of their eyes as they rolled them in terror. She began to share their distress; every groaning pitch of the boat sent her stomach lurching. The captain had asked her to walk around from time to time, to check on all the corners of the hold, but soon she could not bring herself to walk more than a few paces away from the exit and the occasional sea breeze that wafted through it. If she ventured too deep inside, the sense of being suffocated, swallowed up by the heat of frightened bodies, was too much to bear.

In the absence of light there was no way to mark time passing, and Rachel tried in vain to use other cues, counting each roll of the ship on the waves, or every labored breath of the nearest cow. These rhythms could not be trusted—the hour at which she expected to be relieved came and went twice over before she finally heard footsteps descending from above. A young boy, barely older than Nuno, emaciated and angular, took her place, and Rachel escaped into the fresh air.

It was a moonless night, and except for the pinprick stars high above, it was no lighter above deck than below it. A few of the ship's crew were visible only as shadows in the stern or around the mast. The sea could not be seen, only heard, lapping at the sides of the boat. The overall sense was of a vast emptiness, and Rachel was immediately free of the claustrophobia she had shared with the livestock below.

She was, at once, exhausted and restless. Hours of constant, creeping agitation had worn her down, but her mind, released from the narrow constriction of preventing herself from panicking, hopped between thoughts at a breakneck pace.

She decided against rest—she couldn't face going back below deck to find a hammock. Instead, she leaned against the railings and looked out to where she could hear, taste, almost feel the sea.

She could understand why Nobody had liked this life. It had an easy anonymity to it; each voyage felt like a rebirth. The water underneath you was never the same, and yet its gentle, metronomic rocking could almost fool you into thinking it was. A heady combination of familiar and strange.

Rachel looked down at her own hands, and found they had the same quality—the ebb and flow of changed and unchanging. These same hands had gripped the rails of a ship from Bridgetown. They had wiped away tears of sorrow for one son and then joy for another. In the forests of British Guiana, they had dug for cassava root and gathered wild berries. They had clasped together in celebration of her daughter's marriage, and they had held Thomas Augustus close before their parting. There her hands were, still with ten fingers, still with a scar that ran from the edge of the left palm right around to the base of the thumb. And yet, how much they had done, how much they had carried, how much they had grasped. Her life on Providence, frozen in an unchanging twilight of mourning, seemed further away than ever. Rachel was growing again—and there was more yet to come.

As weak sunlight began to spill over the horizon, Rachel returned to the hold and to the animals. She found that it was her stiffness that brought on the nausea. If she relaxed a little, let herself move with the ship, then her body began to adjust. It did not make the job enjoyable, but it made it easier to bear. She gave up trying to count the hours that had passed or that were still to pass until her next break, and instead focused everything on the feeling of fluidity as the waves determined her motion. There would be time enough in Trinidad for the hard choices of where to go, and long, energy-sapping walks around the island. She enjoyed the temporary respite from corralling her body into action, and allowed the sea to take control.

TRINIDAD

AUGUST
1835

30

PORT OF SPAIN squatted in between swamps in the shadow of
Trinidad's northern mountains. Rachel disliked it immediately. She was no stranger to the sweaty, desperate heat of Caribbean towns, but Port of Spain felt worse than any of the others.
Feverish, stifling. On the streets, people gleamed, their skin per-
manently damp with perspiration.

A line of cannons along the quay stared, unblinking, out to
sea—guarding the town against what, Rachel could not say. She
would come to learn, by way of the mix of languages she heard
spoken, that wave after wave of white men had claimed Trinidad as
their own, but she never accepted this as an adequate explanation.
It begged a deeper question—why did they come? What did they
see in this marshy place that made them so eager to kill one another to have it? But then, Rachel had always been confused by the
lengths to which white men would go for the sake of possession.
Perhaps their avarice truly knew no bounds—for, even if Rachel
squinted, she could see no corner of Port of Spain that would have
driven her to conquer it, nor to man the cannons in its defense.

With Nobody's wages from the voyage, they were able to take

up a room in an inn. They settled for the seediest one they could find—hoping the money would stretch further that way—but Rachel knew they could last only a week or two before they would need to find work, and the idea felt almost as oppressive as the heat. Rachel wanted to resist familiar patterns. In Bridgetown and Georgetown, pragmatism had persuaded her to lay down tentative roots. Now, she was unafraid of the nomadic, transient life she knew she must lead, sooner or later, if she was to find her daughters. Better to be free of commitments to Port of Spain, she resolved. They would search all they could, then when the money ran out, they would leave, and take their chances elsewhere.

They arrived on a Friday, and Rachel waited impatiently for a long, humid Saturday to give way to market day. On Sunday morning, Rachel rose early and took to the streets. Even at dawn, she was soon sticky with sweat. Every block had an irritating sameness, and she walked around with no real grasp of where in the town she might be, or which of the identical corners she should turn down next. The buildings she passed—most wood, some stone, all in various states of disrepair—were all ugly to her. She quickened her pace; the sooner she could leave this town, the better.

Eventually, she came upon a square where the market had begun to form. A few intrepid workers from the country, the soles of their feet blackened by the journey, had arrived early to secure prime locations for their collections of fruit and vegetables—or, in the case of one man, a single goat, which he held on a short rope.

Rachel wasted no time. She worked her way methodically around the square, asking about Mercy. Sometimes, she received only stares, or apologetic murmurs in unfamiliar tongues. Some people were a little more sympathetic as they told her that no, they knew no one by that name. One man, squinting, said he had met a Mercy somewhere, but then, after a long, thoughtful silence, he laughed and said that it was a Martha he was thinking of. Rachel's fists unclenched and she pressed onward.

A woman with a meager crop of mangoes, bruised and overripe, seized Rachel's hand when she heard that Rachel had come from Barbados, and began to list with a desperate edge to her voice every single family member she had left behind on the island many years ago. With the roles reversed, Rachel felt an unbearable sense of pity. She pulled her hand back gently, shook her head. No, she did not know any of those people. Yes, if she was ever back in Barbados, if she ever did come to know them, she would mention this meeting. She would pass on the message, that this woman loved them fiercely, and missed them every day.

Over the course of the morning, the market swelled. Vendors and customers spilled out onto side streets. In the thickened crowd, Rachel slowed until she was barely moving, speaking to everyone she could. A dull exhaustion must have crept into her voice, because she began to receive fewer curt replies and a little more kindness. An old woman, bent double under the weight of the basket she carried on her head, insisted on hearing a description of Mercy, and promised to keep a lookout. She suggested that Rachel head toward the fish market on the quay—perhaps someone there might know her daughter.

Resignation threatened to settle in her chest, and Rachel fought it as she walked toward the sea. The sun was heading toward high noon, but there were still plenty of hours in the day ahead. There could be no thoughts of defeat—not yet.

Heat rose from the earth, misting and distorting the air. Despite the bustle of the market, the road was empty. The houses were grander here—two stories, stone, with glazed windows that sparkled in the sunlight. Inside, Rachel caught glimpses of Port of Spain's high society, amusing themselves with tea and sumptuous spreads of food. The people looked like paintings, frozen behind the glass, barely moving except to nibble at pastries or sip from their cups, while dark-skinned maids waited in corners to be of assistance.

But about halfway down the road, there was motion in one of

the windows. The party inside were readying themselves to depart, the women smoothing down their skirts and the men shaking one another vigorously by the hand. Rachel's gaze was drawn to the center of the room, where a woman in a pink dress had thrown back her head in laughter.

The woman turned. Her eyes met Rachel's through the window and the shimmering heat of the street outside, and Rachel knew. It was so impossible, and yet the force of knowing stopped her in her tracks, almost bowled her over.

"Cherry Jane." At first barely a whisper. Then louder. "Cherry Jane!"

They must have heard her inside. A few people were staring. Rachel found herself moving slowly, her limbs heavy as if underwater, as she tried to get closer to the window.

A man stood next to the woman that Rachel was certain was her daughter. His skin was so fair he looked white. He frowned and put a hand on Cherry Jane's arm, his mouth forming words that Rachel could not hear.

"Cherry Jane!"

Rachel was now pressed against the glass, and she watched as her daughter looked to the man beside her, shook her head and turned away. Some of the others in the room were gesticulating to Rachel, their message clear. One of the servants came right up to the window, glaring.

"Go on or me gon' fetch the police," she said, her voice muffled through the glass.

Cherry Jane, her back still turned to her mother, disappeared out of the room.

Rachel stepped back from the window in a daze. The faint, polyglot babble of the market drifted over the rooftops of the surrounding buildings. Everything still had a surreal quality—Rachel rubbed her hands along the tops of her thighs, trying to use the solidity of her own flesh to ground herself.

Had she imagined it?

She doubted her senses. How could Cherry Jane be here? Of all the places, on all the islands—here? And in this grand house, with all those elegant people? Rachel was becoming an expert in all the impossible paths a life could take—away from plantations and across oceans or into forests. Yet this vision of her daughter in a pink dress was the one thing her mind could not accept. Cherry Jane could not have been taking tea in a grand reception room with an almost-white man, when in Barbados she had been little more than a house slave.

But those eyes. Rachel had looked into them when they first opened, almost twenty-two years ago. She would know her daughter's eyes anywhere.

A small stirring in the stifling air lifted the edge of Rachel's skirt—coarse and plain, a world away from the skirts of the women she had seen through the window—and the breeze carried her forward, toward the quay. She kept asking and asking after Mercy. Occasionally, she thought she saw the flash of a pink dress, and she spun round, half-crazed, searching the crowds. But the woman and her pale-skinned companion were nowhere to be seen.

By nightfall, the only thing that kept Rachel from dismissing the woman in the window as a dream was the vividness of the memory. Every time she closed her eyes, she saw her daughter. Rather than fading or blurring, the image grew sharper over the course of the day, until, walking back to the inn with the long shadows of dusk around her, she was as sure of it as she was of her own heartbeat. It was Cherry Jane. She was here.

THE NEXT DAY, as soon as there was enough light to guide her, Rachel went back out again. She had said nothing, either to Mary Grace or Nobody, of what she had seen; to speak of it had seemed to threaten its fragile, implausible truth. She guarded the secret, turning her face away from Mary Grace's questioning gaze so as not to give anything away.

She went slowly, navigating more by sight than by any sense of Port of Spain's geography. By following the little things she recognized—a building with a rotting front door, a rusting anvil outside the front of a blacksmith's workshop—she was able to reach the market square, now deserted except for a man curled up in one corner, sleeping inside an empty sack. From there, she turned onto the road down to the quay.

Cherry Jane was waiting. She stood in the distance, close to where the street opened out into the paved quayside. The morning breeze lifted her uncovered hair and rustled the full skirt of her dress—yellow today, though against her skin it looked a rich gold. Behind her, the sea, speckled with the light of the rising sun, provided an illustrious, shining backdrop to her beauty. She stood so still as to almost resemble a statue, and by the tilt of her head and the way she held her hands clasped in front of her, it was clear she was used to being observed.

Cherry Jane did not move as Rachel approached. Only a slight downward curve of her lips betrayed any emotion—it was either displeasure or pain. Her eyes, two perfect, light brown orbs, gave the impression of feeling, but their depth was an illusion; they gave nothing away.

Rachel paused a few feet away from her daughter, as if there was some boundary she could not cross. She was afraid that with a single breath, she could dispel this vision, and be left with nothing.

Cherry Jane spoke first. "It really is you."

Each word had a richness and a precision that meshed perfectly with the expensiveness of her dress and demeanor. But there was enough of the child Rachel had known, still inside those words, that Rachel could not help herself. Ignoring the fear that the apparition of her daughter might vanish, Rachel rushed to close the distance between them and took Cherry Jane in her arms.

Her daughter smelled crisp and fresh—the only reference Rachel could find for the scent was the memory of the just-laundered
sheets from the master's house on Providence plantation, the smell
of which the wind would sometimes carry over to the slave village.
As mother and daughter embraced, Rachel could feel the sharp
outline of her own body, and she was acutely aware of the layers of
skin between them.

They broke apart. Beside them, a front door opened, making
Cherry Jane flinch. A Black man hurried out, clearly on his way to
work, but his gaze lingered over them. Rachel realized how strange
they must look, and wondered what he would guess their relation-
ship to be. Mistress and servant, perhaps? Though that would not
explain the rigid way they stood opposite each other, like soldiers
negotiating a truce on behalf of their peoples.

"I can't stay," said Cherry Jane, once the man was out of earshot.
"It's too risky for me to be seen here."

"Why?"

Cherry Jane unclasped her hands and then clasped them again.
It was only through these small gestures that Rachel could read her
daughter's growing discomfort; her face stayed as blank and beautiful as ever.

"The people here believe certain things about me. About where
I'm from. Who I am."

Rachel thought back to the elegant man she had seen through
the window.

"What you tell them?" she asked. Coldness had crept into her
voice.

"That I am the daughter of two prominent free mulattoes in
Bridgetown."

Rachel felt compelled to hide how much this hurt her; Cherry
Jane had a gentility that made it hard not to match her serene, ex-
pressionless demeanor. Anything else would have seemed too
rough, too common. But a sharp pain ran through Rachel never-

theless. Her life was irrevocably scarred by the efforts that white
men had made to deny her either forebears or descendants. In leaving the plantation, in seeking out her children, she had defied
them. She had dared to regrow the fragile branches of her family
tree. Now, Cherry Jane stood with a match in her hand, ready to
burn whatever was left between them.

Cherry Jane smoothed down the front of her dress. "I must go."

"Cherry Jane."

Her daughter winced. "Please do not use that name. Cherry
Jane no longer exists." She turned.

Rachel darted forward and grabbed her arm. "Wait."

Rachel expected her daughter to pull herself free, but she did not.
She fixed her solemn eyes on Rachel's hand, on the point where dark,
calloused fingers met skin that was honey-colored and smooth.

Rachel chose her words carefully. She did not want to beg. In a
small way, her pride had been wounded by this daughter who did
not want to be seen with her.

"Me come a long way to find you."

Cherry Jane's lips parted slightly. The tiniest movement, so brief
that Rachel almost missed it. A flicker of surprise, and then it was
gone.

"This is why you are here? In Port of Spain? You came for me?"

"Yes." The corners of Cherry Jane's mouth twisted down further,
so Rachel added, "Me mean you no harm. If you have a new life
here, that is fine. Me not gon' disturb it."

Cherry Jane opened her mouth, caught herself, closed it again.
Rachel kept speaking to fill the silence.

"Mary Grace here, too. She gon' want to see you. We staying at
an inn, next to the jail. You can come?"

Cherry Jane shut her eyes briefly and inhaled.

"I will come," she said. "Tomorrow. Before dawn."

Rachel released her daughter. Cherry Jane was still staring at
the skin on her arm where her mother's hand had been.

"You know it will only be the once?" said Cherry Jane. Another tiny flicker of emotion crossed her face—she looked uncertain. "I can't . . . it's too risky to . . ."

"Me know," said Rachel. "We gon' leave Port of Spain soon. We can leave you be."

They had no more to say to each other.

Walking back to the inn, Rachel's chest began to ache, the way it had so often ached for the sake of her children. This time, the pain was like acid, hollowing out her heart. With a few deep breaths, she was able to banish it. She had come too far and lived too much for such bitterness.

She would see Cherry Jane once more—this daughter who would rather invent a new mother for herself than be seen in the street with the mother she had—and then she would leave. She would climb every mountain and trudge through every swamp in Trinidad if she had to, to find her final daughter.

This was not yet finished.

31

RACHEL STOOD OUTSIDE, waiting for Cherry Jane. The sun had not yet risen, but the horizon had the faint glow of dawn. Opposite the inn, the jail was a skulking silhouette in the half-light—sometimes, at night, Rachel awoke to faint groaning sounds that she was sure were the last gasps of the dying inside that jail. She had met a man in the street, a few days previously, who had told her that far more bodies went into that place than ever came out. The most common cellmate was a corpse, he said. The jailers waited until the flesh had withered off the bones, before using them to beat the prisoners.

When Cherry Jane appeared, she was wearing blue, in a shade so deep she blended into the shadows. She had wrapped a shawl over her head. Rachel knew her only by the way she walked, with an unbroken fluidity of movement like water. She had always carried herself this way, even as a child. Rachel used to tell the other women on the plantation that her daughter did not walk, she floated.

They embraced. It felt different from the day before—still stiff, but it was as if each of them was working to make their bodies fit together. Rachel remembered, in her flesh, how it had felt to carry the baby Cherry Jane inside her. The memory burned so strongly that Rachel knew Cherry Jane must feel it—and feel with it the impossibility of erasing that bodily imprint. No lie was so great that it could destroy the echo of when they had been not two but one, sharing life and blood together.

Upstairs, Mary Grace and Nobody were waiting. They bowed their heads to Cherry Jane, who did not return the gesture. She shrugged the shawl off her head and shook her curls loose, and there was an intake of breath in the room as she bared her beauty.

Rachel studied her daughter's face. The sad thing, she thought to herself, was that Cherry Jane was beautiful in spite of her skin, not because of it, and Rachel was not sure that her daughter knew this. Her eyes and lips, the curve of her chin, were the details that stood out. Her lightness was an afterthought. Rachel was reminded, by the perfect form of Cherry Jane's features, of Hope, though her daughter had none of Hope's vitality. She was just as beautiful, but harder, colder—like marble.

Cherry Jane cast her eyes about the room. Knowing how carefully her daughter could arrange her features, Rachel found it galling that Cherry Jane did not bother to hide the haughtiness in her glances. The acid-like feeling flared up again, gnawing at Rachel's heart. She had borne much in her life, but to have her own child look down on her was at the limit of what she could tolerate.

Mary Grace put her hand on Rachel's shoulder. The tiniest gesture, but through it, she asserted herself. She asserted the worth of all of them, refused to let them be seen as small by her sister. Rachel covered Mary Grace's hand with her own, and she tried to fight the bitterness. For all her airs and finery, Cherry Jane was still her daughter. She made herself focus on the bits she recognized. The way Cherry Jane's curls fell about her face. The dark mole on her neck, only just visible above the collar of her dress. All the little marks of the child she had been.

Cherry Jane's hands were folded neatly in front of her. She was wearing white lace gloves. Finally, she broke the silence.

"Hello, Mary Grace." Then, turning to her mother, "Oh, but can she . . . ?"

"No." Nobody spoke first. "She still doesn't speak."

"I see."

"I am her husband."

"I see. Congratulations."

"Thank you. My name is Nobody."

"How unusual."

Nobody's eyes narrowed ever so slightly. "Not really. I have been Nobody every day of my life, so in fact it is quite usual. At least for me."

Cherry Jane arched an eyebrow. Mutual dislike curdled in the air between them. Rachel was staring at the floor, wondering if she had been wrong to try to see her daughter one last time, when Cherry Jane so clearly wanted nothing to do with any of them.

Cherry Jane adjusted one of her gloves at the wrist. "You said you are leaving Port of Spain soon?"

"Yes," said Rachel.

"Where will you go?"

"We think Mercy somewhere on the island. We gon' look for her here as long as we got money for the room, then we gon' go look elsewhere."

Cherry Jane held herself still in that portrait-like way she had of posing. The mention of her other sister did not seem to move her in any way.

But then, she spoke. "And after that, where will you go? Will you look for the others?"

Rachel was caught off guard. She had not expected that Cherry Jane would think of her brothers. Her daughter seemed too deep into the lie of being a free mulatto to care. The surprise was enough to let a sliver of hope into Rachel's heart.

"Mercy is the last. Thomas Augustus living in British Guiana. We see him there. Micah dead."

The marble cracked; Cherry Jane's lip quivered. Rachel remembered, with all the vividness of a waking dream, the way that Micah would carry Cherry Jane on his shoulders, laughing and telling her that one day she would be as tall as when she sat up there. Rachel managed to hold back her tears, but Cherry Jane did not—a single drop ran down her right cheek, marring for a moment the perfect symmetry of her face.

"I'm sorry," she said. "I didn't know." The words were redundant—how could she have known?—but the sentiment was genuine. For a moment, the artifice was gone, and underneath was a young woman, her emotions raw, who could still feel.

They were all silent. Moved by her daughter's unexpected grief, Rachel reached out and took Cherry Jane's hand.

"Me glad me find you," Rachel said. She put as much warmth into her words as she could muster. After the stilted conversation, long silences and barely concealed contempt, it was her olive branch. Rachel did not want to resent Cherry Jane. Her daughter. Their paths had diverged, likely forever, but it was Rachel's job to teach Cherry Jane that family could not be forgotten.

Cherry Jane toyed with the fringe of her shawl. She did not speak for a long time. Maybe she did not have the words. To live in such deep denial of her past, her parentage, perhaps it took a certain emotional toll. It had shrunk the range of her expression. She could not say she was glad, too, to see this mother, so different from the mother she now pretended she had. But she was, on some level, glad—that much Rachel could see in her eyes. It wasn't much, but it was enough.

Cherry Jane, who had been standing all this time, finally perched on the edge of one of the beds. The knot of tension in Rachel's shoulders began to ease—her daughter no longer looked as if she wished to flee the room at any moment.

When Cherry Jane spoke, it was little more than a whisper. "What—what happened to him?"

"It was the rising in Demerara," said Rachel. These words were familiar to her now—this was not the first time she had retold Micah's story—but her voice caught on them. This retelling felt different. Animal grief tore at her all over again, its claws as sharp as the day Orion had first told her. She had to rest a hand on the bed frame to steady herself. "He fight for his freedom, and they kill him for it."

Through the haze of tears welling in her own eyes, Rachel saw Cherry Jane's face change. The mask of perfect, poised beauty slipped, and there was real anger in her eyes. Hope came to mind again, and now there was not so much between them. One light, one dark, but both fierce, hard-edged women with a sharp instinct for survival. Cherry Jane's hands in their lace gloves were balled into fists.

Rachel drew closer to her daughter. She cupped Cherry Jane's chin in her hands. She did not have to think to do it; the movement came as naturally as breathing. Cherry Jane did not shrink from her mother's touch. The anger ebbed from her face, but her eyes still shone with tears. The two women looked at each other, and felt the warmth of each other's skin.

"Me hear he live a good life," Rachel said. "Many folks gon' remember him, and remember him well."

Cherry Jane's lips quivered into something like a smile. "And Thomas? Is he happy?"

"He is. He find a kind of freedom, and it bring him peace."

"I am glad," said Cherry Jane. But then the smile faded, and she dropped her gaze toward the floor. A shadow crossed her face—her eyebrows drew together, a small sign of some internal struggle.

"What is it?" Rachel asked.

Cherry Jane took time to speak. When the words came, they were no longer smooth and poised but fractured and halting. She had a way of seeming practiced—her looks and her phrases were ones Rachel could imagine she had perfected many times over, in order to pass herself off as the woman she was trying to be. But these words were different. These words fell out of her mouth un-varnished, as if she had been unable to say them before, even to herself.

"Mercy. I . . . I saw her once. A few years ago. I think. I can't be sure. I didn't . . . I couldn't . . . It was only a glance. I was out riding, just beyond the town. I heard a woman laughing and it sounded just like her—just the way I remember, from all those years ago. I turned to look but the woman was walking away from me, next to another man. They were dressed like field hands—so if you're look-ing for her . . . the plantations. You should start there."

"Where exactly did you see her?" said Nobody sharply. "Which way was she heading?"

Cherry Jane shook her head. "That's all I know."

The unsaid words, *I'm sorry*, lingered in the air. Part of Rachel felt she should thank her daughter for giving them some hint that Mercy might yet be found on the plantations of Trinidad, but the angry part of her forced her silence. That Cherry Jane could have been so close to her sister and said nothing, done nothing—Rachel could not fathom it. The callousness terrified her.

After a long silence, Cherry Jane finally raised her head. She looked to Rachel for something—for forgiveness, Rachel realized. For absolution. Cherry Jane had hidden it well, but carrying the secret of Mercy inside her had hurt. She had made her choice, but it was not an easy one, and Rachel pitied her for it. As quickly as it had risen, Rachel felt her anger ebb away.

It was Mary Grace who broke the stillness between them. Mov-ing past Rachel, Mary Grace came close and brushed a hand along her sister's cheek. Cherry Jane closed her eyes and leaned into her sister's touch, then opened them again. The two sisters gazed at each other, and Mary Grace's meaning was clear.

Thank you.

Cherry Jane got to her feet. "I must get home."

Rachel felt a tear in the fabric of herself—she had felt it before, watching Orion walk away all those months ago, in Demerara, carrying the memories of Micah with him. The urge to know overwhelmed her. They did not have much time, and Cherry Jane's expression was returning to its former inscrutable poise, yet Rachel could not help but speak.

"The man me see you with. He your husband?"

Cherry Jane looked surprised. She held her gloved hands together, fingers interlaced, atop her skirt, one thumb slowly circling the lace.

"No. Not yet. But soon, I hope . . ."

"And you happy?"

Cherry Jane was ready with the answer, smooth words on the tip of her tongue. "Henry is very—"

But she stopped. She looked from Mary Grace to her mother, and suddenly she smiled—a real smile, from the heart, lighting up her face, dimming everything else in the room. The smile was incomparable in its beauty—and yet, it was the smile of Micah, of Thomas Augustus, of Mary Grace, of Rachel herself. They were all there, in that smile.

"Yes. I am happy," she said. "I have found my kind of freedom, too. And it brings me something like peace."

Rachel had lost Cherry Jane twice over—once to the great house, and again to the white men who took her from Providence. There was much about her daughter she did not understand, and this elegant mulatto woman before her she understood even less. And yet, in that moment, there was a spark of something between them. Both women softened. Rachel no longer saw Cherry Jane's lie as an act of destruction, threatening the ties between them. It was an act of carving out some space in the world, something it had taken Rachel decades to dare to do. She did not like it—she would prefer that Cherry Jane claimed their kinship openly and without hesitation—but she could accept it.

"Well, goodbye," said Cherry Jane.

Rachel wondered if they would embrace one last time. She noticed how Cherry Jane's arms twitched ever so slightly, but no—they would not embrace.

Cherry Jane pulled the shawl back over her head and moved toward the door, but paused on the threshold.

Looking behind her, she said softly, "I hope you find her."

Rachel smiled.

Cherry Jane left behind her the faint smell of something like morning dew, or sunrise after heavy rain, but it did not last. Heavy, humid air crept underneath the door and through the cracks in the windows, erasing the final trace of her.

Nobody came over and put an arm around Mary Grace's waist. Mary Grace took Rachel's hand and squeezed it. A familiar weariness fogged Rachel's head and weighed down her limbs. It brought with it the sort of gentle and diffuse sadness that spread slowly, like a cloud.

They gathered their things. A blanket, one spare shirt, a loaf of bread they'd been able to buy after selling Mary Grace's wedding dress. There was not much, but Rachel moved slowly, trying to stretch the moment out, give herself time to heal. She thought often of Thomas Augustus—shorter and darker than Cherry Jane—who had chosen a life in the forests rather than in the heart of society, but in her mind they began to blur together as the ones whose futures could not fit with her own. It made her feel a little better to imagine them this way, and the sadness began to lift. They were both young. And however much they tried to propel themselves forward, without any thought of what lay behind, Rachel knew that they would not forget her. They could forget her face, her voice, the feeling of her arms around them, as she had forgotten her own mother. But her warmth, her love and her desire to see them be well, they could not forget.

Rachel imagined Cherry Jane, many years from now, at a lavish dinner party. By her side was the man Rachel had glimpsed with her daughter on market day, pale-skinned, his hand on Cherry Jane's arm.

"Oh yes," Rachel imagined her daughter would say to the other guests. "My mother was very highly regarded. A mulatto, with skin almost as light as mine."

Rachel imagined the way her daughter would pause, and then add, with a smile, "She was good and she was kind." Inside the lie, a kernel of truth. It would be Rachel's love Cherry Jane would feel as she spoke these words. That would never fade.

32

THEY TOOK THE Royal Road east, hugging the foot of the mountains. With Port of Spain behind them, Trinidad reminded Rachel of the wild land beyond the plantations of British Guiana. Although some of the forests had been cleared here, and the landscape was scattered with signs of white occupation, there were long stretches of road where they saw no one and everything around them was untamed. Rachel thought back to Barbados and realized how small it had been—though through the fog of memory, perhaps it seemed smaller than it was. Remembering her life there made her feel trapped and restless. She increased her pace without even noticing, and Mary Grace had to grab hold of her hand to slow her down.

The road forked; based on instinct, Rachel led them south, and they still saw nothing grander than wooden shacks huddled around small plots of land. Nobody had warned them that Trinidad was sparsely planted; he spoke of white men rushing, too late, to crest the great wave of Caribbean sugar, left scrabbling to force a meager profit from the soil. Rachel knew there might be many miles yet before they finally sighted cane fields.

When night fell, they camped on the bank of a river that ran alongside the road. They unrolled a blanket like a sleeping mat and shared it, bodies pressed tightly together. Without the sun, and with the stars remote and half-shrouded in wisps of cloud, the night had a chill to it, but Rachel did not mind. She liked the cool air, and the sound of water running over stones. Her mind felt sharp and clean. She went to sleep with her thoughts whittled down to a single point, and that point was love. The sort of love that, flying like an arrow loosed from a bow, could not miss. She imagined it shooting at speed toward its target, and this image warmed her into a deep sleep.

At daybreak, Nobody drew a knife from his knapsack and used it to hone a stick into a spear. He stood knee-deep in the river and held it aloft, waiting. Every time he shifted his weight, his feet kicked up little streams of mud that swirled around his ankles in the otherwise clear water. From the bank, Rachel and Mary Grace watched as he plunged his spear beneath the surface, and it emerged with a fish twisting desperately on the end, flinging drops of blood from its wound. The fish was small, barely the length of Rachel's hand, so once Nobody had waded over and let the women take it, he went back out to keep trying.

Rachel kept half an eye on the sun as its slow climb marked the hours since they had risen. When Nobody suggested they cook some of their catch and then smoke the rest, she tried to argue back, single-minded in her determination to reach the southern plantations by nightfall, but he wore her down. The little food they had brought with them from Port of Spain would not last forever, and smoked fish would not spoil as quickly as anything they might be able to forage on their route.

Rachel eventually acquiesced, tight-lipped, feeling as though carrying the fish was an admission that they might be weeks or more on the road. She let Mary Grace and Nobody build the fire, and spent most of the waiting hours with her eyes closed and her feet in the river. She tried to keep her mind blank, to control its restlessness, focusing on the simple sensations of the sun's warmth on her face, the cool water lapping around her ankles and the slight burning of the smoke as it filled the inside of her nose and the back of her throat.

By the time they were walking again, the heat was sweltering and they had to move slowly, as if the sun's rays had thickened the air. The small mouthful of bread and fish that had been Rachel's breakfast barely kept her hunger at bay. It was almost like being back on the plantation—sweaty, legs aching, her head throbbing with a dull thirst and an emptiness in her stomach that soon spread outward as if her body was searching all over for a way to feed itself.

A trickle of sweat stung the corner of one eye, and she paused to rub it away.

"Are you all right?" Nobody asked.

She almost laughed. "Me doing fine. This no harder than working the fields."

And it was true. The physical sensations were the same, but the goal was her own. The act of compelling her body to exert itself for a purpose of her choosing, rather than for the profit of a master, was exhilarating. The punishing heat and the sharpness of hunger could not erase the fact that she was free. She would still suffer from weariness, from thirst, from the corners of her vision blackening with dizziness as they went on and on and on. But she suffered on her own terms.

It was close to dusk before they finally reached the plantations. At the first sight of a great house rising from the horizon, with a mill slowly turning close behind it, Rachel almost sank to her knees. Exhaustion hit her, but fear, too. These ugly monuments to the life she had once lived made her realize how vulnerable they were. They had no papers. Nothing that would stop an unscrupulous overseer from claiming them as his own.

She paused, the last of the sun still casting a soft pink glow over the land around them.

"We must wait," she said. "When it get dark, we can go into the villages and not be seen."

In the coming days, by moonlight, they crept into the slave quarters. They stopped workers on the paths, who were using their few hours of freedom to meet friends and lovers in neighboring plantations. They asked—

A woman called Mercy.

Is she here?

Do you know her?

They saw grand sugar plantations, small cocoa ones, fields of cotton, wooden slave huts abandoned or beaten to nothing by a storm. They saw women holding babies barely months old, and men bent by the weight of decades of labor. They met house slaves sneaking out into the fields to see mothers or fathers or husbands or wives. People were warm, people were suspicious, people were kind and people were glassy-eyed, exhausted after a day of work.

They asked, again and again—

A woman called Mercy.

Is she here?

Do you know her?

By day, they rested as much as they could. They kept off the roads and out of sight of the plantations. The fierce heat of the sun made Rachel's sleep shallow and her dreams delirious—Mercy haunted them, and Cherry Jane, too. And Micah and Thomas Augustus. The ghosts of the past were all there. Since they were surrounded by plantations, her history caught up with her and began to drain her resolve. Every time someone shook their head and told them, no, there was no Mercy here, it grew harder to bear.

"The island is large," Nobody said one morning, as the sun rose. "This is only one small part of it. We will find her."

Rachel said nothing. The image that haunted her dreams most

was of her and Mary Grace on some other island, mother and daughter both greatly aged, following some other path. Still asking:

A woman called Mercy.

Is she here?

Do you know her?

EVENTUALLY, THE PLANTATIONS fell away. The land went back to being unclaimed; hummingbirds darted between the trees, and industrious ants marched over the soil like miniature field laborers, carrying their cargo with their pincered jaws. A trail through the bushes led them back to where they had started: the Royal Road. At the sight of it, Rachel could sense the pulse of despair that ran through the three of them. And yet, what could they do but walk on?

Nobody suggested they head farther south still, to where the island began to curve over to Venezuela. Rachel nodded mutely. At previous forks in the road, something had guided her—some sense that Mercy was close. She imagined that she could feel her daughter's presence. Now, there was no such pull.

They had followed the road for a mile or so when they met a man heading north with a donkey that was laden with copper pans. They heard him before they saw him—the pans knocked together as the donkey swayed. When he finally came over the horizon, leading the animal by a rope, they all had to shield their eyes as the burnished copper gleamed white in the sunlight.

The man was strikingly dressed. His clothes were little more than rags, with trousers that were almost severed at the thigh, the bottom half clinging on by a few threads and leaving his knees entirely exposed. But on his head was perched a tricorne hat that looked brand-new, black with a golden trim. Underneath, his cheeks caved inward in a way that suggested missing teeth, and his skin was so lined it looked like dark, crumpled paper.

He pulled the donkey to a stop and stared at them as though they were the true curiosity.

Nobody spoke first, the practiced words falling easily from his lips: "We're looking for a woman called Mercy. Do you know her?"

When the man spoke, his voice was a surprise. It was deep and rich. There did not seem to be enough of him for such a voice; the hollowed lines between his ribs were visible through his open shirt.

"Me don't know any Mercy."

They were so used to replies of this kind that Rachel felt nothing in response to it. There was no surge of hope followed by the crash of disappointment. It was to be expected. Of course he would not know her.

The man was still looking from Nobody to Rachel to Mary Grace, his head cocked.

"Where you heading?" he asked.

"We've just been through the plantations back toward Port of Spain," said Nobody. "We're going to try farther south."

The man rested a hand thoughtfully on the flank of his donkey.

"Me know the south. And the west and north. Me don' walk those roads and trade in those markets." The donkey shifted its weight and a few of the pans knocked together. "Me never meet a Mercy."

He turned eastward. Rachel followed his gaze, the afternoon sun spreading like warm liquid across the back of her neck. The island lay in a thick, uneven line across the horizon. It looked endless, but Rachel knew that at some point the land would meet the sea, and that gave her comfort. It was not endless. It would end.

"Yes," the man continued. "You should go east. Me don't know those parts so well. You might find your Mercy there."

He didn't wait for a reply. He tipped his cap to them and set off at a steady pace, whistling tunelessly over the noise of the jostling pans and the steady beat of the donkey's hooves on the road.

As Rachel watched him go, the sheer absurdity of him was enough to make her smile for the first time in days. Who was he, this ragged man with the hat of a naval officer, and dozens of copper pans? They would never know his story, could never guess at the course his life had taken. After visiting so many plantations and seeing so many workers with the same look in their eyes, Rachel was glad of something so different, so impossible to understand. This stranger was a reminder that out of the deep furrows plowed for them by slavery, they could all still spill over, scattering in unexpected directions. Nothing was set in stone. This man had made his own path, and so would she.

"East?" Nobody asked. The tone of his voice was uncertain. They had no way of knowing if what this man had said was true. Mercy could still be anywhere.

Rachel was thinking of the stories from her childhood that the old women would tell. Stories of heroes and gods and shape-shifters and talking animals. Often these stories featured a journey, and travelers meeting by chance on the road. Secrets would be divulged and weapons would be thrust into the hero's hands. Rachel did not fancy herself a hero, and she had certainly received no great wisdom or weaponry from the man with the copper pans. But the spirit of those childhood tales was there, in the brief moment they had shared.

"East," she said. It was their best hope.

After sunset, they set up camp; away from the plantations, there was no need to hide by day and travel in darkness. Rachel found it hard to sleep. Her dreams were fitful, formless—the idea of Mercy without the image of her, and a sense that there was something wrong. The growing dread jolted her awake, and there was nothing to do but lie there until dawn. The stars, their cold white light piercing through the black abyss of the night sky, twinkled with something like menace, and Rachel was relieved when the rising sun finally banished them.

33

THE SKY WAS low and heavy, threatening rain, as they picked
their way along the eastern trail. The path was well-worn, lit-
tered with the imprints of horseshoes, but uneven. More than once,
Rachel's foot landed awkwardly on the ground and a jolt of pain shot
through her ankle as it twisted. She was lucky enough to avoid any
serious damage, but she slowed their pace, trying to be more careful.
The ability to walk was one thing she could not afford to lose.

Around them, the landscape seemed desolate. Thick woods, interrupted by patches of green marshland, ran along each side of the
trail, but in the gray humidity everything looked like it had been
drained of life. For Rachel, the disquiet that lingered from the previous night of uneasy sleep colored everything. *Infertile* was the
word that sprang to mind, in spite of all the trees.

Nobody stayed quiet. He looked thoughtful, subdued. Rachel
sensed he felt it, too—the inhospitable nature of the island's interior. Mary Grace walked between them, sometimes moving ahead
to be close by Rachel, other times dropping back to hold Nobody's
hand. She was the thread that held them together. Whenever Rachel could feel the warmth of Mary Grace's body, it gave her com-

fort. It was a reminder of something living as they passed through land that, though lush, shivered with death. When Mary Grace walked beside her, Rachel was reminded of all the little ways her daughter had changed since Bridgetown. The parts of her that had unfurled, unknotted. The space she took up now. Her solidity. The way her eyes could hold anyone's gaze, steady, without flinching. Unlike the trees, which seemed frozen, unruffled by the wind, Mary Grace was evidence that things could grow.

When the rain came, they had to slow further. Pools of water, like inverted islands, glistened in the mud. Mary Grace slipped, falling hard, but smiled quickly to show she was unhurt, and scrambled back to her feet. Rachel looked upward, squinting as the rain pounded her face. There was no sign of it easing; the sky was an unbroken gray sheet of cloud, tipping water onto the earth below. Without the sun, Rachel had lost all sense of time. How long before dusk?

"We gon' have to walk through the night," Rachel said. They could try to shelter in the woods, but she knew they would not escape the rain. The droplets were too thick. Rachel could see the trees bending under their weight. The only way was through it.

Mary Grace touched her mother's arm, a gesture that made clear her resolve to walk whenever and wherever Rachel wanted. But there was no mistaking Mary Grace's touch for a sign of meekness, or a willingness to put others' needs before her own. Rachel often worried that Mary Grace was giving up too much to join her on their journey around the Caribbean—a settled life with Nobody, a chance to be happy rather than chasing after brothers and sisters who might be dead or gone, or so deep into lives of their own that they could not be persuaded to rejoin a broken family. Now, in the way the muscles tightened across her daughter's rain- and mud-streaked face, Rachel saw that the search was Mary Grace's as much as her own. Her daughter had lost one brother, said goodbye to another—likely forever—and had a sister turn her back on the family in pursuit of whiteness, accumulated slowly over the generations, until her descendants could pass to the other side once and for all. Rachel had been too single-minded to see that Mary Grace, too, so desperately wanted to find Mercy.

There were dark, puffy rings around Mary Grace's eyes. She was exhausted. They all were. But it was Mary Grace who led the way, started walking again and did not stop, not as the rain pounded their skin, soaked their clothing, their hair, dribbled into the corners of their eyes. Not as darkness fell, moonless and cold, and they had to take one another's hands just to know they were all still there. Rachel lost any sense of where they were, how far they had come, how many hours it had been since they had last seen the sun.

Finally, the rain eased, first to a light mist, then to nothing. Rachel was so drenched that she didn't notice at first. Not until Nobody said, "At least it's stopped raining," and she slipped her hand out of Mary Grace's, holding it up to feel for drops that never came.

They stopped. The ground was still slick with mud, so they did not sit, but they shared between them a piece of smoked fish. Rachel had passed through aching exhaustion to a kind of numb nothingness.

"Shall we keep walking?" Nobody asked. "It can't be long now."

Rachel was about to answer him when the last of the rain clouds parted and released beams of bright moonlight, turning their surroundings silver. Rachel looked ahead, and her eyes were drawn immediately to a crop of shadows in the distance. Trees? She squinted at them. No, the shapes were wrong. Buildings. A plantation.

Mary Grace gripped her mother's arm. She had seen it, too. Rachel exchanged a glance with Nobody, then looked back to the horizon. The eerie lighting made everything ethereal, ghostlike. The three of them began to walk again, but Rachel almost expected the knot of buildings to disappear at any moment. They seemed to recede with the horizon, never coming any closer. But the fields around the buildings did become sharper, more clearly defined, as the three of them approached. Rachel could see the unmistakable silhouettes of sugarcane.

The trail passed between two trees, their branches bent over the path like an archway. With her eyes still fixed on the plantation ahead, Rachel didn't spot the white man behind the left tree until it was too late. Nobody whispered, "Rachel," and then there the man was, stepping out of the shadows. His gun glinted as he drew it upward in a smooth arc. He didn't point it at them, just rested it on his shoulder.

"Out for a late-night stroll?"

Rachel was skilled at getting the measure of a man quickly. She'd had to be. Life and limb often hinged on knowing whether a white man was the type to laugh at you, spit on you or kill you. As soon as she saw this man, she recoiled, shrank, tried to lessen the effect of her height and her broad shoulders. This man was the killing type. Worse, he was the kind of man who did not want to advertise his cruelty. His face was politely blank. Rachel had known plenty of men with a sadistic glint in their eye and a cold smirk on their lips, but they were nothing compared to the men who showed no feeling, even as they committed the worst evils.

Rachel bowed her head and said nothing. Next to her, Mary Grace did the same. But Nobody—less used to discerning danger in the curve of a white man's lips—said, "We are travelers from Port of Spain. We're seeking a woman we believe may live around these parts."

Rachel could feel the heat of the white man's eyes on her, and her alone. She risked a glance upward. He was studying her face, his thin eyebrows drawn together in a half frown. She looked back at the ground, pulse quickening. He could see something in her— something that he had not yet named himself, though Rachel could guess it. He was tracing the line of her shoulders, the breadth of her nose, the shape of her neck. He was wondering if the resemblance was coincidence. Or perhaps, like so many white men Rachel had known, he was not used to differentiating Black features and was trying to puzzle out whether what he saw in Rachel was something common to all Negroes or really was a clue, a family tie to someone he knew.

Mercy was here.

Or had been here.

Or had been somewhere this man had been, wherever he had come from before.

This much Rachel knew. The white man was searching her face for signs of her daughter.

"We are looking for a woman called Mercy," said Nobody.

Rachel glanced up again. The white man was still looking at her. "Mercy," he repeated, and she had to fight against the flash of anger that filled her, that compelled her to reach out and rip her daughter's name out of his mouth.

"You know her?"

Finally, the white man turned to Nobody, arching an eyebrow.

"I am the overseer here," he said. "I have many workers on this plantation, and do not know them all by name. I cannot say one way or another if this Mercy is here."

"Perhaps you would let us walk to the village and ask?"

The white man took a while to answer. He shifted his gun from one shoulder to the other, pausing when he held it in front of his chest to let his eyes follow the line of its barrel up to the sky. Finally, he said, "I'm afraid I am quite particular about who I allow on this land. Especially of late. We get all sorts coming here, stirring up trouble."

"We are not looking for trouble," said Nobody.

With the butt of his rifle resting in the crook of his arm, the white man interlaced his fingers together. Rachel noticed how long his fingernails were, and how pale and soft the skin of his hands looked in the moonlight.

"I'm afraid the only Blacks I will allow here are ones who work for me. Although . . ." He sighed, as if his forthcoming benevolence was a great strain. "I have been looking to fill a labor shortage. Perhaps, if you were interested in employment, you could accept a position here, and see if you can find your Mercy. It would be on apprenticeship terms, of course."

Rachel imagined that Nobody looked to her for guidance. She couldn't know for sure, because her eyes never left this white man. He returned her gaze steadily, probably believing that his expression gave nothing away. But she could still see it. He knew that she was Mercy's mother. What she could not divine from his face was how he knew her daughter. Did she work for him here? Had he come from some other plantation where she was? Or had their paths crossed in a different way?

As Rachel weighed up her options, something rose inside her, like bile but without the bitter taste. It filled her head, pressed against her nostrils. The feeling had no precise name, but was somewhere between certainty and impulse. She knew that she would take the risk. She had no basis for it. But her mouth opened for her, spoke the words.

"We need work, sir," she said.

"Well, then." The white man smiled, and in the moonlight his teeth were the same washed-out gray color as his skin. "Welcome to Perseverance."

He led them up the trail, until they came to a path that split off to the left.

"Follow that and you'll reach the village. You're welcome to any hut that's unoccupied. I will see you in the morning."

"Thank you, sir," said Rachel. She was still slightly hunched, keeping herself small and unthreatening. It was not until they had walked down the path for some minutes that she looked back, saw that the white man was no longer in sight and stretched up to her full height.

"Why—" Nobody began in a whisper, but Rachel cut across him.

"She here."

The light breeze had died away, leaving the night air still, a pause between breaths. The soft earth absorbed the sound of their footsteps. In the quiet, Rachel could hear her own heartbeat and the warm pulse of blood in her ears. She swallowed, but it did nothing to abate the feeling that still gripped her—the thrill of the gamble mixed with the sense that she was right, could not possibly be wrong. Every step took her closer to her daughter. The last child unfound.

Rachel felt a small gust of wind like a whisper on the back of her neck. The ghosts of all her other children came to mind, those dead and left behind, but the ghosts brought no sadness. Only a sense of anticipation—of a door, once closed, about to open. The ghosts were behind her, pushing her onward. Rachel's fingers made brief contact with Mary Grace's, and in that touch, too, she felt something urging her on. She took longer strides.

The path wound its way between two cane fields, and the tall stalks obscured any view of the plantation around them, or any sense of how close the village might be. An occasional breeze rippled the cane, and the effect was like walking through an ocean, bleached white by the moon. Rachel was not especially familiar with Christianity, but she was struck by a dim memory of what Orion had told her about Micah. Something about God and the parting of a sea. Slaves walking to freedom. But no. She blinked and saw the cane as it was—simply cane. There was no parted sea. There was no freedom on the other side. Only the promise of six years' apprenticeship to the cruel man they had met—and, maybe, her daughter.

The cane fields ended abruptly—so abruptly that Rachel halted, disorientated by the sudden appearance of the village. The huts, arranged in a semicircle facing the end of the path, were poorly maintained, some clearly abandoned. Doorframes had collapsed, walls had splintered, gaping windows were so thick with cobwebs that they appeared curtained. Rachel advanced cautiously. Was this the place? Or was this whole plantation an illusion all along? Deserted, decaying, inhabited only by ghosts.

Out of the shadows of one of the huts, a man came, smoke curling from the edge of his pipe. One sleeve of his shirt dangled empty, armless.

"What you want?" he asked, his voice hoarse and his eyes hard. He looked to be about Rachel's age. There was no warmth in the way he stared at the three of them.

Before Rachel could answer, a woman came out from behind him. Younger, but with the same long, thin face, ending in a sharp chin. A daughter, perhaps? She rested a hand on the man's shoulder, above his missing arm, and he softened slightly. She gazed straight at Rachel, her expression blank, like something had sucked all the life out of it.

Rachel held perfectly still, waiting.

Not a single flicker of emotion crossed the woman's face, but she nodded slowly.

"Yes," she said. "Me can fetch her."

She shuffled over to the next hut and disappeared inside.

Rachel could feel parts of her constricting—heart, throat, stomach—even as her lungs were filled to bursting with a breath she did not dare release.

Rachel waited.

She watched the silver lines of smoke from the man's pipe drift toward the sky.

She prayed. There was no other word for the way her mind concentrated itself on a single plea that it offered up to someone, something, she did not know what.

Let it be Mercy.

It was the curve of a belly that came out first. Then the rest. Tall, like her mother. Arms wrapped tightly around her chest. Defensive. Ready for whatever the other woman had told her not to be true. How could it be true?

But it was.

Mercy and Rachel cried out with one voice. No words, just the release of pain and joy all at once. Rachel opened her arms, and Mercy came to her. As they fell against each other, the swell of Mercy's stomach pressed right into the hungriest, emptiest parts of Rachel. They stumbled, almost fell, as Rachel's legs gave way. Mary Grace, who had also rushed forward to greet her sister, was able to help Mercy hold up their mother. As Rachel's body went slack, she thought of how long she had stayed strong, held firm, for her children. How long she had just been waiting for permission to let go.

She allowed herself for once to be weak. She sobbed. Her limbs sank like liquid toward the ground.

Rachel felt her daughters' arms shaking with the weight of her, and she knew they could not hold her forever. She managed to stand.

Mercy was stiff and upright, her eyes glazed. No tears fell. After that first cry, she had been silent. Rachel was still shaking on the verge of sobs; Mercy was still. With one hand, Rachel stroked her daughter's hair—short, like her mother's, hugging the contours of her skull.

"Me here," Rachel whispered. "Me here."

Her chest unknotted, releasing the ache it had held there since the first loss—since Micah, maybe even since her forgotten mother. It was not completeness that she felt, because her heart bore all the scars of the dead, and the ones left hundreds of miles away. But it was the closest thing to completeness she had ever known. It was acceptance. It was peace.

34

RACHEL LOOKED AT what the years had done to Mercy. She was just as tall and solid as she had been before, with sloping shoulders and broad hips. Along with her round stomach, this gave her an illusion of size and strength. Her gaunt face and withered limbs showed the truth—she was wasting away.

When Mercy was a child, Rachel had always worried about her big heart. So much love. Maybe too much. Mercy had been distraught when Micah was taken, and Mary Grace, too. Mercy herself was taken away in the afternoon, when Rachel was up in the boiling-house feeding cane stalks into the press. It was probably just as well; it had always haunted Rachel to think of how her daughter must have cried, how her heart must have shattered as she was dragged away.

Now, Rachel could see it was as she had always feared. Her daughter had been forced to harden in order to survive. It was there in the dullness of her eyes, and the way she held an arm across herself, protecting her heart.

Was it too late? Had Mercy been broken, as Thomas Augustus had foretold?

Rachel reached out to touch Mercy's belly. She saw how Mercy flinched, then caught herself, relaxed, let her mother's hand trace its curve.

Mercy said nothing.

It was usually best not to ask—conception on plantations could be ugly, brutal. It did not do to curse the baby before its birth with the mother's bitterness, by forcing her to speak of how it got inside her. But Rachel recognized the way Mercy's features twisted with a different kind of pain. It was one thing to carry a child inside you all these months, fearing that it would come out looking like someone you loathed. Rachel knew how much that hurt. It was worse to carry a child, wondering if it would come out looking like someone you once loved, now dead and gone forever. Rachel knew that anguish, too—a baby that came from love and then loss in quick succession.

Mercy asked no questions about why they were there, or anything about their journey. Perhaps she, too, looked at her mother and saw grief that Rachel did not have the strength to disclose—not yet.

The old man and his daughter were still hovering outside their hut, impassive as they watched the reunion. The man took a long drag on his pipe and said, "Dawn come."

He was right. To their east a band of milky-gray sky ran across the horizon. Mercy gripped Rachel's arm.

"You must go," said Mercy. "It's not safe."

"The overseer?" said Rachel.

"Yes."

"We already meet him."

Mercy blinked a few times. The words did not seem to sink in.

"We already meet him," Rachel repeated. "He offer us work. We take it so we can come to the village. To you."

Slowly, Mercy unclenched her fingers from Rachel's wrist and brought both arms back across her chest.

"Well," she said, her voice hollow. "Welcome to Perseverance."

———

WHEN THE SUN rose, it revealed cane fields that were spoiling. The ones closest to the slave village were overready for harvest: stalks drooped, and leaves lay rotting on the ground. One field appeared to have been burned, leaving behind only blackened earth.

The overseer also looked worse in the morning light. He was eerily colorless, with thinning blond hair and skin the same shade as sun-bleached bone. Rachel learned that his name was Mr. Thornhill.

She had never seen a man so pale. She was used to overseers who were red-faced from drink and from days outside in the harsh Caribbean heat. This Mr. Thornhill looked as though he spent his time with the women, shaded under a parasol, disgusted at the thought of growing even a single shade closer to a Negro. He paced slowly around the fields flanked by two burly foremen, watching the workers cut the cane. He moved like a white woman, too. Stiff, upright, self-consciously graceful, yet somehow predatory, with a streak of menace.

Nobody and Rachel were ordered to the first gang. They worked alongside the young woman they had met in the village. She kept her lips tightly pursed if either of them attempted any conversation, but around midday one of the foremen barked at her to cut faster and they learned her name was Nancy.

Nancy's father had exchanged a few words with Rachel as they both headed for the fields at dawn. He told her his name was Abraham. He limped behind the first gang, gathering stalks into bundles as best he could with only one arm. Mary Grace stuck close to him, tying up the bundles that he piled on the ground.

The day passed in a daze. In body, Rachel felt like no time had passed since she had left her old plantation—or even since she had first picked up a bill at the age of thirteen and begun to hack at the cane stalks until they gave way. In mind, though, everything had changed. While her body fell into the routine of it all, swinging the bill over and over again, her mind saw every movement in a fresh light. She felt her own strength. In one sense it pleased her, to realize how much power she had, how deep she could drive a blade into the tough green stems. But it also enhanced the dull tedium of the work; she began to chafe against it. This was work that she had done, day after day, month after month, for decades, but she had since tasted something more. She had pushed her body to achieve things of her own free will.

The work was easy because her muscles slipped so readily back into the rhythm of it. But hard, too, because she could not help thinking with every swing—

Why?

Whenever Mr. Thornhill came near, she held his gaze. She could still sense his cruelty, but she was no longer afraid. He always looked away first, finding nothing about her work to criticize, and also—she was sure of it—a little disquieted by the expression on her face. He could tell that she knew her own power, and it unnerved him. Gone was the woman drawing in her limbs and crouching over to seem small. In her place was a tall woman with a knife in her hand. Near the end of the day, as Rachel saw him watching her from across the field, she swung the bill as hard as she could, and brought down a stalk with a single blow. Their eyes met. Rachel smiled. Mr. Thornhill turned and walked off toward the great house in the distance, leaving the foremen to supervise the last few hours of work.

By the time they all went back to the village on the cusp of nightfall, Rachel was flushed with the thrill of her new discovery— that she had no interest in the kind of life she had once lived, resigned to doing someone else's bidding. She had never thought herself capable of great, life-altering change. She had done what she had to do to survive slavery, and then when freedom came she had thought it was too late. But now, she was almost giddy with the sense that change had come without her realizing. It had been there in every step she had taken away from Providence, in every inch of ocean or river she had crossed. The old Rachel would never have dared to look Mr. Thornhill in the eye.

Mercy was already waiting in the village. She did not work in the fields, but watched over the animals kept in pens near the great house. She looked tired and withdrawn, and a wariness flashed across her face as she noticed her mother's good spirits.

"Everything all right in the fields?"

"Hard work," said Nobody, who was kneading the inside of one forearm with his wrist. He had been quiet on the walk back. Rachel realized that, like her, he must have felt a sense of a wheel coming full circle and bringing him back to the cane fields, though for him the arc was measured in decades rather than years. The work had clearly drained him, and Rachel could see in his darting eyes a restlessness. Inside him still was the little boy looking for a way to run like his mother had told him.

"Come," said Rachel to Mercy. "Sit with us and eat. We have some fish."

They shared out the last of the smoked fish and rested their aching feet. Mercy watched her mother closely, her expression guarded.

Rachel took Mercy's hand, and this time her daughter did not flinch at the touch. It was like unwrapping something fragile, peeling back gossamer-thin layers of skin and hoping they would not tear.

"Me must know," Mercy whispered. "The others?" She glanced at her sister. "Did you . . . ?"

Rachel told her about Thomas Augustus and Cherry Jane first. Mercy bowed her head and listened, tracing patterns in the dirt with her finger. She gave away no hint of feeling—either relief or despair.

Eventually, Mercy lifted her head. "Me glad they safe."

Micah lingered in the silence between them.

Rachel began, "Micah—" but Mercy cut her off.

"Don't."

Mercy's hand went instinctively to her stomach. Rachel knew that loss had a way of doing that—each one triggering memories of another, until every death had blurred together into a mass of grief. Mercy was adding Micah to her growing tally of loved ones who were with her no more.

"Someday me can tell you," Rachel said. "But maybe not today."

"Not today," Mercy repeated. Rachel watched as her daughter carefully rearranged her face to hide her pain.

Rachel looked down at her lap. There was so much more to say, but neither of them seemed to have the words. Rachel wanted to warn her daughter that it did not work—keeping quiet, feigning strength, holding back tears and grief. Rachel had tried it for forty years. It was only now, with thousands of miles behind her, that Rachel saw how futile it had all been. She wanted to tell Mercy to let herself feel again, but it sounded hollow in her head. The lesson could not be passed on that way. It was not so simple. You had to live it to understand.

Rachel had convinced herself when she was younger that white men had no power over her if they never saw her cry, never saw how much they hurt her when they separated her from the ones she loved. It made her sick to think of it now, because they had the power all along. There was not so much strength in dignified suffering as she had once believed. The truth was that the white men would not have cared. Screaming or silent, it would have been all the same to them. They would still have taken her children and sold them away, and then expected Rachel to get back to work as if her heart hadn't been ripped out of her chest.

As Rachel grappled with how she could rescue the gentle, kind, loving Mercy, now hardened by labor and by loss, Mary Grace moved toward her sister. She brought their bodies close, touching from upper arm to hip, and they sat this way for a while before

Mercy's head began to droop. She was the taller of the two, but she slumped until her head was resting on Mary Grace's shoulder.

Mercy began to cry. Quiet tears. She closed her eyes and let them fall freely. The skin of Mary Grace's arm glistened with them.

Mary Grace's knowing eyes met Rachel's. There had been two of them on the journey, after all. Rachel was not the only one who had learned to love with her whole heart again. Mary Grace held steady as Mercy melted into her, and Rachel only just managed to avoid weeping herself. Her two daughters were superficially unalike— Mary Grace had a broader, flatter face, and was altogether softer and less emaciated than her sister. But in that moment, as they leaned into each other, Rachel saw a hundred things that bound them together. Eyebrows the same shape, eyes the same color. The same hands, narrow with long, thin fingers.

Mercy sat up and brushed away her tears. She rested her hand on the top of her belly, as if to remind herself of why she must dry them. She suppressed any sign of sadness—her trembling lip, the lines of grief that creased her forehead—and her face returned to blankness. Rachel watched her daughter closely; Mercy had stemmed her tears, but she did not seem to regret them. She was still afraid to show too much, to feel too much, but there was no sign that she begrudged herself that small release of what was left of her heart. It was not too late for her yet.

None of them spoke, but Rachel smiled at her daughters. Mercy returned the smile, not with her mouth but with a softening in her eyes, a glow that flickered there for a moment before it was extinguished.

35

RACHEL NOTICED ABRAHAM, the one-armed man, before he noticed her. She watched him for a while as he sat and smoked, his eyes drifting upward to the night sky. When he finally turned and saw her in the shadow of her doorway, he didn't seem surprised.

"Can't sleep?"

Rachel shrugged in reply.

Abraham went back to looking at the stars.

"So, Barbados?" He glanced at Rachel, noticed her confusion. "Mercy tell me her mother was from Barbados," he said. "Me remember it because Barbados where me was born."

This detail warmed him to Rachel. She looked with renewed interest at his thin face and sunken eyes. Though their routes were no doubt different, they had shared the same journey from one island to another.

"You live there long?"

He shook his head. "Me was eight when they bring me here. But me have some memory of the place. Me grow up in the north."

"Me was in the north, too. Providence was the plantation—you know it?"

"Me know the name. It must have been close."

He was still staring up at the sky. Rachel waited for him to ask about people she might have known, family she might be able to tell him still lived. Or even just to tell her the name of his old plantation, so she could supply the details herself. But he said nothing.

He brought the pipe to his lips, took a deep inhale and let the smoke pour out of his mouth and nostrils. The sight made Rachel think of souls. If they were visible to human eyes, she thought, they might look like that when they left a person's body. Trails of silver, spilling out of someone and lifting to the sky.

"You want to know what happen?"

"With your arm?" Rachel had been watching his empty sleeve swing in the breeze.

"No. To him." He jerked his head toward Mercy's hut. "He was a good man. Cato. It was a shame."

Rachel waited as he took another drag of his pipe.

"They try to run. Well, it was after we were free. How come you still running when you free, me don't know. But they run."

Rachel glanced at the hut where Mercy lay sleeping. The pieces fell into place. The hard shell around Mercy, and the air of resignation to her fate, these were not the work of years but of months—perhaps of weeks. The wound was fresh, and Mercy was trying to heal in the only way she knew how.

"They get caught?"

"In a way," said Abraham darkly. "They don't get far."

He pointed into the distance, out toward the Indian trail Rachel and the others had followed to the plantation. Part of the path was visible above the tall stalks of cane, before it disappeared over the horizon.

"They go that way. Me was out here." In the dark, his face was hard to read. The words fell flat and dull from his mouth, giving nothing away but his deep exhaustion. "Me see Thornhill start shooting. The first shot miss, but the second shot get Cato in the chest."

Rachel felt her mouth contort violently. She took a moment to calm herself, but when she spoke her voice was thick with disgust.

"He get punish for it? Thornhill?"

She already knew the answer. There were supposed to be things that were beyond the pale, but the law had never protected them like it should.

"No. His sister married to a judge. They never get him for anything all the years he been here."

Rachel burned with the injustice of it. This surprised her. She was no stranger to such things. There had been an overseer back in Barbados who was similarly well-connected, whose youngest victim had been only four years old—knocked unconscious by a beating and never woke up. Rachel had spent years numbing herself to the thousands of cruelties, large and small, that made up daily life on a plantation. Yet here she was, rage bubbling up and threatening to spill out of her in a scream, as though she had never before heard of a white man murdering a Black one and getting away with it.

All she could think of was her daughter. Mercy and Cato, whispering at night, a plan forming. Mercy with a hand on her belly, her face set, determined that this child would be the first in generations to be born free. Mercy and Cato, running in the moonlight. Mercy screaming as bullets whistled past her. Mercy crying out as Cato stumbled and fell, blood bursting from his chest.

Abraham was watching Rachel seethe. He opened his mouth, but seemed to think better of it, and closed it again. They sat in silence, the only sound Rachel's breathing gradually slowing back to a normal tempo.

When Rachel no longer looked on the verge of violence, Abraham said, "Mercy get lucky to survive that. Well"—he shook his head—"not lucky. Thornhill can shoot a mango out a tree across three fields if he want to. He know what he was aiming for. He already know about the baby, though many of us didn't. We can't spare the labor round here, so perhaps he think it all balance out. Kill one, but get another one in a few months just the same."

Rachel swallowed the acrid bile that was stinging the back of her throat. Abraham glanced at her, saw the expression still twisting her features, and paused. But his voice was just warming up, losing its croaky edge. Rachel wondered how many hundreds of nights he had spent alone in front of his hut. He was adjusting to companionship, and he seemed to like it.

"You ever think about it?" he asked.

"What?"

"Running."

"Me have to run to make it here."

Abraham took another drag of his pipe. Rachel noticed the way his eyes glazed over slightly every time he inhaled, as if the tobacco dulled his senses.

"Me don' think about it when me was young. When me first get here. Me think about going home. But that's why the white man love to keep us on islands—how can me get home? The sea help them keep us here."

Abraham sighed.

"That was a long time ago. Before Nancy. It's different when you got your own pickney. You get something you want to live for. Cato and Mercy, they was gon' have that here. Have the pickney, be a family. Maybe they think it's not enough. But me never gon' understand why they run. What more they want?"

Rachel could not help staring at him. Abraham didn't seem to notice her disbelieving gaze. He turned the pipe thoughtfully over in his hands, looking over the cracks and worn edges of the old wood.

What more do they want?

Rachel tried to read in his face if he really meant it. Deep lines creased across his forehead, and the corners of his mouth turned downward, toward the tight, graying curls of his beard. He wore every year of his life on his face, and more. The deadness behind his eyes—the same that Rachel had seen in Mercy, too, but his was set deep. Too deep.

What more do they want?

Rachel's mind burst with a thousand answers. There were rivers with mouths as wide as the entire island of Barbados. There was the sea. There were weddings celebrated deep in the forest, away from the misery of the plantations, where love had a cooler, clearer quality to it—like mountain air. There were towns heaving with dirty, grafting people, where the suffering felt different. The work could be as punishing, and the food as meager, but somehow the sheer mass of the hardship, the hundreds of people crammed together in close quarters, made it easier to bear.

The fragile connection Rachel had felt to Abraham evaporated. Their journeys were not the same. Barbados to Trinidad, but along the way Abraham had lost the bit of himself that she had recently discovered. There was fight left in her.

The image of Mercy flashed across Rachel's mind again, cradling the body of the man she had loved. What Thornhill had done, he had done to inspire terror. He knew that murder paid, in the long run. People were afraid. Even in the dead of night, he could strike. From hundreds of yards away, he could kill, and darkness was no protection.

Rachel remembered their eyes meeting in the fields, hers and Thornhill's. Her lips twisted into something like a smile. She felt the limits of his power, and the strength of her own. For the sake of Cato—a man she had never met, but she felt, through Mercy, as though she loved—they would finish it. The desperate wish Cato had formed for his child, for a different kind of freedom than plantation bondage—this wish could still be fulfilled.

The final embers in Abraham's pipe were dying. He sucked out the last bit of smoke, before tipping the pipe upside down and letting the ashes fall to the ground.

"Me guess you gon' be here a while," he said.

"Yes," Rachel lied. "Me guess so."

36

RACHEL'S THOUGHTS OF escape were interrupted by the sharp sound of Nancy sucking on her teeth. It was dusk, on the cusp of darkness. The field laborers had made it back to the village before Mercy, and Rachel had been imagining what she might say to her daughter when she finally returned, how she could impress upon her the need to get away from Perseverance, when Nancy nodded toward the path through the half-cut cane.

"Look like trouble."

Mr. Thornhill had Mercy by the wrist. In his other hand was a length of rope, and the whip.

Rachel stiffened.

Mr. Thornhill was in no great hurry, and if he was angry he gave no sign of it. When he and Mercy reached the village, he did not call anyone out of their huts or demand an audience. He led Mercy to a tree that grew on the outer edge of the village. Rachel had noticed it before and guessed its purpose. Its gnarled branches, barren and leafless, were silhouetted against the evening sky.

Mercy kept her head high, but her hands were shaking.

Nobody took a step toward Mr. Thornhill. Mary Grace put out an arm to hold him back.

They all waited.

Mr. Thornhill lifted Mercy's arms and bound her wrists to a branch that she was only just tall enough to reach. His knots were methodical, and he studied each one to make sure he was satisfied. He stood back. A small crowd had gathered anyway—as if people could sense his presence.

"Today," he said, "Mercy fell asleep while working. As the animal pen was not secured, two of the goats and one of the cows escaped." He paused, and ripped the shirt off Mercy's back. A quick, violent movement that jarred with how slowly he had spoken.

Rachel's hands were balled into fists.

"Let this serve as a reminder to all of you," Mr. Thornhill continued, "that I will not tolerate such laziness on this plantation."

He made another quick movement. Like a viper.

The crack of the whip as it bit into Mercy's skin.

The tangy smell of blood, like metal on the tongue.

No.

Rachel felt it in her own back, flesh made molten, searing, pain that twisted and blinded and cut through bone. Their positions were reversed—it was she who was tied to the tree, her eyes already swollen, almost closed, from blows that had come before the whipping. Her head hung limp against her shoulder. But then, the scream—"No!" Through the slits her eyes had become, Rachel could see the child, slipping through the grasp of her brothers and sisters, tripping over her own tiny feet as she ran. Mercy, still young enough to believe that she might have the power to stop the beating, her eyes wide, her hands raised as if ready to reach up and untie her mother. In the corners of her vision, blurred with pain, Rachel saw the overseer bend, smashing the butt of the whip into the child's face, breaking her nose, spewing blood across the earth, then raising himself and the whip, ready to spill some more.

As quickly and sickeningly as it had appeared, the memory vanished. Mercy was back on the tree, the arch of her back accentuating the swell of her belly, her toes scraping the earth as she struggled to find her footing.

Mr. Thornhill had turned. His pale face was flushed, more with excitement than exertion. He was looking at Rachel. She realized that, all around her, others were looking, too.

How many beatings had she seen? How many times had she screamed silently for it to stop? But this time, the words had come. There was no more terror choking her throat. Only rage.

"No," she repeated.

The whip hung limp in Mr. Thornhill's left hand. Behind him, the open wound on Mercy's back wept blood. Rachel could feel herself trembling, but it was not with fear.

"What do you mean, 'no'?"

He looked more curious than angry.

"Stop hurting her."

The silence was so thick it seemed absorbent. Rachel could not even hear her own breathing.

Mr. Thornhill turned back to Mercy. Rachel moved before he could, darting forward and grabbing his arm in mid-flight. The shock of her touch almost made him fall, contorting away from the wrist that Rachel held firm.

The mask slipped.

"Get off me," he snarled.

He wrenched his arm from Rachel's grip. Every cruel thought he had ever had, every cruel deed he had ever performed, was written on his face. He struck her, not with the lash but with his fist— she felt the hard crunch of his knuckles against her skull, before her body arched backward and crumpled hard against the earth.

Rachel lay still. She was shaking with a power she did not fully understand, and it was only by glancing at Mercy's lacerated skin that she was able to stop herself from rising and returning the blow.

She was ready to die for her daughter, but it would be no use. Mr. Thornhill would kill her, and then he would beat Mercy just the same. So, instead, Rachel closed her eyes and let Mr. Thornhill think he had broken her, as easily as that.

By the sound of the whip and the small whimpers as Mercy fought against crying out, Rachel counted the remaining lashes. In the burning darkness behind her eyelids, Rachel thought of them all free—Mercy, Mary Grace, Nobody and herself. Images floated before her of them bursting from the confines of Perseverance and burying themselves deep in the green landscape of Trinidad.

These images got her through, and Rachel added to the long list of things she had borne in her life the agony of listening to the flogging of her pregnant daughter.

But no more.

She opened her eyes.

Mr. Thornhill cut Mercy down, her legs giving way as she slid to the floor. Her back was a mess of angry red welts of flesh, ribboned with strips of hanging skin. Rachel watched as Mr. Thornhill walked away, all the blood draining from his face again. He was back to being the color of milk. He did not look back, did not even bother to cast a gloating glance her way. Why would he?

But no more.

RACHEL AND NOBODY lifted Mercy and carried her to her hut. There, Rachel dressed the wounds as best she could. Blood was already drying along her daughter's legs; Rachel wiped it away. Nancy, wordlessly, brought a salve for the pain. Mercy winced as Rachel dabbed at the wounds on her back, but made no sound.

To fill the close, humid silence in the hut, Rachel began to sing. One of Quamina's songs. The runaway village seemed like a dream now, a different lifetime. But the song held within it the magic of the forest. Mercy's arms, wrapped across her belly, began to slacken. Rachel, whose chest was still tight with rage, could breathe again.

The song finished as Rachel rubbed in the last of the paste. She sat back on her heels. Mercy didn't move, but a slow breath whistled out of her nostrils.

"The baby," she whispered. "Me can feel it."

Rachel also exhaled. Some of the heaviness in the air lifted. She placed her hand on her daughter's hip, taking care to avoid broken skin, and both women looked to the earth in silent thanks. In spite of everything, the baby still lived.

"You can tell me," said Mercy, her head still bowed. "About Micah."

"You sure?"

"Yes. Please. Me want to know."

Mercy kept still as Rachel told the whole story—the uprising, the battle, the soldiers pulling Micah out of the crowd and shooting him for daring to try to take freedom by force. At times, Mercy's shoulders trembled a little, but otherwise (were it not for the blood still trickling from the deepest cuts) she might have been carved from stone.

When Rachel finished, Mercy sat up slowly, bracing herself against the ground, teeth gritted with the pain. Her eyes burned; they hid nothing. She was not afraid to bare what was in her heart.

"Thank you," she said. Then, lifting her chin, she added, "Me proud. Of what Micah do. He was always the bravest of us all."

37

MERCY WAS AFRAID. There was still a fierce young woman inside her—that much Rachel had seen by the way her daughter reacted to Micah's story. But the scars of the last attempt at escape would not be so easily forgotten.

"He gon' kill us," said Mercy. Her voice was hoarse, as if all the screams she had not screamed while being whipped had weakened her power of speech anyway.

The four of them—Rachel, Mercy, Mary Grace and Nobody—crouched inside Mercy's hut. They spoke in whispers, and Nobody's gaze went frequently to the doorway in search of prying eyes.

"We must get out," said Rachel.

"You don't understand," said Mercy. "He keep watch every night. He gon' kill us all if we run."

Rachel looked from one face to the other. Mercy, terrified, still grieving Cato's death. Nobody, nervous but ready—it would not be the first time he had run. And Mary Grace, her gaze steady—prepared, like her mother, to do whatever it took for the sake of saving them all.

"Then we don't go at night."

Mercy frowned. "What?"

"That's what Thornhill expect," Rachel continued. "So, we go during the day."

"But we gon' be seen," said Mercy.

"No. Tomorrow, the first and second gangs gon' take the cane up to the mill. If we get behind the boiling-house next to it, that can hide us from view. Anybody looking from the great house or the fields not gon' see us. We can run to the woods just beyond."

She waited for the others to give their verdict on the plan. Mary Grace's mouth was stretched into a thin, determined line. Nobody nodded, his eyes wide but filled with grim certainty. Mercy kept her head bowed; she was the only one Rachel couldn't read.

"We can cut through the forest and get back on the road," Rachel said. "Head north to Port of Spain."

"No." Mercy's voice was low. It quivered but did not crack. "We can go another way."

She took a deep breath and sat up a little taller. Even this slight movement made her flinch, the skin on her back still raw and bloody.

"There are free villages," she continued. "Farther east. By the sea."

"You mean there are runaways who live there?" Nobody asked.

"Not runaways—most of them aren't. Most of them are free people. They grow what they can to feed themselves, and anything left they trade along the coast."

Rachel leaned toward her daughter. "You think we should go there? Not Port of Spain?"

"Me don't know," Mercy said. A thin sheen of sweat covered her face. She was clearly in pain—both from her wounds and from the thought of trying to leave again, after last time.

"Abraham tell me. About Cato." Rachel spoke gently. She expected the name to inflict fresh hurt on Mercy, but instead her daughter raised her head. A little of the fire returned.

"We should go east," said Mercy. Her voice no longer shook.

"Cato was the one who think of the villages. His brother don' buy his own freedom, and Cato want to find him there."

The others, who had never known Cato and never would, could still feel the power of his memory. They all looked at one another, forging their pact. Tomorrow, they would leave.

Freedom—real freedom—beckoned.

THE DAY BURNED scorching hot. White rays of sunlight spread like searing daggers over the fields and kept everyone sweating. It was a stroke of luck, for around midday when the heat was most oppressive, Mr. Thornhill retired to the great house and left the foremen to oversee the march of the cane bundles up to the mill. With him gone, Rachel breathed a little easier, although she could not shake the sense of being watched, and without the advantage of being able to watch him in return.

They had no agreed signal and no planned time to set things in motion. Mercy had stayed in the village, claiming the need to recover from her beating. It had been a tense moment when Nancy had relayed this information to Mr. Thornhill—if he forced Mercy to return to her normal task of watching over the animals, it would have made things almost impossible to coordinate. But he gave no sign that he cared one way or another. Perhaps, as a new day dawned and he saw again how short he was of labor, and how thin he must stretch his workforce to bring in and process the harvest, he was more inclined to be lenient. He could ill afford to have Mercy lose her baby. Whatever the reason, Mercy could stay in the village. From her hut, she would just about be able to make out the route from the back of the boiling-house into the forest. When she saw the others, she would run, too.

It was the part of their plan that distressed Rachel the most. Her natural caution struggled against her newfound unwillingness to compromise on freedom. All morning, the thought of Mercy's dangerous sprint across the open fields toward the forest weighed heavy on her mind. But what choice did they have? And Mercy was brave—braver than Rachel had ever been, of that she was sure. All Rachel could do was hope.

In the middle of the afternoon, with the sun still beating down on the workers, Rachel, Nobody and Mary Grace dropped to the back of a group walking over to the mill. Without speaking, without even looking at one another, they knew it was time.

Little by little, they slowed their pace, until there were several yards between them and the rest of the line. Ahead of them, the mill turned—driven by the efforts of workers inside, for there was no wind on that sweltering day.

Rachel led them off the path. She knew they must walk, not run. Running would attract too much attention. So, step by agonizing step, they headed for the boiling-house, for the safety of its back wall.

Rachel saw someone walking out of the mill, and her stomach dropped. She did not stop, dared not stop, but she knew they would be seen.

Out of the shadow of the doorway came Abraham. He stared straight at Rachel, and she dropped her gaze, focused on her feet.

One step. Another.

She looked back up. Abraham still stared. Rachel was too far away to make out the expression on his face, or if he was opening his mouth, ready to cry out.

They were so close, now, to slipping out of his sight. Rachel kept her breathing steady by timing it to every pace she took.

As they turned the corner, Rachel looked back at Abraham one last time. It was hard to tell with the sun in her eyes, but she could have sworn he raised his hand in a kind of salute. He did not understand why they wanted more—why Rachel and the others had to flee this half-life on Perseverance—but perhaps he could accept it. Respect it, even. His silence protected them until they were out of sight.

In the shadow of the boiling-house, Nobody leaned against the wall, panting heavily as if he had held his breath all the way from the fields. Rachel touched him once on the arm, then Mary Grace. They said nothing to one another, but they had survived the first part of the escape.

They discarded their bundles of cane, and Rachel eyed up the distance between the wall and the strip of forest. It looked a lot farther now than it had before. And more exposed. The light from the sun bleached the browning grass and revealed all the patches of bald earth.

Rachel was still readying herself when Mary Grace moved. She ran. She hurled herself out of the shadows and sprinted for the trees. Nobody went with her, only inches behind. Their strides were long and elegant. Rachel took a moment to appreciate their beauty, these two dark figures streaking through the dying grass, their feet kicking up a trail of dust. Then Rachel, too, threw herself forward, into the harsh sunlight and the torturous heat.

As she ran, she felt taller than ever. Her limbs, outstretched in motion, took up more space. She barely touched the ground. She flew.

Before she could draw breath, she was among the trees. She flung out an arm and grabbed a trunk to steady herself. The rush of elation at having made it gave way to the chill of fear.

Mercy.

Rachel spun round, her eyes searching out the village on the horizon.

"There." Nobody pointed.

Mercy was already half of the way toward them. She moved awkwardly, one hand wrapped around her belly. But she moved fast.

Time seemed to slow. A whole age passed with Mercy suspended between one state and the next—between bound and free. A bird on a low-hanging branch began to chatter, and though the sound was nothing like a gunshot, Rachel thought she heard the crack of a rifle in its every call.

Mercy looked behind her as she ran. There was terror in the way she moved. Rachel had to bite back a cry—

Don't look back.

Keep running.

Mercy was almost on them. She was close enough for Rachel to see the tears streaking down her face. Her body shook with sobs and the effort of the sprint.

Then the gunshot came. Real this time, not imagined. The bullet exploded through the wood of a nearby tree. The bird took flight. Mercy was screaming. She stumbled, almost fell, but she was in the forest now—Rachel grabbed hold of her daughter.

There was no time to comfort each other.

Nobody had the wild eyes of a frightened child as he said, "Run."

Moving through the trees was nothing like hurtling across the field. In the dim light, shapes formed and unformed at the edges of Rachel's vision. Where before she had felt stretched out, now she felt trapped. The canopy thickened, until it felt like the lid of a box. Rachel found herself struggling to breathe, some part of her convinced the leaves had shut out all traces of air. Sharp branches tore at her skin, and the uneven soil threatened at any moment to send her tumbling to the ground. But somehow, sheer force of will was stronger than any obstacle. They kept running.

There was no second gunshot. No shouts from behind them. No barking as dogs chased their trail. So when Rachel saw, as they passed through a shaft of light that had pierced through the trees, how hard Mercy was still sobbing, she shouted, "Stop."

Mercy collapsed on the ground, curling into a ball around her stomach. Her shoulders shook. Visible at the base of her neck were the tops of the unhealed welts on her back. The blood had soaked through parts of her shirt, patterning the white cotton with flecks of red that darkened to black where the bleeding had been worst.

Rachel knelt beside her daughter. She stroked Mercy's hair. The memory of the movement was already in her hands, from all the times she had comforted Mercy as a child.

Nobody wrapped a protective arm around Mary Grace. His eyes were fixed on the distance.

"We can't stay here," he said. He, too, was trembling—vibrating with the force of his desire to survive. "They will come."

"She can't keep running," Rachel said to him. "Not like this. Not with the baby."

Rachel watched raw instinct battle with compassion inside Nobody. In the end, his silence indicated that compassion had won. He said nothing more about pressing onward—though Rachel knew, by the knot in the pit of her stomach, that he was right. They could not stay still for long.

Mercy turned her head, pressing her face into the ground. Rachel leaned closer, so that her cheek was almost resting on Mercy's hair.

"You all right?"

Mercy didn't move.

"Can you walk?"

Still, nothing.

Rachel waited. She could sense Nobody's growing agitation, but she ignored him. She focused on breathing in time with Mercy, trying to lead her daughter into slower, deeper breaths.

Gradually, the sobs faded. Mercy sat up and wiped her tears with a muddy hand.

"He's right," Mercy said, nodding toward Nobody. "We can't stay here."

The anguish was draining out of her face, but this was not like all the other times Rachel had seen Mercy hide herself behind a blank mask. This was different. As one emotion ebbed, another flooded in to take its place. Mercy pushed herself to her feet. She stood tall, and there was no mistaking the thoughts that burned inside her.

We must continue.
We must not be caught.
We must live.

38

BY SUNDOWN, THEIR faces were haggard and their feet dragged, but they did not dare stop moving. The close air in the forest carried every sound, from the snap of a twig to the rustling of leaves. Rachel's nerves were frayed, and her neck stiff from all the glances over her shoulder. But still no sign of the drivers and foremen she knew would follow, spurred on by Thornhill himself. They changed direction often, trying to keep their path unpredictable. Nobody scaled a papaw tree and cast the fruit to earth—they all smeared their feet with the smashed pulp, to help mask their scent. Rachel wondered if it would be enough.

Darkness made navigating the trees even harder, and the sight of gaping blackness whenever she looked behind made Rachel's whole body tense with fear. When a bird flew low over their heads, the sudden sound of its wings inches from their faces made all of them jump and grip one another tightly.

"We can't go on like this," said Rachel once she had recovered. "We must rest. Without rest, they gon' catch us for sure."

Nobody, his body slack with exhaustion, looked ready to agree, but Mary Grace held up a hand to cut off his answer.

"What is it?" he asked his wife.

She put a hand to her ear: *Listen.*

The sound of their footsteps had masked it, but now that they were still it could just about be heard. Running water.

They moved slowly, following the noise, until they found it—a narrow river with a racing current. Around it, the forest thinned, and through the gap in the trees, the moon shone down on the water. Something about the sight brought Rachel immense peace. The river, speckled with silver moonlight, so fast-moving that it looked like a living, twisting thing, could offer protection. Under its spell, they would be safe.

They sat on the bank, and were able to breathe. Next to them lay a fallen tree—not cut by men but, by the look of it, blown over by some past storm. Rachel always saw tragedy in trees torn from the earth—things not as they should be, something living laid low where once it stretched to the heavens. Her eyes were drawn, over and over, to the shadow of the thick trunk, with its splaying branches and naked roots quivering in the breeze. She tried not to take it as an omen of what was to come.

They had no food, nothing but the clothes on their backs, so all they could do was sleep. As Rachel closed her eyes, her head resting on the cool earth, she could smell the forest—a gentle, green scent that helped keep her worst fears at bay.

It was still dark when Rachel woke. Beside her, Nobody and Mary Grace were still sleeping, their arms and legs entangled, but Mercy was gone. Rachel scrambled upright, terror flooding through her, ready to cry out—but, no. Her daughter had not been taken. Mercy was sat on the riverbank, with her back to Rachel.

Rachel heard Mercy whimper, saw her hands ball into fists.

Rachel was next to her daughter in an instant. "What is it?"

But Rachel already knew. She recognized the way Mercy's face twisted, as her own had done so many times before.

"The baby," said Mercy. "The pain—it start when we was walking, not so bad. But now—" Her face contorted again. Beads of sweat glistened on her forehead.

Rachel dipped the edge of her skirt in the water and used it to wipe Mercy's brow. She didn't know what else to do. She felt she should talk to her daughter, try to soothe her, but the words were blocked by rising panic. Rachel was no midwife. She had none of the skill of someone like Great Polly, who had delivered most of the children on Providence plantation in Barbados. All she knew were the births she had seen herself, mostly her own. She felt powerless—caught in the grip of forces beyond her control. Things had an inevitability to them. The labor would continue, just as surely as the white men would find them. The corners of Rachel's vision blurred with the thought, her head dizzy with fear, but some small part of her was able to direct her hands to keep wiping the sweat from Mercy's forehead.

Mercy's face twisted again. She cried out, tried to bite back the sound with gritted teeth, only to have it force its way out again. These were strong contractions. The baby was coming.

The noise jerked the others awake. Mary Grace, on seeing her sister, seemed to know instinctively what was happening. She rushed to her mother's side. She began to rub Mercy's lower back in small circles, careful not to stray too far up and catch where the whip had opened the skin.

"The baby," said Rachel to Nobody.

She saw, in the whites of his eyes, that he felt the same way she did. He immediately glanced toward the forest. He said nothing out loud—they did not want to risk frightening Mercy—but a look passed between them. Nobody left the women by the bank and headed for the trees. He would stand watch. If Thornhill came, they could not run—not with Mercy like this—but at least death would not take them by surprise.

Mercy cried out again. This time she made no attempt to stifle the sound. It reverberated through the forest, sending several birds into flight. A sheen of sweat covered her arms, her neck, and dripped down her face. Rachel's mind tripped over itself, searching for what to do. Why couldn't she remember anything Great Polly had done for her? All her memories were clouded by the labor itself, the invisible hands that clamped around her abdomen, the squeezing pain . . .

Mary Grace stopped massaging Mercy's back. Gently but firmly, she guided her sister onto her hands and knees. Rachel, watching, realized—not for the first time—how many gaps there were in her sense of her children's lives. Some she might never fill.

This little action from Mary Grace cut through Rachel's fear. Suddenly, she was alert, purposeful. She was imbued with a sense of what she must do—a knowledge not spoken but absorbed over a lifetime, perhaps even a part of her before life itself had begun. The feeling was at once universal—an animal instinct she knew she shared with all things—and singular. It was the urgent thought that she must deliver this baby that, through Mercy, carried her own blood inside it.

Mary Grace started rubbing Mercy's back again, more insistently this time. Rachel spoke to the rhythm of Mary Grace's hands.

"Breathe, Mercy. Breathe and push."

Mercy's whimpering was punctuated by howls of pain, but the howls, the hands and Rachel's gentle commands all pulsed together. They worked as one to bring the baby forth. The noises Mercy made grew deeper, more guttural. Rachel could almost see the rippling muscles under her daughter's skin. The pressure built. The river itself seemed to contract, forcing water to surge faster and faster between its banks. The women breathed together, in and out, hearts racing, hands gripping at the soil and one another. Mercy pressed her mouth to the ground so that the earth could absorb her screams as liquid poured out of her and ran down the bank to join the river.

When the baby slid out into Rachel's hands, everything stopped. Nothing could be heard—not even a breath, not even the sound of the water. The baby lay still. A boy, Rachel noticed, then wished she hadn't. It made the waiting all the worse.

The baby's fingers curled into fists. With a sharp cry, he announced his birth to the world. The women exhaled. Rachel's hands were trembling. Her tears, falling onto the baby, washed lines of blood off the tiny body. It was a rush she had not felt in years, not since she herself had last managed to produce a living child. The feeling of complete, absorbing, unqualified love. The baby was a stranger, without speech, unknowable. It would be years before he could say what was on his mind. And yet, love did not wait. Love was there in the beginning—even before the beginning. Love needed no words, no introduction. Existence was enough.

The afterbirth slipped out, and Rachel was able to pass the baby to Mercy. There was a moment when all three were touching—grandmother, mother and child.

Mercy held her son. She rocked the baby gently back and forth until his cries gave way to grizzling and, eventually, to sleep.

The three women stared, entranced, at the baby. They took in everything, from the wisps of dark hair on his head to the soft pink undersoles of his feet.

Mercy's smile faltered. There was sadness in the way she gazed down at her son. Grief tugged at the corners of her mouth. Rachel could tell she was thinking of Cato.

"He look like him?" Rachel asked.

"A little." Mercy lifted her head, her eyes meeting Rachel's. "But he also look like you."

Mercy looked back at her son. The grief faded—it would never truly be gone—and she smiled again.

"Micah," she whispered. "Yes. A good name. Welcome, little Micah."

39

BIRTH AND NEW life cast a powerful aura. It absorbed all their attention. But the spell was broken when Nobody came scrambling over.

"They're coming. I saw the lights. They're coming."

Mercy was shivering, feverish. Nobody was beating a fist against his palm, his eyes darting around for an escape but seeing nothing.

A wash of weariness came over Rachel. She closed her eyes. The thought crossed her mind—how easy it would be to slip into eternal sleep.

In the distance, she heard the barking of dogs.

They were coming.

Mary Grace shook her mother's arm. Rachel opened her eyes and there was the baby. He had been born free. Born into the thing for which his father and his namesake had died, for which his grandmother had risked her life, had crossed oceans, had walked hundreds of miles on aching feet. This child could never know bondage. Freedom was his birthright.

A powerful, desperate surge of energy ran through Rachel—the will to live, not for herself but for the baby, and for Mercy and Mary Grace and Nobody. She had searched for them, she had gathered them and she had mended the family she once thought she had lost forever. This was work that would not be undone. Not here. Not this way.

They could all see them now—lanterns moving through the trees, getting closer.

Mary Grace was still gripping Rachel, pointing to the river, to the surging current that moved faster than they could ever hope to on foot.

Mother and daughter moved as one, without the need for speech. They sprang to their feet. Mercy was still slumped on the ground, head bowed, the baby sleeping in her arms. Rachel took little Micah from his mother and held him tight to her chest. Mary Grace lifted her sister.

"The river," Rachel said to Nobody.

He shook his head. "No. We'll drown."

"We got no other way."

Nobody stared at the river. He knew, more than anyone, the dangers that lay beneath the surface of water. Rachel saw the terror in his eyes.

A man shouted from the forest, close enough for them all to hear: "I see them!"

It was as if the world shattered—fragmenting beyond coherent thought. Nothing existed for Rachel but the baby against her skin. Images flashed before her—Nobody bounding toward the bank. Mercy fainting. Mary Grace straining to hold her sister's weight. Nobody, with a scream of fear and effort and exhaustion and the unbearable need for survival, pushing against the fallen tree. It rolled, slowly, slowly, down toward the water.

Rachel turned, dazed, toward the men who hunted them. Saw the dogs loping beyond the trees. Saw, behind, the shadow of a man—was it Thornhill?—and the glint of a gun being cocked.

"Rachel!"

Nobody's desperate scream brought the world back together. She could think again, and what she thought was—

Jump.

Now.

Clutching little Micah, she plunged into the river. Her left hand held him, her right hand swiped blindly through the churning blackness, searching. She could hear bullets, their noise muffled and distorted by the water that surrounded her.

Still, her right hand found nothing. She was buffeted along by the current. She felt as though her body might dissolve. She would cease to be—become one with the river.

Then, something grabbed her by the wrist, dragging her above the surface. Air filled her lungs. The baby was crying. Her hand finally found solid wood. Rachel clung to the tree, holding herself as high as she could to keep Micah's head above water. Nobody and Mary Grace hugged Mercy, still barely conscious, between them, protecting her from the vicious current.

A bullet hit the water, a few yards behind them. But then— nothing. The shouts and barks and gunshots faded.

The water carried them away, out of sight.

THERE WAS NO more they could do. They were helpless. The tree kept them afloat—barely—but the river had no mercy.

Survival was second to second, surge to surge.

All Rachel could do was hold the baby close and pray—not to any God in heaven, but to the water itself.

Please, let us live.

"RACHEL."

The pain in her arms was searing, but she did not dare relax her grip. It took all her remaining energy for Rachel to raise her head and look around.

The sun had risen hours ago. The river was wider now, and the current had slowed to something more like the Demerara, when they had first taken to the water on their canoe, all those months ago.

"Rachel," Nobody repeated. "We've come far. We should make for land."

Rachel could not speak. She simply nodded.

Nobody and Mary Grace managed to kick the tree toward the bank. When her feet met solid ground, Rachel almost cried—her face went through all the motions of it, but no tears came. Little Micah was silent against her chest, but still breathing. His eyes were open, drinking in the world.

Somehow, their legs did not give way beneath them on land—even Mercy managed to support herself on Mary Grace's shoulder. Mercy held out her arms and took her son, to nurse him, as they all stood still and listened to the sound of grass rustling in the wind—the distant call of a bird.

Rachel—who only moments ago had been depleted of all strength—felt a restlessness descend. She wanted to move, to control her own limbs again, after so many hours on the river.

Nobody looked up at the sky.

"We've come east," he said. "The river must flow to the eastern coast."

Mercy raised her head. They all looked at one another.

Could it be? They had plunged, unthinkingly, into the river. Had it really brought them where they wanted to go?

They turned away from the sun. The river stretched into the distance. There was no sign of the land ending.

"You stay," said Nobody, looking around the women. "Rest. I will go and see if—"

But Mercy cut across him. "No. We all go."

Rachel took back her grandson. Mercy could barely hold her

own weight, let alone the weight of the baby. They began to walk. Slow, limping, but alive.

WERE IT NOT for the gentle arc that the sun made toward setting, things would have seemed timeless.

There were none of the usual ways to mark the passage of the hours. They had no food to eat and no work to do except walking.

The only sign of time, the only thing that showed how past, present and future all existed within that moment, were the lines creasing the back of Rachel's hands, the still-swollen bump of Mercy's belly and the wide, fresh eyes of the baby. Time not on the scale of the long, dragging minutes cutting cane in the hot sun. Not even on the scale of the seasons, from harvest to planting and back again. Time on the scale of generations, which could span hundreds of years.

MERCY STOPPED WALKING. She had seen it first, peeping over the horizon. The others stopped, too, and followed her gaze . . . and there it was.

The sea.

They stood close. They were touching—holding hands, hips pressed together, arms around one another's shoulders. Anything to keep connected. To savor, together, the vision that lay ahead. The soft green island giving way at its edge to the glittering waves.

"There." Nobody pointed.

A collection of huts, little more than silhouettes in the distance, facing out to sea. Rachel could see tiny figures moving around the huts—people bent over the soil, a few goats ambling across the grass, a child running out toward the water.

Micah began to fuss, lifting his little fists in protest against the long, hot walk and the fearful, coursing river and everything else that had filled the first day of his life. Rachel rocked him back and forth but it had no effect. He screwed up his face and his cries grew louder and more insistent.

Mary Grace came to Rachel's side and looked down at her nephew. And she started to sing.

Her voice was thin from lack of use, but haunting. Each note wavered, vibrating with a lifetime of feeling. No—not a lifetime. A hundred lifetimes. She sang for herself and for all those who had come before. Her song had pain, frustration and disappointment in it. But also joy, relief, love. Hope.

The world stopped turning. The sun held its place in the sky. Everything was still as Mary Grace sang. Rachel watched her daughter's lips moving, the beautiful shapes they took as they formed the words. Nobody was watching, too, moved to tears by his wife's voice. Had he been able to imagine how it sounded? In his dreams, if Mary Grace spoke to him, did she sing like this? By the way he trembled, Rachel knew it must be all he had ever hoped for and more.

It was a song Rachel recognized. One of Quamina's, an Akan song, a song of their ancestors, a song with a melody that vibrated in Rachel's bones, where it had been sung once before, long ago.

Mercy sang, too. She stumbled over a few of the words, missed a few of the notes. But her voice lifted Mary Grace's up, up, up, higher than the clouds, lifted it to the gods. Micah's cries were fading now. His eyes began to drift closed.

Then Nobody was singing. His voice vibrated through the earth. Not quite the same song—his own, with his own words, passed down from his own people, who had survived all of the chains and the passage and the torture, even death. The two songs blended together to become one because their message was the same. They had survived.

Rachel looked down at Micah, now at peace in her arms. What more could she give her grandson but the fragments of a memory that she had carried with her all this time? The half-forgotten words of a song.

Rachel joined her voice with the others and she sang.

THERE WAS HOPE *for this new world, after all.*

When they sang, we heard them. We sang with them, and welcomed this new life into a world that is cruel, but that has love in it, too, if you know where to look.

This is how we are remembered. In snatches of song, in dreams, in the smile that passes between mother and child. These are the parts of us that cannot be destroyed. These are the parts of us that feed the roots, and keep them strong.

The soil is fertile. Our tree grows on.

AUTHOR'S NOTE

MY GRANDPARENTS WERE part of the Windrush Generation—the wave of migration after the Second World War that brought thousands of Caribbean people to the UK. Though I was born and raised in England, I have always had a strong attachment to Caribbean history. I learned about the formerly enslaved women who went looking for their lost children when I was sixteen and attended the exhibition *Making Freedom* put on by the Windrush Foundation. The exhibition cast emancipation in a new light—not as the gift of white people in Britain, but as something fiercely fought for by the slaves themselves in revolutions and rebellions, from Haiti to Barbados.

A small wall plaque explained that, after emancipation, many women put down their tools and walked all over their islands to try to find their stolen children. I couldn't stop thinking about this remarkable act of bravery, after slavery had worked to destroy people's families so completely, and I later read the book on which this plaque was based, an oral history called *To Shoot Hard Labour* (1986) by Fernando C. Smith and Keithlyn B. Smith. The book records the life of Samuel Smith, who was born in Antigua in 1877 and died in 1982. Smith recalls his great-great-grandmother, Mother Rachael, who walked across Antigua after slavery ended to be reunited with one of her daughters. The true story of Mother Rachael inspired the journey of Rachel in this novel.

Rachel is also inspired by my own family: by the wonderful Black women in my life, including my mother, my aunt and my step-grandmother; and by the stories of my grandmother, who was born in St. Lucia and who died before I was born. Like Rachel, they have had to endure so much. Like her, they can be cautious, quiet, watchful. But like her, they have so much love and strength, and they refuse to be defined by the cruelties they have faced.

River Sing Me Home also draws on my own time spent in the Caribbean, staying in my grandfather's house in St. Lucia. I have such vivid memories of my first visit when I was eleven years old. Of how the thick, humid air tasted when we stepped out of the plane at Vieux Fort Airport. Of how the rain poured so heavily as we ran back from the beach that my mother asked if we'd jumped into the sea with our clothes on. Of the impossible blue of the ocean, a hundred shades that caught the light as the sun set, and the amazing warmth of the water as my sister and I made a game of diving through the waves just before they broke against the sand.

But I developed a new perspective of the place during my most recent trip, when I was researching my master's thesis on the legacy of slavery in the Caribbean. The landscape was just as beautiful, but I now saw the layers of history everywhere. The old plantation houses and the new hotels, both grand and enclosed from the rest of the island. The poverty in a place that is so abundant. The man who stands by the road in the town of Anse La Raye holding a large yellow snake—there are no snakes native to St. Lucia, the man tells you, but they were introduced into the forests by the plantation owners to bite slaves who ran away.

People travel to the Caribbean because it seems like paradise—a place outside time, where they can cast off the relentless rhythms of their own lives and relax on the beach with a cocktail in hand. But to me, the Caribbean is beautiful because of its history, not in spite of it. A place where the past is always close to the surface, and echoes of history are everywhere.

My research trip to the Caribbean allowed me to delve into that history as I interviewed activists, historians and family members in St. Lucia and Barbados to understand whether and how they felt slavery still affected the islands. Two things stuck out for me from these conversations that helped inform *River Sing Me Home*. The first was that people were quick to mention the ambiguities around the end of slavery—the fact that the apprenticeships persisted for so long, keeping people tied to the same plantation; the fact that even after apprenticeships ended, economic exploitation continued and people had little choice but to keep working as field laborers; and the fact that it was white plantation owners who received monetary compensation, while the field laborers received nothing. These conversations showed me that freedom was by no means straightforward in the immediate aftermath of slavery.

But people in the Caribbean were also quick to tell me about the way that people resisted and rebelled against slavery and made their own kind of freedom. In Barbados, I saw the statue of Bussa, the slave who led a rebellion against the plantation owners in 1816. In St. Lucia, family members proudly told me that they lived on land where maroons used to be—the people who managed to escape and make a life for themselves outside the plantations.

I wanted *River Sing Me Home* to build on this idea of what it means to be free, and the ways in which enslaved people made freedom for themselves. I wanted to describe real rebellions, like the one in Demerara that Micah is part of in 1823. Reading Emilia Viotti da Costa's *Crowns of Glory, Tears of Blood* was invaluable for learning more about this uprising. I wanted to write about places like Guyana and Jamaica, with their thick forests or high mountains, that had long-established maroon communities. These real villages inspired the one in which Rachel finds Thomas Augustus.

It was also important to me to include the character of Nuno in this part of Rachel's journey, to recognize the violence done to Indigenous communities throughout the Caribbean. I am descended from the Indigenous people of St. Lucia, and my conversations with scholars of Indigenous history helped shape Nuno's story.

The free village that Rachel, Mercy, Nobody and Mary Grace find at the end of the novel is also based on real places in Trinidad and on other islands, though here I have taken slight liberties with historical timelines, as these places were more common once apprenticeships were abolished in 1838. Some colonies, like Barbados, were so densely settled that there was little habitable land left for people to claim if they tried to leave their plantations. But colonies like Trinidad were not as heavily planted when slavery ended, so it was more possible for people to find land to farm and form villages away from the plantations.

The other bit of historical accuracy I grappled with for this novel was how to write the dialogue. I wanted the characters to speak in a way that reflected the wonderful creole languages of the Caribbean, but also was accessible to non-Caribbean readers. In the end, I went with dialogue that is not always perfectly in line with how someone like Rachel or Mama B would have spoken at the time, but that still follows some of the rules of Caribbean grammar. Languages such as Bajan creole do not conjugate many verbs, which lends an immediacy to Caribbean storytelling, as you have in the novel with Orion's story where it is almost like you get to relive the memory alongside him.

River Sing Me Home also takes inspiration from the present. When I spoke to people in the Caribbean about slavery, they told me how much families continue to fragment to this day. This is something I know from personal experience. While visiting for my master's research, I went to Barbados to meet my grandfather's sister for the first time. My grandfather left Barbados when he was fourteen, moving first to St. Lucia and then to the UK. His mother and the rest of his siblings died not knowing what had happened to him. Only this last sister was still alive to see him when he retired to the Caribbean. Seeing her was tearful and joyful in equal measure, and I got to hear stories about a branch of the family we had thought was lost to us.

On that same trip, while I was signing in to a building for an appointment, the security guard asked me where I was from. I explained that I was British but had family in St. Lucia. He asked where exactly, and what their surname was. When I told him, he went into the back room and came out with a colleague. "You have the same face," the first guard explained. And it turned out we were in fact related through our great-grandfather. That a complete stranger would be so attuned to my features, and that another stranger would be so open to the idea that I was a long-lost cousin, showed me that although Caribbean families may be fractured to this day, there is always the possibility of reconnection—of, as the St. Lucian poet and Nobel laureate Derek Walcott writes, a love that can reassemble our fragments.

I hope this sense of possibility, of love, is something readers will take away from this novel. This is a story that does not shy away from the brutality of slavery, but that ultimately still has something uplifting at its heart. Women like Rachel (and the real Mother Rachael) set out to make a kind of freedom for themselves when they brought their families back together again. There is something so wonderfully hopeful in those stories. They are histories that need to be told.

ACKNOWLEDGMENTS

THANK YOU TO every person in publishing who has believed in this book. Especially to my agent, Laurie Robertson, and to Caroline Michel and the entire team at PFD; to my wonderful editor, Sherise Hobbs, and to Bea Grabowska, Isabel Martin, Caitlin Raynor, Elise Jackson and everyone else in Headline who has made this book possible. Thank you also to Kate Seaver, Daniela Riedlova, Jin Yu, Lauren Burnstein, Tina Joell and everyone at Berkley for bringing this book across the Atlantic.

A writer's life can be a lonely one, so I am forever grateful for the company of Jenn and Indy, who were with me on the journey, and whose own work is such an inspiration.

Thank you to Trixie, the perfect writing companion and the greatest of cats. I was never really alone with you on my lap, and you are much missed.

The research for this book was greatly aided by the following people: Arthur Torrington, for gifting me *To Shoot Hard Labour*; everyone I spoke to in the Caribbean for my thesis research, but especially Anderson Reynolds, Modest Downs, Jolien Harmsen, Sylvester Clauzel, Henderson Carter, John Robert Lee, Pedro

Welch and Rodney Worrell; and all those at Oxford who supported my studies of slavery and reparations, particularly Dan Butt, Blake Ewing and Teresa Bejan.

Thank you to the teachers who helped me to love literature and history: Mr. Douglas, Dr. Brown and Mr. Mann.

I am blessed with so many wonderful and supportive friends who have shared in my excitement at publishing my first novel. I want to particularly thank Dan and Erin, Ellie, Issy, Louis, Will, Lottie, Ameen, Kelsey, Lily, Anna and Joanna. I also want to thank the Thurstons for welcoming me into your family with open arms.

Mum, Dad and Cal, thank you for everything. Jeanette, effectively a third parent to me, and whose book-filled home was such a formative place (especially works of great feminist literature such as *Prince Cinders*)—thank you also. This book is for all of you.

Finally, Charlie—thank you for the all the love and laughter, for holding me when I cry, for cooking for me on all those late nights spent writing and for supporting me in everything I do. I couldn't have done it without you.